JØRGEN-FRANTZ JACOBSEN : BARBARA

Some other books from Norvik Press

Sigbjørn Obstfelder: *A Priest's Diary* (translated by James McFarlane)
Hjalmar Söderberg: *Short stories* (translated by Carl Lofmark)
Annegret Heitmann (ed.): *No Man's Land. An Anthology of Modern Danish Women's Literature*
P C Jersild: *A Living Soul* (translated by Rika Lesser)
Sara Lidman: *Naboth's Stone* (translated by Joan Tate)
Selma Lagerlöf: *The Löwensköld Ring* (translated by Linda Schenck)
Villy Sørensen: *Harmless Tales* (translated by Paula Hostrup-Jessen)
Camilla Collett: *The District Governor's Daughters* (translated by Kirsten Seaver)
Jens Bjørneboe: *The Sharks* (translated by Esther Greenleaf Mürer)
Johan Borgen: *The Scapegoat* (translated by Elizabeth Rokkan)
Janet Garton & Henning Sehmsdorf (eds. and trans.): *New Norwegian Plays* (by Peder W.Cappelen, Edvard Hoem, Cecilie Løveid and Bjørg Vik)
Gunilla Anderman (ed.): *New Swedish Plays* (by Ingmar Bergman, Stig Larsson, Lars Norén and Agneta Pleijel)

The logo of Norvik Press is based on a drawing by Egil Bakka (University of Bergen) of a Viking ornament in gold, paper thin, with impressed figures (size 16x21mm). It was found in 1897 at Hauge, Klepp, Rogaland, and is now in the collection of the Historisk museum, University of Bergen (inv.no. 5392). It depicts a love scene, possibly (according to Magnus Olsen) between the fertility god Freyr and the maiden Gerðr; the large penannular brooch of the man's cloak dates the work as being most likely 10th century.

Cover illustration: Untitled (Faroese landscape at midnight), by William Heinesen.

Jørgen-Frantz Jacobsen

BARBARA

NOVEL

Translated by George Johnston

Norvik Press

About the translator:

George Johnston, poet, translator and academic, studied English and Philosophy at the University of Toronto between 1936 and 1945, a period of studies interrupted by four and a half years of war service as a pilot. From 1947 he taught English and Old Norse language and literature, first for two years at Mount Allison University and thereafter until his retirement as Professor Emeritus in 1979 at Carleton University.

He is the author of seven volumes of his own poetry, a biography, and eight volumes of translations of poetry and prose from a range of Scandinavian languages, both ancient and modern, including Norwegian, Icelandic and Faroese.

Original title: *Barbara*. First published 1939, and reprinted many times since. © Gyldendalske Boghandel, Nordisk Forlag A/S, Copenhagen. This translation © George Johnston 1993.

British Library Cataloguing in Publication Data
Jacobsen, Jørgen-Frantz
    Barbara
    I. Title.   II. Johnston, George.
    839.81374 [F]
ISBN 1-870041-22-4

First published in 1993 by Norvik Press, University of East Anglia,
    Norwich, NR4 7TJ, England
Managing Editors: James McFarlane and Janet Garton

Reprinted 1994

Norvik Press has been established with financial support from the University of East Anglia, the Danish Ministry for Cultural Affairs, The Norwegian Cultural Department, and the Swedish Institute. Publication of this book has been aided by a grant from the Danish Ministry of Culture.

Printed and bound in Great Britain by
Biddles Ltd, Guildford and King's Lynn

Introduction

In the seventeen-fifties, while the Seven Years War was raging, three French warships, having been blown off-course on their way home from America, might well have put in to the Faroe Islands for repair and water. The first sight of their sails would have dismayed the three or four thousand inhabitants and sent them fleeing to their mountains. Jørgen-Frantz Jacobsen introduces such an event early in his story. He tells of a notorious widow of the islands who would not have been frightened, and makes of her one of the most vivid and passionate heroines of fictional literature. His setting is historical, and his characters are convincingly of their time, and they display a fullness of humanity that belongs to any age. Some of them were drawn from life, people he had known in Torshavn or the villages, and they are all clearly-pictured, compelling persons.

Barbara is Jørgen-Frantz Jacobsen's only novel. It was written between 1934 and 1938, the last four years of his short life, towards the end of which he was dying of tuberculosis in a Copenhagen hospital. The manuscript was taken literally from his deathbed and prepared for publication by his close friend and exact contemporary, the Faroese novelist and poet, William Heinesen. Soon after its publication in 1939 by Gyldendal in Copenhagen, it was translated into other languages, and it quickly became recognized as a modern Scandinavian classic. The whole story is set in the Faroe Islands, the author's beloved homeland. He was born in their tiny capital Thorshavn (modern spelling Torshavn) in 1900 of a Danish-speaking father from Copenhagen and a Faroese mother. He and his brothers and sisters spoke Faroese among themselves and with their mother, and Danish with their father. Jørgen-Frantz took his senior schooling in Denmark and graduated Cand.Mag. in History and French from the University of Copenhagen. He became a journalist, and might have taken part in politics, for which he had a bent, except for the onset of tuberculosis in his twenty-second year. He continued to write, and between bouts of his illness he lived an active life until his last four years. He published two other books, one a collection of his columns from the Copenhagen newspaper *Politiken*; the other an account of the Faroese and their land. By trade he was a journalist, but at heart he was a poet, as the classical simplicity of his writing in *Barbara* and in his book about the Faroe Islands shows.

5

The dramatic beauty of the islands is reflected in the novel. There are eighteen islands in the archipelago, lying close together in the North Atlantic, sixty-two degrees north, seven degrees west, between Shetland and Iceland. All but the southernmost are mountainous, and in the channels between their steep coasts the tides make strong and treacherous currents. Many of their shorelines are sheer cliffs, hundreds of metres high, alive with sea birds. Their climate is tempered by the Gulf Stream, but storms and high winds are frequent, and fog and rain are sometimes continuous for weeks. Between the rugged, pyramid-shaped mountains the slopes are gentle and green. These contrasts may be seen in the characters of the novel, though there is no violence in the story except of the weather and of Pastor Paul's feelings, and in his one scene of destructive rage.

Barbara was written in Danish, which was the official language of the Islands when it was published. The Faroese language has since come into its own, though there are still hardly more than fifty thousand speakers of it, the largest number of current readers the fine poets and novelists now writing for it can hope for, except in translation. It is a West-Norse language, closely related to Icelandic and the older dialects of Norwegian, recently combined into Nynorsk. The Faroese poet and scholar, Christian Matras, translated the novel into Faroese, and gave its chief character the Faroese form of her name, Barba. The present translation, though it was made from the Danish, owes much to Christian Matras's fine and illuminating version, which was closely consulted all through.

The novel was translated into English once before by Estrid Bannister, a friend of Jacobsen, and in many respects the original of Barbara. Penguin published her translation in 1948, and it has long been out of print. Christian Matras urged me to make a new translation. I could not have done so without the assistance of Professor Glyn Jones and Kirsten Gade, whose literary sensitivity and familiarity with the Danish and Faroese languages, and with the Islands and their people, made their advice invaluable. I must also thank Professor Christian Matras for proposing the work,, and for giving me so much help and encouragement.

Huntingdon QC   G.J.
Canada   December 1992

Principal characters in the story

Faroese

Barbara Salling, subsequently, Aggersoe, widow of Pastor Niels
Salling, and before him of Pastor Jonas
    daughter of Magdalena Stenderup, widow of the late Judge
    Stenderup
Samuel Mikkelsen, Chief Magistrate of the Islands
Gabriel, Clerk of the Royal Stores
Pastor Wenzel Heyde, priest of the parish of Torshavn
Johan Hendrik Heyde, his brother, Judge, successor to Barbara's
    father
Anna Sophia, Pastor Wenzel Heyde's wife
Andreas Heyde, nephew of Pastor Wenzel Heyde and Judge Johan
    Hendrik Heyde

Danish

Pastor Paul Aggersoe, new priest of Vagar
Suzanne Harme
Bailie Augustus Harme, father of Suzanne
The Company Manager of the Royal Stores
Commandant Otto Hjorring

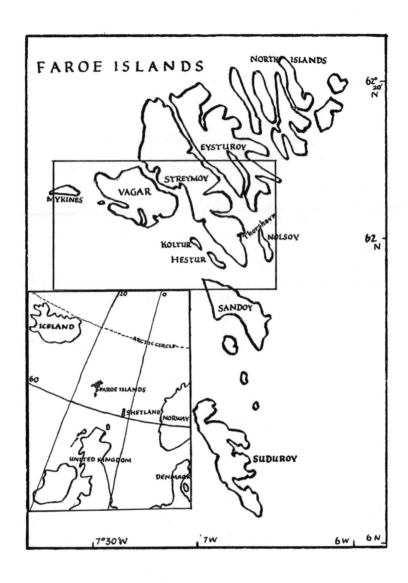

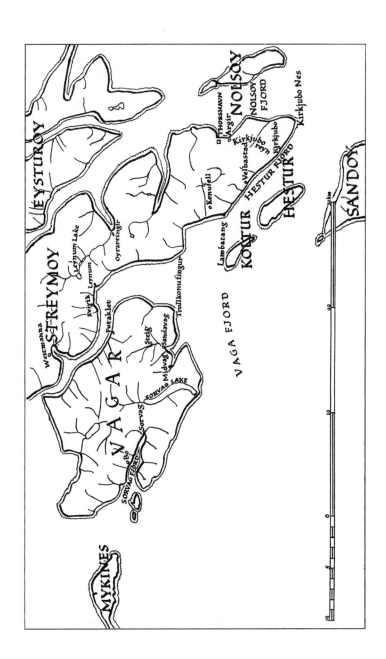

1
Fortuna

The lamps in the Royal Stores Warehouses were nearly blown out by draughts that came with each blast of the gale, but between gusts it was as quiet as the grave. Then the thick beams and rafters would give as the wind renewed its attack on these tarred wooden structures. It whined most grievously in every corner, the warehouse shutters sprang and tugged at their iron hinges, the sod roof waved and flattened like tempestuous flames, and the surf poured in heavy disorder on the flat stone shore of Tinganes and covered all Torshavn in a shower of salt and rain.

In the ships' stores Ole the Sockmaster and Rebekka's Paul were sorting seagoing jerseys. They sat inside in a lantern's small circle of light. Elsewhere the warehouses lay in darkness. But in the shop many were gathered.

There had been news. A boat out fishing east of Nolsoy had seen a ship. They were sure it must be *Fortuna*, due from Copenhagen with goods for the Stores. But she could not come in in this weather. The boat had made land at the last moment before the gale broke.

The men stood idle and talked about the ship. They were all Torshavn men — *Havners* — soldiers at the Fort, porters at the Stores and fishermen on the wild sea all at once, fishermen when weather and their commanding officer permitted. They lounged against the counter. Tallow candles shone on their slack faces and made shadows around their wet, red-rimmed eyes. They spat and yawned gloomily.

11

The news was turned over and over like a quid. Gabriel, the shopkeeper, stood behind the counter at his desk. Now and again he looked up from his reckoning and added his word to the talk.

Was the ship a two-master or a three-master? Two-master. Ay, that must be *Fortuna*.

Katrina of the Cellar fought her way into the shop. The wind was at her heels like an evil spirit. The door slammed shut again. She gave a shy Good Evening, ill at ease about all the bluster she had made. The men spat a little more deliberately and in this way let it be known that they were aware of her. They did not indeed make much of it — neither Springus, Niels of the Field, Samuel of Vippun, or Shrimp. But female participation in serious talk about sea-going would not be gratifying to them. Katrina of the Cellar had a full understanding of this too. She stood meekly a long while and was merely Katrina of the Cellar. It would be more correct to say that for the moment she hardly existed. But her eyes were watchful and stubborn. She had her little campaign to conduct. So when Gabriel once, as it were almost by chance, let his eye light upon her she was right there:

— God bless you, Gabriel, let me get this jug full of molasses from you this evening!

She pushed the jug cautiously across the counter in front of her.

— What the devil do you come stumbling in here for again? Were you not here already today, and bought flour and meal too?

— May God bless you! Just something nice for the little ones this evening.

— Ah, go to blazes! shouted Gabriel impatiently. Why the devil can you not buy everything at once?

— We could not put more in the book this morning, do you see. But now Markus has made such a good catch today, so ...

— Do you think I have nothing better to do than go to that molasses barrel every time Markus hooks a few pollock?

He went with an ill grace over to the barrel, bent his fat back and let the thick molasses run down into the jug. Katrina looked on nervously. It came so slowly. If only he might not change his mind when it was half full. Gabriel groaned and swore quietly. At last he straightened up and slid the jug across the counter: — There, then!

He took her account book and wrote in it. Katrina departed. The men spat.

Gabriel was by nature easy-going but took on some airs on account of his position. He had a big, full-lipped mouth that fairly bubbled with a friendly audaciousness. Idleness had made him fat and under this daily routine behind the shop counter, teasing had become for him something chronic. He was monarch over all his customers and with even-handed generosity he distributed grain and sweets, snuff and sarcasm to his subjects on the other side of the counter.

And now the talk about the ship was beginning to bore him.

— Well, well, he said suddenly, turning his attention to Shrimp. Did you not see any whales today?

Shrimp gave a short spit. He knew what was up. Now he had become a target. His head turned quickly from left to right and his eyes roved watchfully. Were they laughing at him?

— Whales? Whoever saw whales in November, may I ask?

— I thought perhaps *you* did. You see whales when nobody else does.

That story was never to die! Shrimp had once mistaken a flock of eider ducks in the water for pilot whales. In his excitement he had sounded the alarm and caused a deal of commotion. Such mischance had also befallen others. Was that a thing to talk about so many years later? It made him angry every time it was brought up.

The men laughed. Shrimp glared at them, eyed them up and down, first one, then another, with his sour aggrieved look, while he searched for words. His look stopped at Samuel of Vippun.

— You, Samuel, yes *you* had better hold your jaw. Anyhow I do not lie asleep at my post over at the Fort while the whales go swimming by under my nose, the way you do.

— Me?

Samuel was fairly frozen-mouthed with wrathful amazement.

— Me?

There was a cackle of laughter all round. This was a well-known story too. Only Samuel knew absolutely nothing about it. An underworld of injury stood ready to spring in his eyes. He scrutinized the miserable Shrimp. What would he not dare to accuse him of?

13

It became a duel of stares. Then it became a duel of words. They had both tasted the bottle. They were full of injured pride. They were proper men — that they could tell each other. They did their duty. Did anyone dare say otherwise, perhaps?

They banged gingerly on the counter. Gabriel was in his element. Now he had the game going. Now and again he would throw in a serious, utterly matter-of-fact observation, that mightily inflamed their tempers. Then came a turning point in the strife when Shrimp suddenly — as though by a secret inspiration — got hold of the word *contrabandist* and fired that out. He did not understand what it really meant. Silence descended. Samuel of Vippun drew himself up and glared at Shrimp.

— Me? A contrabandist?

Neither did he know what a contrabandist was. But that made the charge no less insulting. Something must be done about it.

— Nay! he burst out, with composure and much dignity. Then he set forth at a walk. Everyone watched in amazement. In he marched behind the counter! In between hogsheads and sacks, right into Gabriel's desk. There he took his stand.

— Nay! *You* are a contrabandist! he roared, and struck a thumping blow on the account books. He turned a paralysing look on Shrimp. Then back he went to his place again, the long way, like a man who has driven home his point.

Shrimp blinked wildly. He had been hit.

— Me? Me? A contrabandist?

Could it really be true? His jaw fell.

— Nay! said he at last, forcefully, and full of recovered conviction. — You, you, yes *you*!

He shuffled out of his clogs, strode in behind the counter, went right through to the desk, thumped it and said in a tearful voice: — *You* are a contrabandist!

Back he went to his place again, circumspectly, and into his clogs.

If Samuel of Vippun had been amazed when the accusation was first hurled, he was no less so the second time. He had in general developed an unusual capacity for feeling amazement at the wickedness of the world — and for meeting it with steadfastness of soul. But this *must* be protested.

So he went deliberately in to the desk again, drew himself up, aimed and fired, like the soldier he was. The desk rattled: — No! *You* are a contrabandist!

Shrimp recoiled a little. That mean flank attack again. His head turned in watchful jerks, to right and to left, his sour eyes spied around him, squinting. Nay, this was more than he could put up with. Clogs off. Straight to the desk. He was a soldier too and knew how to hit a mark. He would show them. He loaded his injured look with the full weight of his ruffled and bullied soul and his fist with the whole of his body's might: — Nay! *You* — are — a — contrabandist!

This last word he shrieked out and followed it with three short extra thumps, a salvo on the desk. Then back he went again. Victorious, he resumed his clogs. Samuel had got it this time.

Samuel reeled under this brutal attack. But little by little he recovered somewhat. He got in motion, still rather bowed, but with renewed tragic dignity. And so they went on. The other men quivered in delighted neutrality. They held their hands before their mouths but their eyes were lively, watchful and gleeful. God be praised it was not them in the line of fire.

Gabriel did not at first like these natural forces being let loose on his desk. But bit by bit he sacrificed dignity on the altar of fun. After all, devil take him, had he not set them going himself? It tickled him, his stomach went quietly out and in. And the Havn men carried on religiously with their comedy, to his high and mightiness' great enjoyment. At last he stationed himself at the end of the counter and controlled them somewhat by virtue of his authority. Neither had permission to go in and bang before the other had come out.

Such was Gabriel. A virtuoso in the art of playing on good folks' weaknesses, stirring them up against one another, making them turn out their hearts' most secret and foolishest longings. What did they want, out in his shop, the poor devils? Life at home with the old woman in the turf smoke, and the bairns bawling was not as much fun. Here there were smells of cardamom and other spices, ay and the prospect of an akvavit bottle. And then, there was news. A glimpse of the world.

And something might well happen.

Once again the door opened to the gale and roar. No-one had paid attention, with the bickering going on — it must be some woman or other. Now they all saw that it was Barbara, the judge's daughter, that had come in.

Everything changed in a moment. Even Gabriel changed. Shrimp was stopped in mid-'contrabandist', his fist fell like an absurd spent shot on the royal desk. There he stood — in his socks — Lord Jesus! — and tried to look like someone.

It was not that Barbara's presence demanded special respect. She talked in a friendly way with the common men and was never proud. But when the sun on a stormy evening suddenly shines on the world of men ...

— Do you have silk ribbon to sell? sang her voice.

— Silk ribbon! Gabriel roused himself: — Silk ribbon, a likely thing!

Barbara, the sun, suddenly made a thoughtful wrinkle between her eyes, pushed out her lips and began to argue. Shrimp sneaked warily out to his place again, but — Barbara's skirt was covering his clogs.

— However we shall have much more silk ribbon tomorrow, said Gabriel. A gleam awoke in his eye.

— Tomorrow?

There was a note of surprise in her voice.

— Ay, or the day after tomorrow.

— What do you mean? Barbara's voice was still more surprised, and at the same time on the verge of laughter.

— Do not fool me, Barbara, said Gabriel, affably: — you will not make me believe that you are the only person in all Havn who does not know that *Fortuna* is lying off Nolsoy.

— God knows ...

Barbara became stubborn, indignation began to rise up against the little laughter that trembled in her throat.

— Ay, now Shrimp broke into speech, his legs apart and making explanatory gestures with his hands. We saw her, Thomas Ole and Marcus of the Cellar and Samuel of Vippun and I, when we were out fishing this morning.

Barbara suddenly let the sun shine on Shrimp.

— You did? But why does she not come in, then?

Shrimp stood in the splendour and shook his head with the glory and excitement: — Nay, there is no lying here in Havn in this weather.

— Ah, of course not.

— And this new Vagar priest who is aboard, — have you not heard of him either, Barbara? asked Gabriel.

— Naturally I know that a new priest is to come to Vagar.

She sounded a little annoyed, and gave up about the silk ribbon.

— As I was saying, repeated Gabriel, when the ship comes in tomorrow or the day after tomorrow, you may have the silk ribbon you wish. But perhaps that will be too late?

— What do you mean? Barbara was again half way between annoyance and laughter.

— Nothing. I only mean that then it will be too late to pretty up for the priest. For by then he *will* be ashore.

The men looked startled at Gabriel. True, he was a cousin of Barbara. But to tease her exactly as he would another ... ! They looked at her out of the corners of their eyes. She stood in the yellow tallow-candle light with a smile on her lips. Not angry in the least. It was almost as though she took a secret pleasure in this shrewd hit.

Then she turned to Niels of the Field and said in a voice full of pleasure: — Is your little daughter getting better, Niels? I shall bring her something tomorrow.

She went to the door and began to push it open. Shrimp, who meanwhile had got his clogs back on, sprang forward to help her. There was a broad smile on his aggrieved face as she went out. There was a smile on all their faces. Some of her laughter, that trembled in her throat, still hung like a tune in the aroma of cardamom. A vision had come and gone. The ragged men had been struck with devotion.

But then Gabriel broke the silence: — Now devil take me if that is not *too* much! Now I will be sworn that tomorrow down she goes to set her snare for the new priest when he comes ashore, exactly as she did for Pastor Niels and Pastor Anders as soon as *they* came!

There was a scandalized note in Gabriel's voice.

Oh, ay. They all knew that story. Barbara was already widow of two priests, Pastor Jonas of the North Islands and Pastor Niels of Vagar, the latter had been dead for only a year. A third, Pastor Anders of Ness, to whom she had been betrothed between the others, had thought better of it in time. For *him* it had not gone badly. But folks said that Barbara had caused the death of both men she had married. There had been much tongue-wagging about it all around among the islands, and some called her *wicked Barbara*. But that was mostly in the outlying villages. Those who knew Barbara said that *wicked* she was not. As for the Havn folk, the folk of her own town, she had never had any quarrel with them, on the contrary. But Gabriel was always ready to make insinuations.

Ole the Sockmaster and Rebekka's Paul came in from the ship-chandler's warehouse with the lantern. They had finished. Moreover it was time to go home for supper. All the men departed, and walked out glumly into the storm, between the warehouses, up over Reyn, past the church and home to their hovels.

All at once Gabriel was alone in his shop. He was big, he was king of those who came to buy, and they had all heard that he could tease even Barbara. But somewhere inside Gabriel it hurt a little. He was only human. Also, in his shopkeeper's soul there lived a hidden streak of idiocy. It was nothing. Perhaps it was only a little dog that howled at the moon, when no-one heard it. He was doing very well, had his earnings and made a little on the side. He would likely be Stores Manager too, one day. Or bailie, for he had good connections. And as for loneliness now, he had Angelika too, who came to him in his rooms when he wanted her. Everything was in order, he managed very well. But then there was that cousin of his, Barbara, who had been married to two priests. She had had amours with many other men, he knew that, he was a clever one, nothing got past him. It was a disgrace to her folk and a scandal altogether. But if there was to be mad goings-on, why had she never done a little marrying with *him*? It lay under their noses. And it would be within the family. It could easily be arranged.

But now comes this new priest.

The little dog in Gabriel set up a howl that was heart-breaking, with his nose up in the air. Then suddenly he got an idea. He gave a little whistle. Of course!

Soon after, when he was in the Stores Manager's office with the keys, he had worked out his plan.

— Where have you been, Barbara Christina? asked Magdalena, the Judge's widow, rather coldly and irritably. She had been sitting by her bureau in her big room, putting some old accounts in order.

Barbara was cold and half wet through from a rain-shower. — You are always sitting at that bureau, mamma. Why do you not sit out here in the smoke room, where there is some heat?

— Ah, Jesus, I lit a fire in the big stove.

— Oh, ay, there is no heat in it, you know that.

They ate their supper in silence. Then mamma went back to her drawing room again, with its bureau and the two ugly miniatures on the white-scoured wall. — Do you not think your papa may have hidden some money in a secret drawer in the bureau? she asked from the doorway.

— You ask me that every day. I do not believe in that story any more. We would have found the place long ago ...

When Gabriel, an hour later, knocked on the door and walked in he found Barbara standing by the fire in a woollen petticoat. A pair of stockings lay carelessly thrown aside where she had taken them off. She was drowsy and bored, and her cousin's coming awoke no femininity in her.

Magdalena came out from the drawing room and asked her nephew about the news. — Do not sit there like that! she directed at her daughter. You could pull something over you!

— Oh, Gabriel is no stranger, said Barbara, shortly.

No, Gabriel was no stranger. He could sit here and see her white arms and neck — as a matter of course, too entirely a matter of course altogether. That was the damnable thing about it. Her skin was so unbelievably bright. Might that be because she had just been in the tub?

Magdalena went back in again after a moment. But Barbara yawned.

— You, Barbara — do you want to have some silk ribbon and stuff and such things? asked Gabriel, suddenly confidential.

Barbara started up, her eyes came to life at once, her voice rang with warmth. — Have you got something?

— Perhaps I can find you something.

— Where? Where? Her whole body was suddenly in motion, her face lit up in shining, almost comical excitement.

— Not a word about it, said Gabriel.

— Of course not, she declared, impatiently; she shivered with delight in the secrecy. The little laughter rose in her throat.

— I have a whole heap out at my place, whispered Gabriel.

— Truly? Out in your quarters? Shall we go right there?

It was a moment's work, open a chest, pull out a drawer and Barbara was in a skirt and shoes again, with a kerchief round her neck, and they were sworn conspirators. Gabriel was somewhat dazed, his big mouth was open.

At that moment in came Suzanne Harme, the Bailie's daughter.

— What a lark, chattered Barbara: just imagine, I am going out to Gabriel's quarters with him to look at some silks and stuffs he has there. Is that not exciting? It was lucky you came!

It did not seem so to Gabriel. Down went a great hope. Devil in hell!

— Out in his quarters? said Suzanne. She gave a visible little shiver. She was a fine-featured brunette. She wrinkled her forehead.

— Is that not madly exciting? said Barbara again.

— I do not know. This very evening? Will it not be noticed? Papa is Bailie, you know.

— You do not usually make so much of that! Gabriel burst out: — But we can quite well go without you.

— No, no, Barbara insisted.

— Yes, but Papa has an office in that building, said Suzanne. And what if you are found out, Gabriel?

— What then? Has the Bailie never sold an ell of cloth? How about that Dutch East Indiaman? But in any case there is no Bailie's office up in my quarters — not this evening, anyhow.

— Mamma, I am going to Suzanne's for a while, called Barbara as they went out. They waded through *Gongin* in the pitch darkness. Rain blew on them in fierce gusts, from above and below. They groped onward and picked their way carefully.

— This is the same as smuggling, Suzanne asserted.

Barbara laughed deep inside. Exciting! Exciting! She had to hold Gabriel's arm. Gongin was the one continuous street in Havn. Otherwise there were only random alleyways between the scattered houses and hovels, *skots*, as the townsfolk called them, often so narrow that two people could hardly pass each other in them. They came up on to the elevation, *Reyn*, where the school, the rectory, Reynagard, and the church were located. They crossed the churchyard. Behind the church, in the church-skot, was the entrance to the living quarters, the northernmost of the Royal Company's buildings. Gabriel turned a mighty key in the lock. The pitch dark, the sudden silence and the oppressive air struck the two young women to the heart as they crossed the threshold of the nocturnal warehouse. Gabriel groped about, at last found a lantern, struck a flame and lit it. They climbed a steep stairs and crossed a long loft. Their shadows flickered across the creaking floorboards. The roofs' grass roots hung down here and there, shrivelled between the rafters. Suzanne clung, shivering, to Barbara.

They stepped into Gabriel's room, far into the one gable. It was a little room with an alcove bed, wallpress and chests.

— Do you never meet Master Naaber here? asked Suzanne, in a tone of giggly anxiety.

— Master Naaber — who the deuce is that? asked Gabriel.

— Do you not know that? Nay, you were not brought up here. All Havn folk are afraid of him. He goes round among the lofts out here in Havn at night.

— I have never seen him.

— He goes about with a black pointed hat and talks to himself. And when he looks at you he has yellow eyes.

She shivered with uneasiness: — Never in the world would I dare to live here!

Gabriel did not like this talk. He began rather noisily to light some candles.

— Have you never seen the *council* either? Suzanne went on.

— The council, what are you talking about?

— The council, you know. Suzanne's eyes grew wide: — The seven men! They sit in one of the houses, I do not know which, at a great table.

Gabriel began to feel cold. Suzanne was spell-bound by her own words. Her features were the least bit twisted. Her voice was low and strained: — Lots of people have seen them. They sit quite still and write and write and seal letters.

— That is enough! Barbara called sharply. A shiver went through her, then she smiled weakly.

— You are not right wise, said Gabriel.

There was silence. The weak illumination from the candlesticks fell far short of all the little room's corners. Bare wood, darkened with age, could be glimpsed through the cobwebby dusk. Suzanne's eyes still showed their queer glint. But now Gabriel began to unpack, and colours blossomed forth from mysterious hiding places. The little room was suddenly transformed, the unearthly spell was broken. Eager women's hands grasped the stuffs, spread them out, white fingers ran over the whistling silks, that gleamed and flashed on the humble table. At first there was only dumb amazement and shining eyes. A quiet springtime was kindled under Master Naaber's sod roof — it raised itself as a mound on four table legs, while the two women sat spellbound.

Gabriel, shopkeeper and lover, played his hand with skill, wasted no trumps but proceeded quietly and let the drama unfold like a splendid ritual. The moment was his. He did not break the silence, but simply let one treasure after another manifest itself.

— Ah, yes, Gabriel, asked Suzanne, suddenly come to her senses: — and how have you come by all this?

— Do I have to say? I have not stolen it.

— You have had dealings with some Hollander or English contrabandist.

Gabriel would not deny it. It sounded all right. Besides the truth was this: it was one of the Royal Company's own skippers that he worked together with.

— And you have silk stockings too! Barbara exclaimed, in astonished glee.

Merchandise is power, thought Gabriel. Barbara's wet wool stockings came suddenly before his mind's eye, as they lay drying by the fire, so dull and workaday. The lead seemed to have come to him and he was playing a winning hand again. — Look here!

He brought out a pair of brocaded slippers and held them to Barbara's feet, which were covered with mud from the lanes.

The two women stared. Barbara withdrew her feet, somewhat embarrassed by the contrast, but then she immediately did want to try the slippers on. Gabriel was not unwilling, he was more than glad to help her, he kneeled and took her shoe off. Barbara's foot was only in a coarse woollen stocking, but the devil — small and nimble as it was it fitted exactly into the fine slipper, indeed the slipper was almost a shade too big. Ah, that blasted Suzanne! Why did she have to come? Gabriel had a sudden dizzying prospect of what spoiled possibilities the moment held. He had many things that perhaps Barbara, otherwise, would not have been unwilling to try on.

His heart thumped. And so it happened that his scheming head for a second misfired. He brought out an elegant garter. Would Barbara like to try this on?

There was a little gasp in her throat, she threw a glance at Suzanne, and then she laughed and said, very friendly: — There is no need to try on a garter, Gabriel.

Suzanne looked up a trifle distracted, with a fleeting furrow in her brow, and then said, suddenly eager: — Let me try on the slippers.

Barbara got up. — How would a dress of this stuff look? she asked, and began to drape some flowered material against herself.

— See, if I had a skirt like this with these slippers, said Suzanne, and pirouetted under a piece of silk.

— Nay, look at *this* now, called Barbara, enthusiastically. She pulled a length out of the pile and held it up to the light.

Gabriel tried to get a word in, but they did not listen to him. And all at once it became clear to him that his wares had quite elbowed him out. The two women had launched into an orgy of clothes talk, they chose and rejected, felt and tried on. Barbara's eyes shone, her voice bubbled like a spring, she grew prettier and prettier in her zeal for beauty.

— I think I want to take my dress off, said Suzanne.

— I think so too, I want to, said Barbara.

Their dark clothes were wet and out of shape from the rain and made the delicate fabrics damp when they tried them against themselves. Suzanne was already beginning to undo her bodice when her eye fell on Gabriel: — Ah, Gabriel, go out for a few moments, will you?

— It almost seems too bad, said Barbara.

Suzanne looked at Gabriel thoughtfully, pondering. Then she came to her conclusion: — No, we cannot have you in here, staring.

So Gabriel went.

Just as though he had been discovered in his own quarters and driven out like an unwelcome dog. It seethed in him. So much for his fine big plan. Here he waited in this empty loft. They had no doubt already forgotten him inside there. Back and forth he paced with the lamp, angry but at the same time properly ill at ease. Master Naaber! The storm had increased in fury and fell like a relentless, overpowering force on the building — an inexhaustible song of thousand-voiced lament. He got to the loft's other end by the room called *Monk's Room* and looked out through a little window pane. West Bay lay in a froth, and foam gleamed through the dark. *The Council* — were they sitting at their table now somewhere or other among the Company buildings? Perhaps only a few yards away from here. That blasted Suzanne — to come out with that story on this of all nights! *She* need not sleep alone in this house tonight.

He went over to his own door again. Women and their chatter inside. Barbara's laughter, capricious and bubbling. Suzanne's rather deeper and more sensible voice. Nay, inside there they were deaf to storm and surf. They did not turn the hourglass, the passage of the night hours meant nothing to them. Least of all did they give thought to Gabriel's hammering heart and burning desire. He was a shadow on a ceiling. But in there it was summer. They gorged themselves on stuffs and dainties and colours. He could imagine how the cloths rustled and crackled. Ay, he could swear to it that they had taken off every shred of their workaday woollens. They were two butterflies who were sunning themselves in the adventure, they wrapped themselves in red and gold and blue, in airy calico and heavy silks — *his* goods. They adorned themselves to weariness in vanity's delights.

It was a long while before it came into the women's heads to open the door to Gabriel again. By then they had chosen what they wanted. It was really Barbara who had come to buy, though the other did want some little things. And what would it cost?

Gabriel, lover and shopkeeper — he *had* thought, in certain happier conditions, to answer Barbara that it would cost next to nothing. But now he was angry, and he named a stiff, almost shameless, price.

The unexpected happened, that Barbara paid cash without a blink, heedlessly from a purse — in silver. Sacrifice on beauty's altar.

Gabriel reddened.

Suzanne had not come prepared to buy, she must have credit. And got it, readily — the town's finest lady.

Gabriel wanted to offer them something for the road. No thank you, no wine at this hour, too late now, said Suzanne. And Gabriel realized that this trump was one he should not have held so long.

As they were going through the long loft, Barbara said quietly and friendly to Gabriel: — I did try on your garter after all.

Was this meant to be comforting? A queer kind of comfort, it must be said. And yet, the way it was spoken, it almost sounded like a thank you. Was it true, as the word went, that no-one complimented Barbara quite unrewarded?

But Gabriel had not complimented her. That tart and priest's hussy! He knew well enough what went on.

In the churchyard the women parted from him. He returned through the graves past the church. Barbara's coins still lay clutched in his sweaty hand. Now he could soon begin to buy property. But the little dog in Gabriel howled. And in he went, into that dark empty house, to Master Naaber and a lonely bed.

And while the storm lay like a nightmare over the town, the two women slipped, slyly and guiltily, full of their doings and carrying a rich plunder, through rain-drenched laneways to their homes.

2
Widow in the Living

S o, you do know that there is a widow in the living?
It was the Bailie, speaking.

The new Vagar priest, Pastor Paul Aggersoe, did know. It concerned him mighty little. Most pastors took the practical course and married the widow. But he was made of no such accommodating stuff. He was not, by and large, in the marrying frame of mind, and it annoyed him when others tried to think that way for him.

He sat in the drawing-room of his colleague, the Havn priest, surrounded by folk who wanted to hear news from the big world. He had been able to tell of battles and generals, of King Frederick of Prussia, whom no-one could defeat, and of King Louis of France, whom no-one could discompose in his debaucheries. His news put them in a state of some excitement, all of them, Judge, Bailie, Stores Manager and Commandant. They kept going and coming and stepping over the high threshold between the drawing room and the study. The women had nothing to say — except for old Armgard, the Chief Magistrate's widow, and her sister Ellen Katrina, with the crutches and happy face. She maintained that no-one nowadays could compare with Marlborough, who had lived while she was young.

Pastor Paul sat and took in all these outlandish folk he had come among. He could still feel the motion of the ship. Four weeks he had been at sea. During the last twenty-four hours the ship lay in a howling gale under a black sharp island that was called Nolsoy. At last this morning the weather had abated and they had sailed in.

Vestiges of the night still hung in the air when *Fortuna* dropped anchor. It was cold and raw, snow showers dragged themselves across the lumpy turf of the hillsides. A black and weather-beaten church-steeple of wood reached up over a few knots of dwellings. This was Torshavn. It was all very muddy. The people who emerged from under the house gables were chilled and pale at this wan morning hour. Pastor Paul had almost felt as though he had come ashore somewhere in the underworld when he set foot on the stone shelf at Tinganes. But when he walked up towards the Company buildings he saw, amid a little cluster of the curious who stood in the doorway, two women in pretty clothing. He was particularly struck by one of them. She was straight and fair-skinned and she held herself with elegant lightness on her feet, and to him she paid not the least attention.

For the whole of the dark, rain-filled day he had been moving among strange folk. They did not stand out sharply for him yet, they were big shadows who spoke a half-intelligible language. Here in the priest's dim-lit drawing room they passed back and forth; a spinning wheel was whirring somewhere in the house, the roof's withered grass hung down before the windows, and the outlook was grey over East Bay to the Fort on the other side, where the flag was flapping. But throughout all this the memory persisted of the woman he had seen. He could forget for long whiles, but she was always there just the same — like something sweet, like a break in the clouds, a comfort.

But it was clear that the Bailie most wanted to go on about this widow in the living.

Bailie Augustus Harme was a Dane; he was a big man, red-faced and a little sweaty. His voice was pompous, friendly enough but always didactic in tone, always knowing. He was everlastingly clearing his throat and taking his time about doing so. When he had a pinch of snuff he let his listeners wait until he was able to speak again.

— Yes, said he, perhaps you also know that this widow is the daughter of the late Judge Peter Willumsen Salling. She is not very old, only twenty-eight, I believe.

— Let you not be praising Barbara Christina, came a stern voice from a pair of knitting needles; she is a slut, everyone knows that. This was the Chief Magistrate's widow joining in. She had a big nose, and her eyes were sharp and cold as a sea-gull's.

— I am not praising Barbara, said the Bailie. But I do not dispraise her either. I just think that our young priest must be apprised of the situation.

— Then you should rather tell him about her doings than about her age, Armgard replied, and rapped with her knuckles on the table: what *she* has managed to do in her eight and twenty years ...

— I wonder, I wonder, said the Judge. It seems to me that Barbara cannot be called a slut. She has her failings, and they are easy to see. But can she help that? Truly, there is not a wicked drop of blood in her.

— Ah, you, Johan Hendrik. You were at home in the old Judge's house like a cat under the stove. You are a fine one to be talking about these things.

— You are right, Armgard. I have known Barbara from the cradle. But you know nothing about her except the slanders you have heard.

— I know the truth. I know how both Pastor Thomas and Pastor Niels died.

The Judge, Johan Hendrik Heyde, said no more. He rubbed his chin, thoughtfully. About his tall, somewhat stooped figure there was a hint of nervousness, of doubt. It was always this way with him. A gentleman, wiser than the others, much too wise to be unbending. But he could be sarcastic, in a dry and biting way. Therefore he was held in respect, even feared.

Like his brother Wenzel Heyde, the parish priest of Havn, he was counted among the better class of Faroese. They both came of an old line, with considerable foreign blood in it, but rooted in the islands. Otherwise there was little in common between the two brothers. The Judge was tall and thin, the priest short and thick. The Judge sceptical, the priest unctuous. And while in Johan Hendrik there was a constant hidden simmering of bile towards his Danish-born fellow officials — the Bailie and the Company Manager — Wenzel bore an equally hidden and equally consuming desire to be of their society. For this reason also Pastor Wenzel was gratified to have them present in his drawing room now, the important Bailie and the witty

Company Manager, with his many comical stories and fine wife, Fru Mathilde, who had little to say and was anaemic as well, but could giggle and faint in a most genteel way.

The talk had died down somewhat among the many people. After the news from the outside world had been told there was no longer anything that quite united them all. In the study, however, there was a clandestine focus, which from time to time caused the men to exchange meaningful glances. There was no rest among them. They kept walking and walking about and drifting across the threshold. It was not merely on account of Barbara that Armgard knit so badly and moodily. She had smelled a device, and was vexed. It was the same with the other women. So it always was when a ship came in.

The Chief Magistrate, too, Samuel Mikkelsen, got to his feet and made a trip into the study. For this massive, immovable man it amounted almost to a whole expedition. And it took long. Armgard gave an ill-tempered grunt when she saw her nephew, her husband's successor, block the whole doorway with his broad back. But her sister, Ellen Katrina, had a knowing glint in her eye. She lay at full length on a bench and drew a giddy drawing in the air with her crutch: — Ah world, world!

The new priest later remembered all this very clearly. But for the moment he had no proper understanding of it. A discreet invitation from his colleague, Pastor Wenzel, first opened his eyes to the fact that there was French brandy to be had in the study.

Neither did he understand this about the widow Barbara: that a fresh breeze filled the conversation's slack sail when the Bailie mentioned her name.

The Chief Magistrate came back out of the study, big and gentle and with some indefinable air or other of renewal about him. He had a broad, wavy, full beard. He looked like the god Jupiter. But his eyes were quiet and gentle. Most often there shone a fine and almost loving smile in them.

He seated himself and said nothing at first. Then he raised his gentle voice: — What Barbara was like in her first marriage I shall leave unsaid, though I have heard some noteworthy things about that. In her second marriage she was not a good wife, I believe so, I dare say so. But to assert that she was responsible for Pastor Niels' death — that is not right, for that was accidental.

Armgard snorted. — Accidental! Ay, then there have been many accidents for Barbara. And they have all come marvellously convenient for her.

Ellen Katrina leaned up from her bench and waved her crutch as though she was signalling: — Hold your tongue, Armgard, and let Samuel tell his story. He knows better about it than you!

Samuel, the Chief Magistrate, sat and looked at his small hands. It was seldom his way to say much. Everyone listened to him intently. He had never before said anything about Barbara. But he must know what was what. His Chief Magistrate's house, Steigargard, was in Sandavag, barely a good mile from the Priest's house in Jansagerd in Midvag, where Pastor Niels and Barbara had lived.

— I do not pretend to understand Barbara. When she came west to Vagar with Pastor Niels, no-one could see but that she worshipped him. Everyone spoke well of her, and for my part I cannot say other than that in all her ways and all her doings she appeared to be an angel.

— An *angel*! Old seagull Armgard gave her nephew a piercing look: Nay, by almighty God, Samuel! Her fist came almost to the table again: Others may not be so wise, but *you* at least ought to know that an angel outward is not the same as an angel inward.

The Chief Magistrate smiled. He held his peace a moment. But no-one broke in, the word was his. Then forth it came, deliberately, with the merest hint of indulgent irony: — Ay, Aunt Armgard, how hasty you are! For that was exactly what I was by way of saying. She *was* no angel, inward. But that does not need to mean that she was a devil, for that was not her nature. I believe that she wanted to be good to everyone. She was down among the folk when they came in from fishing, she was out at the turf-cutting, something that other priest's wives are not used to doing, and she joined in the dances. That did not rightly please Pastor Niels.

— Dear God, said Ellen Katrina: join in the dances, there should be nothing sinful in that — not even for a priest's wife.

— Nay, broke in the Judge: if you were a priest's wife, Aunt Ellen Katrina, and you joined in the dances, then neither would I think that anything sinful would come of it.

— Oh you, Johan Hendrik! You hold your tongue for *once*, with your impertinence! She gave him a tap with her crutch. Her look was at once solemn and giddy.

But the Chief Magistrate's gentle eyes twinkled for a fraction of a second. Then he continued: — No doubt Pastor Niels would have felt more secure with another wife. I do not say that this was Barbara's fault. But so it was, that when Barbara was in the dance, *all* were in the dance, men and women alike.

— No-one will understand that, said the Priest's wife, Anna Sophia, the mistress of the house: it is not always so easy to be Barbara at a dance.

— If Barbara had understood that herself, then she should have kept herself away from the dances, said Armgard. And this time she let her fist thump down on the table.

— How exciting do you think it would have been, evening after evening at home in Jansagerd with Pastor Niels and his mouldy books? said Anna Sophia, with sudden energy.

— Ah, world, world! Ellen Katrina burst out and made signs most thoughtfully in the air with her crutch.

But Paster Wenzel Heyde, the short and unctuous, gave his wife a most disapproving look. She was jolly and plump and had deep dimples.

— Tell me one thing, though, asked Ellen Katrina. Was Barbara not fond of her husband?

— I can assure you, said the Chief Magistrate, that I do not remember having seen a wife so affectionate with her husband, when I first knew them. She would have him near her at all times, and was bound she would help him with everything. And when he was away she always longed for him. And he longed for her too. He would never stay a night with us at Steigargard. In the very worst weather he rode home to her in the evening — in rain, sleet or frost. And so it was, moreover, all through their married life, that she could not bear to have him neglect her. It was on this account that they had their first quarrels — God help me, I think she would hardly give him leave to write his sermons.

— Ay, Barbara! said the Judge: when she is in that mood, she is ready to be jealous of God in Heaven himself!

The Chief Magistrate smiled. — Ay. But what she would not allow her husband, she would willingly allow herself. For many a time *she* neglected him. That was hard to understand. She did *want* to be good to him, of that I am sure. But take charge of herself is something Barbara cannot do. She does exactly what, at the moment, she wants to do — if there was a dance that she would be in, off she went. I believe she was often cut to the heart with sympathy for her husband, God knows she was! But off she went just the same. And then she quickly forgot him. And in the same way, if there was a trip to Havn here, then Barbara *had* to take it. Often she would stay here for weeks and months, as you all well know, who live here.

— No doubt of it! said the Company Manager.

The Chief Magistrate looked at him and scrutinized him for a moment: — How she behaved herself here — you know that much better than I.

— We could not well avoid — hm — not well avoid noticing this or that, said the Bailie.

— That is the gods' truth, said the Company Manager.

The Judge looked at him ironically: — Hm, ay — You did have some interest in the case.

— So, then, I arranged with Melzer of *Jubilee* to make a second trip. Do you have an objection to that?

Johan Hendrik Heyde had no objection, he merely looked more ironic.

— It must be said, the Chief Magistrate continued, that neither did Barbara behave at home on Vagar as she should. That came out all at once, one day, for all that she knew how to step warily. I do not intend to sit here and reckon up everything I have heard, much of it was slander anyhow. But there are different men to whom she has shown friendship.

Armgard had been holding her peace for some while. Now her words burst out: — From all I have heard, Samuel, this is a *slut* you are sitting and talking about!

The Company Manager whistled softly: — No, a priest's wife.

— Jesus forgive me, said Samuel Mikkelsen: she carries herself as seemly and fine as a queen. And she is so friendly and good towards everyone. As Anna Sophia said a moment ago: it is not easy to be Barbara. Everyone flocks around her. She is such that she tempts everyone — and she is tempted herself. It often seems to me that she is like a child ...

— A fine child, ay, eight and twenty years old, priest's wife and biggest whore in the country! said Armgard.

— Ay, ay, said the Judge. And Samuel is quite right. A child — a dangerous child, it is true.

— Ah, world! Ay, everyone tells his own story. But now tell me, how was it with the Priest, Samuel.

— That I shall tell you, Aunt Ellen Katrina: Pastor Niels was an unusually gentle and orderly man. Peaceful by nature. He gave in and tried to look the other way. As I have said, she was fond of him, but by little and little his complaisance must have begun to irritate her. Then he tried taking another line, and answered hard with hard. But that only put her back up. They quarrelled. People say that she once threw a candlestick at him. Gradually it became apparent to all that the Priest was having a bad time. Especially the servants took his part. And the state of affairs in Jansagerd eventually got more and more out of hand.

The Chief Magistrate's voice was deep and bucolic. It would make one think of cattle lowing softly in their stalls, or of the stall doors sounding on their wooden hinges. His words came separately and almost simply. But over his Jupiter's countenance played a fine, disciplined mingling of good nature, irony and wisdom.

— Then it happened one day, he went on, that Barbara was altogether unreasonable with Pastor Niels — in everyone's hearing. She went after him with taunts and that sort of thing. That gentle man had no idea what he should do. He tried to quiet her but it just worked her up all the more. At last she struck him. They had a manservant, Kristoffer by name, a giant of a man. This was too much for him. All at once he goes over and picks Barbara up and carries her out of the house.

— The house-man picked up the priest's wife? asked Fru Mathilde.

— Ay.

— Lord God, what did she say?

— What should she say? He carried her like a little child. She must have looked somewhat surprised. It was not until he got around behind the house with her that she began to struggle. But she was a small thing between his hands. Then he took and put her head-first into a dung barrel. And there she stayed.

— Is that really so, did he do that? they all wanted to know.

— Kristoffer himself told me that, said the Chief Magistrate.

Fru Mathilde took a little spell and had to have her smelling salts brought. — Dear God, if it had been me! I could never show my face before people again!

— It cannot have been a very edifying sight, said Samuel, taking, with a dignified smile, an indulgent attitude to life, whose turns can sometimes be so deplorably drastic. All the household were rounded up — they were fairly thunderstruck.

He smiled again, just perceptibly: — It is not a common thing, either, to see a priest's wife in that fix.

— Who helped her out?

— Kristoffer turned over the barrel and then she crawled out herself.

— She would not be an easy cat to stroke then, would she? asked the Judge.

— She was possessed. She ordered everyone out of the house for the rest of the day. Pastor Niels, poor fellow, he felt the weight of love, he had to help her clean up again. Eighteen tubs of water, they say, he had to fetch her from the river. It was summer time, a Saturday afternoon. His sermon for next day in Midvag Church suffered accordingly. But Barbara ... when the servants came home in the evening she was as clean and pretty as ever and carried on as though nothing had happened. Kristoffer came to me and gave himself up. I took it that neither Pastor Niels nor Barbara would wish to prosecute in this case, and neither they did. Then I took Kristoffer into my household, and from him comes much of what I know about the state of affairs in Jansagerd.

There was a stunned silence. Only the knitting needles could be heard.

— Now then, that is the queen you were talking about, said Armgard at last.

— Queen she was all the same, said the Chief Magistrate. Three days later I was going to Havn by boat. Along came Barbara and asked if she might go with me. But then I said that as it happened I could not have her with me. Other times I do not like to be unaccommodating. But upon my word, that seemed to astonish her amazingly. Ay, that is Barbara for you.

— It is remarkable really that this story has not made Barbara more of a laughing-stock than it has, said Pastor Wenzel. One would think that even the most beautiful woman would have become absolutely impossible.

— Ah, but why not the other way round? said the Judge.

— No, ouf! burst out Fru Mathilde.

— It shows that there is good stuff in her, said Anna Sophia.

— The devil it does, declared the Company Manager; she was simply taking care that folk should have something else to talk about, for it was only a short while after that that she killed her husband.

— It was nearly a half year before all that happened, the Chief Magistrate corrected him, gently. It was in November. The Priest had been with us one Sunday, and preached in Sandavag church. There had been a thaw and rain, but in the course of the day there had come a hard frost and all the roads and paths had become iced over. The Priest was bound he would ride home in the evening, as usual. We tried every way to put him off that. But there was no stopping him. He held to his purpose. Tired of him though Barbara surely was, she would not allow him to leave her sit at home alone.

— So off rode the Priest, the Chief Magistrate went on, and everyone knows how that turned out. At Midvagssand the horse stumbled on some flat rock, and Pastor Niels fell and broke his leg. They say that Barbara was very sympathetic at first, and cared for him so tenderly that it looked as though they were more affectionate than ever. But then it did begin to be tiresome for her. The Priest kept getting better and had come along so far that he could sit up with the broken leg resting on a chair. One day in comes a manservant and says that a strange boat has just pulled ashore down at the landing.

— It must be some gentlemen from Havn, he adds.

Barbara, who had been sitting by Pastor Niels, sprang up and ran to the window — that is her way, to be sure — and in carelessness she happened to knock over the chair in such a way that the Priest's broken leg came down on the floor and broke a second time. Then they brought the Priest to a barber-surgeon here in Havn, but he made such a botched-up job of it that gangrene set in and Pastor Niels did not recover from that.

— Ay, Samuel, said Armgard. And how deeply the widow grieved!

— I do not know how deeply she grieved, but grieve she did, everyone could see that.

— It is true that she grieved, said the Judge. She is not a brute, not Barbara. But she forgets damned quickly, that I shall willingly concede.

— It is just as I have observed, said the Chief Magistrate: she *is* like a child.

— Ah, hold your tongue, with that twaddle. You are a grown man to whom the country and people have been entrusted! Letting the wool be pulled over your eyes like that! A child! Slut, is what I say, the way she carries on, playing up to everyone.

Armgard was indignant.

— Tell me, asked Anna Sophia, have you ever spent any time with Barbara?

The seagull snarled.

— She is so delightful, said Anna Sophia.

— She is a dangerous woman, said Bailie Harme, with much solemnity.

— Ay, said Pastor Wenzel: as the hymn says, 'the fairest flower has a corrosive poison.' Let Barbara be as delightful as she may, Christian folk must stand aloof from her doings.

— She should be locked up, said Armgard, disdainfully. She is a dangerous one to be at large, there is nothing but bad luck to be met with in her wake. She should be sentenced as a whore.

— Now, now, said Johan Hendrik, and shrugged his shoulders, — perhaps there are many others, then, who should be sentenced too. According to *my* understanding of the world.

— Oh ay, oh ay, God have mercy on us, said Ellen Katrina, lame and cheerful on her bench.

— Nay, let the good Lord judge Barbara, reasoned Johan Hendrik. She is so made now, that every man, you might say, ay and every living creature that sees her adores her. And she is aware of it on every least occurrence, if it is only a dog that is worshipping her from a corner.

— Now then, asked Anna Sophia, can she do anything about that? Such is woman's nature.

— Ay, is it not the truth? Johan Hendrik went on, warming to his subject. And such a woman has she become that she needs to have everyone, no matter how small and unworthy, admiring her. Everything in her being wills to prevail — and so has done, to this day. Everyone must love her. And she will love everyone. But it is just this that escapes her, she cannot succeed in this.

— I do not understand such talk at all, said Armgard.

— It is perfectly true and wisely said altogether, declared the Company Manager, but it can all be put in a shorter and more easily understood way. Barbara is downright lecherous. That is my simple understanding.

At that moment women's voices could be heard out in the hearth-room, and two young women came into view in the doorway. Pastor Paul gave a little start — these were the two pretty women he had seen that morning in the gateway of the Company Stores.

— Thunderation! burst out the Commanding Officer of the Fort. He was so full of beer and taken off guard that he stood in the doorway to the study with the bottle in plain sight in his hand.

This was his one contribution to the talk, and it was paid attention to by no-one, for all eyes were suddenly turned to the newcomers, who gleamed in their pretty clothes, and gave off odours of face-powder and filled the air with twittering and smiles.

— Speak of angels — ! said Bailie Harme.

— Were you speaking about us?

— About you, Barbara, ay, said the Judge in a serious tone, but with a half-hidden smile.

This clearly pleased and flattered her, she lowered her eyes and laughed, and her look was modest and fresh.

Pastor Paul was as though stopped in his tracks.

The two young women went round and shook hands with everyone. Barbara Salling was somewhat tall and fair-skinned, her mouth was large and red and she had pretty teeth. She carried herself with an innate naturalness and a gentility that was no less impressive. Suzanne Harme was finer in build and had a much more beautiful face. But her clever eyes were outshone by the liveliness and quick changeableness in Barbara's glance, and her low voice seemed monotonous compared to her friend's, with its unusual turns and breakings. There seemed to be a rainbow of titillating sounds that had arisen amid the dry gossip in the room.

The new Vagar priest stood up and greeted, in a somewhat confused manner, the widow of his living. He was overcome and dazzled. Barbara exchanged handshakes with him without paying him much attention, but she was so natural that he was made to feel at ease. Everyone was made to feel at ease. The Chief Magistrate smiled from the still depths of his good nature, Pastor Wenzel was friendly, though with some reservations on Heaven's account, Anna Sophia was delighted and the Company Manager was gallant to the point of obtrusion. But his anaemic wife, Fru Mathilde, sat with her eyes on stalks and greedily took in Barbara and all she did with curiosity's fiercest demons in her look. But no-one noticed her, for all heeded Barbara alone.

But Barbara turned to Armgard's knitting and was much interested.

— It is a jacket ... or no, a kerchief, or a shawl?

And the pattern was so interesting! Armgard had to explain how it was to be, and pointed with her needles.

— It is lovely! Barbara's eyes gave a lively impression of seeing exactly what old Armgard's kerchief would look like when it would be finished some time.

Armgard's face became pleasant, a smile began to open her tight-shut lips, her old tooth-stumps began to show themselves in mere friendliness and at last she looked at Barbara with more tenderness than one would ever expect of a seagull. They chattered away, they two, about purl and plain.

Old Ellen Katrina on her bench wanted to have a proper look at Barbara. She had never spoken with her before, she lived on the great farm inland on Eysturoy and was seldom in Havn. She held the young woman's hand a long while: — Well, this is Barbara herself, this is what you look like, indeed! Her old eyes were full of attention.

Barbara was ever so little shy under this inspection, she looked down and then up, an almost comical uncertainty showing on her face. She blushed.

— Ay, then, the old dame concluded at last, beautiful you are, as I expected. Jesus bless you! World, world ...

Barbara's errand had been merely to ask the Bailie if a letter had come for her mother on *Fortuna*. She had sought him in vain at his Bailie's house. They told her there that he was away in Havn. She brought Suzanne with her. Now, praise be, she found the Bailie at last on Reyn. But ah, no, there was no letter for Mme Salling, said the Bailie. No, and there was nothing else, and the two ladies departed again.

The Judge said good-bye to Barbara in a certain ironic tone which they had both gradually agreed to recognize as a kind of caress. She responded with a look that might be interpreted thus: Ay, you are the only one who understands me to my depths, and you appreciate me! This rather pleased him. But who could tell? Perhaps she thanked the Company Manager too for his gallantry with some look or other that singled *him* out as the only one or the real one.

That Barbara! — she had sweet confidences enough with them all — bigger or littler confidences.

— How delightful she is, said Ellen Katrina. It may well be that you are right in what you say, but are you so sure too that Pastor Niels was the man for her?

— Nay, said the Judge with a little smile: but — who would that man be?

He stroked his chin thoughtfully, as was his way. There came to be a veritable migration into the study. The Chief Magistrate had been there again and was now walking sedately in a state of large and serene refreshment. It was growing dark, and raining out of doors. The men were of one mind, that they would go down to the Stores and inspect the goods that had come in. It promised to be a wet, a very wet evening. Armgard's needles clicked angrily again at the pattern that had roused Barbara's eager anticipations for a brief moment.

Such was Pastor Paul's first day in Torshavn.

3
Happiness on Credit

It rained and rained.

Pastor Paul Aggersoe took a little walk through the street but found nothing that would lift his heart from the slump it had sunk into on his first sight of this dark and God-forsaken place.

He had not expected this of himself for he had not heretofore been given to hanging his head. He was used to being a happy man, and there were many points in his life already to which his heart could look back and fortify itself in lonely hours. While he was a student, and after his graduation in divinity, as an alumnus of Borch's College, he had reaped many honours for his theological prowess, and this had not been unpleasing to him. He was confident that men in the world of the spirit expected something of him, and in his very assignment to Faroe he had grounds for seeing a significant mission. No, he was not one of these hungry fellows with a paltry third class who would only be considered suitable for a call to Finnmark or Greenland. The bishop had himself summoned him and *urged* him to seek the Vagar call. It would not disadvantage him in the least, on the contrary he would have other calls after that! But the Bishop had learned that things were going badly among the priesthood in Faroe, and he had received complaints on the subject from the provost up there, Pastor Anders Morsing. Now he hoped that he might be able to send one or two of the best among the younger men to bring new strength to the priesthood in Faroe, to give support to the more spiritual and be an example for the weak to follow.

When Paul Aggersoe, after his talk with the Bishop, had come out into the street again, the late afternoon sunlight had just fallen on the heaven-high, gilded spire of the Church of Our Lady. It mounted in one stage and ledge after another, square and closed in below, then, farther up, eight-sided, steadily blossoming and stretching itself upward, each segment rising out of the one beneath in an unflagging and vertiginous reaching after heaven until at last, like the highest note in an aria, it ended in a long point and a pole with three gleaming crowns on it, three hundred and fifty feet in the air. It was a powerful sight, a magnificence, which he rejoiced in daily, and it brought home to him, all at once, how heavy a thing it would be for him to leave Copenhagen. Country dweller though he had been, he became more and more attached to this city, where he could find everything to gratify his heart.

He had a disposition to feasting and splendour as well as to solemnity. He delighted in organ and church music, but also went gladly to the playhouse and opera. And he had taken part in masquerades as well, though he did wonder if such goings-on were proper to a man who had dedicated himself to the Lord's service. For he wanted to serve the Lord, though in all honesty he often felt that his fiery and ebullient nature was, alas, altogether too much of this world.

But he was young and still in comfortable concord with God. Yes, God had helped him, given him rich gifts, graciously strengthened him in diligence and competence and brought him blessedly far in scholarship. And this call out into Faroe could only be construed as a further token of distinction, for it was by no means an ordinary call but must rather be looked on as an upward step on the path of grace which — for all that it was arduous at the moment — would in time bear him onward.

Exactly because it was arduous, he should be heartened in proportion. Was he perhaps a weakling, a lazy and soft man? By no means. He had powers that he was keen to try. It was true that preaching had not as yet shown itself to be his forte. He was strongest in scholarship. But after all, he was not being sent so much to preach as to restore peace and order and decency, and truly he did not mean to spare himself. It should be heard as far as the Bishop's palace in Copenhagen, what he had achieved.

At the same time he would not forget that his own honour was only God's honour. With such thoughts he fanned the flame in his soul, and when he worshipped next day in the Church of Our Lady, and the whole shining congregation sang Kingo's great hymn, *Farewell, World, Farewell*, — then his heart swelled as never before, and with fervour in his soul he took his farewell of the city's splendours and charms to commit himself as Christ's soldier to remote Faroe. Yes, there was a fire in his breast as in the joyful noise of the organ pipes he made his way out of the church. The sun's rays were broken into shafts of uneven length as they shone through the great pillars in that three-fold nave. Mightily uplifted in mood, he stepped out amid the throng at the foot of the tower. Then his determination stood firm and upright as the spire that soared high over his head and reached towards heaven.

But there was a sneaking thought in his heart too that he did not at this moment acknowledge. It was that not *everything* about the town would so strongly have held him back. Over and above the rest there was something that rather urged him away. It was Lucie Gemynther, a respectable and worthy merchant's daughter.

She had pleased him a good deal at one time, and he had thought that this might be allowed to go further. But then Lucie began to think the same, rather too much so, indeed she had shown that she was so dead seriously in love that Paul Aggersoe began to be turned away from her. For she plagued him with her constancy and her sentimentality, which quickly became a tune that he knew all too well. He reproached himself for it, but he knew very clearly that he was not in love with her. For she was like a vine that would wind itself about him, as though about a tree-trunk and quite cover him with her devotion. But that he did not want. He wanted only to be himself, Paul Aggersoe, and he felt affection from others as a burden and a hindrance.

Lucie cried the day he went away, and he was glad, and felt released when the ship crossed the harbour bar and he saw her no longer. The passage went well and was only stormy at the last, as they neared their destination. Pastor Paul still carried the brightness of Copenhagen's spires and towers in his eyes the day they sighted land. But that glum morning when he saw Torshavn for the first time — indeed it was no longer ago than yesterday, though it seemed an eternity to him — it was as though spirit and joy both had been drained out of his heart.

Here he was, walking in the rain among rotten and miserable tarred wooden houses. He could not bear to sit indoors all the while in the priest's house. His host and colleague, Wenzel Heyde, was a Master of Arts and a learned man, but when Pastor Paul would begin to talk about theological matters and give evidence that he too had been a pilgrim in learning's way it seemed as though Master Wenzel became inattentive about it. He was otherwise not unfriendly, but he had very little to say, and shadows kept coming over his water-blue eyes as though incessant hurts and grievances were afflicting him from sources visible and invisible.

Pastor Paul was eager to meet his superior, Provost Anders Morsing, but he was away at Ness on Eysturoy. Pastor Paul spoke of making the trip to him, but everyone assured him that this would be wasted effort, since the Provost was sure to come to Havn in a day or so.

What in the name of Heaven was there for Pastor Paul to do, then? He had paid his respects to the Bailie and the Judge; the Bailie was a turkey-cock of a former toll-collector; the Judge was a fogey, an eccentric and an atheist with whom he was quite at odds; the Chief Magistrate, who was visiting in Havn, was a kindly but thirsty ox who went his own quiet way, the Company Manager was a boor, old Armgard and old Ellen Katrina with her crutches — ah, gemini! And the rest? Dear God, dear God — in Torshavn! Or in Havn, as they all called it.

And yet every time Pastor Paul took his water-heavy black hat and sallied forth in the everlasting rain, he did so with a little hope that something one time or other would happen for him, something bright that would make him laugh, a bit of joyfulness in the gloom. For he knew that here too, somewhere in this labyrinth of narrow lanes, big houses and dungheaps, there must be a nook that housed beauty and elegance. He could not deny in his heart that he would gladly see her again — the widow of his own living. Not that he had any particular intentions. God keep him from those! He could see already what kind of dangerous conjunction fate had brought about between him and her. But at the same time that it made him uneasy it also gave him a touch of pleasure amid this dolefulness. His thoughts played with Barbara. Perhaps she was not after all so dazzling. But, when the sun has gone down the stars shine bright.

It was Pastor Wenzel's wife, Anna Sophia who unexpectedly came to his aid. When he once more got ready to venture forth, she asked whether or not he had paid a call on Mme. Salling, his predecessor's widow. For she thought perhaps after all ...

This was one of the many occurrences that, in the course of the day, were to jar Pastor Wenzel. His cheeks began to redden, his eyes took on a helpless and offended look.

— Pastor Paul, said he, may well make up his own mind as to what he thinks is suitable. So far as Barbara ... Mme. Salling is concerned, nothing has been kept from him.

— For Magdalena's sake! said Anna Sophia, not in the least put off. She added: Ay, Magdalena is her mother — Mme. Stenderup. For her sake in any case, it seems to me! She will feel neglected if you pass them by. Dear God, *she* can do nothing about...

— Well, ay, said Pastor Wenzel, conceding the point and looking still more offended: Mme. Stenderup is truly ... truly to be pitied!

Pastor Paul let Anna Sophia explain to him the way he should go. Straight ahead, along Gongin, in Nyggjustova, as it was called, right across from the Bailie's house, *there* it was.

She said this with a very little smile. There was something both confidential and sly about her manner altogether. It was as though she understood his thoughts better than he did himself. But Pastor Wenzel continued to look offended. Perhaps *he* again recognized his wife's naughty spirit better than she did herself. Perhaps he knew her all too well.

Pastor Paul was received by Mme. Magdalena Stenderup at Nyggjustova, but did not have the impression that his visit had been looked for with special anticipation. She greeted him rather with a sort of half bitter acceptance of the way things go. How she put it he did not remember later, but her words conveyed a weary recognition, as though they would say that this was an altogether too familiar story to her, a new priest in her house.

But this was quickly driven from his thoughts by the unaffected pleasure that brightened Barbara's eyes when he stepped into the room. Indeed she made no least effort to hide her feelings. In her warm, glittering falsetto a childlike note of triumph broke out, as though she had at last, at last! won a long and exciting game, which others had perhaps doubted that she would win — Gabriel, for one, who was also in the room, M. Gabriel Hansen. But perhaps most of all Pastor Paul himself.

And he felt it. It was exactly as though she had said to him: See, how *could* you have waited longer? But he found himself quite undisturbed by this. For at the same time it was as though she had said: It is just splendid that you came! Can you not understand that? She was so natural and seemly that he quickly felt at ease and responsive and as though smitten by her person. She was altogether so fun-loving and candid.

But Gabriel, whose watchful eyes had taken in this meeting, was not amused, and was the last one to find Barbara natural and seemly, the way she threw herself at this stranger. Not that it was in the least way surprising. All yesterday morning he had been sizing up this new Vagar priest and had seen that he was a man with his own kind of look, a somewhat dark and stocky fellow, much unlike the late Pastor Niels. So it was in all respects to be foreseen how Barbara would behave ... it was apparently a matter of indifference to her what men looked like, provided they were ... ay, God only knew what she had seen in many! So long as they were male!

They sat around a white-scoured table, all but Magdalena, who, with a somewhat weary look, thought of an errand to take her out of the room. Barbara was sewing. But her lively eyes were not much on the sewing, they moved about everywhere with their quick green glances, and most of all on Gabriel. She might not know what he was thinking, but she did know what he was feeling. Her hearing was very sharp. When she was sitting like this between two men she could hear the beating of their two hearts. She could play a duet on them, as though on two instruments. And now it was time for Gabriel to be comforted and cheered up a little. She spoke to him, queried him about something and listened to his answer with grave attention. During all this she looked only three times at Pastor Paul, and each time quickly lowered her eyes again.

To Pastor Paul, who had felt all day as though he was dwelling in the uttermost darkness, it seemed all at once as though he had moved into a powerful light. It was not only on account of the white table top, Barbara's white sewing and her very white and warm hands. It was most of all those eyes that shone so bright that she had to withdraw them again every time they looked forth. It was as though they had become much too confident and then turned shy for having done so.

At first Pastor Paul took great pleasure in these glances, until he noted that they played on Gabriel much more than on himself. He noted also that she would often give a pleased smile: the corners of her mouth would curve up, long and red, and make dimples in her cheeks. Pastor Paul could not properly make out what the other two were talking about — it seemed that Gabriel was making sly remarks, taunts even, that Barbara was not altogether displeased to hear. But he was beginning to feel rather left out.

Then all at once his turn came when Barbara seriously and attentively began to sound him out on his voyage, his studies, his probational sermon and many other things having to do with his ministry. It became apparent that she knew the names of many of his professors. There was no limit to her audacity, thought Gabriel. For what intelligence could Barbara have about all this? But on she talked, as though in all her whole life she had had only a priest's wife's thoughts in her head, and at last she asked Pastor Paul if he had ever met her late husband, Pastor Niels.

Devil's own shamelessness! thought Gabriel. It grieved him that no-one else was present to witness her hypocrisy with him.

But for Pastor Paul it was as though for the first time in these islands he had met someone who listened with interest and pleasure to what he had to say, and he spoke out freely and honestly and was flattered in the depths of his heart. For although he well knew that such were unlikely topics for a woman like Barbara, yet he could see in her face and her eyes how lively her attention was and with what closeness she watched his least change of expression, and it occurred to him at that moment, and seemed quite proper to him, that in conversation with womankind the subject was merely a pretext, the true pleasure came in being face to face, in having eyes meet, voices mingle and soul commune with soul. And Barbara's soul, that spoke through her green-golden eyes, was much moved towards him, and blushed sometimes and withdrew, but turned straightway back again and played before him and basked in his strong, eager glance. The corners of her mouth again curved upwards with pleasure, she listened as though to a rare music, and what he said had to do, seemingly, only with priests and parishes but was in truth a long solo aria from the depths of his manhood. An aria that was being listened to.

Then it was that Barbara's eyes suddenly began to flutter away in Gabriel's direction. She lowered them, gave him one lightning glance and made a very soft giggle. The words came to a halt in Pastor Paul's throat: what had happened? Had Gabriel done something, said something? Had he joined in the music? Barbara looked strictly down at her sewing and plied her needle.

— It is a pillow-case, said she, quietly.

But it could be seen that she was full of held-in laughter. Gabriel stared at her with a corrosive stare.

— It *is* a pillowcase, she repeated, stubbornly. Her voice rose into a falsetto and ended in that gasping sound that is midway between a sigh and laughter.

Pastor Paul had become altogether ill at ease. He understood not a word of what they said. At first he thought it was himself that was being laughed at, but then he could see that this was not so. Nevertheless he did not at all like this new flirtatious kind of game between Barbara and Gabriel that had broken right off and made superfluous his own flow of talk.

Suddenly Gabriel pulled at the sewing. Barbara defended herself somewhat and rapped him on the knuckles, but did not succeed in stopping him from pulling the whole white piece of stuff up on to the table. All at once she gave up and said in what she tried to make an angry tone: — You ass, Gabriel. Ay, it *is* a shift! One would think you had not seen a shift before!

Gabriel's fat face looked as amused and bold as could be.

— So I have, he answered, but never *so* fine a shift. Who will...?

But Barbara had suddenly coloured blood-red right down into her neck. She had taken a quick glance at Pastor Paul, it was hardly for a second, and never had she been so quick to withdraw her look. Gabriel could see that something had happened and understood

47

instantly how it was between them. The devil! He had put his foot in it again! Pastor Paul and Barbara had neither of them a word to say, he was the only one to speak, nevertheless he could see that in that moment he was less than nothing. For him it had become an unbearable moment. He said that now he had to go.

— Must you go? queried Barbara, in a casual tone.

— Ay, I must, the Stores, you know, said Gabriel. He was very busy, especially these days.

Pastor Paul, too, made motions to go. He mumbled something, that perhaps it was time he too should be getting back. But then Barbara suddenly found her tongue again and began in a high voice to chatter herself out of her confusion: Nay, he must decidedly not go! Her mother was just then making him a cup of coffee! Indeed she had hardly exchanged a word with him yet, as she surely, *surely* wanted to do. It was only that she had so much to attend to in the house. He must decidedly not go yet!

Gabriel was out in the passage, he stuck his head back in and made a gesture at the sewing: — Ay, good-bye — and good luck with the bridal shift!

Barbara laughed, a little laugh that was also a sigh and rose up in her throat: — Ah, you ass, Gabriel!

She followed him out and stood out in the rain for a moment, full of happiness. Then back in she went to Pastor Paul, the new Pastor Paul. And as it was near the time when it began to get dark she lit the candles.

After this visit Pastor Paul's melancholy became transformed into a quiet cheerfulness. When he departed from Barbara's presence he wandered as though released through the dark town, and desired only to be alone with his happiness. There was just then a let up of the rain. He turned down into a windy passage that led to the water. There he stopped in the lee of a boathouse to collect his thoughts and try to explain to himself wherein his new happiness had its being. But it was not long before he was aware of someone else who had also brought his thoughts to the water's edge at that evening hour. A solitary shape emerged from the dusk, there were greetings, and it was Gabriel.

He was not displeased that it was none other than Gabriel. For all that he had put him out appreciably in the conversation with Mme. Barbara, yet he had been one of the participants in the most pleasurable scene he had experienced since he had come ashore here, and though he did perhaps give the impression of being a bit of a rascal, yet he was a cheerful enough Scapin, who might be worth talking to.

Gabriel, for his part, showed himself friendly, confidential and more than willing to converse. They went on about everything possible having to do with Havn and the islands here, and Gabriel had yarns about many people that made Pastor Paul laugh. But that they avoided speaking about a certain person for a long while made it clearer and clearer to them both that it was around her that their thoughts in a kind of fellowship turned, and when they at last came to the subject Gabriel's voice grew soft and sentimental.

— A lovable piece of womankind, you will say! Ay, and much more so you would have acknowledged her when she was eighteen and blameless. Then Barbara was sweet!

— I can imagine, said Pastor Paul.

— Ay, indeed, said Gabriel. Alas — that she has become so soiled. What a pity it is, God knows what a pity!

— I have heard gossip about that already, said Pastor Paul. There may well be something in it, though I can only with difficulty square it with her behaviour, which seems to me courteous and seemly enough, and not what one would expect of the woman she is said to be.

— Ah, she is full of ... If you knew her rightly you would find it distasteful ... she is full of ... artfulness, as soon as she meets a stranger.

— Artfulness? asked Pastor Paul, very dubious. He remembered Barbara's look, which was so bright that she had to keep lowering it. — On the contrary, he went on, she seems quite natural to me.

Gabriel gave a little snort. — Those eyes! Ay, she is pretty good! I shall tell you a thing, God knows it is the truth: we are often ashamed to be in the family with her. For there are times when she carries on like a veritable ... a veritable ... ay, whore!

— So. I cannot judge about that, mumbled the priest. I hear that such things are being said. But I thought it was chiefly oldsters who were passing judgement on her...

— But it is the young, so help me, who have doings with her.

— Yes, for my part, said the Priest, in my doings with her I have known nothing but what has been decent and lovely.

— God help me! Neither is she likely to practise her wiles on me, said Gabriel, solemnly: I know that side of her all too well ... everyone knows her tricks and artifices. It is truly something one could find entertaining ... if it were only not one's own kin! But I shall say one thing to you, he concluded: lecherous, that is what she is.

Aha, thought Pastor Paul, when they had parted. This Gabriel is not so proof against her wiles as he pretends. Pastor Paul had to concede that neither was he so entirely proof, after this conversation. And his new pleasure in Havn and all this Godforsaken country had not lessened. This surprised him greatly, for Gabriel had said nothing not calculated to destroy the delightful memory of his visit in Nyggjustova. Yet it seemed to him that this delight had merely been made all the greater.

In the time that followed hardly a day passed when he did not see Barbara, and every new meeting served only to increase his happiness. He did not know himself what to think of this. That she was a notorious woman he could not doubt. He had no need of Gabriel's intelligence, he could draw his own conclusions. It was very apparent, the effect she had on all men. She neither said nor did anything blameworthy. Nevertheless! It could not be otherwise. Perhaps she could do nothing about it. She pleased them all, and none knew her ways.

What in heaven's name should he, then, a priest, a man who should serve others as an example to follow — what should he be doing with such a woman? He could already see clearly the snare that fate was laying for him. But he was not afraid of it.

He knew already that he *should* be shy of her, but instead he sought her all the more. His heart was flattered in its depths. His senses were dazzled by the green lights of her eyes, and roused by her glittering voice. And this black and wet country village, with its warehouses and hovels and its wretched fortress, this place that had been at first merely a source of melancholy to him, he now saw as through a shining rainbow.

And so it became clear that this happiness could only be purchased on credit, and that every day that went on like this merely increased its price. He was prepared to pay the reckoning when its time came. He did not doubt that he would be solvent, let it be never so dear. It had not ever been his way to doubt himself, he was used to going under full sail.

On the fifth day the Provost, Pastor Anders Morsing, arrived by boat from Ness. Pastor Paul had heard that this man was once betrothed to Barbara, but had broken with her before the marriage. He had no trouble believing this once he had had a look at him. He was a man of authority, tall and sharp faced. What kind of flirtation could he at any time have carried on with Barbara? His look was like steel, so intensely blue and hard that whomever he talked to must feel that the deeps of his conscience were being plumbed. Yet about his mouth played a little smile that was harsh and sweet at the same time.

Pastor Paul felt brought to attention as soon as he saw him. He felt smartly returned into a former element. The Provost sat with the Bishop's letter open in one hand, and scrutinized him.

— Hm, said he. As you know, something is *expected* of you. Here in the islands it is not the same as elsewhere. It *ought* to be so that there would be priests who ministered to their flocks as models of piety and Christian life, but it *is* often the other way round. I shall not name names but we have one or two brothers here — that is to say, you and I have — of whom one could wish that they were even half so pious as the folk of their parish. Therefore one hopes that the younger priests may be made of different stuff.

He directed his look straight into Pastor Paul's face: — You see, it is hardly a question of having swallowed so and so many big books, or of being well versed in so and so many of the emotional movements that are stirring in Christianity in our days — all these snivelling refinements and subtle sentimentalities! I shall say this to you, once and for all, what I have been saying for a long while: that in rockfast faith and true devotion to God we have more to learn from these folk than they can learn from us. By this I mean properly the village folk. Havn folk ... you cannot consider them the same.

51

What is required of us priests now is not that we outpreach one another in our sermons but, quite simply, that in our lives and conduct we be worthy of our calling, and that in humility and faith we serve, teach and guide our flocks in the commandments of the law and good principles, in such a way that we make ourselves just a little worthy of the incomprehensible trust they put in us.

The Provost had once or twice struck the table lightly; his mouth displayed both firmness and good humour, but his eyes were stern.

— And for the rest, he went on, you have eyes to see for yourself. You will undoubtedly learn quickly what you have to do.

Pastor Paul had nothing else to say to all this than yes and amen. He attempted a few words but they seemed to come out thin and indifferent.

— And now you may betake yourself to your parish at the earliest opportunity, concluded Pastor Anders.

Pastor Paul replied that he had been invited to go along with the Chief Magistrate, who was getting ready to go home to his farm again.

— Hm, said the Provost and smiled: then you will be going to your call in good company. Yes, yes. He is indeed a good man, Samuel Mikkelsen! But he seldom rides the same day he saddles — when he visits here in Havn. Now that is something *you* should be aware of. I am confident that you will in all respects take care of yourself.

Pastor Anders once more looked at him closely and hard — and departed.

Pastor Paul felt overpowered. It was almost as though he had been baptized and confirmed all over again. This Provost was like a spiced and pungent strong dram. Ah well, the hour had struck! He thought, with a sort of elevation, that now he must without delay tear himself loose, say farewell to Havn and begin upon his work. It would not be so hard after all. He went to the Chief Magistrate to make arrangements for the journey. It was then a Saturday.

All the rest of the day he remembered Provost Anders' sharp, searching look, which had cast a light deep into his conscience and brought him to attention. But along with it he also saw Barbara's green-gold shining eyes, which she must always be lowering because they revealed all too much of a secret that could not be spoken, no, hardly thought about, but nevertheless made her mouth curve in a sweet and pleased smile that brought dimples in her cheeks. The sly and eternal secret that Barbara shared with all men.

4
Farewell, World, Farewell

The church bells on Reyn rang for service. Their tone was gentle, it quavered over the rooftops. But the tower they hung in was sombre, and ramshackle with age. It trembled with their motion. The timbers they swung on creaked and groaned, and this dismal undertone, as it mingled with the bird-light notes of the bells, could be heard all over the town.

Gale and rain had let up, and the weather had stiffened to a still cold. The mud of the lanes had become hard and sharp, and the puddles were plated with tinkling ice. The sun shone bleakly on this twenty-sixth sunday after Trinity.

The church was small, thirteen pews on either side and a little gallery above the entrance. Between the bare wood walls it was icy cold. There was no ceiling, the eye looked straight up into the roof's heavy rafters and poles.

Torshavn's poor citizens began to make their way in. The women wore black shawls and kerchiefs, their mouths were drawn shut and Kingo's hymn book was clutched in their hands. The men followed behind, delaying somewhat, as though with a conspiratorial urge to keep in the background. Odd unattached ones among them took the stairs up to the gallery. They were heroes only during the week, both Samuel of Vippun and Niels of the field. Here in the sanctuary it was proper that the old women should take the lead.

The better folk too, and the *fine*, came into the church. They had their regular pews, theirs by right, in which none of the common folk dared trespass. Bailie Harme came, his daughter Suzanne with him, and spread himself out. They sat in the front row. The judge's pew was there too, still occupied by the former judge's widow, Mme. Stenderup, and the Priest's pew too, in which the two sisters, Armgard and Ellen Katrina had their place, as Pastor Wenzel's kin and guests. Pastor Paul as well took his place in this pew.

Many others had their own pews, though they were not gentry: Mme. Dreyer, Sieur Arentzen and the old spinster, Mlle. Kleyn. Solid folk they were, who paid for their pews. This was their pride and token of their superiority over the many, which faintly showed itself on their faces as they sat themselves down.

Common to all church-goers was the grey cloud that issued from their mouths in the bitterly cold air of the church.

Pastor Paul sat and thought of the many times he had attended service at the Church of Our Lady in Copenhagen, of the gallant tumult of carriages and chaises before the entrance and of lackeys who would shut the carriage doors with a crack; of the finery of the well-born and the burghers, who moved in a stately and gratified procession between the pillars of the nave and down the two equally lofty aisles, while the organ sounded its prelude in a solemn thunder under the vault. Alas, here in Havn there was only a poor and bent parish clerk who hacked out, hoarsely, the introductory prayer. Under the roof timbers there was dead silence, none of the coughing and hawking that one might have expected.

Then immediately after, in came Barbara quickly and quietly and joined her mother in the Judge's pew — like a last living glimpse of the world before the doleful hymn began.

Judge Johan Hendrik Heyde had come to church this day at the same time as the Bailie and his daughter. He had greeted them, exchanged a few words and smiled, but when they had gone on through the porch he did not follow them among the pews to his own. Instead he climbed laboriously into the gallery.

Why did he do this? He had nothing against them; nevertheless at this moment, there was something that kept him apart from them. They conversed in Danish. And why not? it was their tongue. And Johan Hendrik felt no dislike for Danish, after all he had lived some while in Denmark and some of his own kin were Danish. Indeed he would have thought it unreasonable for people like the Bailie and the Stores Manager to have spoken Faroese. And yet, here on home ground among the common Faroe folk, the lighter-syllabled language broke the harmony. It grated on him a little, as an instrument would, playing off key. He was in tune with the people. It would have gone against the grain to have put himself in the front row. He preferred to be in the background, in the gallery. Here he could sit in quiet and ponder land improvement, better fishing methods and other useful things tending to the country's betterment.

Soon after the Judge had taken his place the steps creaked heavily and up came his cousin Samuel Mikkelsen, Chief Magistrate of the islands. He was very big and awkward, but he too preferred the gallery, not on account of any subtle ill-will towards other good folk, but out of pure discretion. His comportment was circumspect, he did not make a joke except politely, and when he took a dram during the service he did so with great finesse — not surreptitiously, like a skulker or a schoolboy, but with imperturbable dignity. Johan Hendrik felt himself supported by his presence, but Bailie Harme's view, perhaps not unreasonable, was that His Majesty's Faroese officials did not show a proper sense of their place, obscuring themselves as they did among the discontents in the gallery's six free pews.

It was quite otherwise with the Fort Commandant, Lieutenant Otto Hjorring. He did not hide his light under a bushel, but marched into church in a red dress coat, with sword, mustachios, pigtail and everything that might be expected to appertain to a man of arms. But for all that, did he not go wrong and sit in one of the common folks' pews! Shrimp was both honoured and discomfited and threw many troubled glances in the direction of this overwhelming proximity of coloured finery and costly scent.

So they were all foregathered, the parish folk, high and low. Gabriel in his Sunday best, sanctimonious and unrecognizable, the Stores' men and private soldiers from the Fort, the farmer of Husagard and his household and the farmer of Sund, who had come all the way on foot. The congregation laboured through the first long-winded hymn. There was no organ. The chilled, quavering voices kept bad time with one another. Some sang sweetly and well, notably Sieur Arentzen, about whom it was plain to be seen that he looked upon himself as a leader. Others sang without a note to their names, and the women hardly wailed from under their black kerchiefs. There was inordinate coughing and snuffling when the last interminable wheezing verse was sung to its close. The model of the East-Indiaman, *Lion of Norway*, that hung under the gallery, turned slowly on her cord and her bowsprit began to point to the south.

The priest, who had stood facing the altar, turned towards the congregation: — *The Lord be with you!*

A cloud of vapour emerged from his mouth. A hundred vapour clouds responded from the congregation: — *And with thy spirit!*

Pastor Wenzel was a little too small for the red chasuble, and at every moment he seemed on the point of stumbling over the folds of his alb. He cast a look out over his congregation. The Stores Manager was not among them. Pity. No, that man was unfortunately an indifferent church-goer. Today it was really too bad. The priest felt a sudden disappointment. Today's sermon had a message for everyone, but especially for the great and powerful, who most easily forgot church and neglected its servants. The Bailie was there. But in the moment it took Pastor Wenzel to turn back to the altar he noticed that his own wife was absent. Anna Sophia had not yet come.

— *Let us pray!*

A vague uneasiness began to rise up in him. His mind wandered during the ritual. Then he swallowed and intoned the collect with a weak tremor in his voice. No-one thought this unusual. Pastor Wenzel's talk often sounded as though he was offended about something. His little red-bearded figure always seemed to be somewhat upset.

The service followed its course and came to the epistle. Pastor Wenzel, who had felt himself so strangely absent in spirit, pulled himself together. He turned towards the congregation and intoned in a strong voice: — *The Epistle for the six-and-twentieth Sunday after Trinity is found in St Paul's First Epistle to the Thessalonians.*

Anna Sophia had not come.

— *And we beseech you, brethren, to know them which labour among you, and are over you in the Lord, and admonish you; And to esteem them very highly in love for their work's sake. And be at peace among yourselves. Now we exhort you, brethren, warn them that are unruly ...*

A good while after he had read the epistle, Pastor Wenzel could still, in his inner ear, distinguish the echo of his voice. He had not attached its meaning to a single word he had read. His heart was distressed, his mind empty. Neither had Pastor Paul, who sat in the Priest's pew, paid attention. His thoughts too wandered restlessly on other paths. Indeed, in the entire church there were probably a scant few who had marked the apostle's words. Some were too miserable, some too sleepy. So on went the service as though it was a game that had got started somewhen. *Lion of Norway* had again swung round, unnoticed, and was now steering south-west.

As soon as he had mounted the pulpit and begun to speak, Johan Hendrik in the gallery could tell that something must have disturbed the Priest. There was a note in his voice that he knew well. He had known it since they were boys.

Pastor Wenzel began hesitantly, but soon found the sure clue that he had laid for himself and followed it boldly. This was the sermon he had composed with such diligence and which the Stores Manager especially should have heard, though its message was quite as appropriate to the Bailie and indeed, in its fundamentals, to every one of the congregation, down to the humblest.

— And we beseech you, brethren, to know them which labour among you, and are over you in the Lord ...

It was not every year that there was a twenty-sixth Sunday after Trinity, and it was not every parish priest who was permitted at high mass to preach on the epistle instead of the gospel. But Pastor Wenzel, who was a Master of Arts, was so permitted, and at last, on this rarely occurring Sunday, he found the occasion to say what had been lying close to his heart for so long.

Anna Sophia had not yet come.

She too would have benefited by hearing his word. Though — truly, it would have been no better than water off a duck's back. Nay, it was probably not for that reason that he missed her. He did not permit himself to think deeper on that subject. But his heart knew better, it thumped hard.

He began by rendering unto Caesar what was Caesar's. The King's officials and servants and the temporal authorities in general

— all should be respected and obeyed by everyone. For those in authority were put there by God! But — how was it with the ministers of God's word? Should they not be honoured and respected in the same way? For what was their office? Apostle Paul expounded it in his Epistle to the Ephesians. Respect yourselves, he writes to the foremost men of the congregation, and also the whole flock among whom the Holy Spirit set you as bishops, to feed God's congregation, whom he has ransomed with his own blood.

He looked about him for the first time and raised his voice: — But when the bishops and priests feed you your spiritual food, watch over your souls and justify you before God, should you not honour them equally — yes, at least equally with those who feed your bodies, keep watch over the country's supplies (this was what the Stores Manager should have heard!) look after your Earthly well-being and preserve justice and right behaviour among you?

Pastor Wenzel had warmed to his subject: — Spiritual and temporal are two things, and between them the spiritual is not less than the temporal. When you observe the temporal law, which authority maintains, should you not also obey God's eternal commandments, which I proclaim?

He looked in appeal to the Bailie, and Bailie Harme nodded.

— And when you pay land rent and tax to the Royal Tax Office, should you not also pay your dues to God's Church?

The Bailie nodded agreement again. Pastor Wenzel raised his voice to a loftier pitch: — And when you yield service and pay property tax to the military and its officers, are those who are over you in the Lord not equally worthy that you should yield them their tithe?

His eye strayed to the Lieutenant, who was snoring in his crimson finery. Then he looked back again to the Bailie; it was almost as though the sermon was degenerating into a conversation with him. And the Bailie again nodded graciously.

— For the priest, Pastor Wenzel continued, the *priest* is your spiritual authority, appointed by the Holy Spirit — and moreover also by His Majesty the King — in the same way as the Bailie and the Chief Magistrate, the Stores Manager and the Judge ...

He gave his brother a look in whose depths lay a kind of mild reproach. But then he quickly looked back at the Bailie and continued : ... ah, these spiritual authorities are of the same kind as your temporal authorities, whom you ought to respect and love. Do not be angry with your priest because he tells you the truth. Even the highest ought not to ignore his admonishments, if not for the sake of his humble person, yet for his calling's sake.

Now it had been said. Pastor Wenzel paused, his water-blue eyes wandered a little, uncertainly, as though he was seeking to explore still further the implications of his words. Then he continued: — The Apostle still speaks to us today: *Now we exhort you, brethren, warn them that are unruly ...*

Suddenly it was as though he had lost his train of thought. Anna Sophia — now he saw her! And the Stores Manager, he saw him too. Through one of the church windows he could see beyond the garden of the priest's house and there, in the bed-chamber, he saw both his wife and the Stores Manager ...

He stood and swayed, understood nothing, felt nothing. It was most like, as though he was in a dream. Anna Sophia and the Stores Manager! How was it now ... he did not remember at once ... something had always been going on, he had always known it.

He would take up again from where he had left off, but there was a pang in his heart. It grew. A crippling pain broke out inside him. His heart slowly twisted up till it was an iron-hard knot that squeezed and burned into his throat and shot pains right through his breast.

Anna Sophia!

He heard his own voice, that still stammered: — *Warn them that are unruly ... warn them that are unruly ...*

The whole congregation saw him, how he stood and swayed, helpless, his face chalk-white with a little fire-red spot on either cheek. A few thought that he had become sick, nobody understood the true ground of his deep distress. A good while passed, the Lieutenant's confident snore began to be restless, he mumbled a word or two in his sleep.

Then it was as though the priest himself was struck by the great stillness. He became aware that he was standing in the pulpit — and not preaching. The congregation was sitting in the church — not listening. A shaft of sunlight fell through the windows, he could see every face clearly. Upstairs at the back sat his brother with an uncomprehending expression on his face. *Lion of Norway* turned slowly on her cord, without course or compass. And the whole church was like a ship that, masterless, was running before the waves, full of people, but without a captain.

Pastor Wenzel roused himself. The unruly — now he had it! He let his voice ring out, it trembled with indignation. If there had been much on his heart before, there was no less now. The unruly, they were the great ones! He saw before him the Stores Manager's well-fed, smooth face. Like a flash of lightning it all came clear before him. He had admired that face and cultivated its attention as he would a plant, while its owner, the Stores Manager, had sat at his table over a good roast. Now he saw his own happiness devoured and himself trampled on by this same smug, self-satisfied look. He gasped for breath, his soul and senses turned on the great and snapped at them, as an undeservedly kicked dog. He could see them before him suddenly, an unending procession of the mighty and well-fed. The Bailie, and behind him a string of bailies who had despised the farmers of the land. The Lieutenant, and behind him a platoon of lieutenants who had thrashed army drill into good-natured farm hands. The Stores Manager, and behind him a flock of stores managers who had cheated his worthy and guileless forefathers. Did he not know about the great? King David, who stole Uriah's wife. Herod, who had John the Baptist beheaded. And behind them all, Pontius Pilate, who washed his hands. The great were everlastingly washing their white and elegant hands. Did he not know all about them? They had been the serpents of his life. Until a few moments ago he had stood here and sought to be one of them. And now he had been struck to the heart.

Shaking with bitterness Pastor Wenzel had begun his reckoning with the unruly of this world, but gradually, as he searched his own soul and became aware of the beam in his own eye he began himself to take a greater part in his message. No secret corner in the heart of man, no sneaking selfish thought, no worldly desire, no foolish vanity did he leave in its hiding place. He made it plain that the world and only the world was the course and compass of mankind's heart. For all humankind was born wicked and sinful and did not know *how* deep in sin they were. No-one can be justified by his own strength or good works and all are in need of God's grace. Always when one does a good deed, then along comes self-righteousness, the great flatterer, and reaches a hand to the doer and so turns all the good to bad. Nothing good is said or done but the world, like a filthy hidden motive, underlies it. So limitless is humankind's *incapacity* for the truly good. From the very bottom, all is desire, falseness, self-righteousness, self-love, folly, vanity! Vanity!

— Hm, said the Judge to the Chief Magistrate: so he is on *that* tack today. Ay, then something or other *has* gone against him.

But the congregation in the church below listened with wonder and fear to Pastor Wenzel's words and thought that he was after all a powerful preacher and castigator. For it seemed to them all that he showed them their own images in a mirror, and looked deep into their hearts. It did not occur to them that it was his own heart he was looking into.

The new Vagar priest too, Pastor Paul, like so many others, had to bow his head. For he felt that he too strayed along the same path of vanity himself, and was never wholly pleased unless his heart was flattered, his ambition encouraged and his desire kindled. It was the world, only the world, that played before his eyes, and he was not capable, on his own, of raising his vision higher.

But Pastor Wenzel, who saw that he had the congregation with him, went deeper and deeper into the cellars and perplexed passageways of the human heart, and when he could reach no further and had fully uncovered humanity's incapacity for good, and unworthiness to see God, he let the miracle suddenly manifest itself. And that miracle was the grace of Jesus Christ that took away all our sin! Ay, by grace and only by grace was it possible to raise oneself, lay down the world's burden and despise it for the filth it is and at last, with a true heart, turn one's thoughts towards heaven.

— *Amen!* he concluded in a high voice, and before he began the prayer his pale eyes strayed about the church quickly, but without coming near a certain window. It was a moment of grace for Havn's congregation.

When they came to the hymn Pastor Wenzel said that they should not sing what the book prescribed — he was a Master of Arts and could decide on this — but another well-known hymn from *Spiritual Anthems*, or from the book *Thousandfold*, called 'World-weary and longing for Heaven'.

Most of them knew it by heart. Sieur Arentzen led off masterfully, loudly supported by Pastor Wenzel.

> Farewell, world, farewell!
> How wearies my heart to be quit of your spell.
> The burdens you burden me with, they are vain;
> I cast them away from me now, with disdain;
> I tear myself loose, I am heartsick at last
> of vanity's waste
> of vanity's waste.

The hymn gathered them all, and the whole congregation joined in the next verse with full voice.

> What is it at best
> that makes the world seem so enticingly dressed?

Shrimp took a sidelong glance at the Commandant, who snored steadily with an indescribably unmilitary look on his face.

> What is it but shadows and glittering glass?
> What is it but bubbles on sinking morass?
> What is it but shard-ice and stones and decay
> on vanity's way
> on vanity's way?

Alas, how true! Samuel Mikkelsen was feeling the trace of a headache after last night's quiet indulgence. It had been the fifth night in a row and he was beginning very slightly to tire of the cups and glasses that stood at midnight on the festive board. True it is, no earthly pleasure is without its after-taste.

> What worth are my days
> that slip from me heartless and speed on their ways?
> What all my care-heavy thought, what hopes and fears?
> What joyful reunions, what partings in tears?
> What plans and what labours, what struggle and sweat

> but vanity's debt
> but vanity's debt?

The young did not believe that. But there was not a furrowed face in the church that was not made thoughtful by these words. From Bailie Harme, with his burden of responsibility, down to Samuel of Vippun, with his eight children. The one was brought to acknowledge to himself that his forty years of service stood as though written in sand, the other could expect only three shovelsful of earth as the mortal conclusion of his lighterman's life. But the Judge, that ever sceptical and morose man, was moved to think with acerbity that a piece of useful work on Earth was a happier thing than ten shouts of joy in heaven.

He was a reader of modern books and had arrived at the belief that diligence and patriotism were more blessed than palm branches.

> Oh wealth and display
> oh idol of riches and golden array
> are you not among Earth's most treacherous gifts,
> your waxings and wanings, your dodges and shifts?
> You are the sardonic expression we trace
> > on vanity's face
> > on vanity's face.

This was a comfort for many, who had not had much. But Gabriel — he was so little in control of his thoughts that from this moment they moved into deep speculation on the question, whether certain miscellaneous sums that had recently transferred themselves from other pockets into his own ought not to be invested in five guilders of land that had come up for sale in Mikladal.

> Go, Honour, put on
> your crowns and rewards: ah, their shine is soon gone.
> For Envy rides up on your back with his spur,
> your heart quakes within you, your steps are unsure;
> where others go swiftly, you stumble and fall,
> > poor vanity's thrall,
> > poor vanity's thrall.

Who could feel free? Who did not harbour his worm of ambition — big or little? From the better folks' rented pews to the benches of the poor there was not a soul who did not in secret look askance at a rival or a superior. Envy rode on everyone's back. Who was without pride, who did not have a secret wound?

In Pastor Wenzel's heart, sorrow and a singular comfort flowed together in mighty eddies. The hymn laid balm to his soul. See! Thomas Kingo had felt and lived through it all just as he had.

> Ah, passion, Amour,
> more fleeting than marsh lights your fires endure.
> You strutter and painter, you voice in the wind,
> you thousand-eyed seeker, whose seeking is blind.
> The clear light of day will your fancies destroy,
>   poor vanity's toy,
>   poor vanity's toy.

What had got into Wenzel today, the Judge wondered again. Something or other must have upset the little man and hurt him in his innermost priest's soul. Had the Bailie, perhaps, not liked the tone of his sermon? Something had happened, it was clear, and now there he stood, Wenzel, God help him, up to his knees in earthly passion but with his look turned towards the light of grace — What else? Pah! This hymn was becoming a bore, a kind of dram to comfort good folk when they burned their mouths on the gruel of life. Let a man lose three marks at cards and farewell, world, farewell! Ay, that would be a fat help.

But when they came to the next verse Pastor Wenzel quite broke down for a moment, he forgot about grace and wept, and sang out his pain:

> Ah, friendship and trust,
> you turn as the winds of the world say you must.
> Engaging deceivers, when all is drunk up
> what is it but sorrow that stays in your cup?
> I know you too well, I have supped full enough
>   of vanity's stuff,
>   of vanity's stuff.

And on he sang, burning with righteous wrath and zeal:

> Ah, fleshly desire,
> how many your kiss has engulfed in the mire.
> Your flame-eager tinder, your sparks that ignite
> have lighted souls down into hell's blazing night ...

The invisible aureole over Barbara's head began to glow. For she was the one towards whom, at this moment, most thoughts were turned, in envy, in desire, in condemnation. Gabriel thirsted for her in pain, and even the Judge himself, in the gallery, sat and eyed her. But she sat there as thoughtless as a bird on a fence, never guessing that the fires of hell were flaming around her. The new Vagar priest, Pastor Paul Aggersoe, loved her with dread.

> ... Your promise is honey, but after-taste gall,
> and vanity, all,
> and vanity, all.

Armgard was very little and very old in her black weeds. She nodded in affirmation. She missed in this hymn only one stanza, one about brandy-wine. For that was the devil's distillation and had brought many to their undoing. But her sister, Ellen Katrina, stared ecstatically before her, in the power of her memories: — World!

> Farewell, then, farewell,
> beguile me no longer; I cast off your spell.
> Your tinsel allurements no longer enslave,
> I bury them deep in oblivion's grave.
> My sorrow and need shall be tokens of rest
> on Abraham's breast,
> on Abraham's breast.

And all threw off the yoke of worldly possessions and sang of heavenly bliss. They had cast accounts with their hearts. While the congregation rose and the bells began to ring from the belfry timbers, the hymn's lugubrious notes still sounded in their ears.

Vanity, vanity!

Pastor Paul walked slowly through the church. He was reminded of the Sunday when he, in the Church of Our Lady in Copenhagen, felt that he had said farewell to the world. But the world had stayed with him. Here were no pillars, no aisles, no organ and no vault, only a miserable chancel of wood. And yet the world was as strong as ever, and as hard to bid farewell.

Pastor Wenzel came and took him by the arm, red and flushed and as though not entirely himself. He came as though with authority from a much higher place, humble and yet trembling with triumph.

— Now, Johan Hendrik, he demanded, out in the porch. What do you think of *that* sermon?

— Pshaw, said the Judge, and took his time about putting his hat on his head: The end was not at all like the beginning! *Otherwise* it was enough like you at both ends.

But Samuel, the Chief Magistrate, having emptied the first flask of the day, greeted with a friendly and clear eye his old aunts, Armgard and Ellen Katrina.

It was snowing a little. Outdoors the clangour of the bells sounded freer, it quavered among the white flakes. Everyone felt a particular uplift. They had beheld themselves and one another in the world's beguiling glass, and were numbed and shaken by everything on this Earth. But God be praised! The world had no power over them, they had torn themselves free. Unburdened and released they hurried home. They did not know that it was anticipation of Sunday's dinner that gave them wings.

But in the empty church the East-Indiaman, *Lion of Norway* still hung on her cord, with her guns, pennants and flags, and turned slowly through all points of the azimuth, now to this quarter and now to that.

5
World

Wind blew in every corner and narrow lane, and stank rawly of seaweed. The weather had turned grey again. A south wind came in from the sea and loosened the frost's harsh grip.

A stupor had fallen over the town. In house and hovel the folk sat in their Sunday best. They were replete with food and Sabbath and were beginning to be a little bored. Out in Reynagard sat Chief Magistrate Samuel at a game of chess with his nephew the Judge. There were long pauses between moves and yet longer between words. Armgard and Ellen Katrina sat and talked about the old days and at every word they found some disagreement about their kin. It was a sad privation for Armgard that she dared not knit — it relieved her somewhat when she was in the grip of bad temper; but the Sabbath rest must not be broken by worldly labour.

The priest and his wife hardly looked at each other this afternoon, they had had talk enough in the study. The two old ones thought it was not right for Anna Sophia to neglect Sunday worship. But naturally they said nothing.

Pastor Paul had gone out. He saw not a soul in the deserted lanes. When he neared Nyggjustova he slackened his pace. In the midst of his melancholy he found a deep gladness in knowing that Barbara lived in this house. Would she be at home? More likely perhaps she was at the Bailie's house, with Suzanne.

At Sand, where the brook empties into East Bay, ducks were floating with their beaks under their wings. They made uneasy small noises as he went by, but they were much too sleepy to stir themselves. They were Springus', Vupsen's and Katrina of the Cellar's ducks. Each family had its own, but there were no private marks on them — the town folk knew the town ducks as well as they knew one another. Perhaps Bailie Harme did not distinguish the ducks very exactly, though he lived close by, but then he had weighty matters on his mind. As for Pastor Paul, he did not see the ducks at all that he wandered among. He was wholly taken up with the thought that he was, perhaps, at that moment, being observed from a window. And so indeed he was, he was being watched from many windows. Every old woman's eye in Gongin was much taken up — for the next hour it would be the event of the afternoon, that they had seen the new priest hop from stone to stone across the brook and take himself up on to the outfields.

The south wind kept blowing greyness in over the town. The ducks huddled together in it. But then, suddenly, something happened!

Nobody knew who first raised the alarm — not the watch at the Fort, though he was nearest to it.

Somebody on some errand had first had sight of it ... within three minutes the whole of Torshavn had seen it: knots of people crowded behind house corners, and peered out across the strand.

— Ah, Jesus have mercy on us!

Big sails were emerging above the horizon. They stood there like a dreadful, an all too ominous sign. The old women led the chorus of lamentation. They must be enemy ships. They whined and snivelled, their teeth chattered and they tried to warm their freezing hands under their Sunday aprons.

Ay, it could be nothing else. The last Royal Stores ship of the year had just been. Moreover — *such* big sails, they were no ordinary ships, everyone could see that.

A moment later another ship emerged from below the skyline.

Fear was already crooking their backs. First there was, as it were, a little smouldering fuse, then a flame that stood reflected in every eye, then at last a breaking out into a wild uproar of cries, wails and curses.

There was no uncertainty, however. Now there was only one thing to do. Save what could be saved — household goods, bedding, a little hoarded wool, anything! — and then to the hills. It was an instinct that moved them. Fear of pirates was in their very blood. For centuries the islands had been ravaged. Heavy-booted English and drunk Scots had often come ashore, broken chests and wardrobes open, slaughtered cattle for their cooking pots and pressed men into service in the Iceland fishery. This was something all had heard about. And it was far from being the worst. Once a great horde of heathen — Turks or blacks they were, certainly — harried and burned on Suduroy, killed right and left and carried off more than thirty women and children from their familiar homeland to an unknown and devilish slavery. That was the most frightful story that could be told. Neither had Torshavn always been spared. Some years back some French had destroyed the Fort and plundered the town.

The Faroese, themselves descended from Vikings, had, in the course of centuries, become tamed by poverty and isolation. They had become a shy and dispirited people. Faced with strangers they knew only one defence — flight into the inaccessible mountains. Now the whole of Torshavn was on the point of flight on account of three black sails on the horizon.

A drum had begun to sound among the lanes. Someone had not lost his nerve. Otto Hjorring, that hell-hound, perhaps he was more than just jaw after all. But he was very drunk! With one hand he had the more than half dead drummer by the collar and with the other he brandished his drawn sword. He banged on Shrimp's dilapidated gable until the chimney was ready to topple. But Shrimp was not at home, his old woman had sent him down to Sand to fetch the ducks. As for *her*, though she stood every day in awe of the Commandant, on this day she was afraid only of pirates. And so it was with all the old women. Arms loaded with spinning wheels, babies and dried fish they streamed in fright through Gongin, wailed, fell over, picked themselves up again and called without ceasing on God in Heaven. Their hovels were abandoned with doors open and the fires on the hearths given leave to burn themselves out.

The men were a little slower to flee, and some even wondered *if* they should run away so soon. But to reject flight in favour of wearing a red tunic, white gaiters and grenadier's busby, and standing thus against the foe and defending oneself like His Majesty's soldier — that was more than Otto Hjorring, that drunken pig, could talk them into.

Gabriel had spent the afternoon with the Judge's widow, Magdalena, helping her ransack her old bureau. His fat hands went eagerly back and forth over the wood, he knocked lightly here and there with his knuckles to sound out hollow places, and was indefatigable. There was no insignificant thing, no packaged lot, no gilded security envelope that did not come forth into the daylight. But the treasure in its secret compartment steadily failed to reveal itself. About one thing, however, there could be no doubt — if it *was* there it would be brought forth. This was a quite different ransacking from any that Magdalena, with her withered fingers, could ever have carried out, and she was very grateful to her nephew for the might and enthusiasm he displayed. The bureau fairly groaned under his grip. He was beginning to give up on it. It looked in complete disarray and injured in its pride, with all its drawer-spaces empty and their contents strewn over table and chair.

Gabriel tried and tried and thought and thought. But his thoughts were as much on Barbara as on the bureau. Ah, if he could only have known *her* innermost compartment. For the past few days it had been almost an obsession. This new Vagar priest — was it his turn now? Was there perhaps already something between them? He watched as closely as he could, but the shop took up his days. Every evening he was at Nyggjustova. He jeered, he hinted, he pumped, but Barbara only smiled slyly and objected when he went too crudely far.

Barbara took pleasure in him. She was very musical. There was not a nuance, not an intonation in his voice that got past her. She heard his heart beat. She heard the unhappy little dog deep inside Gabriel that howled and begged: 'Say it is not so'. And how she played with this dog! But then, often, her soft heart took over and she said that it was not so. But whenever she said, that she thought: 'If only it might be so.' And then she smiled and Gabriel's dog howled again.

At last she could hardly do without his chatter, and when he turned his attention to the bureau it was not long before she was sulking. She went out and soon came back with Suzanne.

When the shouting and noise began outside, Magdalena became frightened. But Gabriel had his wits about him. He took old Judge Stenderup's spy-glass and climbed the ladder to the uppermost loft. Barbara and Suzanne followed right after him. But Magdalena had taken to wailing: — Ah Jesus, ah Jesus, pirate ships!

— Damn me if they are! called Gabriel, and stared with a knowledgeable expression out over the sea. But his voice had a note of anxiety.

The three younger ones stood crowded around the little window in the gable and passed the spy-glass back and forth. Barbara was flushed with excitement and fairly hopped up and down on the rickety floor. Suzanne was silent.

— Those are naval vessels, Gabriel declared.

— Are they? Are they? Barbara was beginning to dance: Let *me* see!

— Even if they are naval vessels, maybe it is too early to be glad, said Suzanne. Sailors can plunder and burn a town too. That has been known before.

Gabriel was far from happy. It seemed to him as though the earth was beginning to burn under him. He climbed slowly back down the ladder. But Barbara and Suzanne could not tear themselves away from the window. They stared and stared, both talked at once, breathlessly, and interrupted each other, quarrelled over the spy-glass and kept calling out: — Let *me* see! Let *me* see!

Barbara was not nearly careful enough about her skirts. She did not give the ladder under her a thought. Gabriel could see her legs.

— Ah Jesus, have mercy on us! Magdalena kept wailing. She stared foolishly at her things, all scattered about the room.

— Ay, we had better get all that lot out of the way, said Gabriel, tonelessly.

Magdalena began, idiotically, to gather up the papers.

— Dear God, Suzanne's voice could be heard from above: now I know they *are* pirates and they will come and violate us both!

Barbara laughed in a warm descant, her eyes sparkled: — Oh, you! Just think how sorry everyone will be for us afterwards. That will be almost the most fun!

Gabriel kept looking up at her legs.

— Do not keep standing up there in that immodest way! he called. It was meant to sound manly and joking, but it came out as a cry of distress. He wrenched his eyes away and made for the door.

He had recovered his powers. Like a wounded whale he laboured down through Gongin — against the throng. When he had come out on to Reyn he met the last of the fleeing ones. He hurried through the empty apartments and upstairs to put his things into safety.

But Barbara and Suzanne had hardly been aware of his departure. They became more and more spell-bound by the ships.

— Now I can see one clearly, called Barbara: it has three tiers of guns and a gilded prow! She clapped her hands.

The Chief Magistrate came walking through Gongin. It would not be right to say that he hurried, but an attentive watcher might have observed that he lifted his heels a little quicker from the ground than usual. There was an unaccustomed look of uneasiness on his face.

Bailie Harme was beside himself. His wig was on crooked and he was gesturing with a long-stemmed Dutch clay pipe. He had begun to call for Suzanne, and looked fairly apoplectic. When his eye fell on the Chief Magistrate he calmed down for a moment. That mighty bulk was like a rock in a whirlpool. If Samuel Mikkelsen was downhearted he did not show it. He looked as thoroughly good and gentle as always. But he had no advice to give to the frightened Bailie.

— I do not know, I do not know, said he. I have become so awkward to move, I think I shall stay where I am. But you others may certainly make off, if that is what seems right. It is not easy to know. For naturally — those *could* be hostile ships.

A group of people had paused in front of the Bailie's house. They did not want to appear too afraid. It would be proper to see what the great ones decided to do.

But the Bailie could make up his mind about nothing. He fussed. He had three ledger books under his arm. The Chief Magistrate just stood there. Stood.

Along came the Judge. He was stroking his chin, as usual.

— It would be a disgrace for us all, was his opinion, if they turn out to be friendly warships, and the men on board find not a soul, either in town or at the Fort.

— So it seems to me as well, said Samuel Mikkelsen, quietly.

And there they both stood.

Pastor Wenzel came struggling through Gongin with a great burden on his back. He almost buckled under the weight of good silver, Sunday clothing and eiderdown bedding.

The Judge's lip curled a little. He could not restrain himself. Oh, wealth and display, — oh, idol of riches and golden array.

Pastor Wenzel gave him a look from under the eiderdowns, but kept a bitter silence.

The people were simply frightened. The man of God! They had never seen him like this before. Anna Sophia came up with the two old ones. They looked small and wizened-up in this crowd. The wind blew Ellen Katrina's silver-white hair all about. What a thing to see!

Fright overtook them. The crowd began to set itself in motion again, while the Bailie, carrying the ledger books, never left off calling. — Suzanne! Suzanne!

There came a flash of reflected light from overhead. Barbara opened the gable window in Nyggjustova and leaned out: — These are no pirates! Can you not see that?

Her tone was between impatience and laughter. It sounded as though she had been interrupted in the midst of something amusing and was vexed with them for not understanding that the whole thing was a only joke.

Everyone stopped. Barbara's arms rested on the window sill, round and serene. She was in a blue bodice, her face was fair and rosy, and there was warmth in her voice. Her appearance was like an opening of cheerfulness and mischief amid the chill of fear.

— Can you not understand that? she went on. Such big ships can not be pirates. They must be warships!

There was a silence. The Chief Magistrate stood fixed on the same spot. He shaded his eyes with his hand and stared out over the sea. Then he turned and said with a little smile:

— I do believe that Barbara is right.

Barbara beamed: — Ay, am I not? They are flying a white ensign.

— White with gold lilies? asked the Judge.

— Ay, so I think. She took the spy-glass: Ay, a white flag with something gold on it!

— Indeed! That is another thing! That is another thing! The Bailie recovered his tone of authority: They must be Frenchmen, then; we are not at war with them.

— To the best of my knowledge, Denmark is not at war with anyone, said the Judge, ironically.

There was general consultation and chatter. Folk went back down to the shore to have a look. Curiosity began to displace fear.

— My good men, said the Chief Magistrate to a pair of soldiers, go on back over to the Fort. There must be a salute. Let us not appear ridiculous to these strangers.

Off they went. Order was by way of re-establishing itself. Folk carried their poor treasures home again. Gladness, relief and expectation were in the air. Only a few women were not persuaded, they murmured about hostile ships. But the young were out on Tinganes to watch the strangers approach.

When Barbara and Suzanne came down into the street they encountered Gabriel. He looked as though he had not taken in a word of the whole business.

— How fat you are! said Barbara.

— Yes, why are you so fat?

They felt him. Then they burst out laughing. Suzanne began to haul red silk out of his waist-coat. But Gabriel struck her away and went off, burdened and unhappy. He had ten ells of cloth in his breeches.

Half an hour later all the window panes in Havn rattled with the thunder of the guns. Tinganes and Skindaraskerry were packed with people. Anchor chains rattled, foreign voices gave commands and shouted and out of the gunpowder smoke emerged masts and sails, bowsprits and shrouds, carved galleries and long rows of gun ports. Sailors swarmed in the rigging, busily occupied in furling the heavy sails. Then the Fort saluted back with full armament.

This was life and a feast. Never had such a sight been seen in Torshavn before. Three mighty men of war! From Sand the topmasts of the one could be seen high above all the roofs of Reyn.

The three French warships, *Neréide, Amphitrite* and *Fleur de Lys* were on their way back from the war in America. Storm and bad weather had driven them far north. Now they sought harbour in Faroe to repair various damage and take on fresh water before they continued their voyage home.

But Torshavn was no secure harbour. So long as the wind was in the south-west the ships could ride in the lee of Kirkjubo Ridge, but let it back to the south or east, the sea would come right in to that open roadstead. The Chief Magistrate, the Bailie and the Judge had been on board and explained this to the Admiral. They had advised him to go to Kongshavn or Vestmannahavn, where they could lie secure in all winds. But, the Chief Magistrate thought, they should wait till next day. For it was getting on for dusk now. Navigating between the islands in the dark was no easy matter, and it would be an unusual piece of bad luck if a south-east storm should blow up that very night.

Samuel Mikkelsen could not ever be considered impetuous, but hurry was especially not in him when wine came on the table. He sat in a gilded cabin, whose equal he had never seen before, and though he was a worsted-clad man outward, he quickly became so comfortably adorned inward, that he felt entirely at home.

Wonderful to contemplate, that these Frenchmen had come for water! That was thin stuff for a show of hospitality. But if that was what they wanted, they should not lack. Water there was in God's plenty on Faroe, and when the French gave wine for it into the bargain!

The Judge interpreted his words, and the French officers were astonished that this clan chieftain or Finn, or whatever he might be, knew how to express himself with such elegance. They had been polite to the three Faroe men from the start, but now they outdid themselves in courtesy.

They were themselves disinclined to weigh anchor that evening. They had been two and a half months at sea. Kongshavn and Vestmannahavn were dead places, as they had been given to understand, but here in Torshavn there must be a few people — were there not some girls, could they not have a dance? The Judge was predisposed to answer alas, no. But Samuel Mikkelsen was unwilling to forego an opportunity to repay such dazzling hospitality, and if the officers would find a little pleasure in a dance, that was the least one could provide for them.

And so it was agreed, there should be a ball and a festivity that same evening in the warehouses of the Royal Stores, and boats were soon rowing ashore with lanterns and pennants and wine casks and other things which would serve to make splendid the stone cellar under the outermost of the buildings on Tinganes.

When the time drew near most of the Havn folk gathered out on Tinganes to see the foreign lords come ashore. Rumours went about of magnificence on board. The Admiral, Comte de Casteljaloux, did not have, it is true, actors and actresses in his company, as it was said certain French marshals had with them on their campaigns. But he did have an orchestra and a library and librarian and a butler and many valets. So high-ranking an aristocrat had not been in Faroe before.

The ships swung their high carved poops towards the land. Lights were lit on board, and through the glazed windows of the galleries the interiors of the cabins could be seen. The sea was breaking heavily on the ness. Folk stood in the stiff evening wind and stared out. They spoke of great ships that had been to the islands before, of *Lion of Norway*, that one New Year's night had been wrecked under Lamba, and of *Westerbeech*, the Dutch East-Indiaman, that had scattered her timbers under the cliffs of Suduroy. Some wanted to pass the time in singing the ballad of *Lion of Norway*. But such entertainment was far too glum and far too inane for such an evening as this. What would the foreigners think!

The barge with the French visitors came rowing in to shore; they were carrying flaming torches, and every house and every hovel in Havn suddenly stood out fiery red in the dark. Every head was turned and did not know itself or its world again. Widow Oluva's miserable little shop over on Kag, that no-one had noticed before, stood sharply lit up, and grinned out over the bay. It was like a dream. It was as though the widow herself had broken free of her thirteen years' mourning, thrown over the traces and got drunk. Ay, it was the same with the old church tower, it too stood darkly red in the skies, like a portent. No-one had seen the church tower like that before.

But no eye lingered on the skies that evening. The Frenchmen were already shouting in the surf. They hurled their mooring lines with mighty casts and swarmed ashore quickly, laughing, with flashing teeth. Havn's women folk were transported. Their cold everyday eyes eagerly drank in the fierce sun of the foreigners' glances, the summer of their tanned faces. It was like a fire that filled them. The women's ears rang with the tramp of boots and clangour of rapiers, a rhythm of virility carried them with it.

When the oboe's animal cry soon after began to sound through the stone cellar, every heart was filled with folly.

Except Gabriel's. It could not rejoice. His eyes did not stray from Barbara. She was wearing the stuff that he had sold her. Ah, she remembered no more the one who had supplied her splendour. There was not a particle of gratitude in her heart. She did not know, she did not see Gabriel. Her eyes widened and shone, they were unrecognizable, she did not know how she stood or went, she became more and more beautiful. She was shameless, that tart, that born whore!

One of the French officers came by. Ay, of course, it must happen, it was as sure as tinder and spark. Gabriel turned away, ugh! he did not want to see.

It was Capitaine Montgaillard who bespoke Barbara for a gavotte, and with that the dancing began.

Soon there was not a girl, ay, not a young wife, who was not on the floor. But the menfolk of Havn gave themselves up eagerly to what they had been dreaming about all the late afternoon. The wine casks were aside in the one alcove, and here they flocked, while the Admiral's men served them drink in golden streams. Chief Magistrate Samuel Mikkelsen had ensconced himself by a cask, and there he sat, still and Olympian, and helped himself.

But Gabriel paced about and thought. He reckoned and reckoned, but however the devil he reckoned he only came to one and the same answer for this sum. It was sure and certain. He saw Barbara gaze in admiration at Montgaillard's eyebrows. Tcha and Tcha! His heart was pierced.

There was another too who was not happy. It was Pastor Paul. All this had taken him so entirely off guard. He had permitted himself to think that he was himself a luminary in Faroe's dark sky, in noteworthy conjunction with Venus, indeed only a moment ago he had imagined himself in a dance with Barbara. Alas, for vanity, which exacted its penalty. Now he was watching Barbara's golden head swing slowly about among white perukes and hair bags that were also swinging about just as blissfully, while he, like a student of theology, leaned against the wall and looked on.

— Hallo, brother! What kind of a face is that to present to such an evening?

He felt a hard slap on the shoulder. It was none other than Pastor Wenzel who had bobbed up, red-faced and cheerful.

— Nay, we shall enjoy ourselves, that is what we need, God knows! he went on, and conducted Pastor Paul to the alcove, where the drink was.

All the better folk were there, toasting one another. The Bailie was as red as a port lantern, but he was not well pleased. This was not according to his notion of things. Truly! There were important personages here but the guests took no heed of them at all. Look at that lieutenant there — he did not think he was too good to flatter, yes even caress, Lumpfish's Sara!

The Stores Manager did not express his views on the subject. His face was grey, and sweat stood out in a thousand little pearls on his face, his bespectacled eyes glittered loweringly out over the dancers. If one had followed his glance one would have seen Fru Mathilde. She was obviously exhilarated in the arms of one of the French officers.

The judge leaned up against a post; he was stooped and had an amused look. But Pastor Wenzel was gleeful, and he observed to the Chief Magistrate: — Oho, if the Stores Manager gets cuckolded tonight, then I shall not feel so badly about being a cuckold's cuckold, ha ha ha!

The Chief Magistrate had little to say to this. He sat like a Buddha by his cask, self-sufficient, while the dance whirled past him.

Pastor Paul was not much in the mood for drink. The music sounded tuneless in his head and the wine was tasteless. He heard a voice just by his ear: — Look at that Barbara! Now she is dancing with someone else. It would be a lark to see who finally bangs it into her tonight.

He turned. It was Gabriel speaking, his tone was spiteful and slanderous, but then all at once it altered and became soft and solemn: Ay, just study her closely this evening — you will learn a thing or two!

He went away, he was close to tears. He had drunk several beakers. This was not his usual way. He was used to leaving such stuff to the less clever. But this evening the world was upside down and all shop reckonings were invalid.

Barbara danced with her head in air, she went through the steps and figures, turned and went through them again — this was a quite other arithmetic. All at once the folly of the dance took hold of Gabriel. His heart ached, but pleasurably. He heard the oboe, as it told the same brief tale over and over, while the bassoon, in a clowning mood, chuckled and answered back. He felt himself being celestially fooled, his head was turning, he had to chuckle too.

Faces revolved and swung around him, familiar and strange. The stone walls shrieked and roared with music. Yonder stood his girl, Angelika, being kissed by a comte, was that not laughable? Opposite in the doorway stood Vupsen and many of her kind, everyday gossiping nymphs from the shop — God help us! Their eyes were out on stalks, they were all gestures, but they had only one another to flirt with, they were quite no-account. And behind them, out in the dark, stood their husbands like wolves, the brightness reflected in their eyes as they stared hungrily in at Canaan's land. Through a trap door high up in the ceiling could be seen Shrimp's melancholy features. His sour eyes were as though rivetted to the wine. And yonder sat the Chief Magistrate, immobile by his cask. But both the Chief Magistrate and the cask he sat by and the keg he sat on and Shrimp in the trap door and the women in the doorway and Angelika and her comte whirled around in a mighty circle. And the bows of the fiddlers went slowly up and down.

Gabriel had tears in his eyes. His heart ached, but pleasurably, pleasurably! He grasped it all, ay, the meaning of life itself. He knew what beauty was too, something he had not understood before, but now his brain sang and his bosom heaved.

It was quite otherwise with Pastor Paul. He could not drink, he heard nothing, he saw nothing, a greater and greater sorrow welled up in him.

Suddenly the room went still. The music died out, the dancing ceased. Something was going on outside. A word passed from mouth to mouth.

— The Admiral!

In a moment a passage was cleared, rapiers flew from scabbards and the Admiral, Comte de Casteljaloux, stepped in. He greeted and smiled at the company and all the foreign officers stood straight as candles.

The townsfolk looked on, very solemn. They would not have believed that so important a man could be so ugly. The light fell on his deeply-pitted face. His nose was big and crooked, his eyes popped out, and his broad lips moved ceaselessly, as though he was always remembering a delicious sauce he had tasted. But he bore himself with such cheerful dignity that it was a pleasure to watch him, and afterwards everyone had to confess that a finer man they had never seen.

Some of the officers gathered around him, talking and laughing. Capitaine Montgaillard made a proposition, but the Admiral looked doubtful. Then the Admiral began to be reassured, and became very serious.

Gabriel had made his way to Barbara, who had suddenly been left disengaged, and said something frivolous to her. She smiled and merely seemed pleased to hear what he said. At that moment up came Montgaillard and carried her off to the Admiral, and Barbara dropped the most elegant curtsey she knew how.

A signal was given to the orchestra. The musicians bent over their folders and turned the pages. On every music stand burned a wax candle, whose yellow light shone on white perukes, blue velvet coats and great lace cuffs.

The conductor raised his baton. A deathly hush fell on the cellar. The surf could be heard pounding outside.

A flute began its trembling note in the room, then another answered and it was as though two lone birds were calling each other; then suddenly the delightful voices of the violins broke in with a flowery tune. It was the Admiral's minuet, he danced it with Barbara.

A moment and it was over, and did not take up again. But the brilliance of Versailles' *roi soleil* had been reflected briefly in the

Cellar out on Tinganes, where the surf on winter nights would splash up on the windows.

Pastor Paul went out, he felt entirely superfluous. How had his heart ever flattered itself, thinking that there might be something in common between him and this woman? He now saw the gulf between them. God had torn the veil from before his eyes, and exposed his folly to him.

But he felt no gratitude towards God. His mortal being burned.

He walked and walked. The night was not pitch dark. But everything he saw, houses, gables, window-panes, reminded him of the bliss he had borne within him when he last came by.

At last he returned to the ball. Nearly everyone was down on the ness to see the Admiral on board again.

Then Barbara came over to him, warm and glowing, and whispered in his ear: — Shall we take a little walk together, we two?

She said it with child-like familiarity.

They walked. And behind them stood Gabriel. He grew pale and quite sober. This was beyond all reckoning. The bitch!

Houses, gables and window-panes in the town now reminded Pastor Paul of a happiness that he had lost, and behold, found again. They hardly spoke. Suddenly Barbara said: — You are not enjoying yourself at all this evening!

It sounded almost a little submissive.

Pastor Paul felt her hand, he seized it hungrily, but she played with his fingers. She looked up at him for a moment, with uncertainty in her eyes, then slowly looked down again.

— But the Frenchmen were enjoying themselves well enough, he replied at last. He was not in control of his voice.

A little smile spread over Barbara's mouth. She was still standing and looking down: — Ay ... but ...

Suddenly a ringing note came into her voice: — Tomorrow they will be gone! Will they not?

She looked at him. Again there was an almost comical uncertainty in her look. She pressed his hand lightly and repeated: — Will they not?

Pastor Paul's head was in a whirl. When Barbara said she wanted to go home he went with her. Then he too went home. His instinct kept him away from the festivity. He must protect his happiness, he felt that it was made of the merest fragile glass.

But Barbara went right back to the dance.

The whole cellar was a lurid tumult of drunk folk. The oboes were still speaking their peculiar, seductive speech, but no-one here needed seducing any longer, everything had let go. Only the Chief Magistrate sat immobile in his fixed place. He brushed his hand across his forehead once, as though he wanted to brush something away. Those woodwinds! They made such a din, it rang in his head.

Johan Hendrik, the Judge, came weaving towards Barbara. She had not ever seen him so degraded. She slipped away and made straight for Montgaillard, who was leaning against a wall with his arms folded. His strong lips sharpened into a smile, he took her by the arm and spoke. Barbara understood not a word but she recognized the tune. She saw his face very close to hers, his laughing eyes were golden and as though full of light, she felt his lips, he kissed her, hard and hot.

Gabriel saw. He went out and confided to Shrimp, without mincing his words, that now he had given up, once and for all, all effort to make a lady of Barbara. He would henceforth not concern himself about her in the least, for she was not worth it.

Then he went in again. He saw Barbara in Montgaillard's arms. They were sitting together by a cask and beginning to drink.

The place was a cauldron of yelling and stamping. The wind was blowing in through the door. Lanterns swung slowly from the ceiling and the shadows of their glass frames crossed back and forth on the wall in a dance. Gabriel went down into the store-room, which was adjacent. It was almost dark, but the whole room was alive. Round about among the hides and tallow-casks and butter-barrels sat couples. He felt the official rise up in him — this room was under his jurisdiction — he stumbled about on a tour of inspection. But who took heed of Gabriel on this evening? On all sides he heard gasps and giggles, cooing in French and squealings in Faroese. He saw his girl Angelika, dead drunk and in a sinful state of undress in the middle of a circle of Frenchmen. But what did Angelika matter to him? She was just Angelika! He recognized a skirt. He had sold that skirt to Suzanne Harme himself. It was unbelievable what the haughty Suzanne was letting a young French officer do with her. But what did

Suzanne matter to him? She was just Suzanne. He was drunk, he was weak, he was despondent, his eyes were dim, his hands were numb.

He went back out and again passed Montgaillard and Barbara. He pulled himself together. He could say something to her! Of course — what would be more natural? But he could not find his voice, and when at last he did find it he could not recognize it. It was like nothing in the world. But then up came the Judge — and his tongue was not quite tied.

— Ah, Barbara! said he: here you are broaching the wine cask. Have you not had enough of breeches?

— Depends on what is in them, Gabriel blurted out, rudely.

Barbara stared at them, drunk and scornful. Montgaillard did not understand what these sots were talking about.

Gabriel and Johan Hendrik walked out on to the ness. They were lifelong friends, this came over them suddenly. At other times they had never a good word for each other.

Nay, let Satan worry his head about Barbara. They were both agreed about that. They confirmed it with many embraces and looked deep into each other's eyes. And that new Vagar priest. If he imagined he had a look in, ha ha ha! Gabriel had to laugh. He stood in the middle of Tinganes and laughed to high heaven about the new Vagar priest, that damn fool!

And God be praised that they were not married men — Johan Hendrik and Gabriel! God in heaven be eternally praised! They were all but the only ones here in Havn that were not cuckolds this evening. So God be praised for that.

But then Johan Hendrik said that it might very well be so, but before the good Lord he was just the same a miserable cuckold. And Gabriel confessed that if he were to tell the truth, then he too in his heart, which the good Lord could see into, was a miserable, miserable cuckold — though he was still Gabriel on the outside.

They were both deep downcast, and the night was long.

When they came back to the cellar the festivities were done. The candles were burned down and one ceiling lantern was beginning to flicker. There were no musicians and no dancing. Only a few lone figures wandered like shadows on the empty floor. Someone was coming up from the store-room. It was Capitaine Montgaillard and Barbara. She teetered, holding his arm, shockingly disordered and unfastened. The red silk bows down her dress hung rumpled and lifeless, like crushed roses. Her shoes squelched with wine.

Suddenly she stopped, threw her head back and laughed. She pulled off one of her shoes and emptied its red contents out over the floor. At that moment her eye fell on Johan Hendrik. Quickly she hid her flushed face against Montgaillard's shoulder and gave a long laughing sigh. Her wet and glistening stockinged foot hunted for the shoe that had fallen on the floor.

Gabriel and Johan Hendrik stood and looked on. But Montgaillard became impatient, he wrapped Barbara in his cloak and carried her out. One of her stockings had slid down to her ankle, her bare leg hung and dangled. Wine dripped from her feet.

Johan Hendrik had collapsed on to a cask with his face hidden in his hands. Suddenly he looked up. In a dreadful falsetto he sang:

> What is it at best
> that makes the world seem so enticingly drest?

Gabriel leaned upright against the wall in an extremity of brandywine tears. Occasionally he joined in the hymn. In his hand he was holding a garter. He had found it on the floor. It was one of the pair he had sold Barbara, not long ago.

The hymn quavered unevenly on. Sometimes it almost came to a stop, sometimes it picked up with an unexpected spurt. It was like a difficult sail in heavy seas. But they helped each other, the two of them, and often looked each other deep in the eye — they understood each other so well, their souls wept together, while they sang and confessed:

> For envy rides up on your back with his spur.
> Your heart quakes within you, your steps are unsure;
> where others go swiftly you stumble and fall,
> > poor vanity's thrall,
> > poor vanity's thrall.

Gabriel held fast to the garter. Often *it* was what he sang to. He scolded it and pulled at it:

Your flame-eager tinder, your sparks that ignite
have lighted souls down into hell's blazing night ...

The quavering tones slowly died away in the cellar. Gabriel and the
Judge had set out for home. There was emptiness now, the last
lantern was just burning out. There was a soft rustle in an alcove. It
was the Chief Magistrate, Samuel Mikkelsen, who was getting up
from his keg. He was very awkward — though not much more so
than usual. But over his face played a subtle smile. Up in the town
the hymn could still be heard:

Farewell, then farewell,
beguile me no longer; I cast off your spell ...

6
Rain

The large Fort boat had been launched and was moored off Vippun, waiting to carry the Chief Magistrate and Pastor Paul, who were to have conveyance to Vagar.

It was a long and troublesome journey that lay before them. The first day they must go by boat to Kollafjord and from there on foot through the dale to Kvivik. The next day they must cross the Sound to Futaklett on Vagar and from there over the hills to Sandavag. The Chief Magistrate did not gladly choose this route, he was no keen walker and would rather have gone all the way by boat. But it was winter, and the sea passage south around Kirkjubo Ness was not advisable.

The ten soldiers in the boat waited and waited. This was something they were used to, not least when they were conveying the Chief Magistrate. They sat and talked about not missing the favourable current. It was a thing they were always talking about. For the current would not wait on the Chief Magistrate's dilatoriness, even though everyone else did. The fact had been demonstrated more than once.

It was two days after the visit of the French ships, and everything was more than usually normal. The town had slept most of Monday. In the evening tongues had been loosed, and surprising things had come to light. But today was Tuesday, and grey skies.

The Priest came on foot. Soon afterwards the Chief Magistrate appeared — in no hurry.

— By the way! he remarked, as though he were telling them an almost pitifully trifling thing! Barbara asked if she could come with me. She will be here presently.

He turned his back and looked as though he had said nothing.

A cloud of dissatisfaction passed over the men's faces. — Eastfall will soon be past, observed Niels of the Field, sullenly and sharply.

Samuel Mikkelsen made no response. The crew murmured their discontent. Wait for the Chief Magistrate could be, then, what it would be. But wait for women folk! They knew about that. There was no end to that. However you look at it — women and boats! Women folk should not be allowed in boats, women folk were a nuisance in boats, nothing but trouble, with their kerchiefs and shawls and their cackle. Worse than hens.

Gabriel came out of the shop, pasty-faced and rotund. Nothing doing today. He exchanged a few flat phrases with the Chief Magistrate and the Priest. There were some things he ought to have told Pastor Paul but the Chief Magistrate was standing there. Never mind, Gabriel was just as glad — if Pastor Paul wanted to be made a fool of, God bless him! he *had* been warned.

Half an hour went by before Barbara appeared. Eastfall had past a while ago, spit after spit had been spat in East Bay on that subject, deep and philosophical and argumentative and bad-tempered spits. There would be Westfall to row against, no doubt about that. But Barbara came walking, quite easy. She reached out her hand to Niels of the Field and asked him to help her down into the boat. Her voice was fresh and playful.

The boat gave a mighty roll when the Chief Magistrate stepped in, and rocked violently from the shock, but the Chief Magistrate's face was unmoved. He settled himself in the stern. Then they pulled away from the shore. Gabriel stood alone on the quay and grew smaller and smaller to the view.

Oars groaned and creaked against thole-pins. The boat flew onward in swift spurts. The river, the Bailie's house and Nyggjustova disappeared behind Fort Head. Gongin followed quickly after, gable by gable, then Reyn followed with its black church steeple, then the Stores Buildings out in Havn, then the last of these, the outermost building, where the dance had been held, and finally Tinganes' low-lying point. The town was gone. They rowed along an empty shore.

When Pastor Paul first saw Torshavn it seemed to him that it was a place in the kingdom of shadows he had come to. But now he felt that he was taking leave of the world itself. He sat in the stern of the boat with the Chief Magistrate and Barbara. They were being ceaselessly lifted up and down. The Chief Magistrate steered. One moment his great form could be seen high up against the grey sky, the next moment he was sitting deep down between walls of water, with a wave top frothing over his gentle head.

Pastor Paul had made the long sail from Copenhagen to the islands, but never had he felt the sea as today. He was so near it he could feel its strength quiver in the strakes of the boat, yes, and up through his very spine. He need only stretch out his arm for his hand to be in the waves; he looked right into them, where the light was refracted green.

But not a drop of water came into the boat. The men sat dry and comfortable and chatted with one another. The sail was raised; it stretched out over their heads like a bird.

— Do you not get seasick, Barbara? asked the Chief Magistrate.

— Who ... Barbara? shouted Ole Atten in his husky voice: never have I seen a woman so able at sea. Do not tell me that anyone has seen her seasick, do not tell me that!

— Nay, she is soon used to the sea, agreed the Chief Magistrate. He gave Barbara a friendly look. But in his venerable eyes flickered the shadow of a smile.

— And she is never afraid, either, Ole went on with his twaddle.

— Oh ay, God knows I am afraid! Barbara burst out suddenly. I hate Holma Sound!

She had taken Pastor Paul's arm. He felt that she truly was anxious. Before them lay a black rock island. The seas were breaking heavily around it, fountaining up in their excess and giving the stone no time to dry off again. Between this island and the shore was a narrow sound, full of skerries, which the seas boiled over. Pastor Paul felt a tremor too when he saw the boat turn in towards this turbulent strait. He looked at the Chief Magistrate, but Samuel Mikkelsen just nodded back:

— The weather is favourable. After a moment he good-humouredly went on to the crew: — Your Eastfall is holding longer today. It is not past yet.

Perhaps a little too much had been made of that Eastfall. Niels of the Field admitted that there was a touch of it left yet. They had just made it!

The current was indeed still running like a river northwards through Holma Sound. The boat danced like a cork. It came so near the rocks on the port side that the blades of the oars all but touched them. Pastor Paul kept feeling Barbara's anxious grip on his arm. But the Chief Magistrate sat as unmoved at the tiller as though he were playing chess.

All at once the waters became smooth. They were out of the sound. Northwards stood Eysturoy's peaks, black and sharp. But the men were expecting rain. Clouds were hanging low over Nolsoy.

It was past midday when they reached Kollafjord.

— You can easily row us right the way in to Oyrareingir, I know, said Samuel Mikkelsen, guilelessly, to the crew. It is a tedious walk along the fjord.

— We have a long way home, murmured Niels of the Field. And a contrary wind ... and Westfall will not lie still and wait for us.

— Westfall — dear God, Niels, said the Chief Magistrate; Westfall will without doubt take its full time. It has hardly even begun.

No-one had an answer to that. The oar strokes became a little bad-tempered perhaps. The Chief Magistrate sat and looked dead serious, though he might have been smiling a little, inwardly. They came ashore at the very end of the fjord. The crew carried the baggage from the boat. The Chief Magistrate was the one who had brought the least with him, all he had was a box. But he told them to be very careful with that. There was chinaware in it for his wife. Then he set out walking forcefully. Pastor Paul and Barbara followed after him.

Oyrareingir Farm lay a little way up in the midst of a small piece of level ground. Over it hung mighty rock faces. They towered into the clouds and were lost to view. The river murmured; otherwise there was not a sound to be heard but the rustle of the pale grass against their feet. The farmer came out to meet them. Would the crew not like to come in too?

— They will not say no to that, Samuel Mikkelsen assured him.

There was a crush in the hearth-room when all the men came crowding in. They were shy and awkward on land, they stood in a row and one after the other threw back the snaps the farmer poured out for them. Niels of the Field stood foremost with the warmth on his face. Ay, ay, said he, many thanks. But Westfall...

— Westfall will hold till six o'clock, said the farmer: will you not have a bite to eat before you go back again?

Pastor Paul felt the need to slip out for a moment. He found a small passage between some out-buildings. Everything seemed utterly still and comfortable here. The Chief Magistrate was standing there already.

— What a rare, fine place this is! said Pastor Paul.

— Ay, the Chief Magistrate answered, and smiled a little dubiously; when it is properly run, mind you.

He reached a flask to Pastor Paul. The priest was amazed that here, in a land where there was so often occasion to drink there was so seldom opportunity to attend to drink's consequences. He swallowed a small mouthful and walked uneasily farther along the walls of the building, which was constructed of loose stones and sods. But the Chief Magistrate seemed to suffer no such mortal weakness. He resumed his fellowship with his flask.

The rain had begun to fall. Oyrareingir Farmhouse lay at peace on its bit of level ground. Grass covered it like a carpet right to the ridge of its roof, and up through its smoke-hole curled turf smoke in blue rings. Cows bawled in their byre. In the hearthroom pots hung over the fire. The Havn men looked at them with eager eyes — it was not every day that they had farm fare in prospect.

When the Chief Magistrate came back in again he opened the subject of a horse with the farmer. Might he not borrow a horse? He was so awkward and slow on foot. It would be tiresome for Barbara and Pastor Paul to have him in tow through the dale in the rain. But if he had a horse to sit upon, they could keep together more easily.

Assuredly he could have a horse, with pleasure. The farmer asked if Barbara and Pastor Paul would not want horses too, but Barbara wanted no horse to sit on and freeze. Pastor Paul felt the same as Barbara.

It was a miserable downpour that they at last set out in.

Was *that* a horse? Pastor Paul had never seen such a horse. Nor did it look happy. It stood there with its eyes shut. Its tail hung straight down, its mane hung straight down and its ears hung straight down. Likewise the rain fell straight down.

The Chief Magistrate asked the carriers to be careful with that box. There was a little chinaware in it, he said. For his wife. Then up he got into the saddle, but the horse was like to capsize. A half-hidden smile crept from face to face. Perhaps there was a flicker of the same in the Chief Magistrate's eyes. He might well guess what he looked like. But his voice was as benign and undisturbed as ever when he bid farewell, and the farm folk said good-bye to him with great respect.

The dwarf horse put one foot before the other, the Chief Magistrate's gigantic bulk swayed slowly on its back and thus he went gently out of sight into the smoky rain.

Pastor Paul and Barbara followed behind, the grass whistled softly against their legs, and right away their feet became soaked. Barbara kilted up her heavy overskirt above her knees and went in her striped petticoat. She was full of life. Her face was wet but her eyes shone.

The two carriers came somewhat behind with their packs. They were not happy about the walk in this weather.

The rain poured down. In the heavy mist they could see only their immediate wet surroundings of heather and turf diggings. In order to keep from straying they had to stay by the river all the while. Its waters rose higher and higher and became gradually more and more turbid with soil and mud. Every moment they would come to a freshet that ran down the hillside into the river. The Chief Magistrate's horse trudged on through thick and thin, while Barbara leaped over the freshets. Pastor Paul often stood and hesitated before he dared follow her.

— Jump! she called to him, and laughed.

He was not used to such footing, full of stones and tussocks, bog and lumps of turf. He had to admire Barbara's feet, how they found, without hesitation, the right place to step, and her legs, how gracefully they carried her. She walked upright over all unevenness, holding her bosom high and looking straight ahead. But about her mouth a smile played constantly, as though she was making towards something happy.

Pastor Paul suddenly felt that water had begun to run down his spine. He was wet through.

The Chief Magistrate sat in this driving rain and swayed and nodded, but his expression was imperturbable. — Now you are wet right through to your shift, I would guess, Barbara, said he from his height.

Barbara, through her wetness, gave a gleeful laugh that rose from her throat: — Ay, right to the skin ... just look!

She pulled her skirt aside, her petticoat was clinging to her knees.

— You should do your walking in man's clothing...

— I do not know so much. I think it is more fun to be a woman! She laughed again and took Pastor Paul's arm — then off she went. They had been on the way for an hour, and now could not become wetter. It was just beginning to grow dark. They had crossed a watershed. The river they were following flowed the other way through the dale. Before them gleamed the surfaces of two small lakes. The carriers declared that they had come halfway.

The Chief Magistrate was no impatient horseman, he gently let the little beast walk at its own pace, but it was beginning to flag all the same — it was not even as big as its rider.

They had made their way onwards to a larger lake, Leynum Lake. Cliffs hung over the water, and the path wound its way underneath them along the shore. Here they must not call out or speak loud, the carriers said, a stone might come loose and fall down. But this was an unnecessary warning; for a long while no-one had spoken a word.

Pastor Paul and Barbara, who had been near each other all the way, sometimes before and sometimes alongside the Chief magistrate, as it grew darker kept closer together. Sometimes, when they came to a little obstacle, they took hands with each other. They waded in mire, the insides of their shoes were full of mud, that squelched and slid under their arches. The rain was now full in their faces, it was hopeless to try to talk, and sometimes they could hardly draw breath in this stormy weather. Yet Pastor Paul felt fresh and in good spirits. It was as though he was being led into a new and significant life which in its depths hid something sweet and precious.

A little way below in the thick darkness glimmered one or two weak lights. Barbara shouted to him that those were the houses in Leynum. They halted for a moment to let the others come up. Samuel Mikkelsen looked like a tame and mighty centaur.

— We should go in to Ole Jacob's in Leynum, said he. He can easily put us up. The rivers are very full this evening. It will be impossible to cross them to Kvivik.

The carriers came up. They were of the same mind, and so was Barbara, it was a delightful idea. Overnighting with the priest and his family in Kvivik was always so boring ... whatever anyone might say, it was. But Pastor Paul was all at once aware of feeling disappointment that this walk was almost over. He would gladly have gone through swollen rivers with Barbara.

A quarter of an hour later they stood in Ole Jacob's yard in Leynum Farm. The Chief Magistrate softly lifted the latch and passed hugely and carefully through the low doorway. The others followed in single file and stood in a group just inside. They looked as though they had been fished up out of the deep. The fire was burning brightly on the hearth and the room was full of people who all stared in silence at the intruders.

— Good evening, said Samuel Mikkelsen at last, softly and sedately.

The housewife took a step towards them: — My Lord and God, is this the Chief Magistrate, out travelling in such weather?

— Ay, five of us, said the Chief Magistrate, and then gave a weak smile.

— But bless your hearts ... come right inside!

Ole Jacob, the farmer, had got up and come over and shaken the hands of the newcomers. — Had we known that we might expect such important visitors this evening we should have laid a fire in the best room, said the housewife. But Barbara laughed: — We shall be more at home in the hearth-room.

Supper pots hung over the fire. The girls went back and forth and busied themselves. But the men mostly sat on benches alongside the wall. Some were carding and spinning, two or three older men were knitting.

The visitors were seated. Warmth hit them and their clothing began to steam.

— You need dry things, I would say, said the housewife.

A little smile appeared on the Chief Magistrate's face. There could be no doubt that he was in sad need of a change, but it was also well known that in the whole land there was only one other man with whom he could exchange clothes. And that man lived on a farm far in the North Islands.

— I am not so very wet, said he. I can sit here quite well in my clothes. Maybe I shall soon have leave to go to bed.

In came the housewife with an armload of woollen clothing. She began in a friendly way to help Barbara off with her things.

— How lovely, said Barbara. She smiled with pleasure and let herself go slack and weary in all her limbs.

But Pastor Paul was suddenly struck with the most powerful uneasiness. It was like a shot. He started up and was immediately in the middle of the floor without knowing how he had got there.

Barbara was already partly naked, she was so white that she shone in the hearth-room. She was not at all shy about the entire naturalness here at Leynum, she was natural herself and easy. Yet as though without noticing she took care always that no-one saw anything improper or secret, or too blindingly much of her bare skin. Once she slipped up a little. She covered her bosom quickly again. But Pastor Paul had seen. She suddenly blushed deeply. Those who were aware of it were somewhat surprised — after all they had heard they would not have expected Barbara to be one of those who blushed.

Pastor Paul had gone back to his place. His heart was beating so hard it almost hurt, and his body trembled weakly. Two of the servant girls began to help him off with his wet things. He hardly knew how the change of his clothing was made.

Barbara had already been dressed again for some moments — in thick and heavy farm-wife apparel. But her face was trim and bright and cheerful.

The Chief Magistrate thought that he would rather go and lie down — if they would not take it ill. He had a box that it were best he take with him, there was cough medicine in it, good to take at night.

They asked him if he was ill. No, ill he was not. He was shown into the best room and a candle was lit for him in a candlestick.

Talk, which had died down a while with the arrival of the unexpected guests, began to liven up again. All had heard, with astonishment, of the French ships that had come into Havn, but indeed they thought it a much more important event that they

95

themselves were visited this evening by such great ones. The Chief Magistrate was the island's foremost man. His mighty breeches were at that moment hanging up under the roof to dry. They swung majestically back and forth. But a shining new priest was also someone worth seeing. And most of all their curiosity gathered about Barbara.

She felt this and was radiant. She knew well how to talk with everyone, and had a particular gift for finding the insignificant among them and flattering them with a few words. She basked in their gratitude and admiration. It was not long before she discovered that old Tormod had been interrupted in a yarn when the guests arrived. She sat on a stool in front of him and asked him to go on.

Old Tormod sat by the fire. Turf crumbs and ashes clung to his clothing, and his white aged head nodded slowly all the while. At first he wanted to be excused. It was only an old story, nothing but lies, said he, that nobody wants to hear, least of all a priest, a learned man, who surely knew much better things. But he was not hard to coax, and soon he was off again, yarning about earth folk that men and women might encounter out in the outfields when they least expected to.

The housewife was busy. She called to Tormod and told him he should leave off such twaddle. He was in his second childhood, he should remember. What was he thinking of, did the visitors want to listen to such stuff?

But Tormod did not hear her. He sat with a far-off look and half-shut eyes and told how Pastor Rasmus Ganting, one summer's day, was walking alongside Sorvag Lake. A green mound was there and the mound stood open. A woman stood in the doorway and asked him in. Another woman came with beer in a silver beaker and gave it him to drink. But before he drank, Pastor Rasmus blew all the foam right into the earth woman's face. 'That was cleverly done,' said she. 'If I were not cleverer than you I should not have come into this mound,' said the priest.

The fire blazed under the pot. Shadows danced their black dance along the walls. Up under the roof wagged the mighty shadow of the Chief Magistrate's breeches. Tormod yarned on and on. Knitting needles clicked and spinning wheels hummed. He told about a man in Goosedale who had an earth woman for a lover. She came to him during the night. The true wife knew nothing about this, but one night when she lay on the inside of the bed beside her husband she was suddenly aware of a cold hand. It was the earth woman, who had laid herself on the bed board on her husband's other side.

Everyone sat silent and listened. A few had experienced one thing or another that they did not think hung together just right. Thoughts began to stray out among the mighty hills to dark heaths and troll-sized boulders where the heathen lived their silent lives... Then the housewife called them back to reality, for supper was ready.

Pastor Paul felt very queer. He almost felt as though he too had come into a mound. His heart was full of a great uneasiness and peculiar comfort. As soon as he had eaten he asked if he might go to bed. He wanted to collect his wits if he could.

He was shown into the best room and asked to share a bed with the Chief Magistrate. The candle in the candlestick was lighted again. It was placed on a scrubbed board between two windows. Walls, ceiling, all were of white-scrubbed wood. On one of the side walls was a cupboard and an alcove bed. On the other side wall were two alcove beds end to end. The Chief Magistrate was snoring in one of them.

While Pastor Paul was undressing he read the inscription on the stove in the partition wall:

> When I caught my Master's feet
> he flew away with me;
> my friend, I counsel, take good note
> yourself in me to see.

A bas-relief pictured an eagle that was flying off with a man in its talons. What one was expected to see oneself in was the man's backside. Ole Jacob explained that the old ones used to say it was Griffenfeld who got into that trouble.

Pastor Paul crept into the alcove bed. The Chief Magistrate took up much of it, but there was still an adequate warm space for the Priest. His feet came against something hard and flat ... this soon identified itself as two pint-and-a-half flasks. And they were empty. It took a while for the Chief Magistrate to wind down from a visit to Havn.

Light from the hearth-room came in through chinks in the door. On the other side were life and voices yet. From time to time Barbara's laughter could be heard, gratified and happy. Pastor Paul lay in the warm dark and endeavoured in vain to call his soul to devotions. God in Heaven, what state was he in to be journeying to his new call? His blood burned with desire for Barbara.

The day's events began to come back before him. He felt the boat's rhythm and saw the island that the surf splashed up around. He leaped over all the brooks in Kollafjord Dale while the rain poured down. Barbara took him by the hand, she was so wet that her clothing clung and slapped around her. She said 'jump', 'jump', 'jump' in a different voice every time. She asked him in and gave him ale and he forgot to blow off the froth.

He woke up when something rustled near him. Somebody was getting ready for the bed next to his. He saw a gigantic indistinct shadow on the wall. Suddenly it dawned on him that this was Barbara. He heard her lie down and push the sliding door to, but the noise continued, close by. His heart hammered.

Others came in. He heard the farmer and housewife talking very softly. They must sleep in the bed on the other side. Everything had become still in the house. Everywhere folk rustled and went to bed. Only one girl was still working in the hearth-room, putting bread to bake in the hot ashes.

Pastor Paul felt something scratch very quietly on the pillow. He thought it was a mouse and made a grab for it. He caught a hand. He turned towards the head-board and looked right into Barbara's eyes. A board or two were missing between the two bunks, her head was only an ell away from his. The last of the remaining light through the door chinks fell on her face, she was deadly serious and quiet, he could see that she was as intent and roused as himself.

They caressed each other's hands and arms without a word and stared at each other as though in fear. The light through the door grew weaker and weaker and at last they lay buried in darkness. Now there was nothing in the way between them. But the Chief Magistrate snored on.

7
Coloured Stones

At ebb tide the whole of the wide Midvag Sand lay white and dry. It was then that Barbara would cross over to Pastor Paul in Jansagerd from her widow's house in Kalvalid on the other side of the bay. For it was a lovely short-cut this way, said she. Often it would sound as though it was only for the short-cut's sake that she came. The sand was so flat and so white! And it was such a short way — was it not? She always brightened when she explained this.

Barbara had many glittering explanations to give of her life's dodges and short-cuts, she had as it were a wallet full of pretences that shone like coloured stones and sparkled like her own yellow-green eyes. But although Pastor Paul knew well that it was wholly for his sake that she crossed the sands every day, it hurt him a little when she talked like this. For his heart was full of a great disquiet.

His life was not days and nights, but rather flood-tides and ebbs. He sat through the long summer day-light at his table and read in *The Garden of Paradise, Treasures of the Soul* or in *Faith's Precious Gem.* But his heart was empty and responded only to the shell-curved waves, as they came sliding slowly, and broke along the beach. His heart was on that white sand below, which widened and then narrowed, and when the tide went out the last murmurs of his devotions too, ebbed out of his mind. Then he could only wait and wait.

Before him on the table stood two brass candlesticks. In the foot of one was a big dent. He knew well that this had come when Barbara, in a fit of temper, had thrown the candlestick at his predecessor, Pastor Niels. But he never dwelt on this. All he longed for was that Barbara should come, as she had yesterday and the day before, and play with the inkhorn and *The Treasures of the Soul*, and let her light hand stray among his miserable learned things and brighten everything with her lively yellow-green glance. In one of these painful times of waiting he had begun to scribble some verses about her.

> My beauty,
> my sweet one,
> my joy and my goal,
> my Earth-dwelling Angel
> and most precious soul,
> you have touched me and won me
> my heart and my all
> your ways that are lovely
> and form beautiful...

But even these verses to Barbara could not concentrate his attention. His eyes were unceasingly down on the sand where he expected to see her.

And when she came she was an erect and graceful presence among all the youngsters who were running and playing down there. She always walked so erect. Once he seen her bend down and tie up her shoe-lace that had come undone. She went mostly, like other women in the village, in shoes of soft, pale sheepskin with red laces that were tied around her ankles. Her step was so light that it left no print; the sand remained firm and rippled like the waves, just as the tide had left it. Pastor Paul often thought of the discomfort her footsoles must feel crossing this rough ground, and how the gravel and pebbles must cut into her heels and the balls of her feet. He loved her feet, that made all these steps every day to come to him, and leaped so lightly across the river. When she got there he could always see her face for the moment that she passed by the window. Her look was deadly serious, her eyes flashed and she hurried.

Yet every day he feared that she might not come, that the ebb might run out like an hour-glass and the flood then submerge the whole sand. But what least ground did he have for such a fear? It had never yet happened that she did not come. On the contrary, she had sometimes come unexpected, having taken the long way, out around the bay, and surprised him with a surge of affection. And once, when she had not found him at home, she had left on his table a little note, which read: 'My dearest friend, I cannot wait so long so do come over at once, because I most want to be where you are, but you were not here your loving heart Barbara Christina Salling.'

It was horrendously badly and hastily written. But Pastor Paul became dizzy and all but terrified when he read it, for he felt that this was a quivering reality of flesh and blood, and not just a glittering stone from Barbara's make-believe wallet.

But it had also happened that he, in the middle of one forenoon, had walked over to Kalvalid to see her and had said: — I have such a longing for you. And she, in an unrecognizable tone of voice, had answered: — That is *good*!

When he left her again she was high-bosomed and red-cheeked as a goddess, and her eyes shone like bright flames.

Folk in the village believed that Pastor Paul and Barbara were betrothed, and reports of this had long since reached Torshavn. All nodded their heads and said it was just what would have been expected. But the truth was that neither betrothal nor marriage had at any time been mentioned between these two. They had never had time for that, for they were always more than betrothed and married when they only saw each other.

But in lonely moments it would happen that the priest would suffer qualms that dismayed him. When he sought to draw some Christian words and sentiments for his sermons from that weighty tome, *Treasures of the Soul*, he most often found only condemnations of his own way of life. There it stood that chastity was essential in a believer, that it could not be separated from fellowship with Christ, that it was the fruit of faith. And the means for achieving it were 1) a holy and upright intention, 2) immediate suppression of unclean desires, 3) avoidance of all occasion for them, 4) avoidance of idleness and laziness, 5) discipline of the flesh by fasting. As though he did not fast! Often his flesh would hardly allow him to eat, so sick with longing was he in his anxiety over Barbara's coming. And when he did eat, it could happen that he would bring it up again.

Alas, he was a wretched priest, and it was meagre comfort to him that about *chastity* there also stood: few can boast of it. For he was a pure-hearted man and did not know *how* few.

He read often till the sweat broke out on his forehead, to see if there might be some small thing wherein God might find the least pleasure in him and Barbara. Because they did love each other with heart and soul. But he could not bring Barbara and God together. How could he even speak to God about Barbara? And how could he talk to Barbara about God?

He could find no defence for his behaviour, yet it was impossible for him to do otherwise than he was doing. He did not have the power over himself.

Yet he could indeed enter into matrimony with Barbara. Then everything would be different. Because a woman was also a most provident creation to counter adultery, fornication and loose living. He read this in a little old book that he found among Pastor Niels' relics. It was called *The Righteous Woman's Mirror*, and it was, all in all, a delightful book, with all the beautiful things it said about the married woman. 'Surely,' it said, 'there can never be or be found such bosom friends, whose intentions are so heartfelt and true towards each other as righteous husbands and wives, who are one flesh, one body, and one heart, and have one will, who bear joy and sorrow, good and ill together, and especially the woman, with her beauty, grace, love and blissful ways, her sweet and pleasant voice and words, is for the man the greatest refreshment amid his burdens — next to God's word.'

When Pastor Paul read this his heart was filled with sweetness, but at the same time with a vertiginous dismay. For he knew Barbara's history, and he knew her at first hand far better than his heart would acknowledge.

Woman is like a hind, which has a keen and ready hearing, especially when she pricks up her ears. But when she lets her ears drop, she is all but deaf. Like the hind, woman should prick up her ears both when she hears God's word, and when her husband admonishes her, and listen well to what folk say about her reputation. But she should be deaf to all the sorts of blasphemy that the hedonists speak of God, to the fool's shameful words and desires, which provoke to unchastity and looseness ...

But alas, Barbara, Barbara! Was there a single hedonistic word that did not immediately catch her ear and make her senses quiver? Was there any artfulness that did not immediately waken life in her eyes? Was there any game that she did not immediately want to play?

Pastor Paul was like a bird catcher who hangs on his line and dares look neither up nor down. Because if he looks up towards the heavens his line seems lost in the distance, and it is as though he is hanging by a severed thread. But if he looks down, he becomes aware of the horror of the abyss.

He hardly dared think. He only dared live. His happiness drew him without mercy through the summer days and nights, his happiness was a trembling and fickle hind whose ears were always pricked up and alert.

Except in church. But then, Pastor Paul's sermons were not good.

Barbara, who missed nothing, did not miss sensing her beloved's disquiet, and she felt this as a deep injury. One day, when they were speaking of their love, she said: — Every time I reach you my whole hand, you reach me only your little finger.

Pastor Paul was so astonished by this that for a long while he was silent. He had not seen it this way at all, far from it, he had seen it the other way round.

— You do not reach me your whole hand, said he, you do not because you cannot.

Now it was Barbara who was astonished, she reddened a little and said quickly: — I give you everything that I have to give you.

She looked a little pained. Pastor Paul paced up and down on the floor. Then all at once he burst out: — Barbara! You know that I have my work to do.

— Ay, but can I not help you a little?

She ran over to him, put her arms around his neck and asked very earnestly: — Can I not help you a little?

Pastor Paul remembered that brief letter from Barbara, how horrendously badly it had been written. It was as helpless as a prayer, it was the most touching thing he knew about her — he treasured it as a piece of her very soul.

Barbara looked at him with childlike enthusiasm. The look in her eyes was droll: — I can write well, when I am told what to write ...

The Priest felt something like elation. Master Chr. Scrivers' *Treasures of the Soul* lay on the table delightfully sweetened. Barbara clapped her hands. She thought that they should compose a sermon at once — this very moment. But Pastor Paul did not want to do that. He wanted to think first. They should begin work tomorrow.

Barbara said that she would come first thing next day. She was so heart-happy that she kissed and kissed him when she went.

— Now I know that we shall have a wonderful time together! For can you see, she added confidentially: I shall have a part in everything you do, can you understand that?

Pastor Paul went about a long while and did not know either what he was doing or saying. He came to himself in the middle of a hymn:

> Hallelujah, our God is mighty,
> and Heaven replies: Amen!

Next day Barbara came to write. She had so many quills that the Priest had to laugh. He asked if the geese up at Kalvalid were not all naked now because Barbara wanted to write a sermon. But she explained that she was a terrible one for spoiling pens because she wrote in such a hurry.

She sat impatiently at the table, laid the paper at an angle in front of her and held her head at an angle too, and as soon as Pastor Paul began to dictate she settled in eagerly and wrote freely, with her tongue slightly out of her mouth. Her hair fell down a little over her forehead, she grew redder and redder in the face while the pen scratched and spluttered.

Never had Pastor Paul imagined such a thing — that this beautiful woman should become his obedient and enthusiastic instrument. His happiness grew and grew like a bubble and became as fragile and empty. Suddenly his feelings all left him, his mind wandered and he received an inspiration. Barbara's literary competence — God better it! — it was not very impressive. Yet seated there as she was, she might well do. Even the innocent geese were instruments of the spirit and of learning, for they were full of quills. Pride rose up in him for a moment. Then just as suddenly he became downcast. He had not before associated pride with Barbara, only adoration. He was conscious of a deep loss and went and stood by the window. There he cleared an opening in the moisture. Outside everything was green and flourishing, mist was drifting across the grass.

Barbara marked a full stop, lifted her pen and looked up: — What more, then?

She stroked the hair from her brow and was red and happy with enthusiasm.

— Let me see what you have written.

She handed him the paper. It was marked all over with great letters, that danced eagerly and straggled out of place and all slanted up towards the right-hand corner of the paper. The spelling was so-so, but intelligible. Then he came across something and burst out, with pain in his voice: — Jesus!

Barbara did not understand at first what he meant. She blushed deeply at once.

— Barbara! Ah, can you not once spell Jesus?

— Oh! She snatched the paper from him, sat down again and, with the tip of her tongue between her lips and her pen spluttering, quickly and violently stroked out her *Hjesus* and wrote the correct word above it. Then she happily and almost triumphantly handed the paper back to him.

But Pastor Paul would not take it. He sat pale-faced in his chair and stared at her. Barbara became confused. It seemed at first that she was searching her wallet for a bright stone that would make his face light up again. But her heart was wiser than that. She suddenly understood who Jesus was and began to feel miserable.

She went over to Pastor Paul, but he hid his face in his hands. She picked awkwardly at his shoulder, toyed very lightly with his hair and his cheek and at last whispered quietly in his ear: — You must not be angry with me.

He made a violent movement.

— Leave me, you... you... it is not of *me* that you must ask forgiveness.

Barbara went over to the window and drew helpless drawings and lines in the moisture. She was miserable with desperation and shame. The Priest too was filled with greater and greater distress. He sat slumped in his chair. This was the first time there had been a hard word between him and Barbara. He forgot his anger entirely. Yet he could not bring himself to go to her.

— Of course, Barbara murmured at last, in a broken voice: — of course it was dreadfully stupid of me, all this. For I am not worthy of such work ... I am indeed a sinful woman.

And she drew a mass of long streaks in the moisture. It looked as though what she was doing was a very important piece of work.

Pastor Paul sat for a while in silence. Then he asked: — Are ... are you a great sinner?

Barbara turned to him. She looked at him with burning, frightened eyes.

— Ay.

Then she ran over and kneeled at the priest's feet and hugged his knees and hid her face. And so she lay a long while, and neither of them uttered a word. But this time it was he who played just a little with her hair.

He was perplexed in the depths of his heart. What had he done? He did not know what it was that this reminded him of. Perhaps it was some dream or other. But in any case it was something very shameful. He began to see himself as a small, small man with a pharisaical accusing finger. And here was a great sinner, in tears.

Suddenly Simon the Leper's house came into his head, and his heart was lifted. He had found it! He got up and leafed through the Bible to the seventh chapter of Luke's Gospel.

— Barbara, will you listen to something? he asked.

She nodded, without a word.

— 'And behold, a woman in the city, which was a sinner, when she knew that Jesus sat at meat in the Pharisee's house, brought an alabaster box of ointment. And stood at his feet behind him weeping...'

Barbara sat dead still while he was reading. Now and again she looked up at Pastor Paul with a hurried, frightened look. And he went on reading to her about the woman's humility and the pharisee's self-righteousness, and he came to Jesus' parable of the man who had two debtors. 'The one owed five hundred pence, and the other fifty. And when they had nothing to pay, he frankly forgave them both. Tell me therefore, which of them will love him most?'

Barbara gave a start — it was as though something had suddenly opened before her, she was on the point of exclaiming something.

But the priest read on from Jesus' words: — 'And he turned to the woman, and said unto Simon, "Seest thou this woman?" '

Barbara began to tremble and she became very shy. For she was indeed a woman and her heart had become an alabaster box. Never had she given, and never had she received as now.

— 'I entered into thine house, thou gavest me no water for my feet: but she hath washed my feet with tears, and wiped them with the hairs of her head. Thou gavest me no kiss: but this woman since the time I came in hath not ceased to kiss my feet. My head with oil thou didst not anoint: but this woman hath anointed my feet with ointment. Wherefore I say unto thee, Her sins, which are many, are forgiven; for she loved much; but to whom little is forgiven, the same loveth little.'

With the last words Barbara began to brighten up. Her yellow-green glance shone frightened and at the same time pleased. But Pastor Paul sat still and silent. He had been shaken through and through. He had learned something quite new of God's inexhaustible grace.

— Thank you, Paul! said Barbara. She was desperately shy. I thought that God had long ago abandoned me, she whispered, and hugged him blindly and strongly as never before.

But Pastor Paul was forced to say to her: — My dearest! It is not *me* that you must thank. I shall go outside now for a while, so that you may be alone, as though in a secret chamber, and thank God for his word.

How Barbara went about thanking God she hardly knew herself. But though it was sweet — and there can be no doubt of that — it was also short. For one, two, three and she was out in the green out-of-doors with Pastor Paul and chattering like a bird.

The mist was clearing off and the sun's rays were beginning to shine through it. A comfortable warmth wove itself into the fine rain and softly heated their skins. And Midvag's green pasturelands laughed through their maskings of mist. Buttercups and primroses shone yellow in the grass. Every blade was still weighed down with a drop of dew.

It was ebb-tide now, but that no longer had any significance.

Barbara was so happy, she took Pastor Paul's arm and said that now they must go up to the lake, to Sorvag Lake.

When they came out upon the brown heath, the sun was shining full and the heather and ground were drying off and easy to walk on. Pastor Paul walked and turned over in his mind what had happened. It was such an inconceivable happiness for him that he hardly dared believe it. Now was the pearl found, for God and Barbara had come together.

But Barbara was not so thoughtful. She skipped and ran. She was a great sinner and Jesus was her friend. It seemed to her that Pastor Paul was not nearly happy enough. She pressed close up to him, took fast hold of his arm and twined her fingers with his. Then she smiled comfortingly at him and said to him, as though to a child: — You are a sinner too, Paul, are you not, now? Yes, you *are*! We are both great sinners!

Pastor Paul did not know whether he should cry or laugh. He said, Ach! and was both heavy and joyful. And Barbara smiled and comforted him still more and was on the point of bringing forth something from her make-believe wallet and saying that if he did not owe 500 pence his debt was pretty close to 450! But she checked herself and looked rather compassionately at him. For in her heart she knew that he did not even owe 50. Poor good Pastor Paul — she loved him!

Pastor Paul had more than a suspicion that her Christianity would hardly stand under a theological scrutiny. But he only smiled at that and remembered the Good Book's words: — 'Whosoever shall not receive the kingdom of God as a little child ...' That dry-as-dust *Treasures of the Soul* back home on his table had only confused him and hidden God's true love from him.

They came to the lake. It lay dark and shining, and the green and brown ridges roundabout mirrored themselves in it. Pastor Paul had often been in these parts. When he was on his way to the sister parishes in Sorvag and Bo or out to the lonely island Mykines, the way came past here. Also in lonely, troubled times he had wandered here. But with Barbara he had never come along Sorvag Lake, and it seemed to him that it was a new and solemn world that he was leading her into. He had had many beautiful thoughts out in this terrain, and he longed to tell her about them.

There was a cluster of small buildings along the shore. They were not dwellings, only houses for storing turf, and boat houses. Even so, they looked like a proper little town. At this moment too, many people were busy among them. Midvag folk cut their turf in summer on Sorvag outfields on the other side of the lake, and now, in these days, the first turfs were dry and ready to be ferried across.

Pastor Paul and Barbara sat down in the heather. A single heavy-laden boat was nearing the shore.

— When I come here, said the priest, I always think of the Sea of Galilee. I do not know why that should be. When I first saw this lake it was like an old dream coming back to me. But then I understood that I was only thinking of the Sea of Galilee.

Barbara had nothing to say to this, and perhaps did not understand at all. But her lively eyes declared how much she admired Pastor Paul, and how her heart hung on his words.

— These little buildings now, he continued, put me in mind almost exactly of Capernaum.

— Capernaum! cried Barbara, happily. It was as though she understood better, and it seemed all at once that she could take part in the talk. Capernaum! Was it not in Capernaum that ... that ...?

She began earnestly to pull up heather and look down at the ground: — Was it not there, it happened, you know...? She was shy again.

The Priest thought about it and replied that there was nothing in Luke about the place where it happened, but it might well be that it was Capernaum, for Jesus often came there.

Barbara said that it was *surely* Capernaum. Her whole face shone and she became excited, for now *she* was in the story that Pastor Paul was telling. This was a big splendid stone that she bestowed on herself, and her eyes shone golden in the sunlight.

— Altogether, said Pastor Paul, Jesus went round among all the small towns by the Sea of Galilee, and sometimes he was on the other side in the wilderness, preaching. I always imagine that place to be over there, where we see the people going and working.

Barbara sat and chewed on a stem of grass. Then suddenly she said:

— You remind me of Jonas — my first husband.

Pastor Paul did not know what to think of this, and made no answer.

— You *always* remind me of Jonas, Barbara continued. I thought so right away! — the very first time I saw you!

— Did you? That time down in the gateway at the Stores?

— Ay, I had gone down only to see what you looked like.

— Were you very fond of Pastor Jonas? asked the Priest.

— There is no-one I have ever been so fond of as Jonas. We used to talk together all the time, as you and I have been doing today, about every kind of thing, and we never tired of being together. That was at Vidareidi ... it was wonderful. But then he died and I missed him dreadfully. Always, always I have wished that it could be like that again, as when I was married to Jonas — but it never has been.

She brushed a tuft of heather from herself.

— What did you talk about, you and Pastor Jonas? About God?

— Ay, about God too. About everything. I do not remember exactly now, I was so young then, but when Pastor Jonas talked about God it always made me happy. It was not as when ...

She stopped, abruptly.

— As when? asked Pastor Paul, disturbed.

— As when Anders began with his everlasting warnings and sermons and ...

— Pastor Anders? The Provost at Ness?

— Ouf, ay, now he is Provost. They will have been good enough to tell you that I was once betrothed to him. But I could not bear him. Always full of ... of punishment and damnation ... and he was wanting to make me better.

— Did you so badly need to be made better?

Barbara looked down: — I needed a man like Jonas, that was the one thing I longed for, and the one thing that could have kept me from ... from sinning.

She got the last word out with a kind of reluctance. It sounded altogether foreign in her mouth. But then she suddenly cleared the skerry and added: — He gave me stones for bread.

— Did you become so tired of God's word? asked the Priest.

— I did, said Barbara. Sick and tired. But I never forgot Jonas, and I kept thinking that perhaps another might come ... one who would be like Jonas and could make everything good again.

110

— And then came Pastor Niels?

— Pastor Niels! It was as though Barbara had forgotten that she had once been married to a man whose name was Pastor Niels. But then she all at once burst out: — Poor Niels! Ay, that was frightful. And it was that surgeon Balzer, it was all his fault. He was so clumsy with that leg. I hate that clown!

The priest sank into a deep thoughtfulness. Then at last he questioned her: — But could Pastor Niels not lead you back to God's word?

Barbara at first made something like a grimace, but then her look softened and she said, quietly: — I was truly terribly fond of Pastor Niels, that you may believe, though I was often a beast to him. We were terribly good friends. But ... but ... you understand: he had such an awful tiresome and squeaky voice.

The Priest turned away and looked dispiritedly down at the ground. There he saw a little spider that was working between heather and dead grass.

But Barbara stood up, brushed her clothes off a little, and called: — Come, let us go down to the water. Perhaps we can go over to the other side with that boat.

Pastor Paul followed her. She took his arm again and folded her fingers in with his, looked up at him and said: — Now we are by the Sea of Galilee and are going into Capernaum, are we not?

And when they came into Capernaum she hugged him and said: — You must not die, do you hear? I cannot be without you.

She was very serious, and trembled.

When they got down to the water the boat had been unloaded and was ready to push out again. Pastor Paul and Barbara were told they could come too. They sat on the sternmost small thwart and were pressed a little against each other all the way. The boat was full of turf crumbs, and the oars creaked and groaned against the bone-dry thole-pins.

Round about them the lake was a wide shining surface on which the image of the afternoon sun glittered, and hurt their eyes. But across from them the mountains cast their dark shadows in the water, and the ripples left by the oars were circles of cool darkness. Barbara held her hand in the water and let it course between her fingers.

The peat-bog was a dark land with black diggings that looked like wounds in the earth. But the air was bright and ringing with the voices of grown-ups and children who were working round about. Curlews and plovers stood on heather tumps and uttered their cries, and here and there, where people were cooking, smoke curled upwards. It was a smoke that smarted and made the eyes water, but it was sweet and strong, like a kind of brandywine. There was thyme in it.

Barbara said that this was one of the things she liked best, going out for the turf. She took Pastor Paul round from one family to another and asked them in a concerned way how far the work had progressed, and how soon they thought the last of the turfs would be dry and could be carried over. With one of the families they ate a little lunch. They were poor people, but Barbara praised their offering and got the Priest to do so too.

There was an old granny who helped carry the turfs down to the shore. She did that, as everyone else in the country did, in a *leyp*, a big rectangular slatted box, shaped to be carried on the back, held by a knitted wool tump line that went across the forehead. The old woman was almost sinking under the burden. Her neck was strong and springy enough, and her face was a knot of determination. But her legs could hardly carry her.

— Let me try carrying the *leyp*! said Barbara.

— Nay, nay, nay, said the old one, that would never do.

But Barbara lifted the *leyp* from her so slyly that nobody was aware before she had fitted the coarse woollen tump line over her forehead and bent her fine back in under the heavy burden. She walked without faltering down to the water, unloaded the turfs and came sauntering back with the *leyp* hanging over one shoulder. Now Pastor Paul wanted to carry one too. They loaded the *leyp* on him and fitted the tump line over his forehead. But no sooner had he felt the full weight before his knees began to shake. His neck was too weak, and suddenly he sank down backwards and sat on his rump.

— I knew it! shouted Barbara, gleefully.

But the folk were polite and explained that no stranger could carry a *leyp*, because his neck sinews were not developed for it.

Then Barbara carried another load. There was no stopping her, she laughed gaily, and everyone admired her. And every time she set down the empty *leyp* she was always as upright and high-bosomed as ever. Her eyes shone, she was like a lighted candle among them. She was as though charged with strength and good will, for God, this day, had accepted her heart.

As soon as the work was done she brushed the turf crumbs from her neck. She told them she had got some crumbs down her back, and laughed and shook herself. Then she went over to Pastor Paul and was unceasingly full of warmth and radiance.

They walked southwards and came to the end of the lake. But there was no River Jordan here. The still, shining water fell outward in a mighty waterfall into the great ocean. It darkened and foamed far below them. Thus ended the Sea of Galilee — not in a narrow valley but in a roaring eternity.

They sprang from stone to stone and came to the other side of the short stretch of brook that led from the lake to the waterfall. It was evening now; all the heath birds were silent. When they reached Midvag it was nearing midnight. But the tide was in, and Barbara found that an excuse to stay a little longer with Pastor Paul. They walked in the dew-wet grass, and everything northwards, houses, rocks, and wooden crosses in the graveyard, were all lighted by the great beacon fire of the sky over the mountain tops. There was such a dead stillness they only dared whisper. They sat down and talked and talked and were in agreement about everything, and meanwhile the heavens' light moved farther and farther towards the east.

When Pastor Paul lay down to sleep, nature's power was still over him. His senses relinquished only gradually the dark earth, the brilliant sky and the bright voices that had sounded over the heaths. But that sudden waterfall to the sea was the end of everything. Indeed, God's grace and God's goodness were so great and so strange, that one might well think that the angels in their heavenly hymn books had *spelled* the words a little bit wrong. Yes, it would have been strange otherwise.

Barbara too, went to bed renewed by this great day. She did not remember it all so exactly, but her heart still treasured these words: 'Her sins, which are many, are forgiven; for she loved much.'

And she did love much.

8
Akvavit

T he grass on all the roofs in Torshavn stood green and flourishing in the fog. It was a dry and mild fog that wet the paving stones not at all, but it was so thick that it closed the whole of the outdoors, everything and everyone, as though in a cupboard full of white murk. The noisy play of boys out on Tinganes and the shrieking of terns over their heads was damped and stifled in the impenetrable atmosphere. Yet other noises, which came from far away, could be heard with sharp clarity. Time and again during the course of the day rhythmic oar-strokes could be heard from out in the fjord, and time and again the boys stopped their game and listened and peered out until a fully-manned boat took shape in the fog and pulled in at Vippun or one of the other landing places in East Bay.

It was the day before St Olaf's Wake. In all the town's lanes gathered a quiet throng of villagers. They had come to Havn to meet friends and see the Council opened. They sauntered up and down in their heavy silver-buckled shoes, met at passage-way corners and stood in knots and exchanged news. A dawning hilarity was showing its first rays in many eyes. But they started no loud talk, and made no disturbance. They were full of occasion and dignity.

Housewives of the town found a little entertainment in opening their windows and spying on the village men, as they gathered inconspicuously in a corner or alleyway around a bottle. But they were not very disposed to meet the Olaf visitors face to face. Villagers had a strange simple-minded way of putting questions. They would sit and look innocent, as though they had not learned to count to three. But watch them! They could very well count to three and up to nine, and what gossip they were after today no-one need be in doubt about. The town's big scandal had already reached all the islands, and now they had one thirst in every last village, to learn what they could of the more explicit details.

Ay, it was the devil's own scandal — there had never been anything like it. It touched not just a few, it took in the whole town. Gabriel was the one who had first given the story legs to walk on. For months now he had been telling the farmers who had come to the shop about the many *French bairns* that were expected soon in Torshavn. Just wait till August, he had said, and see how busy the midwives will all suddenly be. He had given a big grin and the village men had returned home quite wide-eyed with these tidings of Sodom and Gomorrah.

It was reported also that Barbara was soon to be married to the new Vagar priest. Ay, that was nothing unusual for her. She never seemed to have enough of priests, the farmers thought. But Gabriel was not right sure that her appetite was so great this time. There might well be other causes than hunger. Let us see then, he said. He knew what he knew. And gradually they came to understand that Pastor Paul was about to marry a French bairn around his neck.

Ay, is it not the devil? Gabriel would say to the customers. He never wearied of talking about Barbara's inexhaustible store of amorous wiles. With a balance-weight or a meal measure in hand he would often stand and simply fall into a reverie over her goings-on, and he would shake his head and snicker; the devil, eh?

During the summer it had been unusually convenient to come to the Stores, and this twenty-eighth of July the shop was therefore the first place the St Olaf visitors made for as soon as they came ashore. The first to come was Niels Peter of Myrin from Lorvik. He was a notorious wag, but most people were just mildly amused by his curiosity and his big mouth. French bairns, he blurted; the words were out of his mouth almost before he was through the door. But Gabriel told him short and sharp to hold his jaw and go to the devil. Niels Peter was so flattened that he slunk off. He was baffled altogether by Gabriel's words and could think of nothing better than to thank God that no-one had been present when he had made such an unlucky inquiry of a person in authority. That was an experience he would keep strictly to himself.

By and by in came other villagers to the shop. They had a better understanding of right behaviour. Their talk was slow and circumstantial and dragged itself out with this and that about wind and weather and crops. But not a word did Gabriel vouchsafe about the great crop of humanity expected in Havn. This was extraordinary, it was a proper let-down for St Olaf's Wake. A few went so far as to ask if there was anything new. But that was as far as they would venture. They were respectable farmers, who stuck their fingers in the earth and smelled where they were at. They got a powerful feeling that the set of the wind in the Royal Stores was not favourable to much questioning this day.

They came out as wise as they had gone in. They were bursting with curiosity. They went uphill and down in town, peering on all sides and outstaring every miserable window-pane. They hailed other groups of Olaf visitors at random and asked them right out if *they* did not know something about these blessed French progeny. But no, nobody knew anything, even Niels Peter knew only casual gossip about this and that and the other, things they all knew already. And that was precious little to have learned, now that they were on the very scene. Vupsen came by and she was big all right, that she was. But Vupsen had been that way many times before in her life.

There was no savour in the akvavit. Nay, a dull Olaf's was in prospect. Neither did anyone invite them in, and a man could not see his hand in front of him in this fog. They could think of nothing better to do than go back and forth through Gongin — out on to Tinganes and back again.

— Can you not get a word out of Gabriel? one of them demanded of Niels Peter.

He shook his head: — Nay, that I can not.

— Get away! That would be a small thing for a man like you!

— I could easily have asked, said Niels Peter, but I do not think that he will say anything to me. He says exactly nothing unless a friend makes him. You, Hans Lavus, you could ask him, you are his cousin.

Hans Lavus turned his head slowly, stared thoughtfully in front of him and closed his eyes once or twice. He had white eye-lashes.

— Ay, ay, he nodded at last, but it sounded rather as though he was talking to himself than with one of the others.

— Ay, for you really are his cousin, are you not? Niels Peter went on.

Hans Lavus was not in the least Gabriel's cousin, he was a weak-minded tramp, known over the whole country and put up with because he was inoffensive. He believed that he was some-one important — most often he called himself Chief Magistrate. But he was a gentle and melancholy authority who had only the one weakness, he was susceptible to flattery. And now that all proclaimed him the only one among them to whom Gabriel would spare a word he was not the man to say no. A spark of life began to show in his eyes, he looked about with a pleased expression: — Hm, ay, good men. Hm, ay. What is it that you would have me ask him?

Niels Peter as good as put the words in his mouth. He should say: 'Hm Gabriel, hm, good chap, what can you tell us about the French bairns today?' And then he should offer him a pinch of snuff. Thus. Niels Peter straightened himself up and showed how an important man offered a lesser man a pinch of snuff. The farmers smiled secretly at one another. What a devil's own clown he was, that Niels Peter! Just the same, it was beginning to shape up as a proper Olaf's. They all got into a corner, Hans Lavus was given a snaps too, and then off they wandered out on to Tinganes.

Gabriel did not look closely at this procession that with Hans Lavus at its head began to fill the shop. He stood and weighed out barley for Vupsen and was silent and officious. Only when he was quite ready did he deign to cast a glance at the invaders.

— Hm, Gabriel, hm, good chap, sounded Hans Lavus' gentle simpleton's voice: what can you tell us about the French bairns today?

He smiled foolishly and fetched an absurd snuff-box out of a red and foul pocket handkerchief.

Gabriel was ready to explode, but restrained himself. His quick wit had in a second read the conspiracy in the villagers' all too numerous and all too solemn faces. Especially there was no misinterpreting Niels Peter's face in behind all the rest. That broad grin lay in wait and alert for every word. Many seconds passed without a sound to be heard but Vupsen's asthma. Then Gabriel said at last in a weary and quiet voice: — Get away with you, Hans Lavus. I have not got the time to stand around and talk foolishness with you this morning. Here you go!

He dropped a piece of loaf sugar on the counter. Hans Lavus grabbed the white lump eagerly and viewed it with gluey, infatuated eyes. The villagers stood helpless and looked on. Their whole enterprise had stranded. They felt like fools and had no notion how they might slip away again with their dignity intact.

It was at this moment that Vupsen put in her word. It began with a wheeze in her narrow chest, then her speech began to come clear: — Ay, you had better get along, Hans Lavus, and you had all better get along, the lot of you! You did not know that the pipe is piping a new tune here in the shop. But I can tell you that Gabriel now has a right to talk about French bairns. He has been like a scourge of God all summer, scoffing and telling lies about us common folk and putting bastards on to us. But the scoffer comes to the scoffer's house and burns the scoffer in! You can go home and tell that in your villages. For now Gabriel has hung a French bairn around his own neck, and you can say good day to them and tell them that from Vupsen. He is going to be married to the Bailie's daughter on Sunday! And there is to be a confinement already, next month! And you may swear to it that the Bailie's daughter is not the lady to have bedded with Gabriel at any time. Nay, it was a high-born lover, and French, that is who it was, though Gabriel may be written a thousand times husband and father in the church book.

During all this Gabriel had stood pale and silent. When Vupsen had finished he said in a soft and uncertain voice: — I shall go in and fetch the Stores Manager, so I shall.

— Ay, go right in to him, Vupsen started in again; he will not be so keen to come out and talk about French bairns, no more than you. The fine folk have all turned lambs this past while. Vupsen is not the only one, madame or miss, that will give birth this August.

— You are a slanderer, said Gabriel. The thought, that it was not just himself but everyone in authority that was being slandered, gave him new conviction. — You shall mind your tongue, said he, in an ominous tone, or I shall see to it that you have your confinement in the dungeon, do you understand.

Vupsen had gradually approached the door.

— Ay, ay, you can put me in the dungeon a thousand times, or upon the Peak, she bellowed, but make a French child into a Gabriel's child, that you can not do. Good-bye!

The villagers' eyes had gradually grown bigger and bigger. They were almost dismayed, and when the dungeon was mentioned it made them feel quite ill. Slowly they stumbled out of the shop, weak in the knees from shock. On the steps stood Niels Peter, bent over, his shoulders working slowly, as though he was sobbing. And the foremost of the villagers were beginning to cling together. But not a sound from them. They just got moving, the whole lot got moving and fairly streaked away, and not till they found a secure corner did they come to a halt and begin to snicker. They were so agitated that it was all they could do to have a drink, and it was a long while before they found their tongues again. But then a great cheerfulness began to spread among them, the news and the akvavit filled their breasts with warmth, and one of them struck up a ballad. And in the course of the day, more and more frequently a snatch of ballad would rise into the air among the tarred wooden walls. The milk-white fog closed all the passage-ways in, a man could not see his hand before him, but the town was full of hidden mirth.

Gabriel was left in his shop alone. With an old sack he went about and cleaned up all the leavings of barley and sugar and snuff that had been spilled on the counters. This turn of events had been worse than expected, and he could see that a couple of cursed days lay ahead. But there was no help for it. He had reckoned everything up and he would stand by his reckoning. Only it behoved him to be in charge of himself. The damnable thing was that he had not been used to restraining himself with these clowns. But the more successfully he restrained himself the less power there would be in their mirth, and the lighter the costs would be.

The profits themselves were sure enough. He had weighed it all up carefully, debit and credit. Suzanne Harme was a good match, the best match in the islands. It was understood that advancement came with her, and he had stipulated from the first that the Bailie should promote him to his full clerkship. From this it followed with reasonable certainty that he should also be his successor. To be sure the Bailie had not undertaken to die soon, but he had already suffered a stroke.

That was the most impressive entry, but along with it came the consideration that Suzanne was a both beautiful and sensible woman. Gabriel never wearied of repeating this to himself. She was no Barbara — God be praised, she was no Barbara! Certainly, she was not undamaged. But when a man takes damaged goods, exactly on the understanding that they are damaged, he can not at the same time demand that they be undamaged. Suzanne was after all only a *little* damaged, and it was an everlasting plus that no-one *here* in the islands could brag that he was father of her child. Damnation, what a thing that would have been!

Finally there was this entry, that Suzanne, though she was not exactly Barbara, just the same she was almost Barbara. She was a considerable someone, ay she was at bottom a kind of Barbara who did not have Barbara's weaknesses. How could it be better?

On the other hand, on the debit side there did stand the entry that when he was married to Suzanne he could not be married to Barbara. This was an entry that he did not fully understand. For had he at any time wished to marry Barbara? Assuredly not! Was it not on the credit side not to be married to Barbara? Assuredly yes! This was rather a muddle, this bit. Why should it stand under debit that he was not married to Barbara when the same circumstance was implied in several entries on the credit side? He puzzled more and more over this and was quite uncertain about himself and his reckoning. At last he comforted himself that the whole thing was only an anomaly of the double-entry accounting. Exactly. It was not unlike the problem about a surplus. Or a cash balance. That was entered on the debit side too. Strangely enough.

Another entry on the debit side was the mirth. It was truly only a minor entry, that could hardly be calculated along with the others. But one thing was damnable about it, it had to be paid out of hand, in cash. The worst of it, however, was surely over and done with. What was yet to come would hardly be very much. So long as it was enough to bring it to an end. Outlay was naturally always painful, but when one considered what one received for the money ...

Gabriel never wearied of reminding himself of this, he comforted himself with it and thus kept up his nerve in his fortress. It was not always easy to look the enemy in the eye, the people were drunk and unruly today ... that she-devil Vupsen had kindled the torches of mutiny, so to speak, and made the common people quite disrespectful. The decent villagers too, were they not coming into the shop and making impertinent insinuations? Ay, and he had some inklings of a sort of secret gathering around the corner, where the mirth was on the boil, and whence, from time to time, spies were sent into the shop to bring report of its mood.

There had not been such a mirthful Olaf's Wake for years. The Havn dwellers had had their party in the winter while the French ships lay in the roadstead. Now it was the villagers' turn. They had nothing better to drink than akvavit and nothing more elegant to dance than their Faroese dance. But they also had their advantage, they had their great advantage, and they were fully equal to the occasion.

Niels Peter was the one who began the dance. That lucky turn in the shop had made him the day's man, and he was not one to hide his light under a bushel. With ringing voice he struck up:

> — The King asked his daughter fair
>   matrori, matrori,
> — whose is your eldest son, my dear?
>   Torilori gekk gekk gekk
>   torilori gekk gekk gekk
>   torilori gekk.

There was no harm in this. But it was impudent just the same, and a spectacle, to be dancing out in Havn, right in front of the shop. More and more took their places in the ring and the wantonness and boldness mounted minute by minute. A few staider men declared that it was no mere joke to be teasing Gabriel like this. They knew that he was a man who would become more powerful and eminent, and who could take his revenge when the time came. But the younger ones would not listen. They were full of akvavit and would think of nothing but their fooling. When Gabriel, pale with anger, came out on the steps and told them in the devil's name to hold their peace, Niels Peter looked him in the eye and sang:

> — Bailie, he to his daughter said
> matrori, matrori
> — what have you done with your maidenhead?
> torilori gekk gekk gekk

With this Gabriel went back in. But Niels Peter made more verses and became cheekier and more personal. He sang:

> — Bailie, he to his daughter said
> where is a husband for your bed?

This was too much for Gabriel. He fumed down the steps and swore he would bring this unruliness up short. He could taste blood. He would call out authority and commandant and soldiers. But he came nowhere near doing that. Two of the strongest villagers grabbed him by the arms and forced him to dance with them in the ring:

> — Bailie said to his daughter fine:
> matrori, matrori
> — your bairn comes of a noble line!
> torilori gekk gekk gekk
> torilori gekk gekk gekk
> torilori gekk.

The men swung and made mighty jerks on Gabriel's arms, looked deep into his eyes and sang like madmen. Then suddenly they all stopped, the words dried up in their mouths and not another sound was to be heard but the shrieking of the terns in the fog. The Chief Magistrate had appeared in their midst. He moved so unobtrusively that only for his great bulk they might not have been aware of him. Behind him in the fog outside the Royal Stores' gateway, up the slope came Barbara, and Pastor Paul with her, and the sheriff of Vagar. They had just come ashore at Vippun.

— Lord Jesus bless us, said the Chief Magistrate in his gentle ox voice, and looked about, astonished. What is going on here?

All looked crestfallen. Gabriel had escaped back into the shop. Hans Lavus too had slunk off. He was the only one in the islands who could not bear to see the Chief Magistrate, in him it always brought on a fit of the deepest melancholy. But otherwise there would normally only be confidence wherever Samuel Mikkelsen appeared. His enormous quiet gave a comforting strength to all hearts. Nor was it long before Niels Peter had got hold of himself sufficiently that he could offer a kind of explanation.

— We ought all to be rejoicing, said he, in a flippant tone. It is not every year that such a distinguished marriage is arranged in Havn.

The shadow of a smile showed in the Chief Magistrate's eyes. It was clear that he had guessed the drift of things, but he showed no change in his look.

— You had better go up to the Council Chamber and dance a respectable Olaf's dance there, said he. This is a queer dancing place altogether.

A moment later the shop was full of cheerfulness and pleasant talk. Gabriel found it a relief to be among polite folk again who understood the proper way to congratulate him. The Chief Magistrate had been informed in a letter from the Judge of the forthcoming marriage, and on the way to Havn he had told the news to Pastor Paul and Barbara.

— What fun! said Barbara to Gabriel. Her laughing voice was perfectly candid. Just think, you are to be married to Suzanne. Then you shall be almost my brother-in-law!

— You are to be married too, I am told, said Gabriel, feebly. The moment permitted him no malice. Nay, in every respect it was Barbara who would have good reason to smile. He had taken her measure at a glance. It was easy to see that *she* was not with child.

— Ay, what fun it is! said Barbara:— We shall both be married! She was happy and quite without guile.

That evening the Chief Magistrate made a call on Bailie Harme. The Bailie had aged, visibly. During the winter he had had a severe stroke and been laid up a long while. It was late before he was informed of his daughter's condition. She had been considerate in not wanting to expose her father to this shock before he had got back his strength. But a good way out would have been costly. It being summer he might have thought of getting his daughter away on one of the merchant ships. Unfortunately he had no kin whom he was willing to entrust her to. Besides, there was the bairn. It would be best all round that this acquire a father. He had thought of the Judge it is true, but this might well have been an insulting proposal to make to him. Then there was Gabriel ... Alas, it was indeed not because the Bailie had a high opinion of that Gabriel. And his opinion had not improved since, on closer acquaintance. But something had to be done.

— Ay, said Samuel Mikkelsen. I shall not say otherwise than that I too could have wished another man for your daughter than Gabriel. To tell the truth, I have not ever had much faith in him. But what does Suzanne herself say?

— Naturally, Suzanne is not enthusiastic over this way out either, said the Bailie. But now that Barbara has come ... perhaps she may comfort her a little — God help us!

The Chief Magistrate smiled a small, unhappy smile. He sat a while in thought.

— Perhaps, he said, — perhaps you should have spoken to Johan Hendrik just the same. I would not be sure, but he is a sensible man and at any rate he would have given you a courteous no. And if he had said yes, it would have been very much better for everyone. What is more, I am sure that *he* would not have been thought less of on account of it. People are very different and they are respected in different ways.

At that moment in came Gabriel. He was much upset and hardly acknowledged the presence of the Chief Magistrate in the room.

— The common people are out of hand today, said he. The devil seems to have got into them. I think it is too much that I am the one to suffer on account of Suzanne's damned loose behaviour.

The Chief Magistrate stared and almost forgot to hide his astonishment. What airs! Was this fellow already beginning to talk about the 'common people'? He had to smile a little. Well, well, thought he; give a small man power and watch him take more.

— I demand to have Niels Peter of Myrin put in the dungeon, Gabriel went on. Today he has slandered and ridiculed everyone in authority. It is all very well to sit here and be comfortable. Why do *I* have to bear the brunt of it, I who have done nothing but good? *I*,

124

this day, have had to listen to a slandering ballad about the Bailie and Suzanne.

— If the ballad had nothing to do with you, Gabriel, said the Chief Magistrate, in a friendly voice, surely you need not have taken it *so* hard?

Gabriel stared enraged at Samuel Mikkelsen's imperturbably gentle face:— Nothing to do with me? Nothing with me? Of course it had something to do with me too ... what the devil ...?

— Did it then? asked the Chief Magistrate. His eyes were entirely good-natured and beautiful.

— And now I am demanding a warrant for the arrest of Niels Peter of Myrin, said Gabriel, angrily, to the Bailie. I shall then take it to the Commandant or to Hans Constable and see that it is carried out.

Bailie Harme began to stir himself. He was ill at ease and indecisive. He breathed heavily and fiddled a little with a pen. Then he began to pace up and down on the floor and became very red in the face.

The Chief Magistrate had all the while been sitting in exactly the same position. Now he raised himself slowly from his chair, whereupon the little room grew dark. For a while he stood and looked out the window. Then he said:

— Ay, this is a case that does not involve me — not for the moment at any rate. But if you will listen to my advice, Gabriel, you will do nothing about this. After all, you cannot put all the Olaf visitors in the dungeon.

Samuel Mikkelsen departed. He was not happy. Dear God, thought he, enough of one kind or another will land in the dungeon in the times ahead.

Round about in the town he could now and again hear the chorus:

Torilori gekk gekk gekk.

He wished it would let up.

Folk greeted the Chief Magistrate with gladness. His presence was the authoritative sign that it was now properly Olaf's Wake. But the Chief Magistrate went directly to his lodgings and lay down. Among all the noteworthy things that were happening at the Olaf's feast, perhaps this was the most unusual.

9
At a Diocesan Meeting

Olaf's Day began with bright sun and the sound of bells.
Pastor Paul, as the newest priest who had come to the islands, read the service in the church, and all forgathered to hear what admonitory words he would have to say to the members of the Law-Thing. After the service the Chief Magistrate proceeded to the Thing with the Law Book under his arm, and the church bells rang again. Behind the Chief Magistrate came the Bailie, the Judge, all seven of the country's priests and the six sheriffs and at last came the forty-eight members of the assembly with white ruffs around their necks. The farmers were solemn today: and sang no more torilori gekk. Gabriel had recovered his composure and given up his demand for Niels Peter's incarceration in the dungeon. The womenfolk of the town leaned out of their windows with curiosity, but called no gibes at the passers-by. Only the church bells were to be heard, and the scuff of holiday buckle-shoes.

The Chief Magistrate proceeded into the Council Chamber, and all the authorities and members of the Assembly followed after. The common folk stood out-of-doors in Gongin. Through the open windows they could distinguish the dark outlines of King Frederik's portrait with his queen, Juliane Marie.

The Chief Magistrate rose to his feet and cleared his throat.

— The peace and blessing of our Lord Jesus Christ, he began, in his deep and gentle voice, be with us and with all those who make this goodly Thing journey now and always, amen.

From a book he read out the long formulary by which the Thing was called to order in peace. The words were hard to decipher, his voice, from time to time, became weak and unclear. But at last he laid the book down and concluded:

— Herewith all, in the peace of God, be seated.

The Thing was now in session, and its business began. Bailie Harme was the first to take the floor. He supported himself a little against the table and his head trembled weakly. It was apparent that he had failed badly during the past year. His voice had suffered as well. It was almost painful to hear him clear his throat and say Ahem, for there was no strength or dignity in it any more.

The Bailie asked, as was the custom, if anyone in the Thing or among the common folk had any complaint to bring forward about the handling of supplies for the country, or about service in the Royal Stores, whether as concerned demeanour, measure or weight. There was a general murmur. No doubt many in the course of the year had sworn to wait no longer than Olaf's to complain about the good stockings that the Stores had rejected and refused to accept in payment, or about the supply of akvavit, which had run out. Plug tobacco too, had been poor and mouldy for a while. Not to mention Gabriel's maliciousness many and many a time. But now that they were asked and the Bailie was standing there and looking to left and right, they all held their peace. It was no small thing to come forward in this gathering, it was not easy to express oneself the correct way, and if one said something stupid he would be sure to be a laughing-stock all over the country. Nay, it was best on all counts to be quiet. As the old ones used to say: Silent you suffer one injury, speak and you suffer two.

So this first day of the Thing was almost always short, it was little more than a formality.

After the Thing came the diocesan meeting. With the greatest uneasiness Pastor Paul accompanied his colleagues out to Reynagard — Pastor Severin from Suduroy, Pastor Marcus from Sandoy, Pastor Wenzel from South Streymoy, Pastor Gregers from North Streymoy, Pastor Anders from Eysturoy and Pastor Christian from the North

128

Islands. Barbara he had had hardly a glimpse of today. God alone knew how her paths wandered. Pastor Paul was always ill at ease when he did not have her with him, and here in Havn her lively goings-on caused him more anguish. Provost Anders Morsing complimented him on his sermon, but he hardly listened. As he walked he searched to right and left in case he might see her in the crowd. But all he could see were unknown farmers.

— Ay, if you will be so good as to take pleasure in my poor little house, said Pastor Wenzel, as they stepped into Reynagard. He was short, red-haired and unctuous as always.

— Poor little house? Indeed! So said Pastor Severin. He emitted a long asthmatic wheeze and then broke into a rattling laugh: Verily verily I say unto you ... well, God forgive me! No, what shall I say ... poor little house! Dear colleagues! Which of us has such a house as this? Upon my word!

He rubbed his hands and paced quickly up and down the floor. He was a very short and very thick man with a kindly, pleased expression.

Reynagard was no poor little house, and its drawing-room, which they came into, was a large, four windowed room. The sun shone through them and laid bright rectangles on the white scrubbed floor. Through them could be seen the church, the churchyard and the *Corps de Garde*, with its dungeon.

— Eh, what? Pastor Severin went on, what if we two had such houses, eh, Pastor Gregers?

He went over and tried to thump Pastor Gregers on the shoulders, but he could only reach part way up his back:— I say: what? What do you think? Eh? Eh?

With every word he gave Pastor Gregers a whack and with every whack the dust whirled up like smoke from a gun in thick clouds out of Pastor Gregers' cassock and danced in the sunlight. Pastor Gregers lost the drop that was hanging from his nose and pulled himself together with a start. He was a lean, rheumatic man with a wrinkled face and ragged wig. He tried to speak, but not until Pastor Severin had ceased to whack him and had broken out into his violent laughter did he get his words out.

— We have the dwellings the Lord has called us to, said he, in a hollow and mournful voice.

— Yes, yes, yes, yes, said Pastor Severin, but I could just wish that the Lord ...! He was seized by a violent attack of coughing: ... What I mean to say ... eh? Have the moths been into your wig too?

— Not moths. With me it is mice, they have been at it.

— No, truly, upon my word ...!

They had both taken off their wigs and fallen into a deep conversation about household afflictions. A new, clear drop formed under the tip of Pastor Gregers' nose. He had many tribulations.

So had they all. The lofty, long-legged Pastor Marcus from Sandoy complained to Pastor Christian from the North Islands of the many children the Lord had given him, and which were a blessing truly enough, but hard to get launched into the world.

God be praised — one son had married himself into a good farm in Skalavik, another, with the Bailie's help, had got a good place on Suduroy, and three daughters were well married. But there were still nine children at home. It was not easy, no it was *not* easy.

Pastor Christian had no children and was not married. He would much rather talk about the Moravians. He said he had a good *understanding* of the Moravians, he felt compelled to say so, and he was sympathetic with such men as Zinzendorf and Spangenberg.

Yes, said Pastor Marcus, his daughter Elsebeth was now nineteen, he had brought her with him to Havn, she would learn nothing if she just stayed at the priest's house down there at Todnes, so if Pastor Christian might just talk to her a little about things of the spirit, then ...

— To be sure, Spangenberg, said Pastor Christian, and stroked his chin with long, sensitive movements of his hands. He spoke the name in a soft, reverent tone, as though he was whispering a sacred word. His face was pale and solemn, but otherwise he was a tall and well-formed man with a thick head of curled and powdered hair which he had plaited in a neat little whip that stood straight out behind over his clerical ruff.

Pastor Wenzel had abandoned his guests for a moment. He had gone into the study and there the sound of many voices came to him, and an aroma of chocolate.

Fru Anna Sophia showed herself in the doorway of the study, her red face spotted white from a mouthful of sugared bread.

— Well, I must say, said Pastor Wenzel, looking much offended, — we are living well here, I see.

— And what of it, said his wife, it is only once in the twelve-month that all the priests' wives come here, so ... And I wonder if I should not have asked Barbara too, although they are not quite married yet.

— Well, her too! Her too! A little red spot had formed on each of Pastor Wenzel's cheeks, and he departed, angrily. His wife stood for a moment, chewing, and watched him go. Then back she went to all the priests' wives.

In the drawing room Pastor Anders had settled in to an earnest conversation with Pastor Paul. He had taken him by a pleat in his cassock and drawn him over to one of the windows. He spoke to him with an authoritative air, his eyes were blue and sharp under their bushy brows.

— Ah, yes, I too have been in your position, said Pastor Anders. I was, as you well know, at one time betrothed to Barbara ... Pastor Niels' Barbara, so I have experienced what I am talking about.

— Yes, I did know that, said Pastor Paul, briefly and respectfully.

— I expect that you will not take ill my speaking to you as one who is older and has been through more than you — the Provost cleared his throat — and as your superior.

Pastor Paul inclined his head.

— It is in *fraterne* that I address myself to you but also indeed in *serio*, and I must in the most solemn way admonish you to reflect on what it is you are on the brink of committing yourself to.

Pastor Paul looked up.

— This I have been weighing most seriously over the whole summer, said he. His voice quivered and was close to breaking.

— Yes, I too had to weigh this matter once, said the Provost. I have never regretted the decision *I* came to.

Pastor Paul felt disconcerted by the Provost's exceedingly steady and blue eyes. His thoughts flitted briefly to the Provost's wife, whom he had caught a glimpse of during the morning — she was stout and sharp-nosed and had a strident voice. He was surprised that his mood could be so flippant at such a serious moment, he was close to laughter. He was suddenly reminded of his school days and of his rector and was all the while no less disquieted by the blue eyes. But he was required to find an answer. So he said:

— I can not, neither will I go back on a promise I have given.

— Indeed, said the Provost, and withdrew his eyes.

Pastor Paul was amazed that his answer had had such an effect. It was almost as though he had told a lie, and he felt a little ashamed of himself — he did not himself know why.

— So, indeed, the Provost went on again. He was rather nonplussed, but it was clear that he was not defeated. After a moment he asked:— Are you quite certain that the woman you intend to marry takes her promises as seriously as you take yours?

It occurred to Pastor Paul that he should be angered by this question, but he was not. He did not even succeed in feigning anger. He merely said:

— I know that Barbara means it very, very seriously. But of course she is a weak vessel, I know that too.

The Provost made no answer. He merely turned his disconcerting blue eyes on Pastor Paul.

— But perhaps one may be allowed to trust in God, added Pastor Paul, suddenly.

The Provost again withdrew his eyes and Pastor Paul again felt rather ashamed. Then the Provost stood stiffly upright and said, in his authoritative tone:— Now you listen to me! You need not imagine that the Lord will trouble to lift a finger about your damned gamble of yourself and your sacred calling in a marriage that ... that ... are you out of your mind, man?

— I know it is hazardous, said Pastor Paul, and I know as well as anyone that Barbara is ... a sinner ... of course ...

He tried to collect his wits by drawing on the window pane, but it was clear and quite without moisture. — Ah, well, he went on, more calmly: we must not forget that the Lord himself did not consider himself too good to associate with sinful women and ...

— Yes, he did not go and marry one of them, damn it! said the Provost.

— No indeed, he married none of them — which is to say that he was the bridegroom of sinful women, and therefore it behoves us all to keep from thinking ourselves too good ... I mean simply that one should guard against any self-righteousness.

— Hm, said the Provost, and nodded once or twice. Then it is perhaps on account of her sins that you are marrying her?

— My hope to God is that this will prove to be a blessing.

— I see. Nevertheless, it is by no means a Platonic — I mean a purely spiritual marriage that you are intending.

The irony in the Provost's voice was apparent. Pastor Paul was not slow to answer.

— No, it is God's truth that we are both wretched, sinning mortals. But all rests in God's hands.

— God has nothing to do with it, said the Provost, sharply. What I mean is ... he corrected himself in a loud voice: thou shalt not tempt the Lord thy God!

— So this is the young man here, is it?

Pastor Severin had come up. He laid a sharp whack upon Pastor Paul's shoulder, breathed a long asthmatic wheeze and then broke into his noisy laugh:— No. I mean to say: is he tempting God? Is he tempting God? Is it not himself that is being somewhat tempted, eh? eh? eh? Eve and the serpent, eh? Beware of the serpent! Marry her? Not wise, dear friend, not wise, say I. No, take example by the Provost, he was one too many for her, he was ... too clever, I mean to say ...

Pastor Severin shifted his attention and began to thump the Provost on the shoulder:— He knew more about women, upon my word! Look at Madame Provost!

Pastor Severin was out of breath and broke into a long fit of coughing:— I mean to say. There is an aroma, so there is, of ... of ... upon my word! Of chocolate, is there not?

He beamed about him with pleasure.

— Ay, so there is. My good wife ... said Pastor Wenzel in a polite and restrained way.

— Now *that* is what I call a diocesan meeting! roared Pastor Severin and rubbed his hands.

— Yes, yes, said the Provost, and gave Pastor Severin a sharp look: we have not come to the chocolate yet. There are still a few matters ...

He went over and began a conversation with Pastor Wenzel, which was clearly a source of gratification to the Havn priest. He had, till now, been quite out of it in this gathering.

— *Faith's Priceless Gem!* could be heard suddenly in Pastor Christian's voice. He was caressing with careful fingers a book that he had just drawn out of his pocket:— Do you know it?

Pastor Marcus peered near-sightedly at the book's spine. Hans Adolf Brorson he spelled out slowly. No, said he, with indifference, I do not know it. No, you see, he went on, the two gylls of land in Depil, they lie right in your parish and they would be something for you, if ...

— How is that? called Pastor Severin. Upon my word! Has my good colleague acquired land way up in the North Islands?

— Only two gylls, said Pastor Marcus. No lordly estate, it must be said. But better than nothing, better than nothing, he added, with a glance at Pastor Christian.

— True enough, like a little dowry, said Pastor Severin, slyly.

— Fruit of two funeral sermons, with their toil and trouble, said Pastor Gregers, a note of bitterness in his hollow voice.

— I got them for only *one*, said Pastor Marcus, and glanced first at the Provost and then up at the ceiling.

— For *one!* Pastor Severin broke into a roar of laughter. For *one!* He began to thump Pastor Marcus on the shoulder:— Two birds with one stone, eh? eh? Well done! We should all have a try at that! Get land for our funeral sermons, eh? eh? From dust you came and to dust you shall return, and dust shall pay for your burial. Ha ha ha! Not just *one* but *two* gylls of land for one funeral sermon ...

Pastor Severin was interrupted by a cough.

— Not quite, said Pastor Marcus, with a look over to the Provost and Master Wenzel. Only in certain cases. Alas, many pay absolutely nothing for a funeral sermon. It is *not* easy.

— No it is not easy for those who have no land, said Pastor Gregers, in a dry, hollow tone. Where there is nothing the emperor himself loses his tribute.

— I have nine unprovided-for children, said Pastor Marcus, glumly.

— Tell me, what do you take for a requiem? asked Pastor Severin.

— I am no papist, said Pastor Marcus, shocked, and what I earn and have, I have worked for honestly and had registered. It is not easy for me. My parishioners are not as generous as yours. They tell me that no-one puts less than a bad daler in your parish offering.

Pastor Severin broke into a frightful laugh. He put his hand to his mouth and coughed and protested and looked as though he might choke to death. — That is a lie! he barked. That is the blackest lie! For the last marriage I got only three marks, God knows I did, and one eight-shilling piece.

— So, did you get that at last? said Pastor Gregers, with melancholy dryness; that was the last eight-shilling piece on Suduroy — you will not get another of those.

— Yes, the devil knows, said Pastor Severin, suddenly serious: no, there may well be no more of them. But marks I still see regularly, he added, regretfully. There is no seeing the end of them yet, though I have changed a good many.

— Something like that, said Pastor Marcus, in a matter-of-fact voice, could never come to pass on Sandoy. It is only because Suduroy is so far away that it happens there. The Sandoyers can easily man a boat for Havn to change their money. But Suduroy is much too far away.

He stroked under his chin: Imagine, getting nothing but silver in the offering! But today the Suduroyers have filled their boat right up with copper. What else should they do? And you will see! Then they will have their revenge. For a long while you will have nothing but shillings on the altar ...

Yes, let me see now, said Pastor Severin, and made his pocket jingle; for the time being I have made provision ... ah, yes. He gave a look at the Provost and became a little more cautious. But then, he added, and winked his eye: this is a matter in which we can help one another.

He broke into a laugh and turned towards Master Wenzel. He was the only man in the group whose back he could thump without having to reach.

— I keep above such things, said Pastor Wenzel, in his offended tone.

He backed away from Pastor Severin and stood near the Provost.

— Yes, perhaps *you*, said Pastor Severin and turned towards Pastor Paul: take my advice, young man. Hold fast to the copper, do not let it get away. Mind the shillings and the dalers will come of themselves. You shall see, you shall find a use for them.

— Hm, said the Provost, shall we at last have a diocesan meeting out of this gathering?

He looked about with his authoritative look, and his glance fell on Pastor Marcus, who was bringing his daughter in.

— Now, Elsebeth, said he, pay your respects to the gentlemen, as your mother taught you, and say your best how-do-you-do in the room. See, this is Pastor Christian from Vidoy.

— Eh, verily! Pastor Severin came trotting up. Verily, verily I say unto you, Lord forgive my talk — now, *that* is what I call, *that* is what I call a lass, eh? eh?

He began to thump Pastor Christian with all his might so that his head rocked in time with the blows, and his little pig-tail swung like a pendulum:— Now that is what I call a sweet maiden!

Elsebeth blushed very red. Her clear eyes were slightly slanted, she had a look of purity, like a young deer. Pastor Severin pinched her on the cheek several times, and she stared with a frightened look at the floor. Pastor Christian blushed a little too. He was standing with *Faith's Priceless Gem* still in his hand, and his face had taken on a courteous and timid expression.

— Come, speak to her then, now speak to her, damnation! crowed Pastor Severin. What kind of a way is that? Upon my word! If I were only your age ...

— Come, come, do not spoil everything when it has got off to a good start, said Pastor Marcus, anxiously.

— Yes, Severin, be off with you now — what business have you got with the young?

This was Pastor Severin's wife, who had made her way into the drawing-room. She was short and square and like her husband in every way.

The Provost threw himself into a chair, hopelessly, and stretched his legs out in front of him. Master Wenzel paced quickly up and down the floor.

— Disgraceful, he whispered, disgraceful!

A red spot had again appeared on each of his cheeks. A strong aroma of chocolate filled the drawing-room. The priests' wives were already in the study, they approached in a wave of talk, sweat and coloured shawls. Madame Wenzel Heyde, well-built, weary and over-fed, Mme Anders Morsing, stout, sharp-nosed and shrill, Mme

136

Gregers Birkeroed, merry and manly and Mme Marcus Faroe, small and over-worked.

Pastor Gregers turned his red-rimmed eyes upwards and lifted his crooked hands in the air:— God have mercy!

A new race had filled the drawing-room, taken it over as a flock of parakeets takes over a tree. It was as though the priests had paled and dwindled. Only the Provost sat like a hawk, with watchful, ungentle eyes.

Pastor Christian made an effort to smile. But it looked rather as though he was about to faint. A cloud of feminine ways and chatter surrounded him. Gradually he became more confident. The many enquiries by which he was beset were so warm and so simple-hearted, so easy to answer, that he felt himself quite pleasantly comforted. It was as though he was wrapped in a warm blanket of sympathy and motherliness. Moreover, everything went forward naturally. Mme Provost had put her arm around Elsebeth's waist and was rocking her back and forth like a child that needs to be soothed and quieted. Elsebeth too had begun to smile. She lifted her limpid deer's eyes from the floor and looked into Pastor Christian's beautiful and dreamy countenance.

— Ah, yes, look you, whispered Pastor Severin to Pastor Paul: when it comes to women! There *is* a thing that must be handled the right way! You would never have missed out if you had been in Pastor Christian's place. And what a darling lamb she is!

— *De gustibus et coloribus non disputandum*, said Pastor Paul.

— What is that again? What? Now, now, said Pastor Severin, and started to laugh. But his laughter was a little less boisterous than before. What shall I say, of course, it is never easy with a widow in the living. No question about that!

The Provost had stood up. He made a sudden loud throat-clearing:— As concerns this betrothal, it may perhaps wait until later ...! This is meant to be a diocesan meeting, I must remind you, he added and looked Pastor Marcus sharply in the eye.

The ladies were a little offended, they betook themselves loftily out of the drawing-room, they were not ones to make an interruption. Pastor Christian was left behind alone, red and pale by turns, and with his *Priceless Gem* still in his hand. Master Wenzel, Pastor Gregers and Pastor Severin recovered their usual air of importance. The Provost sat at the table and opened with a smack the book of ecclesiastical meeting procedures.

— We must see that we bring this forgathering to a Christian conclusion, said he.

— Yes, yes, indeed yes, said Pastor Gregers, and quickly folded his hands: the spirit does really demand its part as well!

The Provost smiled a stern smile. All the priests took their places around the table and began to cough and sneeze and unfold great red pocket handkerchiefs. They also brought out large sheets of paper. These were the ecclesiastical and sacramental records of their parishes for the past year.

— Does anyone have anything more to bring forward with respect to these matters? asked the Provost.

None had.

— My brothers, said the Provost, I shall close this diocesan meeting then by reminding you of certain words that I also reminded you of last year, and, if I remember right, the year before that also and all the preceding years.

He smiled again and surveyed the company with a caustic glance:— These words are indeed only the Royal Synod of Rendsburg's admonitions to priests, wherein it says thus: 'Then it is truly our irremissible duty to bear in deepest consideration that God has instituted the office of preaching and inducted us in the same not for the sake of worldly things — the Provost raised his voice — but in order that he might be glorified of mankind through us.'

There was a pause. Provost Anders allowed his strong blue eyes to dwell a moment on each one of the priests, and for an especially long moment he fixed them on Pastor Paul.

— Truly, a by no means uncalled-for word, said Master Wenzel, solemnly, and looked meaningfully at Pastor Severin.

— Alas, alas, said Pastor Severin, and rocked his head in his hands; we are all weak and unworthy creatures ... that we are. God knows that we are.

— True, true, agreed Pastor Marcus. He held his hand before his mouth and turned his eyes upwards towards the ceiling.

Pastor Gregers said nothing. He merely nodded. But Pastor Paul's and Pastor Christian's thoughts seemed to be far away.

— Moreover, said Provost Anders, and began to turn the pages of his book:— Here is another point in the same admonition, which perhaps also deserves to be remembered.

He smiled again, almost fiercely. — It has to do with safeguarding the dignity of our office, said he, and singled out Pastor Paul with his eyes. But then he suddenly looked at Master Wenzel and read: 'This is not accomplished by acquiring certain titles and ranks for ourselves, not by importunate, insinuating, flattering and worldly sociability with the eminent and powerful in the congregation, with confessed worldlings, so as to win advantages, temporal honours and privileges, not by placing oneself on equal terms with the world in free, loose talk, costly fare and clothing.'

Master Wenzel had turned chalk-white, he sat and gasped. His blue, somewhat watery eyes had taken on a miserable expression, the red spots on his cheeks made a sickly flush. He said nothing, he looked as injured as a blameless whipped dog.

No-one could doubt that it was Master Wenzel at whom the Provost had aimed this last admonition, and it seemed to everyone clearly unjust and excessive. Dear God, Pastor Wenzel was inoffensiveness itself, the most Christ-like of them all.

— Ah, said Pastor Severin, forthrightly, — if only my sins had been no grosser than Master Wenzel's! He was ready to break out into his usual laughter, but restrained himself.

— Indeed, said Pastor Marcus too, and turned his eyes up towards the ceiling again.

Master Wenzel sat and fumbled with the clasps of a book. His hands were shaking violently. But all at once he said, in a curiously cracked voice:— Who cannot see into a man's heart, neither does he know his sins. Many small sins in the open, other great sins in the dark.

All were startled, they stared at Master Wenzel. He sat and gazed down at the table. It was impossible to be sure whether or not a thin and timorous aureole flickered for a moment over his thin hair.

— We have all sinned, he went on, and are in need of God's grace.

The Provost's look was ill-tempered.

— Well, we must close with a little devotion, said he.

Master Wenzel began zealously to leaf over the book that lay in front of him. Pastor Christian too came promptly to life. I would like to propose a hymn from *Faith's Priceless Gem*, said he.

— No, said the Provost, harshly, and mumbled a few scornful words about Gems.

— Here in the *Spiritual Choirbook*, said Master Wenzel, leafing steadily, there may be one *plaint* or other that will be suitable.

— Yes, said Pastor Gregers Birkeroed in his careworn voice; one or other of the *plaints*. For example: Perils every hour I face, Always in the need of grace, All my days are full of woe ...

Pastor Anders Morsing looked as though he wanted to say: hold your jaw. He took the *Spiritual Choirbook* from Master Wenzel and began leafing through it himself:— We shall have no *plaints* here! Much rather a penitential hymn!

He pronounced the word with a mouth full of severity and scorn.

— Here, for example, is one: *The second hymn is a hymn of repentance and betterment.* He turned a few leaves: It is as long as a bad year, this one, but nevertheless, desperate diseases ...

He looked up, his eyes gleamed with a kind of grim enthusiasm under their bushy brows.

The priests coughed, sneezed and unfolded great pocket handkerchiefs. Master Wenzel passed around copies of the *Spiritual Choirbook*.

Pastor Severin was the one to lead off. He sang in a powerful voice.

> Come soul, and make our weeping,
> with body, weep our woe!

And now Pastor Gregers' hollow mournful tones began to be heard as well:

> As fountains ever leaping
> our grief let overflow.

Now all joined in the singing.

Empty the sinful heart out
of all its filth and shame;
weep every mortal part out,
cast off the robes of shame.

The priests sang high and slow, dwelling with interminable quavers on every note.

They were, so to speak, a boatload of penitents, pulling with uncertain and lingering oar-strokes across treacherous waters. Only the Provost sat as a kind of helmsman, with sharp, commanding eyes. From time to time he beat the rhythm on the table.

Beware of bold temptation
with fleshly goods to sell,
take shelter in salvation,
send them all back to hell.
Come, let me cast behind me
the world and all its gain.
So may my Jesus find me
a penitent again.

As they came to the twelfth verse, bitter tears flowed down Pastor Marcus' cheeks. But Pastor Severin sang with exultation in his voice and radiance from his face.

By thievery my coffers
were filled, not honest trade;
by underhanded offers
and bargains falsely made.
My neighbour's goods and purchase
by usury I bleed
and all the while look righteous,
and sanctify my greed.

141

His house and lands I covet,
the comforts of his life;
his honour, I would have it
and have his loving wife;
I envy his contentment
and what I dare or can
I filch, in my resentment
of that good, happy man.

The twentieth verse was the last. They sang it with undiminished force and the comforting certainty of deliverance.

When, with late footsteps creeping
towards thy Mercy Seat
I beg forgiveness, weeping,
oh may I hear the sweet
unmerited words clearly
'You are forgiven, go!'
then shall my heart sincerely
with thousand thanks o'erflow.

The priests stood up and blew their noses.

— Ah, yes, said Pastor Severin. Truly it does one good from time to time to take refuge in God's gracious saving bosom.

— Yes, grace, said Pastor Marcus. Where would we be only for grace?

The Provost nodded at him, sardonically.

— Now, it does not seem necessary to me that you should ask about that, Pastor Marcus. Moreover, you are not to feel too sure of yourself. Moreover, we should none of us feel at ease, he added in a louder voice; God is not mocked.

Pastor Severin was just putting snuff up into his wide nostril. He looked a little reproachfully at the Provost and sneezed violently.

— Ay, said Master Wenzel, and opened the door to the study. If you please ...

Aroma of chocolate and the sound of women's voices once again invaded the drawing-room.

— Now, then, burst out Pastor Severin. This is something like ...
I mean to say ... the temporal also makes its claim.

And he broke into his usual laugh, and thumped Pastor Christian
on the back.

10
In a Garden

B arbara was in a green silk dress with a white calico fichu that day. She was discontented that Pastor Paul had been occupied the whole of the forenoon, she said it was all stuff the priests wasted their time over. They talked of nothing but tithes and wool and then wool and tithes again. It was always the same with priests when they came together. And that was surely one thing Barbara ought to know. She was sitting in the Bailie's house with Suzanne and listening to her unhappy story. She did not know what to answer, she was so happy herself and had never known unhappiness.

— It is all right for you, said Suzanne, and smiled a little sadly — you are always newly in love and newly betrothed. You do not know what it is to be not at all in love and yet betrothed.

— Oh, ay, God in heaven knows I do, Barbara burst out suddenly, with conviction. That is something I do know, so it is!

She sighed happily and lightly. — I was married for years without being in love.

— Ay, but not with Gabriel.

Barbara's expression became thoughtful for a moment. True enough, she had never been married to Gabriel. Then she said in a knowing tone:— Gabriel! ... You can keep him in his place all right.

Suzanne shook her head slowly:— You have no notion how I dislike him.

Barbara's look was straight-forward, as though she was weighing and measuring Gabriel. She did not dislike him. He was always so jeering and so sure of himself, but it was not hard to have him at a disadvantage. Oddly enough, she had never tried it. She had never had the time.

— Gabriel, said she, — you can surely get your own way with him. You only have to tease him.

— Yes, but I cannot bear him. I cannot stomach him.

— Nay, then, said Barbara. But there is no call for you to like him — is there?

This was unexpected from Barbara. Suzanne had always admired her and considered her worldly-wise. And now she was talking like a child. There she sat in the sunlight by the window, looking out, and only wanting to chatter whatever came into her head. When she saw Gabriel coming her whole face lit up and she called out to him:

— Good day, Gabriel!

Gabriel had no sooner stepped in than Suzanne felt that he was not his usual self. There was a pleased, almost good-natured smile on his fat face. He rubbed his hands. Ah, Barbara, how is it with you?

He said no more. His eyes said the rest. With friendly boldness he gazed at her slim form. The familiar, bubbling laugh welled up in Barbara's throat, great pleasure lighted up her face. Gabriel grew warm with it, but at the same time he felt a little stab in his heart.

— Ay, Barbara, said he, it is all right for you. You come lucky out of everything.

Barbara again gave a laughing sigh. She tried to look serious. — What do you mean?

But she was too happy to hide anything. She blushed and looked very beautiful. Gabriel's bold stare was on the verge of breaking, his heart burned. The devil! What could he hope from this rose on which he always pricked himself?

But Barbara had suddenly thought of something and hurried over to Suzanne. She kissed and hugged her again and again.

— Adieu, Gabriel! she called, and departed.

Gabriel stood for a moment and chewed his lip. He kicked at a stool and then went over to the window. — Dear God! said he, and shook his head. Now she has gone to chase after him — the priest. Ouf, what lechery! I hope there will not be too much conviviality between you and her henceforth, Suzanne, you will learn nothing good from her.

Suzanne had stood up. She threw her head back, her eyes were half shut with scorn: — Barbara is at all events in love with the man she is going to marry. That is more than can be said about me.

She went out and slammed the door hard behind her.

— So, so, so! called Gabriel, and dropped himself into a chair. He crossed his legs and was quite at home in the Bailie's house.

When Barbara came out into Gongin she met Johan Hendrik, the Judge. He greeted her with his usual ironic smile: — Well?

Barbara laughed with pleasure.

— Ah, when we see you look like that, we all know what hour the clock has struck, said the Judge. Tell me, now — is he very much in love?

Barbara laughed again. She did like Johan Hendrik, she often felt a desire to confide everything to him.

The Judge stroked his chin. — This Gabriel, he muttered. I do not know. Unpleasant business.

— Why in the world have *you* never thought of marrying her, after all? said Barbara, and laughed. But she blushed a little too.

— I. Who do you think wants me, an old man?

— Get away, Johan Hendrik! Barbara gave a loud laugh and turned quite red.

— Now, what kind of a husband do you think I would truly be? asked Johan Hendrik.

Barbara looked down at the ground. Then she said, and nudged her foot a little against a stone: — That I do not know. I dreamed once that you were married.

— To Suzanne?

— Nay, to me!

— Indeed, indeed, said Johan Hendrik. Are you sure I can bear to hear of such a thing?

Barbara had turned quite pale. She tried to look the Judge in the eye, but could not keep herself from blinking; she was at the same time a comical and touching sight.

146

— Nay, but what I was meaning to say, she stammered at last: ...
I think that Suzanne would be a thousand times happier with you
than with Gabriel.

The Judge stroked his chin.

— The Chief Magistrate said the same to me this morning. Have
you laid your heads together, you two?

— No, not at all. Not at *all*! Barbara laughed. It just came into my
head the moment I saw you. And so I thought I should propose it to
you like that. Imagine, the Chief Magistrate had the same idea!

She was rosy, and pleased looking, and she had quite recovered
her composure.

— Ay, is it not amazing? said Johan Hendrik. For the first time
in my life I was under the impression that the Chief Magistrate was
bent on something. It was not that he *said* so much, as you may
guess, but ...

— Ay, but will you not do it? asked Barbara. Her feet were
dancing up and down, her voice was brimming over with ardour and
expectation.

— Now, then, so far as it concerns me ... I have always had a good
feeling for Suzanne, and even supposing they had made a ballad about
me too ... though I wonder, they might hardly have done that. But,
you understand, the matter is not so easy to arrange now.

— Oh, you must try, Johan Hendrik, will you not?

— We shall see, said the Judge, and his look became thoughtful.
Suddenly he brightened up and eyed Barbara.

— But then there could be no match between us two!

Barbara gave a lightning glance downward. There was a chuckle
in her throat.

— Adieu, Johan Hendrik! she called, and hurried away towards
Reyn. Pleasure radiated like sunshine from her voice.

The first thing Pastor Paul saw when he stepped out of Reynagard
after the priests' dinner was Barbara in her shining green silk gown.
He felt, as it were, a slight shock of contentment, as so often when
he had hoped but not expected to see her. She came to meet him,
smiling, took him by the arm and was full of gaiety and quivering
vitality. The falsetto in her voice was like a rainbow of sound that
titillated his ears. He kept up with her, she was lively and light-
footed, but his joy was burdened with an anguished happiness.

— Now where shall we go? she asked.

They wandered through Gongin all the way to the river above the town. Pastor Paul told her about the diocesan meeting, about Pastor Christian and Elsebeth and Barbara laughed and said that was cruelty to Pastor Christian.

— Did they say nothing about me? she asked, suddenly. Her voice had a note of humility in it and she bent her eyes downward.

— No. I should say — Pastor Severin said something nonsensical, you know well enough how he is.

— What did he say?

— Ah, he just laughed in his noisy way and declared that it was foolishness and so on.

Pastor Paul noted a slight pressure on his arm. Barbara looked quickly up at him. In her look there was something both uneasy and thankful. There was a pause. Then she asked off-handedly:

— Did the Provost say nothing?

— Nothing, answered Pastor Paul, decisively. But Pastor Severin, he added quickly, Pastor Severin thought *I* might rather have married Elsebeth, Marcus' daughter from Sandoy. He said that she was a darling lamb.

Barbara looked like a child that has been done an injury. But it was hardly more than a shadow that passed across her face. Immediately after, she laughed and said: — It seems to me now that Elsebeth is very sweet, and she would do *famously* for Pastor Christian.

Barbara became thoughtful. Then she added: — But Pastor Severin is and always will be a clown. He always plays a game with me and calls me Chrysillis and Amaryllis.

They had stopped for a while at the river and then turned back again out on Reyn. They did not know where to go next. Then Barbara got the notion that they should go into the Rector's kitchen garden and sit a while. It was quiet there and they could be alone.

The sun shone straight down into the Rector's garden. It lay behind the school under a steep slope on the west side of Reyn. There were no trees, but various ornamental shrubs, and everywhere stood man-high angelica plants with white umbels of bloom. Nowhere in the Faroes had Pastor Paul seen such thriving plant life, he was almost stupefied by the warmth and the spicy aroma from the growth.

Barbara sat down. She was at home here, as everywhere in Havn.

— Do you have a knife? she asked.

He handed her his knife. Barbara cut through one of the tall angelicas, took off the leaves and offered him a piece of the thick stem. — If you please, said she. Have a taste of that!

Pastor Paul bit into the stem. It was exceedingly green and juicy.

— Does it not taste good? laughed Barbara. She had begun to chew some too.

The angelica had a strong flavour, sharply fresh and darkly spicy at the same time. Pastor Paul did not know at first whether he liked it or not, he was quite taken by surprise, it stung in his mouth.

— It tastes of summer, said Barbara. She sat with the greenish-white flower head in her hand and twisted it between her fingers.

— It tastes as it looks, said the Priest, contemplating the plant's violent green colour and luxuriance. Green was all around them. They sat as though at the bottom of a bottle.

— Can you imagine, said Barbara: I proposed marriage today — proposed to a man.

— Proposed — what do you mean? asked Pastor Paul. Proposed to whom?

— To Johan Hendrik, the Judge.

Pastor Paul's heart had begun to thump. What was this then? He was always full of uneasiness, never did he feel secure.

— Oh, Paul! Do not look like that, cried Barbara. She took his head between her hands and looked into his eyes: You must not look at me like that, do you hear?

— No, but ... he mumbled, and was quite perplexed.

— Did you truly believe what I said? Barbara continued, and would not let go of his head. Her voice was both glad and indignant.

— Of course not, said Pastor Paul, and pulled himself gently away: I only became so ... startled.

— You are an awful idiot, you are, said Barbara. You must not be like that. It is not nice of you. It is naughty, do you hear? I did not propose for myself, of course. I proposed for Suzanne. Can you not understand that?

And then Barbara told the whole story about Suzanne and Gabriel, from beginning to end, how repulsive he was and what a shame it all was, and meanwhile she twisted and twisted, light-heartedly, the big greenish-white flower head that she held in her hand.

But Pastor Paul thought back to the Sunday afternoon when the French ships were at Havn.

— And what did the Judge answer? he asked, in a preoccupied tone of voice.

— Oh, yes, he said ... he said yes, that naturally ...! But that he would much rather be married to me.

— Did he? said Pastor Paul.

Barbara's eyes fluttered a little, then she tried to catch his eye, but he was staring at the ground. Then she took a straw of grass and tickled him a little on the neck.

— Idiot, idiot, idiot! she whispered into his ear.

It was a while before Pastor Paul raised his head, but in the very second that she could see his eye Barbara threw herself impetuously on his neck and kissed him long and moaned at last with love sickness. Finally she left off, looked him in the eye and asked — Did you truly believe?

But in the same moment she snuggled herself in against him again and moaned at him and would hardly let him go. Pastor Paul sat quite dazed in the intense heat, he could still feel the angelica's sharp sweetness in his mouth, his heart was burdened with anguished happiness.

Gabriel happened to be standing in the Bailie's window exactly at the time when Pastor Paul and Barbara came by. The sight of the two of them struck him like a blow, though he knew quite well beforehand that they at this moment must be together. Nevertheless, it was more than he could bear to see, it hurt him not only in his heart but in his gut, yes, down into his legs. It was damnable, that it was. He paced restlessly up and down the floor. Then he went out. He did not want to go too quickly, he was afraid of overtaking them and seeing them again. Why was he going at all? he could not help himself, the lower half of his body propelled him, took him straight through Gongin.

He stopped in the middle of Reyn. He could not see them anywhere. The sun burned on his head, he had forgotten his hat. He was altogether confused and indecisive and he could feel a dull sensation in his thigh. He walked around among the houses, but kept coming back to the highest point of Reyn, School Reyn it was called. His nostrils quivered. All at once he heard Barbara's laughter. It stabbed like a little sharp and shining arrow somewhere in his body. Nay, he could not endure it. He went into the Rector's garden and made his way among the currant bushes. For a moment he stood and listened. Flies buzzed and the sun blazed down. Now he could hear Barbara's voice quite near by. And there she sat, in her green silk gown and white fichu.

She and Pastor Paul.

The moment the Priest saw Gabriel he took on the dark, strained expression that as much as said that once again he would keep a tight rein on himself. But Barbara laughed and said, surprised:

— Gabriel! You here?

Gabriel smiled awkwardly and took his stand before them. Pastor Paul felt as though a cloud had come across the sun. He stared bitterly at Gabriel's thick legs and said not a word. Gabriel, too, was very angry. He would not look at the Priest at all. He was repelled by the sight of him, as by a blow-fly on a fresh berry.

Barbara was the first who began to talk. Will you have some angelica, Gabriel? she asked, indifferently.

The Priest looked angrily at her. Nor was Gabriel in a mood to show the least politeness. Perhaps he was upset by some note or other in her altogether too natural tone of voice, perhaps he was irritated by a look in her friendly eyes. The devil! He knew quite well that he looked ridiculous standing there.

— Angelica, he grimaced angrily, I do not eat churchyard plants!

Barbara looked as though she had taken a blow. She was not used to having people speak so sharply to her.

— Ay, but Gabriel, said she, this has nothing ...

— It is a corpse plant! said Gabriel. Do you not know that this was a plague cemetery here?

— Nonsense, cried Barbara. The plague cemetery was not here, it was down below in the corner.

— No matter, it is repulsive nevertheless, said Gabriel.

His anger was directed at the Priest, but he would not look at him, he would not acknowledge his existence here in the garden. Therefore it was Barbara at whom he directed his scolding, and he felt a certain sweet release as he observed the effect of his words. He laughed softly and without smiling and continued: — You must know well, Barbara, that angelica is a foul plant. You can get leprosy from it! Ha ha ha! Ay, where the devil else would the leprosy come from that sneaks about here in Havn? It is repulsive — *repulsive*!

Barbara was truly upset. Never had anyone said that something she did was repulsive. She hurriedly twisted the great angelica flower and threw it from her.

— You are a fool, Gabriel, said she, with a little unhappy laugh.

Gabriel was so gratified by his victory that he sat down beside Barbara.

— Ah, said he, for something to say, and gave a small groan. He did not look at Pastor Paul. Neither did Pastor Paul look at him, he was seeing black with anger.

Gabriel laughed again, very lightly, and said, mollified: — Nay, of course it is not certain that angelica is what causes leprosy. But ... Niels of the Field's son Hans, who went into the leprosarium at Argir last year, he had stuffed himself rotten with angelica just before, everyone knows that!

Barbara answered nothing to this, but suddenly she said: — Are you pleased that you shall be married, Gabriel?

She badly wanted to talk about something besides angelica.

— Pleased, said Gabriel, what the devil should I be pleased about?

— Ay, pleased to be marrying Suzanne, perhaps?

— Hm. And should I also be pleased to be getting the bairn, do you think? Well, think again!

He sat with his elbows resting on his knees and stared down into the grass. Suddenly he looked at Barbara and laughed: Ay, it may be said that someone was clearly much cleverer that evening.

A gasp that was part laughter came from Barbara.

— You are quite wrong! she cried. Laughter and indignation contended in her voice, she began to turn a little red. But she did not succeed in being angry.

Gabriel sat and looked her over, laughing silently. He had the same friendly, impertinent air as in the morning. He gave the Priest a single, searching look. It was the first time he had looked at him. Pastor Paul had not altered the enclosed expression that meant that he was restraining himself.

But Barbara hastened to change the subject.

— Do you not want to marry Suzanne? she asked Gabriel.

— Ay, the gods know that, he sighed, candidly. There is no denying I would have preferred something else.

A pleased smile lit up Barbara's face. Once again a little laugh escaped from her.

— Ay, but Gabriel, said she, and shut her eyes many times: perhaps ... perhaps you can get out of it?

Gabriel's face took on a very strange expression. An overpowering vain thought flickered for a second in his brain. His under lip went slack.

— Get out of it? said he, in an uncertain tone of voice.

Barbara kept looking at him and lowering her eyelids slowly. — Ay, I mean that perhaps it is not necessary, said she, slowly and rather hesitantly.

— God knows it is necessary, said Gabriel, without conviction. But all at once his face became pale and strained. — Tell me, what are you driving at? he said.

— I only mean that you do not have to, if you do not want to, said Barbara, quickly.

Gabriel sprang up.

— Who the devil says I do not want to? I mean ... who the devil says that I ... that I do not have to.

— Nobody says so yet, but perhaps the Judge will marry Suzanne, if she will have him. Both the Chief Magistrate and I have talked with him about it, and ... and ...

Barbara shrugged her shoulders and looked teasingly up at Gabriel: — And if you are so fed up about it, then ...

— I must thank you, Barbara, said Gabriel, on his dignity. I must thank you, he repeated, almost in a bellow, that you have told me this in time. Devil take me, I shall never forget this low trick of yours!

He was already out of the garden. The sod loosened under his feet and rolled down the slope. Barbara stood and stared scornfully at the powerful play of muscle in his backside. Perhaps she was angry at the same time that he had left her so unceremoniously. She noticed that his breeches were of thick, very solid stuff.

But suddenly a yellow butterfly flew up from the bushes and began to flutter about the garden.

— Oh, look! she called.

Pastor Paul got up slowly. The sun blazed down. In his mouth lingered the sharp sweetness of growing flowers and black earth.

11
Eddy

Pastor Paul woke up. The sun shone in through the window and cast its light on to Barbara's clothes, which lay in a heap on a chair.

He was married now. Barbara was sleeping by his side.

Some of Barbara's clothes were of white linen, others were of coloured stuffs — they were her yesterday's fell that lay where they had been hastily stripped off and thrown aside, a disorderly but not unbeautiful display. Pastor Paul lay for a moment and looked at those garments. Perhaps she would have placed them a little differently if she had been thinking about it. But did Barbara think about anything? The clothes, as they lay there, were an utterance of her heart, caught and exposed in all its strong, thoughtless nature and grace.

Pastor Paul was filled with a marvelling tenderness and gratitude. These garments lay there like an intimacy, like a kind of touching declaration to him. He turned towards her. But her face in sleep was not like her waking face. He had made note of this before. When she slept there was a kind of grief in her look, something helpless and suffering. This too she was letting him see. But ought he to see it? Was this a confidence she would have conceded if she were awake? His heart beat for her.

Who was Barbara? Was it she who, the evening before, had undressed by the chair over there, or was it the woman who slept here with woe in her face? What if everything he knew about Barbara were only an outer skin, a many-coloured shell, like her clothing?

She opened her eyes, and in that second she was another person. She smiled at him as though she had suddenly got him back after he had been away from her for a long while. She was warm from sleep, and she put her arm around his neck. Then she looked at the sunlight and said that it was time to be up.

Barbara got out of bed. She walked about, in full flowering naturalness, with nothing on but her shift, only her feet curled up a little in response to the cold floor. Pastor Paul lay and admired her. Here, outside Nyggjustova, less than a year ago, he had paced and trembled at the mere thought of Barbara. And now she stood before him as his married wife, naked and flushed with warmth from their connubial bed.

All at once a pang of disappointment went through him. Was this indeed all? A bed, an embrace and a wonderfully sweet air, which he had for some while become used to — was there no other content in the fantasies that had taken hold of him for the past three parts of a year?

Barbara pulled off her shift and stood quite naked on the floor. Pastor Paul felt a violent start of desire, but then the emptiness in him made itself felt again. So that was what Barbara looked like. She was lovely, he was fully conscious of that. But he felt nothing towards it.

He met her bright glance in the glass and heard the urgency in her voice:— Nay, dear one, today I must bestir myself. We must be on our way.

— How tiresome, he heard himself say. He was quite amazed. He had not felt the need to pretend to her before. He remembered how wild out of his wits he had been one winter evening when he had caught a glimpse of her nakedness in a hearth-room. Now there she stood in the morning sunlight and doused her rosy body with Eau de Cologne. And he was so unmoved that all he felt was the absence of his torment and longing.

Barbara blew him many kisses and laughed. But all at once she stopped: — What is wrong, dearest? Are you cross about it? But I do *not* have time!

She ran to him and gave him a kiss with pouted lips. Her body smelled sweet and fresh. But for Pastor Paul it was as though a great soap-bubble had burst. He was full of painful pity for Barbara, and reproached himself bitterly.

But Barbara had no inkling of his thoughts, and began to dress herself. She buttoned her underskirt over her hips, looked at herself quickly in the glass, sat down and pulled on her stockings. Already Pastor Paul had begun to feel a change of mood. But Barbara took no heed of him whatsoever. With one quick movement she wound the garters around the hollows below her knees. Then she picked up a comb and began to do her hair.

He tried to catch her eye in the glass. But she looked only at her own reflection and smiled to herself while she arranged her coiffure. He tried to talk with her, but she answered only in monosyllables, and raised a cloud of fragrant powder around her.

— May I kiss you? he asked.

He could see her laughing mouth, red and white, in the glass. Carefully she set a little black patch on her cheek.

— May I kiss you?

She rubbed off the patch and put another a little nearer one corner of her mouth. Then she turned quickly towards him, her bosom breathed scent, her eyes burned in her powdered face. She gave him a hasty, absent-minded kiss and went straight back to her glass.

— How you paint, said he. I did not guess that one painted so much in the Faroes!

She did not answer. He could think of nothing better to do than pull on his breeches. Then he sat on the edge of the bed and contemplated love. It was like sun and hurrying shadows.

Barbara had put on her blue gown. She tied a silk kerchief around her neck and shone, and breathed scent. Then she opened the window. A mild breeze began to clear away the clouds of powder. Torshavn's roosters crowed, ducks swam on East Bay's gleaming mirror of water.

— There goes Gabriel! said she.

Gabriel was on his way through Gongin, in peruke and tricorne. He had become a fine man. His very shadow was as sharp and *distingué* in the morning light as any of the silhouettes on Bailie

Harme's tapestry-hung wall. Folk greeted him with respect and he responded by touching the silver-plated knob of his ebony cane to his hat. It was one of the Bailie's canes.

Gabriel was married, and on the first morning of his marriage he had been presented a son. The bairn had come a little too early into the world, it was not strong, it had to be baptized at once. It was named after the Bailie, Augustus Gabrielsen Harme.

— Adieu, said Barbara, and blew a kiss. — I shall be frightfully busy today.

Pastor Paul ran to catch her but she slipped away and was gone like a startled bird. He was left behind in his socks, like a half-clad simpleton. The usual vague uneasiness began to torment him again. He wished the moment back when he — just now — had cared nothing about her at all. He looked through the window and saw her go into the door of the Bailie's house from which Gabriel had recently issued. Well, at least he knew, for the time being, where she was to be found. How had the absurd notion, that he did not care about Barbara, ever come into his head? He lit a pipe of tobacco and slowly dressed himself.

He felt a longing to talk with someone. But, dear God — with whom could he talk about Barbara? His colleague, the Havn priest? Master Wenzel would answer from Heaven every time he asked from Earth. The Chief Magistrate? Samuel Mikkelsen's good face presented itself to him. He would smile gently and indulgently over love's subtle ways. The Judge? He would open a philosophical book and throw light on the case by means of examples and like instances. But when one came right down to it, was that so little to be desired? He had heard so many of God's words, he now desired to hear an earthly sermon. He did like the lean rationalist very well. But there had been little time for him, hardly time to breathe.

It was a remarkable new thing for him, that he had begun to reflect today. For the past three parts of a year he had done no reflecting. Was this not a sign that the fever in his heart had begun to cool? He was glad of it, and yet at the same time did not like it.

When, half an hour later, he stepped into the Judge's room, he at once felt an air that had been familiar to him. It was something from Copenhagen, it made him think of Regensen and the colleges in the students' quarter, and in a flash brought back to him the gilded, heaven-aspiring steeple of the Church of Our Lady. He felt as though he had now returned to an earlier, forgotten time, when much had not yet happened.

The Judge met him in partial undress, holding a book in his hand.

— You will excuse me, said he. It is not that I am a slug-a-bed. But often I become so absorbed in a book that I do not remember to get up.

Yes, thought Pastor Paul: Regensen! He began at first to talk about the weather, and the Judge talked about crops, which he expected to be good after the favourable summer.

— You are a man who is rational about everything, M. Heyde! said Pastor Paul, without further ceremony.

— I try, in the interests of my calling, to be that, said the Judge, in his unassuming deep voice.

— Yes, said Pastor Paul, and gazed absent-mindedly out the window. You must surely think, then, that I am a very unreasonable man.

— Why that?

— I am thinking of my marriage.

The Judge sat down, crossed his right leg over his left, leaned forward and sank his chin in his hand. Then he changed his legs over and leaned back and at last he said, while he pulled a silver snuff-box from his pocket: — He who does nothing foolish in his life is not so wise as he thinks.

Pastor Paul looked at him, astonished. The Judge stood up, made a defensive wave of his hand and laughed: — Ay, you must not think it was I who found these words — I am not so clever. No, it was *La Rochefoucauld*.

— Laroche ... I see, one of these modern French philosophers?

— Nay, not so modern, but he will never be *demodé*. I make a point of reading a word or two of his, often, as I take a pinch of snuff. It is so healthful!

He offered his little silver box to Pastor Paul: — It is so healthful now and again, to hear a word of truth, about oneself and about mankind in general. The Judge sneezed heartily. — These are subjects I never tire of pondering.

— So I have thought of you, said Pastor Paul. Therefore I am the more astonished that you recommend for me what you yourself call foolishness.

The Judge sat down and laughed. He crossed his legs again and rubbed down the length of one of his stockings.

— Ay, here is what I mean, spelled right out: go overboard! It takes something to live life, and those who avoid foolishness, in my opinion, go aside from life. I shall tell you something. I shall freely confess to you that I not only admire, but I also envy you. Ay, now, you must not misunderstand me. Above all I can see clearly what a risky game it is you are playing, and you will surely come to find it no path of roses. But to express my feelings precisely: I envy you the experiences you will undergo.

— Even if I lose?

— Exactly if you lose. If you win this game, then something must be wrong with you.

— I do not properly understand you.

— You will understand afterwards — if you survive.

The Judge suddenly sprang up and went over and gave Pastor Paul a clap on the shoulder: — Now you must recognize a joke, — of course you will survive. You must not let yourself be influenced by superstition. Courage, then! But this much you know, beforehand, that an adventure is what awaits you.

— You say you envy me the game I have committed myself to. Now, I cannot help asking, why you do not risk an adventure yourself?

— Alas, smiled the Judge: I am much too sensible. Good sense stands in the way of acquiring wisdom. You must not see yourself in me, I am no better than a pedant. Here I have been sitting year after year and fairly killing myself with curiosity about mankind, and on that account I have read God knows how many books! And do you suppose I have become wiser?

He blew out a breath or two and laughed. — I shall tell you one thing: what a man understands from a book is only what he agrees with, and what he agrees with is only what he, by whatever means, already knows. Or whatever suits his purpose. The rest is smoke.

The Judge had come to a pause. He sat, seemingly wool-gathering, and whistled out of the side of his mouth. Then he stood up all at once and began to pace about.

— Do you understand what I am saying? Here I sit and study charts of the ocean that is called human life. And here you come suddenly out of the blue and stand under full sail out to sea.

— Towards my shipwreck, you say.

— Ah, yes. But do not misunderstand me: a philosopher never suffers absolute shipwreck. And here is something more I want to tell you: since you are aboard this vessel you must sail as a philosopher. Make philosophical and moral notes of everything you see and hear and, every day, measure the force of folly's wind. Then you will one day return to shore, having lost your vessel perhaps, but in exchange you will smile an omniscient smile and shake your head and say 'world, world!' like my aunt, Ellen Katrina.

Pastor Paul felt no less confused.

— It is something new for me to hear, said he, that folly should be a way that leads to wisdom.

The Judge paused and laughed. With his lean finger he made a gesture as though he were a preacher: — For a man of God like you that should not be so hard to understand. You surely have observed that the way to salvation lies through sin, so likewise the way to wisdom lies through folly.

It seemed to Pastor Paul that there was something familiar in this line of thought. He felt its seductiveness, it helped him through something difficult.

— I thought you were a disciple of Baron Holberg and such men, said he, whose morality is said to rest entirely on reason.

The Judge suddenly sat down. He looked as though he had a stomachache, he grimaced as though in pain:

— Ah, yes, what shall I say? The one thing a man can stand by is his miserable reason. Therefore he reads Holberg and Bayle and Locke and all those men. But if I, in my ignorance, were to dare criticize these *authors* a tiny bit, it would be in this respect, that they in all their reasoning forget that mankind is at bottom unreasonable and cannot live without unreason. I am not far from believing, with my brother Wenzel, in original sin!

— Original sin?

— Ay, or in original-unreasonableness! Sin and folly are only two names for the same thing. My brother Wenzel frets himself bloody over this and calls it sin, and plagues heaven about it with a circumstantial report of his own heart's miserable and unreasonable condition. I do not feel that I am a hair better than he, but cannot indeed find myself other than laughable and foolish. Truly, my dear Pastor Paul, we are all clowns. Mere envy, greed, desire and vanity rage in us. Especially vanity!

He shook his head and laughed: — But such is our nature, whether it is the devil, now, or whoever it is, that put this clown mentality in us.

— That is so true, so true, said Pastor Paul. What would we be at all if God had not in his love given us grace, that makes all our sins white as snow?

— Grace, said the Judge, poh, grace, excuse me. What is grace but a bottle of smelling salts that one sniffs when the stink of sin's sweaty feet becomes too strong?

Pastor Paul could not restrain himself from smiling. He thought of Pastor Severin's and Pastor Marcus' hymn-singing. But this was terrible, this talk, it was heresy, it was not allowed.

— Ay, Johan Hendrik continued, a bottle of smelling salts will perhaps take away the stink, but damn it, the sweat is the same. That is smothering the one folly with the other.

Pastor Paul gave a toss of his head and said: — What you say there hits only the orthodox. The modern Christian does not believe in grace except in one who, at the same time, with an honest heart, repents of his sins and seeks to better his life. Without that one does not *have* grace.

— What is an honest heart? Ah, excuse me, I ask like a Pontius Pilate.

The Judge stood up and again began to pace about slowly. Pastor Paul thought of his own heart. It could not be honest, this morning it had been shamefully fickle and flighty even about Barbara. At this moment he could not be sure that he loved her at all, or whether the whole thing might not be some kind of witchcraft. He could think of no answer for the Judge.

— Ay, there you see, said Johan Hendrik. We cannot run from the clown in our own hearts, whether we are Christians or atheists.

Have you read Pascal? No, you have not. My brother Wenzel has not read him either, and that is a lack. But he has read Kingo and he says, Farewell, world, farewell. That is to say, he says devil take it, he does, but never mind, he is only a clown like all the rest. I do not know, truly, how the good Lord can find any difference between us. My own poor reason has carried me so far that I acknowledge my folly, but never far enough that I amend my unreasonable heart. It has been no more helpful to me than grace. Nevertheless, I see no better way of serving God than searching out, with the light I have been given, the fool in myself, and trying to be useful to the world in which I have been put. In my condition there is little to learn and less to achieve. But you, my dear friend, you must know that those who encounter true grace are those who have been taken hold of by fate and played upon, as upon an instrument. If only they will be willing, then, to learn something from it.

— I consider you a heretic, M. Heyde, said Pastor Paul. Yet I must acknowledge that I have learned something from you.

The Judge made no answer. He stood at a small table and busied himself putting a flute together. When he had done so he put the instrument to his lips and blew a long cadence.

— See, said he. This, now, is one of *my* follies. I cannot give up playing, though there is neither reason nor morality in it.

Again he blew a long, quavering trill and then stood thoughtfully with the flute in his hand: — Even Holberg, that stick, had a passion for music too. One would never have expected that. Did you ever see him?

— No, he died before I matriculated.

— Ah, yes. *I* have heard him play ... one evening, as I passed by his mansion in Copenhagen.

Johan Hendrik blew short phrases and talked between them. He spoke about his nephew, Andreas Heyde, who played with such skill on the violin. His father was dead. Andreas was now studying economics in Copenhagen.

— Economics? asked Pastor Paul, surprised.

— Ay, nodded the Judge, I recommended that. With that perhaps he can be of some use to his motherland. Wenzel, of course, wanted him to study theology. He thought the other was a far too worldly subject.

163

— So I can imagine, said Pastor Paul.

— And what is more, he said that theologians at any rate did not starve.

Johan Hendrik made a face. — World, world! he added, and shrugged his shoulders.

— You are not very fond of priests, I see, said Pastor Paul, and smiled.

— Not so fond as Mme Aggersoe!

The Judge suddenly lowered his instrument and made a deep, extremely ceremonious bow towards the open window.

— Good morning, Johan Hendrik! sounded Barbara's voice from outside: I have been charmed this way by your playing!

— Hm, said the Judge. Perhaps you think you can make me believe that. I know well enough why you come. But there is nothing wrong with longing for your husband!

Pastor Paul had at that moment stood up. His wife blinked her eyes when she saw him, and laughed, but without conviction.

— Just the same, said she, and blushed, — I did come on account of the playing! I had no notion that Paul was here.

— Ay, but come in, said the Judge. Then I shall play for you both. But it should be on an *Oboe d'Amour*!

Barbara looked at the Judge and laughed. To Pastor Paul it seemed that there was a confidence between the two of them that he did not know about.

— *Oboe d'Amour*, — do you know what that is, Barbara? the Judge went on. You do not understand the words, eh? But you always know the tune!

— Nay, I must move on, said Barbara. I have absolutely no time to be staying here, I have *so* much to do. Besides, a ship is coming! They say it is *Fortune*.

She waved good-bye and smiled once more at the Judge. But when she had gone a little piece down the lane-way she turned and blew her husband a kiss. By then the Judge had withdrawn to the inside of the room.

— Ay, said he. That is a lovely woman, you have. I have paid court to her since she was a little girl, and she has always been kind enough to pretend she did not know how old I was.

Pastor Paul contemplated him with uncertainty. These easy-going words pleased him but they did not satisfy his hunger for reassurance. He was strongly minded to open his whole heart to the Judge, to, in any case, enlist this man as his ally. But he was fearful of receiving all too shattering truths. He had already learned that Johan Hendrik was a surgeon who wielded a merciless scalpel. So he turned the conversation to more commonplace subjects, and then shortly he took his leave.

— Good-bye, said the Judge. If there is anything I can do to be of help, I hope that you will come again. I shall follow your course with interest.

Pastor Paul did not know exactly how he should value this interest. He felt as though he was a paper boat that had been launched to sail in a stream. So far the stream was quiet. He lay to, and turned this way and that in love's eddying current.

12
Fortuna

In the lanes of the town there was a certain restlessness to be felt. Windows opened, folk peered out, a few hurried down through the narrow, stepped passageways that led to the shore. When Pastor Paul came downstairs in Nyggjustova he could see that a ship was sailing in. He recognized it as *Fortuna*, the ship from which he, three-quarters of a year ago, on a gloomy November morning, had come ashore.

Neither Barbara nor her mother were at home. He got an impression of the whole town on foot. The sun shone and the Fort was flying its bunting. Everyone seemed on holiday. On the way to Tinganes he overtook the Chief Magistrate and fell in with him. He asked him whether they would not soon be setting out for home.

— Bless you, answered Samuel Mikkelsen, and eyed him with a smile: When the ship has just come? Nay, *today* I at any rate am sure that we shall not be going.

Pastor Paul had always, in an indefinable way, disliked this ship. Now he was feeling very ill-disposed towards it. The desire overcame him suddenly to be away as quickly as possible, he was nervous and anxious about having to stay longer in Havn. His discomfort increased when he came out on Vippun ... here he found Barbara in the midst of a crowd. She hardly noticed him, she was walking about, and had eyes for nothing but the ship.

Dear God, thought he. Must I learn what it is to be jealous of a ship? He shook his head over himself. They were surely no great griefs he was troubling his heart over.

When, after a short while, the ship had cast anchor in East Bay, an unfamiliar man could be made out on deck. A passenger, assuredly, but no-one was able to say who it was, for no-one was expected in the islands. Folk stood in groups chattering with curiosity and making guesses. The Fort boat put out from shore with a flag at the stern post and a red-coat trooper at the tiller. There was a long and restless wait. When the boat was at last on its way in to shore again with the skipper and the unknown one aboard, a shout of recognition suddenly went up from the eager knot of women farthest out on Vippun:

— Andreas! It is Andreas!

And now everyone could see that it was Andreas Heyde, the student, who had come home again.

The Priest, Wenzel Heyde, who had also come down on to Tinganes, immediately acquired the two red spots on his cheeks: — This was not the intention ... this was not the intention!

Even the Judge's face took on a disapproving look. He had always understood that his nephew should finish his studies before he came home again. This did not look like taking things seriously, it must be said. But it was clear that other Havn folk were glad to see Andreas again, they thronged down to Vippun and surrounded him the moment he set foot on shore.

Andreas Heyde moved jauntily through the crowd and greeted them and laughed. He had a bright, manly countenance and very big, merry eyes. His clothing was gallant and well-tailored, but he wore it in his own careless way. His hat was on at an angle, and snuff lay in the folds of his waistcoat. Its lower buttons had, moreover, not been buttoned, so that his shirt bulged out a little over the belt of his breeches. He went straight over to his uncles and greeted them cheerfully, but thereupon became so busy shaking hands with everyone, high and low, that he had no time at all to answer questions.

Not until the activity had quieted down somewhat around him, and he had got a bit of snuff brushed away, did he look up with a sudden lift of his head at his uncles and say: — Ay, you had not expected this, I am sure! His voice had a bright, cheerful, rather challenging tone.

— Your uncle and I ... began Pastor Wenzel, seriously and with dignity.

Andreas interrupted him with a little laugh. He stood with both hands in his pockets and bent his knees, first one and then the other, with a little jerk. — Look at this, said he, and brought forth a paper: Royal Exchequer — Resolution! You did not expect anything like this.

Havn folk were standing about and exchanging forthright, loud-voiced observations on the new arrival. They all knew him, he was one of the town's children, and they were proud of him. — It was a proper lad like him who should have married the Bailie's young miss, one of them said, — instead of Gabriel, that lunkhead.

— No such thing, said another: Andreas is used to mamselles finer than the Bailie's miss.

— Puh, said a third. Finer than the Bailie's miss? If Suzanne is not a fine lady ...

— Well, fine here in Havn, but out in the world ...

— Havn folk are never too fine for Havn folk, declared Vupsen. Poor Suzanne, it was never sung to her in her cradle that she would have to marry a village lump, and I have told himself so.

— You are off your head, that is what you are — he will soon be bailie!

— Well, I do not care even if he ...

— Mind your tongue, the Chief Magistrate is standing right here!

— I am not afraid of the Chief Magistrate. He is a blessed kind-hearted authority to have over us. If they were only all like him!

Samuel Mikkelsen had been amusing himself for some while in silence over this talk. Now he turned his bearded face towards Vupsen and said, with his gentle smile: — You seem to forget that I am a villager too.

— Ah, said she, what does that matter? You, Samuel, and the Judge and all of you! A darling family, God knows you are, and never do you forget the common folk.

The Chief Magistrate smiled again. He was familiar with this talk. It had to do with the fact that Vupsen and other poor folk would take themselves out to the villages to ask for a wool tuft or lump of tallow or such other things as the countryside produced. They never came away empty-handed from his or his kinsfolks' farms. Dear God, Havn folk had very little to live on. One had to help them out, for all that they were often rather sharp-tongued.

The Judge and Pastor Wenzel had been reading with mounting astonishment that We Frederick the Fifth, by God's grace King of Denmark and Norway, of the Wends and the Goths, through our Exchequer do appoint that student Andreas Heyde shall make a journey to the Faroe Islands in order to explore and report of the land's nature, its flora and fauna, its inhabitants and its economy.

Pastor Wenzel was dumbfounded and silent. The Judge stood and swung his arms, enthusiastically. Then he put his hand to his chin, in a dubious way, and asked: — Do you think, now, that you *can*?

— Can? laughed Andreas.

— It will be hard, said Johan Hendrik. But it will be pleasant work, God knows it will. How the devil did you manage to get it?

— It was Professor Oeder who managed it, said Andreas. He is my patron.

Johan Hendrik looked about in a daze. He most wanted, at that moment, to find somewhere that he could sit down and ponder this astonishing development in quiet. But on all sides were chattering people. And Andreas himself was just like quicksilver. It was impossible to get any kind of straight answer from him in the midst of this confusion. That would have to wait.

Pastor Paul, for the rest of his life, never forgot this moment. In the very second that Andreas Heyde stepped ashore his heart was filled with a dreadful anxiety. He saw at once that a dangerous bird had come flying in, against which he could never defend himself. He knew now that he was committed to a game of incalculable odds.

His eyes sought Barbara. She stood a short distance away from him, up in the gateway to the Stores, the very place where he had first seen her. She seemed to be deep in conversation with Mme Anna Sophia Heyde. From time to time, she turned her head and gave a glance, first over the water and then back again over the assembled crowd. Then back to her conversation. He could hear her voice and her laughter. Her whole being shone.

She was at that moment his enemy, he could feel it. It would be a hopeless undertaking to go up to her and try to lure her away from this place. He had no power over her; in everything she did exactly as she pleased. She was a cat, she was frightful.

Andreas Heyde came nearer and nearer to the gateway, talking all the while and laughing. He was perhaps not aware of Barbara yet. Pastor Paul took a closer look at him, noted his sturdy, sauntering gait, observed his friendly and at the same time entirely indifferent air. He was attracted by the brightness of his presence. But at the same time he knew that it betokened the end for him.

The inevitable was about to happen. Andreas looked up with a start, and then his expression became alert. Barbara turned her profile towards him and looked at nothing. Anna Sophia began to be playful and to ask if Andreas could no longer recognize his old aunt who had come down to meet him. While all this welcoming was going on Barbara was standing with a steadily distant but polite look on her face, and her head held at an aristocratic tilt. Then Andreas turned quickly towards her and smiled a candid and slightly impertinent smile. His bearing was negligent, but the moment he saw her face he became serious and drew himself up hastily to make her a bow.

— Ay, do you recognize ...? said Anna Sophia.

— To be sure, said Andreas, and bowed: from my school days ... I recognize very well ... Mme Salling.

— Mme Aggersoe! Anna Sophia corrected him, with a smile.

— Mme ... Mme Aggersoe? asked Andreas, surprised, and bowed again. His bright countenance had a fixed look of puzzlement.

Barbara blushed suddenly.

— I remember you well, she hurried to say, and closed her declaration with her little laugh.

Pastor Paul heard it. That familiar sigh which ended in a falsetto note, ah, — he understood her. Now their game was begun.

Both Andreas and Barbara were a little shy, but she was the one who soonest found a few trivial words to say. And she drew him out, listened carefully to what he had to say and approved of his words with little bursts of laughter. Very quickly he was cheerful and easy

170

as before. But he never quite recovered himself again. In whatever he said there was now a faint note of seriousness and courtesy.

— I presume you will be satisfied to stay with us, Andreas? asked Anna Sophia. They began to move off, Pastor Wenzel, the Judge, Andreas Heyde, Anna Sophia and Barbara. Everyone was now going home. A broad stream of folk flowed between the Company buildings and up into the pathways between the churchyard and the Corps de Garde. Pastor Paul followed with them and came over beside his wife. She looked at him as though she was a little surprised, but said nothing.

— We shall hardly start homeward today, said Pastor Paul.

— Nay, she answered, unconcerned.

— I suppose it is not such an important matter to you.

— What? To start for home? Nay, you may be sure we cannot leave now, not when the ship has come in. Tomorrow, dearest! Or another day.

She spoke to him as though to a tiresome child, friendly but absent-minded.

— Will you not come in with us? asked Anna Sophia. You, Pastor Paul, must meet our nephew!

Pastor Paul wished to excuse himself, but Barbara said: — Do come in, Paul!

Pastor Paul followed as the last of the guests, unhappy and with fearful forebodings. He felt quite superfluous. He was all too forcibly put in mind of the afternoon when the French ships came to the town.

Andreas Heyde was not the sort of man who could sit still in a chair in the priest's living room. He was all over the house at once, talking with everyone at once, this moment on economics, next moment on the opera, and on the whale hunt in between. He had brought a new book with him, he said, that the Judge would be curious to see — he had it here in his chest, he would look for it right away. Without ceremony he took off his coat, hung it over a chair and began to unpack. Meanwhile he sang in his light voice: La la la la la la la la!

Then he got up and looked with sudden deference at Barbara.

171

— Ah, Mme Aggersoe, you must excuse me for being so *sans façon*! I forget to shed my raw undergraduate ways. I shall make a stern effort to remember ...

It seemed to the Judge that Andreas looked less like a student than a *petit maître*, with his extravagant shirt-sleeves and lace. Perhaps these were bagatelles that could be put down to his youth. He did not want to judge rashly. But he had intended something rather different for his nephew.

So had Pastor Wenzel, only more so. He was by now deeply offended, the red spots glowed like geraniums on his cheeks. He could not decide which he was more exasperated by, Andreas or his wife, Anna Sophia, who was hopping about and making herself a fool for this coxcomb and scatterbrain they had got into the house. This was the fruit that Johan Hendrik was harvesting from his great plan for setting the boy to such worldly and vain studies.

— La la la la la la la la, Andreas was already singing again.

— Ay, la la la la! thought Johan Hendrik. He could not deny that he had been made angry. La la la, pouf!

Pastor Paul observed his wife. She was sitting straight up in a chair, saying nothing, but in the corners of her mouth played a little smile. Andreas did not pay attention to her, did not once look at her. He looked at everything but her. Yet she was the pivot around which all his fooling turned. Pastor Paul could see this with diabolical clarity, and he could see that Barbara saw it. She was enjoying every bit of it, economics, the opera, pilot whales, the chest, the flowing sleeves and the singing, all were as a comedy that was being played for her benefit. What had the Judge once said: that a dog could not admire her from his corner without her noticing and taking pleasure in it. But this was a young Apollo who was making himself into her clown.

Andreas Heyde began smartly to empty all sorts of things out of his chest. He was impatient and hasty and let fly about him with stockings, waistcoats, books and music paper, buckles, pistoles, small boxes with miniatures painted on their lids and many other manly and gallant things. A sweet and ardent scent drifted up from the chest. At last he hauled out an instrument, it was a lute.

— Well, I must say! burst out Master Wenzel, bitterly. You have gathered yourself some goods!

— Ay, so, said Andreas. But I am still lacking a sort of — he made a circular movement with his hand: a sort of mill-stone, you know, uncle, like the priest's ... I mean a sort of priest's ruff, that uncle would like to see me strut in.

He made a comical innocent face and threw a confidential glance at Barbara. Pastor Paul could see her quickly bite her lips and suppress a laugh. Then she immediately blushed and became serious. Master Wenzel turned on his heel and paced quickly up and down. A moment later he was out of the room.

The Judge smiled a little to himself. He stood and examined the lute.

— I had always thought you played the violin, said he.

— I play that too, answered Andreas. But the violin is by itself in a proper case. I only play the lute when I sing.

— Do you sing as well?

— Ah, yes — only trifling songs.

— Hm, said Johan Hendrik, and stroked his chin.

— Do sing a song for us! called Anna Sophia and Barbara, almost in one voice.

They had both become excited and could not sit still, their eyes shone with eagerness. Andreas began to strum and tune up his instrument. A thoughtful wrinkle formed between his eyes, as he sat on the very edge of his chest, one leg swinging free and the other firm on the floor. He looked straight ahead for another few moments, then he glanced up in his brisk way, played a loud chord on the strings and sang:

> Columbine, Columbine
> Do you ever think of me
> Think of me, think of me?
> What a loving glance was mine
> Loving glance I used to see
> Used to see, used to see.
> Came I early, came I late
> Was my welcome always sure

> Always loving was my fate:
> Ah, between us, what *douceur*.

He laughed and looked at Barbara with a droll despair in his big eyes.
Then he began again, with a sobbing note in the strings:

> You could like me well before,
> Now your taste is altered quite,
> Altered quite, yes altered quite;
> Now you fancy me no more,
> Columbine, ah, is it right,
> Is it right, and is it right?
> Were we not a constant pair
> Not a loving pair, we two?
> Why am I in this despair,
> Such despair? My heart is true.

Pastor Paul wished himself far away. He felt that his heart was an
open book, which all could read and be amused by. Desperately he
tried to put on a cheerful countenance, he knew that he looked like
an unhappy wretch. Then suddenly the Judge clapped Andreas on the
back and said: — Ay, indeed, Master Harlequin, that will be enough
for now. You must take heed of your uncle, he will have no use for
that. You did say that you had a book for me?

Andreas put the instrument aside. It was as though he had
immediately forgotten all about singing and music. He quickly bent
over the chest, rummaged in it for a moment and brought forth a
book: — My compliments, uncle, do not refuse to accept this as a
little gift. It is a quite new and much discussed book.

Francois Quesnay, Johan Hendrik read.

— Ay, he belongs to the new school of economics that they call
the physiocrats. They propose that everything should sound a new
and as it were more natural note here in the world. They say that the
use of the land and cultivation of the soil are the true sources of all
wealth and also obviously ought to play first violin in every well-
governed nation's economy.

The Judge stood and held the open book in his hand. His eyes grew brighter as he looked at his brother's son, who with mounting enthusiasm explained how everything in the world would work of its own volition if only the farmers, by whose sweat all men lived, became enlightened, efficient and industrious.

— *Pauvre paysan*, said he, *pauvre royaume. Pauvre royaume, pauvre roi!* Ay, we can see that here in our islands. If our farmers were so efficient that they could grow all the grain they need for their bread, there would be no need for the king, at considerable loss to himself, to sell grain down here in the shop, and our country would save many a shilling thereby.

The Judge wanted to bring his hand up to his chin many times, but he would forget, his hand would stop half way and then drop again — this was absorbing. Only Barbara had no taste for such talk. A shadow seemed to have fallen on the room just where she was sitting.

— Nay, we must be going, said she.

Andreas suddenly broke off. He hardly knew which way to turn, it looked as though he would like to talk with everyone at once.

— Nay, must you be off? said Anna Sophia: will you not stay and eat? The meal will be ready in a moment. Come, Andreas, let me take you to your old room!

— My old room! said Andreas: I was going to ask if I might have another, not in the garret. For certain reasons, for example ...

He went out with Anna Sophia. The Judge stood in deep thought, then he went into the study to join his brother.

Pastor Wenzel was pacing agitatedly back and forth on the floor.
— I do not know what *you* will have to say about this young lord! he hissed. Now you can see what comes of these meaningless studies. Eaten up his patrimony, that is what he has done. And my money and your money. And so he has learned to sing immoral jingles.

— Ay, said Johan Hendrik, he has his bad habits. But what the devil have they to do with his studies? The boy has some bent for economics.

— Ay, one can see that in his foppish get-up, said Wenzel, with the utmost bitterness.

175

The Judge turned to him: — Just the same, I am damn well glad that we have not had him come home a pedant or a bookworm! He grimaced angrily: Or a prig! The country will benefit by his studies. We shall give the farmers a leg up. You will not understand that. But let me tell you something that you will understand: the tithes will get bigger too. Goodbye.

In the drawing-room Pastor Paul and Barbara had been left alone together. She was not looking at her husband, she was startled when he suddenly stood in front of her.

— Ay, but sweetheart! she burst out. Why do you look like that? Paul!

She stood up and caressed him, her voice was full of tenderness: — What is wrong, dearest?

Pastor Paul did not answer, did not stir. His features were unmoving, but his eyes were dark with anger. He was on the point of striking her. But suddenly he broke and said simply: — Barbara!

She hugged him quickly and looked at him. There was deadly fear in her eyes.

— Will you come away with me today? he asked, tonelessly.

— Ay, she answered, still frightened. Then her face quickly lighted up: — Ay, do let us go! She laughed and kissed him over and over: Of course! What else but go?

Tears were starting in her eyes.

Pastor Paul's mood was wonderfully lightened, and it seemed that Barbara's was too. They paced quickly back and forth on the floor and smiled at each other as they met.

— But the Chief Magistrate! Pastor Paul remembered. It is not likely that he will want to go today.

— Pooh! said Barbara. We shall go without the Chief Magistrate! We shall get a boat for ourselves.

Andreas was beaming happily when, a moment later, he stepped into the room.

— Were you given good quarters, monsieur? asked Barbara.

— Could not be better! In a priest's house one ought always to lodge on the ground floor ... especially when the priest is one's father's brother, Wenzel.

— Ay, then you may come home at night when you please, said Barbara.

— Exactly, said Andreas. You understand me, madame.

— Ay, Barbara continued. Her eyes were full of life: and then you may ...

She stopped herself.

— Precisely! said Andreas. That I may too!

They both laughed. Barbara blushed a little. But all at once she reached him her hand, looked at him and said: — Now, good-bye, monsieur, and a happy sojourn. We are departing now.

Andreas' face went like a turned-down lamp.

— Are you leaving? he stammered. I thought ...

A little pleased smile spread itself at the corners of Barbara's mouth: — Ay, said she, in a tone that was at the same time teasing and apologetic: we must *truly* go now.

— You cannot leave today, said Anna Sophia, who had come into the room. All the men will be off-loading. You will not get a boat.

— Nay, you will not get a boat, repeated Andreas enthusiastically.

Barbara looked somewhat perplexed: — What must we do then? said she. We must stay, then. She gave a look to her husband, and there were both laughter and tears in her eyes: — How tiresome, Paul!

Pastor Paul was desperate. He felt that this was a life and death matter.

— We shall walk to Velbestad, said he, and take a boat from there. That will be quicker as well.

— Ay, that would be a good plan, said Barbara. It will be quicker and pleasanter both. What a dolt I was not to think of it right away.

— Ay, but all your bags, you cannot take them with you that way, Anna Sophia objected.

— Nay, that is impossible, said Andreas, persuasively.

— Then we are not better off than before, said Barbara.

— The Chief Magistrate can bring our bags when he comes, said Pastor Paul.

— Ay, indeed, to be sure! said Barbara. The Chief Magistrate can certainly bring our bags. Then we had better go after all.

She gave Andreas a look that was both laughing and sad.

— Well, then, good-bye, monsieur!

In a short while the necessary arrangements had been made, baggage got ready and Barbara changed into her travelling clothes. As they passed the westernmost houses in the town she took her husband's arm impulsively and laughed an intimate laugh. — How exciting it is, all this! It is almost as though you were carrying me off!

She pressed herself a little against him before she let go of his arm. The wide land lay before them in the light of the midday sun. They crossed over green flats and brown heath and became more and more alone with nature. Brooks gurgled and plovers sat on their tumps of heather and made their cries. It was a beautiful afternoon, warm and fresh. When they had reached the mountain-ridge over Velbestad they could look out westward over the open sea. The islands, Hestur and Koltur, rose steep and foam-ringed out of the water, with afternoon clouds on their eastern slopes. To the north-west the mountains of Vagar were blue. Pastor Paul and Barbara looked at each other and laughed, as though they had escaped a great danger.

13
Christmas

The first months that Pastor Paul spent as a married man in Jansa-gerd priest's house were the happiest of his marriage. At that time the days were growing shorter and shorter and the weather harsher and stormier. During the few hours around midday when there was light, men could be seen with leyps on their backs climbing towards the lake to get turfs from the little town of store-houses that had resembled Capernaum. But it was a desolate and wet Capernaum, and when the men, in the cold and showery half-light of dusk, came home with their burdens they looked grey like cats against the dark land.

The winter gnawed at many tempers. But for Pastor Paul the darkness was just like a warm nest into which he sank himself deeper and deeper. His days were sweet and good. Wherever he stopped or went, whether in the hearth-room, in the pulpit or in cottages with the sick, he thought of himself as a man who had newly left a good haven and would quickly return to it again. Barbara always waited for him with longing. She sewed clothes for him and tried them on him and was only in a bad humour when he had to be from her on longer visits. Then she could hardly bear to pack his chest and put food in it for him. But he did have to visit the remote parishes of Sorvag and Bo and be away for some nights, and twice a year he must also cross all the way out to the island of Mykines.

He might perhaps have felt all too happy, as had occurred for him once or twice before, but now he knew how fragile happiness is, and the insecurity that resulted from this kept him alert and watchful.

He perceived now, something that in his younger years he had not heeded, that love is like a flame that will not burn bright and clear unless it is fanned by the breath of anxiety. But this anxiety, which had heretofore been uneven and capricious, had now become a firm and steady blast. He knew now that a single danger threatened him. Andreas Heyde was always in the back of his mind, though he never named him. Neither did Barbara name him.

Yet he was present, for all that, in their talk. Sometimes, when they were happiest, Pastor Paul would feel as it were a stab in his heart, and then he would regularly ask her: — Do you think you will always feel towards me as you do now?

What Barbara answered to this varied somewhat. When she was most content she would answer nothing. But other times it would happen that the look in her eyes became uncertain, and in a deeply emotional voice she would say: — I hope so.

When the Priest became disconsolate over this she would try to comfort him. She said he should give up asking such foolish questions, it was too bad of him, now of all times, just when they were so happy together. And when at last she did not know what more to say, she would end with these words: — God in heaven, Paul, it is not something to keep fretting about. There are just us two, at this moment, are there not? Can you not be glad about that?

Pastor Paul could see the wisdom in this. They were both helpless and defenceless creatures. He knew what Barbara was, dear God! She meant no less well than he did, her heart was many times better than his. But she had no control over her heart, it always went its own way. They both trembled on account of that heart, it was so wilful and so blind, and they had only God's grace to look to in their human weakness.

Pastor Paul learned in this way to accept every new day as a gift of God. In the dark mornings he would read devotions by candle light for the folk of the household, but afterwards he would go down to the sand to make his own devotions there. And while the day, like a blood-red rose, unfolded in the south-east, he walked back and forth on the dark sea shore and brought to mind the words of the morning hymn:

Each morning fills my cup
With Grace unmeasured up
That from above pours down.

The golden mornings were frequent in December and were for Pastor Paul a source of great joy. But for most people the days came to be no more than narrower and narrower openings of light in the heavy oppression of the dark season. All longed now for the joyfulness and release of Yuletide and made ready for it in their different ways with slaughtering of sheep and with baking. Two boats had been to Torshavn for Christmas drink, and one brought a letter for Barbara from her friend Suzanne.

It was a most enthusiastic and gleeful letter. 'If only you could have been here,' wrote Suzanne, 'you would hardly have known Havn. Everything has changed here. We have had a ball and soon we shall present a comedy in the Council Chamber. It is called *Herman v. Bremenfeld*, and all we young people are to have parts in it. As you may guess, Andreas Heyde is the man behind all this.'

Barbara was at first exhilarated by the letter, but then she became thoughtful. Pastor Paul did not have much talk from her that day, she answered him as though from another world. In the evening he asked her if she regretted not being in Havn for the comedy. But she hugged him and said that she would much rather have Christmas with him in Jansagerd. He dared not tell her that it could only be a short Christmas that they would have together. The day after Christmas high mass he must go to Sorvag to say Evensong and if the weather were favourable he must go on the second day after Christmas out to Mykines. He dearly hoped that it would not be favourable.

Among those who made the sea trip to Havn at this time was the Chief Magistrate. He was the last to come back. Not until Christmas Eve at nightfall did he land at Sandavag. Festivities had already begun

181

and few observed that he had a guest with him. This had not been anticipated in the Chief Magistrate's establishment, but as soon as the sons of the family saw the newcomer they guessed that it must be Andreas who had come for Christmas. We thought as much, said they, as they gripped his hand. Andreas would not come back to the islands without paying Steigargard a visit too! And Andreas laughed and was straightway the same as he had been in their boyhood days, when he had often been the guest of his kinsman, Samuel Mikkelsen, and got into uncountable bad scrapes along with his four unruly sons. He remembered them one and all, and went at once round the hearth-room and greeted each of the domestics.

Old Armgard was having this Christmas at Steigargard. Andreas was less courageous when it came time for him to go into the great room and greet her. He made a shrinking grimace at his cousins when he took hold of the door latch.

— She is in a good mood, said they. She will be in a good mood with you this evening, you may be sure.

And so she was. Her expression melted with tenderness and pride when she recognized her sister's son's son. She held his hand a long while between her bony hands.

— Nay, Andreas — is it you? So now you have come back, Jesus bless you. I cannot tell you how happy that makes your aunt! But see here now, dear Andreas, sit down now and talk with your aunt. Let me hear about you.

Andreas sat down and gave an account of himself in his frank way, but in a polite tone of voice. Sometimes he had to repeat what he had said, but not often. Armgard was not deaf, but she did want to be clear about everything.

— I am very glad, said she, that you are thinking of this poor country. We shall see how your potatoes, or whatever it is you call them, will grow. You are like your great-grandfather, Paul Caspar, the Chief Magistrate. He was the first to plant a proper vegetable garden here in the islands, as you know. The berry bushes around the house here, he brought them. But dear Andreas, you will not be offended if your aunt gives you a piece of advice? You must also give a thought to yourself. Do not neglect to acquire a profession in time!

Andreas' heart was touched by the sight of his aunt's face. It was so old and full of affection. When she smiled he could see the stumps of teeth in her mouth.

— Well? asked the Chief Magistrate's sons: she did not bang the table at you today, did she?

Andreas felt somewhat embarrassed. The Chief Magistrate's wife, Birita, shushed her sons: — Be still, you! What terrible tongues you always have! Samuel, you should say a word to them.

Samuel Mikkelsen smiled: — Andreas will not take them seriously, I am sure. He knows them of old.

— He knows them all too well, I fear, said Birita.

The Chief Magistrate had four sons, but the eldest, Peter, was married and in charge in his father's stead at the great family estate over on Eysturoy. The other three, Mikkel, Jacob and Samson, were all unmarried and lived at home with their parents, went out fishing a great deal, helped in the running of the farm and were otherwise the heartiest participants in all the wedding feasts on Vagar. There was a daughter as well, Armgard Maria, a pretty, dark lass. But she seldom had a word to say. It was always her brothers who were talking and tormenting in the hearth-room.

— Tell me what we must do with them, Andreas, asked the Chief Magistrate's wife. Their father and I have wanted to set at least one of them to learning or official duties, but they do not want that. And they cannot all be farmers, God help us, unless they can marry into a farm, but what do you think? Would you expect any proper farmer's daughter to care for these hardened good-for-nothings?

Mikkel laughed: — What do you know about it, mother? I have not yet seen that the girls do not like me well enough. What is more I have just now been thinking of getting myself a sweet-heart for Christmas.

— Ay, I believe that, said Birita. You petticoat chaser! Your Christmas sweet-heart is hardly ever your Easter sweet-heart too. When are you going to think of betrothing yourself to a decent girl?

— Devil a one of your Christmas sweethearts or your Easter sweethearts for me! said Samson, the youngest son. I shall go to sea. I want to get into a war, that I tell you. You, Andreas, perhaps you could take me with you and get me into the navy, could you not?

The Chief Magistrate stopped in the middle of what he was doing:
— Leave off this kind of talk, Samson.

Samson had got up and was standing, like a playful giant, in the middle of the floor. He was swinging his arms.

— Ay, you are a peerless fellow, said Birita. Andreas will not thank you for your company, making him look foolish in Copenhagen.

Samson did not answer her. He closed his eyes, began to rock his shoulders, and sang to himself in a powerful voice, Forth sailed the nobles from Norway!

— Here comes Aunt Armgard after you, Samson, Mikkel shouted at him.

But Samson paid no attention to him. He rocked like a berserk all around the hearth-room, flapping his giant arms in the air and keeping on with his singing.

— You must speak seriously to him, Samuel, urged Birita.

The Chief Magistrate smiled good-naturedly in his full beard. His beautiful clear eyes followed, with scarcely-hidden pleasure, his son's outsize capers. But at last he cleared his throat and spoke out in a deep, half-sorrowful, half-admonitory tone: — Lord Jesus, Samson, what a way to behave, with Christmas right at hand. Be still, now, Samson, do as your father asks you.

Soon supper was ready. Quiet fell slowly over the hearth-room, everyone ate devoutly the over-abundance of good food that first marked the approach of the great feast. The Chief Magistrate conducted the evening prayers as was the custom. His deep voice was blurred, and although he read very slowly he stumbled twice over the words. But he was tired, he had just come home from the Havn expedition and longed for his rest. The great house began to settle down for the night. Next morning everyone would be up early, for it would be Christmas morning.

The Chief Magistrate's sons and Andreas went out into the yard for a moment. There was a light frost. The jagged silhouettes of the mountains cut big, sharp pieces out of the starlit sky. — Shall we have a dram now? asked Samson, confidentially. He had opened the door to a hay-barn. A heavy and sweet scent of hay breathed out from the dark. — Nay, wait rather, said Jacob. Christmas has not begun yet.

— You and I, Andreas, — we should stay up till midnight, Samson proposed. Then we shall drink a skoal together.

— Do not bother Andreas now, said Jacob, he is tired after his trip.

— Ay, the deuce, said Samson, we can lie here in the hay and sleep. Then we shall be up all the earlier! Shame on those who lie and doze on Christmas morning. I do not know that that will suit you so well, Andreas? You are used to another kind of *bedding* down in Copenhagen.

In Regensen Andreas had often dreamed that he was home again and sleeping in a fragrant hay-barn. It suited him very well, his blood was stirring and he was longing, moreover, for the night to pass. It was not just for the Yuletide drinking that he had come to Steigargard, there was another little motive for his trip to Vagar.

A warm fragrance emanated from the cattle stalls. The cows stood in the darkness and munched, and from time to time lowed softly and then breathed deeply in again. Andreas found something so familiar about this noise that it made him feel at home again at Steigargard, and he was filled with gratitude for the place where he had passed so many of his childhood days. The Chief Magistrate's imperturbable, heavy and gentle shape rose up in his mind's eye. He had the same mild-mannered, thoughtful tone of voice as the cows, he was a farmer at his heart's core. But he was a farmer of the great, open-handed and hospitable kind, and the smile, that always played a little shyly over his worthy face, was an affectionate, a humble, an ironic and indulgent smile. It took a living part in everything that happened to him, it was like a flame that flickered with every word that he spoke, ay, almost with every thought he thought. So much wisdom, such fineness and so much fun lived in this heroic bulk. Andreas felt a little ashamed. What kind of look would Samuel Mikkelsen have given if he had known the true purpose of his visit? He did not want to guess. He laid himself down to sleep in the Chief Magistrate's sweet hay. Through a hole in the stone wall he saw a star twinkle.

He awoke, shaking with cold. Outside, the stars were still twinkling.

— Happy Christmas, said Samson, in a hoarse voice. Did you have a good sleep in the hay? Now I am sure you need a little something to warm yourself! He handed him a keg that gurgled: Skoal!

— Skoal! said Andreas. And happy Christmas! He put his mouth to the bung-hole and swallowed a gulp or two. They were like a fire in his stomach.

They both stood up and brushed themselves off. It was still night, not a light to be seen in Sandavag.

— We must have something to put our teeth into, said Samson. He opened up a drying house. The door creaked on its hinges. Inside hung dried sheep carcases in a row; there was a musty, sour smell of meat. Samson took his knife from its sheath and with sure and skilful strokes cut away a leg.

— Meat is good, said he. Good for hunger, for cold, for weariness, for bad humour ...

— For love? laughed Andreas.

Samson made a manly grimace. They ate and pared off meat and ate again. Andreas felt a fiery comfort from this meal, the hard sheep flesh buckled between his teeth, its rancid juice intoxicated him, his stomach cried with delight and hunger. — Eat, said Samson. We shall eat up this leg ... my oath on it, father will not grudge it us.

They each sat on a keg. Between them on the floor stood a tallow dip, and shone. Suddenly they heard a footstep in the roadway. Samson listened. — It is Ole of Lida, said he, I know him by his footfall. He is seldom the last to come and wish us a happy Christmas.

They went out and listened to the steps, which came nearer and nearer. In the village, solitary lights were now to be seen; also in the Chief Magistrate's house, there began to be a stir.

— Ay, soon all our Christmas guests will be here, said Samson.

The worthy farmers, who came in the earliest hours of the morning to wish the Chief Magistrate a happy Christmas, were all shown into the innermost room, where Samuel Mikkelsen himself poured drinks for them. The younger ones came no farther than into the great room, where the sons were hosts, and a few poor folk were hardly to be persuaded farther than into the hearth-room. Still, they were all alike amply served, and at last sat up to the table before splendid legs of dried meat. Candles burned in candlesticks, and people's shadows played like trolls on the white-scoured walls. But there was no loud talk to be heard, all were sober and well-behaved in their Christmas cheer.

The younger ones felt no such quiet in themselves and were soon away on other Christmas visits. The older folk, on the contrary, were wholly absorbed in all kinds of memories, and lingered around the Chief Magistrate's silver flagon. He filled for them often, and at last invited Farmer Halvdan and Farmer Justinus to remain and hear the Christmas reading. They were by now both rather set in the eyes and full of deep Christian thoughts. They did not say nay to a reading of God's word.

Guests and household folk gathered slowly in the great room, where they reverently took their places along the walls.

— You have become such a learned man, Andreas, said the Chief Magistrate. I think I shall ask you to do the reading for us today. I am sure you will give us that pleasure.

Andreas was perplexed — this was a hitch in his plans. At first he thought of objecting that he had meant to go to high mass at Midvag, but he soon understood that this was an honour the Chief Magistrate was doing him. He felt like a fraud when he sat at the table with the candle and Jesper Brochmand's great book of homilies. Over by the wall-stove sat Armgard, her cold eyes half closed, her pale, bony face, with its hooked nose, unmoving as a mask. The last of the domestics came in and sat noiselessly by the door.

— Since it is so great a festival today, perhaps we should sing a hymn, said Samuel Mikkelsen, and began to leaf through the hymn book.

They joined in softly:

> The blessed day again is here,
> Sing we with gladsome voice,
> For Christ is born, our Saviour dear;
> Let every heart rejoice.

The Chief Magistrate led the singing. His voice was hardly melodious, but there was a note in it that touched Andreas and made him think of a bassoon, a horn or some other unsophisticated pastoral instrument. He felt a moment's reverence, but awoke to cold reality when the hymn had been sung. Before him lay the open book. Brochmand's homilies were notorious for their length.

— And it came to pass in those days, that there went out a decree from Caesar Augustus ...

He read in the light, brisk manner that he had acquired, and could hear immediately that his tone was false. It was not the heart's clumsy and simple Danish that he had just heard Samuel Mikkelsen sing, it was a profane and conceited speech. He made a pause when he had finished the Gospel passage. All his listeners sat unmoving, most buried their faces in their hands. Farmer Halvdan sat with glassy, running eyes and combed his fingers through his white beard.

— I think I shall go into the bed-closet, mumbled the Chief Magistrate to himself: I shall hear just as well there ...

At that moment Andreas' eye fell on Samson, who sat, well sheltered, with the wall-stove between him and Armgard. He was sure that he saw a lightning smile vanish from his face. He felt himself humbled and laughable in this dignified station where he, against his wish, had been placed.

— Come, ye that are God's children, he began, and lament the world's heedless failure to accept Jesus Christ, the Saviour of the world and King of Kings. Lo, now is fulfilled what Isaiah clearly prophesied: the ox knoweth his owner and the ass his master's crib, but Israel doth not know, my people doth not consider.

No, — the Chief Magistrate should have been reading this. Andreas did not know how to strike the right note, he blushed over his enforced priesthood and only wished that it might quickly come to an end. He might have been half way to Midvag by now. He read straight on over stock and stone, he no longer understood the words, his thoughts were wholly on how he might shorten this torment. But round him sat his listeners, absorbed, with their faces buried in their hands.

From within the bed-closet came a sound, faint at first but rapidly growing louder. It was all too clearly a snore. Andreas took a glance in its direction and saw, at the foot of the bed, Samuel Mikkelsen's crossed legs. Laughter boiled up in him, his voice became for a moment weak and unintelligible, sweat broke out on his forehead, he read on and on while the house shook with the Chief Magistrate's snores. But all the listeners sat in unaltered reverence, with their faces hidden. Only Armgard looked straight ahead, and her face was as though of stone.

Andreas let his voice run on, but inwardly he was numb. Laughter came in assaults, it was a sickness, a spasm. He had read many pages but as yet he could see no sign of an amen. He was like a wreck which, far from sight of land and without a compass, tossed on the wild ocean of the Brochmand eloquence. At the end of the next page he leafed over several at once, he did not know whether two or four, it seemed to make no difference, there was still no amen in sight.

He read and read, and the longer he read the worse it got. Lord, Brochmand! He had always heard that he was everlasting reading, but so long a reading had he never before seen. Christmas was a high festival, that must account for it. Outdoors it was now broad daylight, roosters crowed and the candles flickered pale on the table. He leafed over double again, but still no amen.

Then Armgard spoke up. — Here, Andreas, said she. Turn back again!

Andreas turned back one page and found to his joy an amen. He looked gratefully at his aunt and was about to read the last bit of the sermon.

— Nay, Andreas, said Armgard. You have not turned back to the first day of Christmas yet.

Andreas gazed into the book, bewildered. At the top of the page was printed *Lesson for St Stephen's Day*. Not a word of it all made sense to him.

Armgard had stood up. She thumped the table so it thundered: Keep turning back, keep turning back, you young devil! God forgive my tongue! There you sit and read up the page and down the page about St Stephen on the first day of Christmas. What can you be thinking? Turn back to the place where you first cheated!

Andreas turned back in confusion, page after page, all of which he had read. Then at last he found the amen to the first day of Christmas. It was on one of the pages he had skipped.

Armgard had gone back to her place. — Read from the place where you cheated, she said again, sharply.

Andreas began to read again, obedient as a little boy. A pin could have been heard drop when he at last pronounced amen. Then the Chief Magistrate appeared all at once at the bed-closet door, slept out and smiling.

— Many thanks to you, Andreas, said he, that you have taken this on. Whose tongue would have spoken such fine Danish as yours?

— Ay, bless you, agreed Farmer Halvdan, in his high-pitched old man's voice. A heavenly tongue you read, ay, just like a Danish priest. But for my poor old ears it was rather quick ...

Andreas was still somewhat embarrassed. His listeners came one after the other to shake his hand and thank him for the reading. Last of all came the Chief Magistrate's sons, dignified and quiet like the others, but lighted up inwardly with laughter.

Farmer Halvdan and Farmer Justinus had begun to say their good-byes. The Chief Magistrate urged them to stay, and said that they had not partaken of Christmas hospitality.

— Bless you, they objected. Christmas hospitality? Have we not had all that heart can desire? Snaps and the Gospel both?

They went out, augustly but cheerfully. Andreas stood out in the door-yard. He was in good spirits; he was already by way of shrugging off his bit of bad luck. When it came right down to it, it was not to read from prayer-books and homily books that he had come to Vagar.

Samson came out. He clapped him on the shoulder: — You are not the emperor's friend now! said he, and laughed.

— Would I have become that, anyhow? thought Andreas. In the distance he could hear the church bells at Midvag.

It was a hasty noon meal that Pastor Paul ate on that first day of Christmas. The service at Midvag had dragged on and he had hardly come home to Jansagerd before the boat crew appeared that was to convey him to Sorvag. The day was so short, said they. Best to travel by daylight. But they had a long wait in the hearth-room just the same, which they, perhaps, did not mind so very much.

190

Barbara was in a proper sulk.

— You must admit, said she, that there is little pleasure for me in this kind of a Christmas. And afterwards you insist on going out to Mykines! I assure you, it has not happened before that a priest has been on Mykines for Christmas. Even if you get there you run the risk that the sea will come up so that you do not get away in months. You are mad to do such a thing.

— Yes, but my dearest, said the Priest. You would not let me go out there in summer and not in the fall either. Now it cannot be put off longer. The good folk out there have not yet seen their priest, though I have been in the living for more than a year. Children run about unbaptized out there like heathen! Some couples have not been able to marry, other folk lie in their graves without Christian burial, no casting of earth on them. They have cause to reproach me out there for all this; you must understand that I was constrained to promise them this.

— To come at Christmas?

— Something had to be done. To make up for my neglect, you understand!

— No priest has ever been there at Christmas!

— For that very reason, Barbara! However, there is no certainty that the weather will be favourable for me to get away in the morning. Then I shall come straight back to you, you know that ...

But Barbara was not mollified, she was half sullen, and the meal ended as it had begun, bad-humoured. The Priest had just changed into his travelling clothes and stood ready to go when he happened to look out the window.

— We are having visitors, said he. Or rather, you are having them. If I am not mistaken, those are the Chief Magistrate's sons that are sauntering in across the sand.

Barbara brightened up. She was over at the window immediately.

— Ay, said she, there is Samson ... and Mikkel, and ...

— And Jacob, is it? said the Priest.

— Nay, said Barbara, it is not Jacob, it is ...

At that moment the Priest could see that her face was quite changed. She turned from the window, wordless and utterly

191

confused. She looked almost as though she had been given an unexpected blow on the face.

The Priest took a hasty glance out again. A dreadful foreboding had struck deep in him. He soon recognized Andreas Heyde's carefree stride and bright face. He it was who went foremost of the three.

Pastor Paul turned to his wife. She was still terribly upset, and when she began to talk she was hardly in command of her voice.

— Never mind, said she. The men will not find anyone at home. I shall come with you ... up to the lake. They will have to wait, if they have so much time.

She was very hurried, and as though dismayed. In a moment she had found something warm to put over herself, and went quickly out with Pastor Paul. The boat crew followed, amazed.

The weather was still and cold. Hoar frost covered the ground, and the small puddles all had clear plates of ice on them. Barbara took her husband's arm and often pressed close to him. Gradually, as they got farther away from Jansagerd, she eased her pace and at last walked slowly.

— You must come straight back again. That you must promise me!

She spoke this in a quiet voice, and as though full of anxiety. Other than this she had said nothing. She was very serious, and looked at him with a look full of pain.

— I shall return the quickest way I can, said Pastor Paul. Perhaps I shall be back tomorrow, if the weather changes.

— Ay, it will do that, it will surely do that! Barbara insisted.

— Ah, Lord God, Barbara! the Priest exclaimed. Will you have forgotten me in three days?

Barbara did not answer this at once, but after a moment she said:

— Dearest Paul! You know what I most wish. That is all I can say. Do hurry home again!

While the boat crew went ahead for a moment she put her arms around his neck and hugged him fiercely. Then she stroked his face and looked at him with grief in her eyes. They had crossed the ridge. The great glass of the lake spread itself out before them. When they reached the little cluster of buildings that they had once called

Capernaum, the boat crew hauled a little boat out of a boat-shed and launched it into the lake. The thin ice along the shore splintered with a tinkling sound. Pastor Paul said good-bye.

— Come back again! was the last that Barbara said. She was very moved.

The boat glided quietly from the shore. The cold winter light lay over the lake's surface. Barbara went home. Pastor Paul sat and watched her, as she walked up across the heath, brisk and straight. She did not look back.

14
Weather-fast

P astor Paul was wakened early next morning by his host. The weather was still and the stars shone clear. If it was his wish to go to Mykines, said the Sorvagsman, the conditions could not be better at this time of year. He offered to have him rowed there at once.

Pastor Paul asked if he also thought they could row him home again the same day. To this he answered that all rested in God's hands, but if he got ready for Mykines quickly they would try to wait for him at the landing place. If only a sea did not get up. This was the one thing it all hung on. For if the sea was not still at Mykines it was as impossible to come away as to get ashore.

This being so Pastor Paul had no alternative: he must keep his promise that he would come to Mykines over Christmas. But he remembered with a shudder all the stories he had heard of people who had been weather-fast out there for months, only on account of the sea at the landing place, and he knew that he would feel no security till he was away from that island again.

Their passage out through the long Sorvag's fjord was in darkness. It was a long row that awaited them, which was otherwise almost never undertaken in winter. Mykines lay a good way over open sea, it was the outermost of all the Faroe islands. And the village and landing place lay far out at the western end. In all there might be eleven or twelve sea-miles to row out there from Sorvag.

The men looked up at the starry skies and guessed that the good weather perhaps would hold for the day. They pulled manfully on their oars and were in good heart. On both sides dark nesses and frost-covered fells glided by. When they came into the mouth of the fjord they could discern the distant Mykines in the starlight, thrusting up like a single mountain out of the western ocean, shining white at the top. But its sides were black and steep, and allowed no place for snow.

Soon the stars began little by little to grow pale, and when the boat came into the open sea, day broke. Mykines grew bigger before the bow in the early winter sunshine, flame-red and crude in its wild, jagged might. It was a vision and terror all in one.

The hour was still early when they reached the little village at the island's western end. There was a great commotion when the boat came in sight, and Pastor Paul had hardly set foot on shore before the bell in the wretched little sod-roofed church began to ring joyfully and scatter its tones into the bright morning air. It was a glad day for everyone on Mykines.

The climb up to the village was long and steep. Pastor Paul went into the church-warden's house and allowed himself a hurried meal, then proceeded straight to the church, where everyone was gathered — all but the Sorvag's men, who had gone back down to their boat again.

Pastor Paul read the service and made it brief, though without unseemly haste. The sun shone the whole time through the small windows, and bore witness to the steadiness of the weather. Right after the service four children were christened and a young couple launched into married life. Then there were only a few castings-on of earth on buried folk left to do. Pastor Paul went between the withered grass tumps of the graves in the pale sunshine, and once again the little church bell rang out over the whole village. When this was accomplished the Priest's visitation had been fulfilled. The weather had not changed. Pastor Paul went into the church-warden's house again and got ready to leave. He had feared that they might want to delay him with attentions and entertainment, but his host seemed to understand that he wanted to leave again at once.

He was already on the path down to the landing place when a man came running after him, and with confused words stopped him. He wanted him to turn back and come and christen a child.

— Christen a child? asked Pastor Paul. Why was the child not at the church?

— Bless you, — it was not yet born!

The Priest became impatient. He understood from his companions that they too were impatient with this man, and would have sent him away. But he did not want to appear ill-tempered.

— Let me christen it at once, then, said he sharply, and turned back.

— The Priest need only have said no, murmured the church-warden. This dunderhead should see that the Priest has no extra time ... a winter day! ... so late, what is more.

— Where is the child, then? asked Pastor Paul, brusquely, when he walked into the man's house.

The man made a comical, beseeching gesture: — The child ... the child is not born yet ... that is, I mean: not altogether ... not altogether come into the world. But I assure you, he continued, entreatingly, that my wife is always very quick about this business. It will come right away!

— God's death, Hanus Elias, are you not in your right mind? the Church-warden burst out. Are you wanting to make a fool of the Priest? What are you thinking?

— It will be no time at all, none at all, pleaded Hanus Elias.

Pastor Paul at this moment was of a mind to go. He was angry enough for that. Why he did not do so he could never explain to himself later, though his thoughts often allowed themselves to go back over this unlucky hour.

They had waited a full quarter-hour in Hanus Elias' best room when a sudden gust of wind made the house tremble. The Priest looked out and observed that the wind, for a moment, was waving the withered grass on the roof of the neighbouring house. The sun was no longer shining.

— I shall go now, said he, sharply, and got up.

— Ay, there is no waiting any longer, said the Church-warden. A south-west wind is rising, that is clear.

At that moment Hanus Elias came in, begging and pleading: —
Bless you, do not go now! The child *is* born! If you will only wait a
moment ... bless you ... is there such a hurry?

— Hurry? said the Church-warden, angrily. You have always been
dimwitted, Hanus Elias, do not be dimmer than you are, you know
well how much it matters.

Hanus Elias made a despairing gesture or two. In his fatherly
agitation he was like a lost soul, he fairly danced with nervousness.

— Bring the child ... in the devil's name! said Pastor Paul, and
stamped on the floor.

He gave in to his anger and paced back and forth in the room.
The Church-warden had gone out to have an eye on the weather. He
came in again and said: — There is little time to spare.

— It is going fine, it is going fine, stammered Hanus Elias.

Once again a gust flattened the grass on a neighbouring roof. The
shrill cry of a new-born could be heard. Three panting men came
running from the landing place: they came to fetch the Priest. At that
moment the child was brought in. In all, a half hour had passed.

Pastor Paul christened the child like lightning and thunder. When
he asked for its name, the god-mother stammered a little over it. The
child was to have five names. Pastor Paul gave it three, and the
instant the amen was said he was out through the door. All the men
ran with him.

When they came in sight they saw, far below, that the boat, fully
manned and rising and falling, was hoving out from the landing.
Elsewhere the sea looked calm, and, out over its surface, rays of
sunlight could still be seen.

Pastor Paul ran as though for his life down the steep bank. The
whole village was on foot, all had one wish, that the Priest should
succeed in getting away.

He came to the farthest out ledge of rock. Two fathoms from him
heaved the boat — he need only make a bold spring. Pastor Paul
knew that his happiness was at stake, his heart was in his throat.
Time after time the boat came close to shore, but had to be rowed
quickly away again so as not to be smashed. More and more violently
it cut into the rising swell. Once he perhaps might have made a
spring, had he been an experienced seaman. But that he was not. By

now the stoutest Mykines men were gathered around him. They were ready to help him by whatever means offered; they called to the men in the boat that if the chance came they would throw the Priest on board to them and they should take care to hold him. But no such chance offered itself. The moment had passed. The suck and splash of waves against the shore was beginning to drown the men's voices: a surf was setting in. Again and then once again the Sorvag boat made bold attempts to come in close. But these moves were hardly more than courtesy. There was no hope in them.

Then occurred a mishap. One of the Mykines men who had been gesturing and calling most zealously slipped on the smooth stone and fell into the water. In a moment he was seized by the others and pulled, dripping, to shore again. It was Hanus Elias.

The Church-warden cursed him up and down: — That served you right! It was you that spoiled everything, you Jonah. Why can you not be like everyone else? Get home, now, and shame on you! See the harm you have done!

Abashed and dripping, off went Hanus Elias to his house. Harm? What harm had he done? Made the Priest stay on Mykines. What was the big harm in that? When he was a priest after all, and could be put up by such a man as the Church-warden. At Christmas, too!

But the Priest stood as though he had been lamed, and with despair in his heart he watched the boat row off. It had not gone far out before they set the sail and scudded away.

— Ay, one of the watchers said: they got a good wind and the current is with them too.

The Church-warden turned to Pastor Paul. — It was too bad, said he. Perhaps the Priest will not mind staying in my house?

From that moment Pastor Paul spoke few words. As recently as twenty-four hours ago he had been a happy man, and only an hour since he had been full of confidence and hope. Now he had fallen irretrievably into a pit. His ill-luck was so great that he could hardly grasp it.

Farmer Niklas, the Church-warden, thought in his quieter mood that the Priest was now making more of his mischance than was reasonable.

— The weather is after all not really bad, said he, and so far as I can see it shows no sign of becoming a storm either. It is only this wind direction that is so miserably unlucky. But — suppose your delay does not last longer than a day or two? We must hope for the best.

Pastor Paul gave Niklas a friendly look but at the same time shrugged his shoulders, as though he thought it was rather hopeless even so. He went over to the window. The weather, it was true, went on looking reasonably good, there was no motion to be seen on the endless grey face of the sea, where patches of sunshine gleamed here and there.

He felt that he had fallen under a kind of spell.

Farmer Niklas had the table set with the farm's best food. Pastor Paul was friendly and polite but he had no appetite at all, and at the first sign of the early twilight he asked Niklas to show him where he was to sleep.

It eased his feelings somewhat to be alone. Slowly a dull calm came over him. And even supposing the worst did happen! Ought that to break him? Was he not a man and a priest?

In any case, what had happened was a testing, a hard testing. He prayed God to support him. It grew into a long and heartfelt prayer and he felt strengthened by it. — We must let be, he whispered to himself. We shall wait the time out. God's will alone must be done.

When he awoke next morning he did not feel the pang of despair in his heart that he had feared. On the contrary, he felt comforted and composed. The weather had not changed appreciably. A little wind, otherwise the same red daybreak as yesterday. Pastor Paul joined in some chat with the Church-warden. After breakfast they went around together in the village. The Priest wanted to visit the sick and the aged. It took up his attention. Gradually he got used to thinking of this mischance as, perhaps, when all was taken into account, not a mischance but rather a testing for him and for her. He imagined his homecoming. Barbara comes to meet him, she smiles and it is as though he can see already in her smile that all is well. Yes, perhaps Barbara had changed in the course of those deep, happy winter months that they had lived alone together in Jansagerd. Perhaps she was no longer the old Barbara but a new, an enlightened, a faithful and longing Barbara!

Eleven days passed before the weather permitted the Priest to get away. In compensation the weather became so fine that it might have been high summer. The broad sound between Mykines and Vagar was ruffled by no more than a light chop and by the rustling and sparkling path of the current that bore the boat swiftly on its way. Sorvag fjord was as calm as a lake, and mirrored the clouds and cliff-rock. At Sorvag the captain got a horse for Pastor Paul and rode with him up to the lake. A little group of oarsmen was there already, standing by with a little boat. The Priest had said that there was need for haste.

At the beginning of this homeward journey Pastor Paul had felt gratitude and lightness of heart. He had been conscious of the help of God and man. But as he approached Midvag and Jansagerd his spirits began to sink. The picture of Barbara coming to meet him gave way to another, which moreover was no picture at all but only an emptiness. Emptiness! Empty rooms! And a voice that said in empty tones that Barbara was not at home. That Mme Aggersoe had gone to Havn ... on a visit.

Barbara is not at home! went through him like a shiver, as he hurried down towards Midvag. The village was behind him, then the sand, then came Jansagerd. Barbara is not at home!

It was true — Barbara was not at home. So it turned out to be. The old half-deaf servant-woman Kristina was the one whose voice was to give him this news, in a commonplace, affectionately dutiful, servant's tone of voice. Barbara had gone to Havn. She had not left a message.

For a while Pastor Paul went back and forth through the empty rooms in travelling clothes and carrying a blanket over his arm. Barbara! kept sounding hollowly in him in sobs.

He went into the hearth-room to ask Kristina if Barbara had travelled alone or with someone. But he could not bring the question past his lips. All at once he thought of the Chief Magistrate! Samuel Mikkelsen ... Samuel Mikkelsen would surely be on his side! He must ... he must not have given his consent that what had happened should have happened!

Pastor Paul threw aside the blanket and undid his heavy travelling clothes a little, but did not give himself time to take them off. He was quickly through the door and on his way to Sandavag. He looked on it as a kind of rescue, to talk to Samuel Mikkelsen. He ran most of the way, and when he reached Sandavag he was wet through with sweat and had hardly breath to talk.

In Steigargard's dooryard he met Samson. He said that his father was down at the boat sheds. He was expected back at any moment.

Pastor Paul sat on the nearest stone. He was dead tired.

— Will the Priest not come in? asked Samson. You must be uncomfortable here.

— I am sitting comfortably enough, said Pastor Paul, shortly, and as though distraught.

Samson saw the look on his face. He left him in peace and went into the house. He told them only that the Priest was sitting outside.
— He does not want to come in, he added. Nobody said much about it. One or two of the curious peered out. They could see the Priest in the gloaming, sitting with his elbows on his knees and his face hidden in his hands. No-one wanted to disturb him.

Below on the slope to the shore something came in view over the edge; it emerged slowly, first a head, then a pair of shoulders, then gradually the whole form of a man that unhurriedly came nearer and nearer and moment by moment grew larger in the half light. It was the Chief Magistrate, on his way home. The Priest became aware of him all at once as a huge shadow before him, and got up. Samuel Mikkelsen wished him a good evening.

— Barbara has gone away from me, said Pastor Paul.

The Chief Magistrate answered nothing. He stood with an unhappy look on his face.

— Will you not come in? he asked at last, softly. Please, let us go this way.

They entered by a special door into the Chief Magistrate's study ...

201

— I am very distressed by this, began Samuel Mikkelsen, after they had sat quiet a good while. It was not with my consent that they went to Havn together, but I could not keep them back. I tried to bring them to their senses, but, as you may imagine ... it is useless to talk to folk when that madness is on them.

The Chief Magistrate spoke gently and hesitantly. Nevertheless the Priest's heart ached, and when he heard the words *that madness* a shudder of dismay went through him.

— Andreas is so impetuous, Samuel Mikkelsen continued. I should not have invited him west here ... but not for a moment did I think ...

— He would have come sooner or later just the same, said the Priest. It *had* to happen.

— Will you drink a snaps? asked the Chief Magistrate, almost pleading with him.

He opened a cupboard and filled a silver beaker to the brim. The Priest put it from him. — No, thank you! Not now ... I ... no thank you.

— You are like me, perhaps, said the Chief Magistrate. I have no mind for spirits if I am not in a good humour.

— I am not up to it, mumbled the Priest.

They sat silent for a while. The beaker stood between them on the table.

— If it comes down to that, you might drink it as medicine, the Chief Magistrate suggested.

The Priest did not answer. Suddenly he emptied the beaker.

— It does the heart good, said the Chief Magistrate.

The Priest felt that it did the heart good. He smiled. He smiled like a dog, his eyes were expressionless and hungry.

— Ah, said he, yes, yes! It does not *surprise* me in the least now, no it does not. For I always knew it.

The Chief Magistrate perhaps smiled too, just a wrinkle. He too felt that he had always known it. Or if not exactly this, then something like it. Then he went and fetched the flask and filled the beaker again.

The Priest sat and mumbled to himself. He repeated mournfully:
— But it had to be this way. Though I knew all the while so well, I could not have done otherwise.

— Nay, said the Chief Magistrate, neither you could.

— Neither I could, neither I could.

Pastor Paul emptied the beaker again. His eyes were as though blinded, he drank eagerly. Ah, yes, said he.

The door opened slowly. Armgard came in with a candle; she was bent over and deliberate in her movements as she went about. She screwed up her cold eyes at the Priest.

— Good day, Pastor Paul, said she, a little sarcastically. And how is *your* life these days?

— Good, thank you, said the Priest. And yours?

Armgard had sat down with her knitting.

— What kind of life is it when one's kin ...? She broke off.

The knitting needles had come into play, they went like a machine. Her eyes were half shut.

They all sat silent for a while. The Priest had fasted since the morning. He was aware that the Chief Magistrate's cognac was beginning to stupefy him. A black snow was snowing against his eyes, the hard ache in his breast had loosened just a little.

— When I look at it rightly, said he, then the whole thing is not so overwhelming ... what I mean is, a man may rise above his own fate. I can see what is laughable in it. Ha ha ha! What is more, a cuckold is always laughable.

He laughed again, and the tears stood in his eyes. He drank another beaker and said: ah, ah yes, ah yes.

— Ay, we must wait and see, said the Chief Magistrate. It may all straighten itself out again, I think it may. Barbara is so ... she is so ... capricious, often.

He glanced over towards his aunt. Old Armgard's eyelids were almost tight shut. Had she not been knitting so briskly, one might have thought that she was sitting and dozing. But he knew her better, he knew that at any moment a pronouncement might be expected from her.

— Yes — Barbara! said the Priest, and suddenly an altogether fatuous look came over his face. He seemed to have had a vision. All at once he broke out: — Do you think so indeed? Do you think she will come back some time? No? No?

His voice was quite out of its usual register, it was wild and beseeching, as of one who suddenly cries out in sleep. Then he added, in a calmer tone, almost himself again: — If I might only *once*, one only time in this life ... yes, then I would not ask for more. Ah, Barbara, how I long for you!

Armgard had looked up. She cleared her throat, but stopped herself and went on knitting. There was a scornful expression about her nose and mouth.

— You see, said the Priest, and turned confidentially towards the Chief Magistrate: you understand ... I must explain myself ... you have the right to expect an explanation from me. I knew in my heart all the while that this had to come, I was quite clear about it all the while.

— Ay, then Armgard interrupted him, drily. So that was why you had to marry her at last, I suppose.

The Priest surveyed her with a drunk man's loftiness. He merely turned his back on her still further and steadied himself on the Chief Magistrate's arm.

— That is, I was expecting this all the while. As a punishment, let me say, because it was all far too good, it was far ... far too epicurean, luxurious, delicious. He stumbled heavily over the words. You understand, it had to come, that is. It was expected. Just the same, it came unexpected. I mean, it came unexpected on *that* day, that is. I was not prepared, it was too sudden. If I just once ... I mean if I might in any case be allowed to ... I do not wish to be spared my punishment, but first, first ... I do *wish*, that is! he cried, and banged his fist on the table.

— Aunt Armgard, said the Chief Magistrate, the Priest must have something to eat.

— That I *have* taken care of, said Armgard.

The Priest sat leaning back and staring in front of him. — Barbara! he mumbled. If she knew how I think and feel for her now, if she knew my heart now, she would come to me. Skoal! Skoal, Barbara! do you not hear me?

He had raised the silver beaker, and he sat and cried. Armgard
turned her chair away with an embittered motion. A housemaid came
in and laid the table for the Priest.

Pastor Paul was sitting crumpled up and looking as though the
whole thing did not concern him. The Chief Magistrate had stood,
and put his hat on a shelf under the roof.

— Please, said he. God bless you, eat now, Pastor Paul. You must
need something to eat, do you hear?

He spoke in a gentle, almost beseeching tone and smiled
helplessly. Pastor Paul took a piece of flatbread and laid it on his
plate. No places had been set for the Chief Magistrate and Armgard.
They both sat a little away from the table, as the custom was for the
host and hostess.

The Priest hardly touched the food. He sat with a dried leg of
lamb before him and made a few indifferent and clumsy efforts to cut
pieces from it.

— Bless your heart, eat, said the Chief Magistrate, it strengthens
both body and soul to eat flesh.

But the Priest did not touch the meat. It looked as though he was
already beginning to fall asleep. Suddenly he roused himself a little,
clenched his fists and sang with wide movements of his arms:

Ah, Lord, your rods chastise
And make me manly and wise ...

Armgard looked up, surprised. — That is a new hymn, surely! she
remarked.

Pastor Paul's look was idiotic. — Is that not good? he asked. Ah,
Lord, your rods chastise and make me manly and wise? Yes, that is
how it should go. Now I have found it! Ha ha ha! It came to me all
of a sudden!

— Listen to me, you poor Pastor Paul, said Armgard, in a pointed
school-teacher's tone: You are a simple-hearted man and it can surely
never come into the Good Lord's mind to chastise *you*. Nay, nay, she
continued, in a mocking falsetto, that sounded like a sea-gull's laugh:
You, who cannot even keep your own wife in line! But *she*, who has
been corrupting the youth here in the islands, God forgive me, now

205

she cannot even leave *our* family alone! ... when *she* comes under the Lord's chastisement ...!

And old Armgard struck her fist on the table. Then he said: — Yes ... devil take her! The devil carry her off for what she has done! That hell-wife she is ... that bitch!

Thereupon he fell asleep. The Chief Magistrate smiled unhappily, and discreetly called in his sons. They carried the Priest carefully into bed. They were not at all ignorant of what had been going on in the Chief Magistrate's study.

— You should have seen, said Samson, with a wry smile: you should have seen when he proposed a skoal to Aunt Armgard! He was sure she was Barbara!

15
Tempo di Menuetto

P astor Paul woke in the middle of the night and at first his mind was blank. But suddenly it all came back, everything that had happened. It came like a violent blow in the stomach. After that there was no more sleep, he lay in a state of the greatest disquiet, with a spasmodic pain in his breast. He longed eagerly for the household to wake up and for day to begin.

He was first up of all that morning, and his first wish was to ask the Chief Magistrate's sons if the weather would permit a journey to Havn.

He went out and in and then out again, held out his hand in the half-light, felt a fine drizzle on it, looked up at the heavens and tried to guess at the wind's quarter. The thought that he might perhaps see Barbara again before nightfall was nearly enough to choke him.

But the Chief Magistrate's sons were late out of their bunks, and when they at last came forth under the eaves they declared their conviction that the weather was not fit for Havn today, with such a strong wind. Around Kirkjubo Ness was out of the question in any case, now that the days were short, though a landing might possibly be managed at Velbestad. They would speak with their father about that, they said.

The Chief Magistrate had never been an early riser. When he eventually appeared his deeply phlegmatic being wore an air of uneasiness. One could imagine that he might have looked so if Steigargard had been in flames around him. He was on the verge of being in a hurry.

Pastor Paul had, during his long wait, ceaselessly wandered out of the house and in again. He had by turns stared at the weather and stared at the people. He was like a dog that, speechless and frantic, tries to enlist human aid in a desperate situation. Now, when he at last saw the Chief Magistrate come, he hurried straight to him. An indomitable eagerness emanated from the Priest, his will was so strong that it acted on the others like a force.

— The weather is not good, indeed it is not, said Samuel Mikkelsen. He leaned forward on a stone wall and observed the heavens with care.

A short while passed.

— Perhaps the Priest would be best advised to go by Futaklet, said the Chief Magistrate's son Jacob, tentatively.

Pastor Paul said nothing to this. But he may have made some gesture or other. His whole being expressed the strongest aversion. He knew this would mean at least a two-day trip. And must he now make the heavy journey back to Futaklet, to Kvivik, to Leynum, to Oyrareingja, all that long way that he had, in a happy time, taken with Barbara? And that she had just lately taken with Andreas! His heart knotted up in despair.

— I see how it is, said the Chief Magistrate, with the profoundest thoughtfulness, Pastor Paul is perhaps in rather a hurry today.

He looked enquiringly at the Priest, as though to ask whether this might not be so. His eyes expressed simple good will and courtesy.

— God's own hurricane is blowing! Jacob burst out. He puffed a little; it was his way to puff, when he became excited.

Samuel Mikkelsen did not answer. The Priest stood and fidgeted uneasily. He was beside himself, it was as though his spirit wanted to wrench itself out of his body and take its solitary flight over Vagarfjord.

The Chief Magistrate gave one more weather-wise look at the clouds: — The wind *is* strong, said he. But it is from the most favourable quarter for us, so long as it holds north-easterly. And it was half-moon yesterday, so the current should be right ... though it is not what could be called weak. The moon is so near to the Earth.

He stood a moment and pondered, his features were unmoving: — If we were to wait till Westfall slacks off, it might just be possible, he added.

It sounded casual. Not until the Chief Magistrate and his sons were on their way into the house again did Pastor Paul understand that this was the last word that would be said, and that the matter had been decided. He hung back and could hardly believe he had got his wish. This evening he should see Barbara again!

But among the Chief Magistrate's household there was no little agitation that morning, as the Priest could not fail to see in the look on the housewife's face. And Samuel Mikkelsen had to shush his son Samson once, who was not usually a faint-heart, but who damned and blasted just the same about making this pig of a trip on account of that cursed bitch. But the Chief Magistrate said that they would go for the Priest's sake, because it was such a shame for him. And Armgard thumped the table and her face was like flint as she said that they should go for *family's* sake, so that whore should not corrupt Andreas entirely.

It was nearing midday when Samuel Mikkelsen, with ten men, pulled away from shore in Sandavag. He sat in the stern himself and steered and the Priest sat next him. The wind was blowing in gusts out along the bay. They set the sail and the big boat was blown along, and all the houses in Sandavag and Midvag quickly mustered themselves into small, insignificant clusters, while the peaks above began to reach their black fingers up over the bluffs that had hidden them. In Pastor Paul's heart the knot began to loosen little by little, he was sailing, he was flying towards his goal. This evening ... he hardly knew whether he should dread it or rejoice.

Soon they were by Klovning, an abrupt headland, whose extreme point was cleft from the land and stood and lowered over the deep. They turned into the open Vagarfjord and rowed eastward along the steep shore. The wind was coming in broken gusts from above, so they lowered the sail. The water was smooth and dark. Trollkonufingur reached up like a dark spire a thousand feet over their heads and behind it was the sheer fell, much higher still.

The men rowed. They struck their slender oars into the waves with short quick strokes, the boat drove forward in strong tugs, the Chief Magistrate and the Priest nodded involuntarily with each tug. The men talked in hoarse voices and spit tobacco-juice into the sea. They kept looking at the weather. — The sky is like a sooty pot, said one of them.

So it was, the sky was very dark. And against the foot of the cliff the water boiled softly. But the Chief Magistrate smiled out of the depths of his good nature, his hand lay authoritatively on the tiller. His red-headed son Samson rowed like a Viking. — Forth sailed the nobles from Norway! sang he, and gave the Priest a mighty look and winked at him. The Priest smiled back. It was as though a healthy breeze was blowing into his anguished breast. He would gladly have been such a man as Samson.

They rowed for an hour and at last left Vagar behind. The wind was blowing somewhat against them down Vestmannasund but it raised no sea worth speaking of. Then one of the men said: — Look, is the wind not veering to the east!

— I see that, said Samuel Mikkelsen. It means that we must row in closer to Streymoy. Then we may be in the lee all the way to Velbestad and have Eastfall with us as well.

But Streymoy's sheltering coast was still far ahead, and the way to it became wet and salty, for the wind stood more and more against them, and the water splashed so heavily into the boat that a man had to be set to bail from time to time. But the high-swept stem rocked defiantly up and down, up and down, and ploughed its way eastward fathom by fathom while the oars slapped into the waves.

— Forth sailed the nobles from Norway! sang Samson once again, and laughed through the salt water that was coursing down over his face. But the Priest no longer felt exhilarated, he became impatient that they were moving so slowly.

— It is veering, veering all the while, said the men anxiously, meaning that the east wind had swung further and was now veering towards the south. Their senses were open only to weather and current, they were on the watch constantly and took heed of many

210

small signs in the passage of the clouds and the going of the waves. Out of the restless surface of the sea rose the islands like high, rough-hewn blocks. To the south-west, Koltur lifted his wild head, rearing towards the heavens, and Streymoy, which lay in front of them, was like a long row of battlements and chasms, steadily changing castles and chasms.

When a snow-flurry suddenly curtained everything from before their eyes the boat seemed all at once alone. Only the splash of the sliding wave-crests could be heard between the oar strokes. The Chief Magistrate soberly rummaged out a compass and steered by that. The wet snow whipped him harshly in the face, but not a feature did he move.

It is veering, veering, thought he, and kept his eye on the wandering compass needle.

Barbara, Barbara, thought the Priest, and stared blindly into the snow.

It had been Samuel Mikkelsen's plan to row the whole way in the lee of Vagar's and Streymoy's high mountains, which would shelter them against the strength of the north-east gale; at the same time he expected to take advantage of Eastfall to carry them southward through Hesturfjord. Now he saw this plan brought to nothing. Within half an hour the gale had swung to the south-east and now blew unhindered up the length of Streymoy, exactly counter to the flow of the current. It was the worst that could have happened.

When the snow-flurry had passed, their predicament became apparent to them all. They were now under Streymoy's mountains, but out on the fjord the gale was in a raging strife with Eastfall's strong flow. The boat was working against a stiff head-wind, but in by the land the current was less strong. Few words were spoken. All knew that turning back would be desperate, there was no alternative now to creeping slowly ahead along the shore against the gale, and hoping that a landing would be possible at Velbestad. But three sea-miles yet lay between them and that village.

They had now rowed a full three hours. Suddenly the mighty Konufell lifted out of the clouds overhead, like a petrified roar. Rags of cloud still hurried by this broken mountain, hid the gigantic bluffs and then uncovered them, wrapped the crags and then laid them bare again, danced, drifted and mounted like smoke up through wet crevasses and fissures. The crew looked up as though into a giant organ, that was playing an inaudible but visually wild music.

The Chief Magistrate held the boat as close to shore as possible. They rode over wave crests at the edge of the surf and it often seemed as though they were about to be thrown in against the rocks. But on the other side of the boat frothed Eastfall, whipped up by the opposing gale.

The Priest sat and viewed the wet shore. Its brown seaweed was exposed deep down as the waves drew back. There is the island that Barbara walks on, thought he, it is hardly three fathoms from me. If only I might come ashore, then I could hurry to her, wherever she is. Further he did not think. What should happen thereafter he did not know. Yet he was already thinking too far. The Chief Magistrate's thoughts went no further than Lambatang, which they soon must pass. That was a notorious storm head.

— Ay, ay, thought Samuel Mikkelsen: Eastfall is at the full. Yet there was only a half moon yesterday. Least current! Should be. But ... the moon is nearest Earth these days. So the current will be strong enough, for all that.

Samson rowed like a madman. A vein low on his forehead swelled. It swelled as Roland's jugular did, when he blew the blast on the horn, Olifant, at Roncesvalles. All ten men rowed and gritted their teeth. The boat crept forward, fathom by fathom.

— Like a fly on a tarred stick, groaned one of the men.

— Ay, like a fly on a tarred stick, groaned another. At that moment they were labouring by the great chasm that was just north of Lambatang.

— Dirty weather we are having today, observed the Chief Magistrate, helpfully, to the Priest.

In another moment the first breaker in the cross-current, with its roaring crest, reared itself before them above their heads. The Chief Magistrate gripped the tiller hard and said — somewhat louder than was usual for him:

— Now pull!

The men struck their oars into the water. They were as though flogging the boat forward into this frothing death.

212

— Now — now — now — now — row — hard in — row — row — row! groaned an old man in time with the strokes. The Chief Magistrate steered the boat straight for the middle of the breaker, it rode up in the boiling sea, lurched and took water over both gunwales, while everything vanished in foam, froth and stinging salt rain. The Priest sat death pale and hung on tight. A tune was going round and round in his head. Might he fail to meet Barbara this evening after all?

Suddenly everything went still. They lay on a surface of foam, and rocked. The two men nearest the stern bailed, the rest pulled fiercely on their oars. The lull lasted only a moment. Then the Chief Magistrate called out:

— Now, hard as you can!

This time he shouted, and his voice broke. Before them a green wall of water rose up, it was breaking slowly and beginning to lace itself out deliberately in a wide and elaborate crown of foam and bubbles.

— In Jesus' name! said one of the lead men.

There was a sudden lull in the wind. They were in the lee of the wall of water that hung over them, they could see the green daylight through it, the oars creaked savagely against the thole pins. Then the boat reared and stood on end almost upright.

A prolonged sound of crashing thundered about them. The Priest felt the harsh, ice-cold water on his thighs, and he was blinded by foam. Koltur's stormy profile and Konufell, that giant stone organ, towering amid its vapours and smoking clouds, were the last things he saw. He felt a stinging, ice-cold pain, and exulted, amid a shower as of splintered glass, and he wondered, is this the end? So this is what it is like, he went on, and felt unburdened and free, but at the same moment he saw the stem thrust itself defiantly up out of the water, and all the men in the boat had sea-water streaming from their whiskers.

They tore the lids from their food boxes and emptied them of their contents and began to bail with them as though possessed. Samson bailed so manfully that he made an arch of water rise out of the boat, and when a young man from Sandavag in a half-crying voice said: — Jesus, we are lost! And what for? then Samson took time to roar: — Hold your jaw, chicken-heart, and bail!

All bailed and rowed and bailed again like madmen. Even the Chief Magistrate bailed, uncomfortable as his bulk was, and Pastor Paul, too, found a box to bail with. Water surged around their legs, flat-bread, dried lamb, knives, sheaths and other contents of the food boxes swam about, but the boat, that for a moment had lain as though dead, came to life again, the stem righted itself and began to shear into the waves once more and the Chief Magistrate bid them all pull now in God's name, then they might soon be away from all danger. In a few moments they had cleared the crest, just as a new chalk-white peak broke into bloom and spread itself out over the dark waters.

— Ah — you were afraid that time! Samson laughed, and laid his hand cheerfully on the shoulder of the young man whom he had shouted at. But Farmer Justinus, who was also in the boat, said quietly and solemnly to the Chief Magistrate: — That time I was sure we would founder.

— I thought the same, answered Samuel Mikkelsen. Troublesome place, that Lambatang.

— The Lord will not take us before his time, one of them said.

But the Priest was aware of the same tune, going round and round in his head. It had been there all the while. It was a minuet. He remembered it from the time when the French had danced on Tinganes.

Another snow-flurry came and hid everything, mountains and sea. The boat struggled farther out along the Streymoy coast. Like a fly on a tarred stick.

The breakers on the submerged skerry by Velbestad shone through the dusk when they at last came to them. The surf was running far up into the grass, there was no possibility of their coming ashore here. The Chief Magistrate tried at several places to come in, but had to give it up. Higher on land some men were walking and shouting something which could not be heard. More than half an hour passed this way, and gradually it became quite dark.

— Now I can see nothing to do but try to beach at Kirkjubour, said the Chief Magistrate.

214

This 'beaching' talk sounded bad. This was something only resorted to in case of distress at sea. To land twelve men high up at a place never intended for it went against Samuel Mikkelsen's sea-farer's grain. And the errand too! What will the Kirkjubour folk think of them, out here, paddling about like clowns on such a day — the Chief Magistrate too — to carry a desperate Priest whose wife had run away? Would it not be wiser to wait for Westfall, and for the sea to quiet down, and then set sail and run home with both wind and current at their backs? Nay, it would not do. The poor fellow must be put ashore somewhere on Streymoy or he will go out of his mind.

There were two sea-miles between Velbestad and Kirkjubour, dead into the gale. The Chief Magistrate's men rowed, groaned over their oars, gritted their teeth and leaned back in their benches with the full weight of their bodies. And the boat had to be bailed constantly. Samson's brow swelled. He made one more effort:

— Forth sailed the nobles ... from ... Norway!

But his voice was hoarse and his eyes dazed. They rowed in silence. Only a minuet went round and round in the Priest's despairing brain. Then — well on in the evening — the Chief Magistrate suddenly turned the boat into the lee of Kirkjubour Islet. They glimpsed, through the darkness, where they were — the looming great farm-house and the church ruin. Soon the boat was hauled, in good trim, up on shore, and Samuel Mikkelsen and his crew walked, quiet and dripping, into the farm-house, as sea-faring Faroe men often go — almost as though they were a little ashamed about this.

The Kirkjubour farmer received them with warm-hearted friendliness, and explained to Pastor Paul right away that here in this place, in days of old the bishop's seat of the Faroes had been. He pointed to the great cathedral, whose empty windows glared dismally in the darkness. But Pastor Paul was in no mood for antiquities, nor would he have dry clothes, he hardly gave himself time for a little supper. The farmer could not believe he meant seriously to go to Havn this evening, in this God's own storm and at night. But the Chief Magistrate took the farmer very gently aside and told him it was wasted effort to be talking with folk when this madness was on them.

This madness — the farmer understood. Ay, what could that woman not do! Now, today, she had all but been the deaths of twelve men besides — there could be no doubt about that. The Kirkjubour farmer stroked his white beard. He said nothing. Moreover it was not necessary; men like Samuel Mikkelsen and himself might well exchange thoughts without saying anything.

But there could be no arguing about one thing: if the Priest was *determined* he would go to Havn this evening he must have a good escort. The farmer sent his best mountain man with him. They must go over Reyn, *Kirkjuboreyn*. For there would be no swollen streams that way, no mud holes or swamps.

They struck out at once, each with a small horn lantern, whose weak circle of light fell on turf and stone. The Priest stepped forth quickly, he hurried impatiently on up the steep path. Only in the most difficult passages up the bluff did he let the farm-hand go ahead. A minuet was going round and round in his head, he was hardly conscious of it, he did not think, he was full of nothing but longing. Short of breath to the limit of endurance because of the steep climb, and hindered by one obstacle after another, on he went and on with the tune repeating itself inside him. It had become the theme of his distress, it led him onward as, like a sleepwalker, he clambered over Kirkjuboreyn's cyclopic bluff to the beginning of its great stony plateau.

— Now we must keep the path in sight, said his guide, for if we do not we are in a bad way in this darkness.

The path was an indistinct trampled down track that twisted over gravelly flats and among heaps of boulders. The farm-hand wanted to go forward cautiously, and he noted carefully every marker cairn they passed, but the Priest kept running ahead of him, and only by the glimmering of their horn lanterns did they find each other again. Then it happened that the Priest's lantern blew out in a gust. They were in the middle of an open flat place, that was scattered with big stones. Pastor Paul was not immediately aware of his mischance, he simply went on, wildly and as though in a stupor. Then he heard the farm-hand shout and saw that he was swinging his lantern. He had apparently climbed a high boulder. Pastor Paul turned and went towards the place, but then immediately the light went out. The shouts kept on and Pastor Paul shouted too. He ran blindly. And in this way the two men went about in the coal-black of the night, each with a lantern that had gone out, and shouted hopelessly at each other among the great boulders and shattered rock masses. The sounds of their voices were carried away in the noise of the gale. They did not find each other again. But Pastor Paul set a course as his half-asleep brain directed him, and he walked and fell and got up again and trudged on through chaotic fields of stones and great patches of scree without being able to see his hand in front of him.

Once, when he had come out on to a flat space, he suddenly heard a loud and steady hissing. Slowly this loud, sorrowful noise made its way into his consciousness, he stopped, and the dread that he had hitherto not for a moment felt crept slowly up into his heart. He ran for a piece, but always this note of whispering woe was beside him, to the left. Then the sky brightened a little, moonlight grew white under the clouds, and he could see that he was standing by a mountain lake. Its waves were hurrying onward, and washing against the empty stony shore. It was something alive that he had found here in the wasteland — an agitated lake, and all its passion was loneliness.

He hurried onward, the sky grew brighter and brighter, the half moon broke through the clouds, and Pastor Paul could see in the sharp, lingering rays of its light where he was: on a frozen sea of stones, a sea with great waves, a whelming surf of rock, and foam of sliding gravel. Boulders grinned at him; the rocks had such frightening forms that a panic terror seized him and he ran as though for his life.

He ran for a long while. But at last the land sloped down a bank into a softer earth bottom, and when he stumbled he no longer bruised himself, but immediately he felt wetness come through his clothing. He waded through swamps and stood at last by a lone house in which a candle was burning. When, out of breath, he knocked on the door he became conscious of the minuet and knew that it had been going round and round in his head all the while that he had been running and moaning and groaning and — who knows? — perhaps howling.

He asked as soon as he came in where was he and where was the way to Havn, but then the words came suddenly to a halt in his throat. For, round about him in this hearth-room, he saw nothing but dreadfully ravaged or idiotic faces, and all stared, gaping and foolish, at him.

— Lord Jesus! said a man with a chalk-white face at last. His voice had an unreal melodiousness. — Lord Jesus, he repeated. This is the hospital! The hospital at Argir!

— The leper hospital, burst out Pastor Paul, and his knees went weak.

— Ay, bless your heart, the leper hospital! came the voice of a man who sat like a beast and gnawed at something over a feeding-trough. There was a foul smell in the room that Pastor Paul found suffocating. It was all a nightmare.

The pale man with the melodious voice said that he would see the Priest on his way. Sand River was not so easy to go over this evening, he would show him the proper crossing.

— There is a comedy in Havn this evening, said he. He looked very knowledgeable, and talked much and at length in his mild-tempered way. They met someone in the dark. — That is one of the patients, he explained. They walk and roam about around here, but they are not allowed to be among people. And he explained that it was no pleasure for him to be one of the patients. But no-one would have him in the house, though he had only a light case of the disease.

He went on talking, full of knowledge and unhappiness, until they came to the roaring Sand River, whose swollen eddies tumbled in the moonlight. Here the Priest thanked him for his company and got well beyond the river.

His heart was beginning to thump dreadfully, for now he was quite near to Havn. He could already see lights here and there, yes, and now he would see Barbara again. He could not think beyond that moment. She was sure to be at the comedy ... so there would be no possibility of having a talk with her. He went breathlessly on. He and the minuet.

He passed the houses on the edge of town and remembered the afternoon only five months earlier when he had taken flight past here with Barbara. Every house was shut and empty. Nyggjustova too was in darkness, nobody was at home. Pastor Paul trudged on through Gongin with his blown-out lantern.

In the Council Chamber there was light and festivity, and a crowd of people. The first his eye fixed on when he stepped in was the Judge, who was solemnly sitting and bowing a violin, and giving forth a *douce* music. He sat down in a place at the back and in another place at the back a group stood and snickered, among them Gabriel, big and portly, in a shining new bright red tail coat. It dawned on Pastor Paul that he in a way recognized the scene, but he was dropping with weariness, and with the deadly thumping of his heart. Then it came to him — it was, of course, *Jeppe on the Hill*, and Gabriel must be Baron Nilus. For in a large bed in the middle of the space lay Andreas Heyde, pretending that he was trying to control himself and saying, in a drunkard's voice: — But can I be dreaming? It seems that I am not. I shall try pinching myself in the arm; if it does not hurt, then I am dreaming, if it does hurt, then I am not dreaming ...

At that moment Pastor Paul's eye saw Barbara in the midst of the crowd. She went out of the hall; he thought she must want to get away from him, and he followed after her. But she was standing in the entrance and waiting.

— Ah, my sweetest, she cried: are you out of your mind? Are you quite out of your mind?

Her voice was almost tearful with concern, she felt his torn and soaking wet clothing and stroked his face: Are you quite mad?

— Barbara, I have come ... to you, stammered Pastor Paul, brokenly.

— Have you come to me? She spoke as though to a child, and a gladness began to bubble up in her voice. But how in the world did you come in this weather? Dearest! Did you come by Kirkjubour? You must be mad!

She seized him fast by the arm: — Come! Come home, my dear!

She twined her hand down around his and seized it and clasped it lovingly with her other hand and led him, meanwhile, through Gongin, and supported him and pressed her whole body against his and looked quickly and shyly up at him many times and beamed. But Pastor Paul, all the while, carried in his left hand the blown-out lantern.

She took him into Nyggjustova, lit candles, helped him off with his clothes and gave him something to eat, and she did all this with a quiet good will, a submissive zeal, that he had never known in her before. It was as balm to his soul. But while he, slowly and as though in his sleep, was eating the food, he brought himself to ask her:

— Are you — in love with him?

Barbara immediately became serious. She looked down and said, hurriedly:

— Ay.

That is to say she whispered rather, she all but did not say it at all, she hardly breathed it, it was so quick ... it *was* undeniably 'ay' but it could almost have sounded like 'nay.' Her eyes were full of contrition.

Then there was a pause, after which she asked: — Paul, may I drink a little of your beer?

She took the mug, drank a little, handed it back to him and said: — Now, you drink too! You must be very thirsty.

Pastor Paul drank and was again as though revived. He felt it as a caress through the dulness of his fatigue.

— I am glad that you are with me again, said Barbara, suddenly humble. She looked down.

Pastor Paul was no longer in despair. Yet it all seemed to be something he was dreaming. He ate quietly, ate till he was full.

— Now you must surely go to bed, said Barbara.

Pastor Paul went to bed.

— Shall I sit by you till you fall asleep? asked Barbara, persuasively: Shall I?

Pastor Paul felt desire stir in him. New discontent, new uneasiness.

— Barbara, what is to become of me? he asked, in a subdued tone.

— Ay, but sweetheart! she broke out, in her most sympathetic treble, crying and laughing at the same time. There was a tremor in her throat. She sat on the edge of the bed and bent over him: — You must not be so unhappy, do you hear! She made her tone very intimate: — I shall tell you something; you have no reason to be unhappy, none at all. No hint of a reason! I feel about you exactly as I did. As always. That is very truth!

She gave him a hurried look. Her eyes were still full of bashfulness, contrition and a droll fearfulness. She had put her hands in under his shoulders and was playing convulsively on his back with all ten fingers. She was triste and comical, blushing in shame-faced anticipation.

Pastor Paul was very tired, his thoughts moved slowly. But he took hold of her and pulled her to him, and suddenly he was aware of how fully she was responding to him. A joyfulness welled up in his breast, an overwhelming tide rose slowly and flushed him all through with elation. Dear heaven! He had been granted everything, yes, she was helping him moreover, undressing herself with meek haste and lying beside him. He saw her eyes right close to him, green as the deep sea, every time she glanced up at him; her face was unrecognizable, not beautiful, doting with rapture.

Ah, ah, ah — all that he had endured, suffered and fought through, it had all only happened so that they two should know this moment of incomprehensible union. Ah — she was compensating for Mykines, for the cold ashes in the earth at Jansagerd, for the sore distress at Steigargard, for the peril under Konufell, for the terrifying wastes of Kirkjuboreyn, for the lepers at Argir ... and for the minuet, plin-plan-plon! Ha ha ha! Barbara was rewarding Pastor Paul, she was submissive to him, she was loving to him, she exulted in ecstasy with him, while the Havn folk were on their ways home from the comedy ... yes, half the night through.

He fell asleep as one drowned in a tide of joy, and Barbara's eyes still sparkled sea-green as he drifted away from her.

16
China

Pastor Paul was beginning to waken, but he lay for a long while before he was conscious of anything. Then he came suddenly to himself with a violent beating of his heart and immediately he remembered Barbara. There she lay beside him! Yes, it was true, all was well, there had been no such betrayal as he had believed. He gave a released, a disburdened sigh, his heart beat again at its good footpace. Pranced, rather, like a horse that has been retired from work and loosed into a green meadow. He turned over and went to sleep again.

When he awoke a second time it was almost daylight. Barbara opened her eyes, stared at him confusedly at first and then recognized him with great delight. She put her arms around him and kissed him.

I am glad you have come, said she, and looked shamefaced and a little foolish. She played shyly with his shirt button.

Pastor Paul said he was glad too, he could not remember that he had ever been as happy as last evening.

— Nay, was it not good? said Barbara, eagerly: Never, ever, have we both been so blissfully happy! Do you know what it makes me think of? Do you remember that time in Leynum?

She lowered her eyes and pressed herself in close to him.

— But how about ...? said Pastor Paul, then broke off immediately. Laughter, an enormous laughter, all at once filled his being, yes the horse that his heart had become ran a gleeful gallop around his green pasture. Ah, Andreas Heyde! thought he. Ah ha ha! But he would not let his pleasure be seen, and not a sound did he utter.

Yet Barbara had understood him so well that she quickly, and almost as though in a fright, broke out: — You must not talk about this to a soul, do you hear. It is a secret between us. Ah, I cannot think how desperate he would be if he knew about it.

She stared thoughtfully in front of her and paid no further attention to her husband.

Pastor Paul lay without a word for a long while. His heart's horse stood still, and behaved as though it had become frightened. This mention of Andreas Heyde was the first he had heard from her, and the tone of voice in which she spoke was quite strange to him.

— Barbara, are you regretful? he asked.

— Ach, nay, dearest, said she, and smiled at him. But then straightway she began to stare again, as though she was seeing a vision.

— I am so afraid he has drunk himself senseless! she said. He was certainly drunk last evening.

She gave a little shiver.

— *I* was drunk the evening before last, said Pastor Paul.

— Were you? said Barbara, absently, and went on staring.

Pastor Paul did not know whether he was angry or unhappy, he turned away from his wife. She was in love with Andreas Heyde! But that was no other than he had known all the while, indeed what she had said herself. Had he thought for a moment that it might be otherwise? Had he perhaps come here to fetch her back to Jansagerd? Had he truly been such a fool? No, he remembered well what he had thought. If he could only *once* more, one single time.

Well, then, he had accomplished his errand, accomplished it with vigour and flourish. What more did he ask? Yet *another* time?

— Why have you turned your back on me? asked Barbara. There was a hint of injury in her tone. Pastor Paul felt happier and made no answer.

— What a sour one you are! she whispered in his ear.

He turned towards her again and smiled.

—I am not sour, said he. I was just thinking. You are in love with someone else and I know that I am in your way. I shall not try to hinder you at all, for I would gain nothing by it. But then I must put you out of my thoughts and forget you entirely. Does it not seem so to you?

Barbara did not answer, she shook her head helplessly, hardly enough to be noticed but enough that Pastor Paul could see. She was very serious, her eyes were full of a great distress.

—Yes, but Barbara, Pastor Paul continued, since you now ... since it is no longer me that you are fond of.

—You must know how fond I am of you, said Barbara. That you *must* have understood! If not, what happened last night would have been out of the question, not to be thought of! You have no reason to ... between us everything is as it was! Do you not *understand* that?

She spoke with fierce urgency, she took him by the wrist and let her hands slide up inside his sleeves. The she added all at once, in a lighter tone: — If you had not gone away from me. Then nothing at all would have happened!

She smiled happily over this find that she had made, this little coloured stone. She believed it herself: We two should only have lived here together in Havn, perhaps? I cannot thrive in the villages. Now you must stay here for many days, — must you not, my dearest?

A full hour later Pastor Paul was on his way to the Judge's place, satisfied, but hardly comforted. His wife had gone to Andreas Heyde. He might well be in need of her visit, poor chap. Pastor Paul granted him this, ah yes! One must be magnanimous to one's enemy. He had already fixed a fine horn in his forehead. But why should he be a unicorn? One horn was no horn! No, it must be a *pair* of horns ... at least. Pastor Paul tormented himself with this line of thought. Was he already one of those — a libertine? Alas, the thoughts were swarming furiously in his head today, he was in a strange mood, miserable, ardent and proud. He let himself sink into one of the Judge's chairs, threw off his hat and said: — Yes, a man has now succeeded in being his own wife's paramour! And another man has succeeded in being his own cuckold's cuckold! Which do you think is worse?

A light came into Johan Hendrik Heyde's cheerful, lined face, he came to life at once, he sat up, put his book aside, rubbed the tip of his nose with his finger and said: — Now then, that is what I call a jovial way of looking at things!

Then he screwed himself up in his chair and supported his chin in one hand.

— Pshaw! Ordinarily one would say that the husband is the only one who can be a true cuckold, because he is the only one who is married to the woman in the case. His own cuckold's cuckold a man can not be, because ...

— Ah, you see things too legally altogether, Pastor Paul broke in. It is only before God and man that Barbara is my married wife. In her heart she is another's woman. The other is therefore the true cuckold because he is the one who ...? Do you not think so yourself ... that they are much in love?

— Ach, ay, too much in love altogether, sighed Johan Hendrik. Andreas is not lifting a finger, though he is capable of great things. Imagine — appointed by the Exchequer! That was a great mistake.

— Yes, I agree. A great mistake indeed! laughed Pastor Paul, inordinately, with a knife-sharp pang in his heart: — In the highest degree, a mistake, ha ha!

The Judge looked at him intently.

— Ay, said he, now you find yourself in dangerous waters, as I knew you would. You seem to be taking it well ... hm, how shall I put it? To be taking the rough seas well.

— I am in a stormy passion, said Pastor Paul. In a desperate passion! And yet an exultant passion. I would never have believed that I could house so many strong feelings at once.

— Ha Ha! Ay, so I thought. Then it may be that the good Lord has not poured his misfortunes on you in vain! But as yet you are only in the first stage.

— I well remember what you said to me when we were last together. That people who encounter the true grace are those whom Fate takes hold of and plays as though upon an instrument.

225

— Ay, provided that these people are fine instruments and not reeds, or firebrands, or woolgatherers.

— God's death, I am an instrument! said Pastor Paul. A wind instrument! And the Lord blows me powerfully! Like a whistle, an entirely worthless whistle.

— Now, now, you may not be a bassoon, and moreover you must guard against being a trumpet. Johan Hendrik gave an ironic smile: — But a woodwind, ay, let us say a woodwind. A trifle monotonous it may seem at times, yet it is the sweetest.

He stood suddenly and paced energetically up and down the floor.

— The important thing, he continued, standing before Pastor Paul: the important thing is that one should have a temperament that does not give in to but is inspired by misfortune. Desperation and rage are the best winds to sail by, if only one understands that. But do not sail too close-hauled! One *can* capsize. I assume that you will commit one folly after another, eh? But whatever you do, keep yourself from killing my nephew.

— I assure you, said Pastor Paul, that I have almost a colleague's affection for him.

— But how long will that last?

Pastor Paul immediately felt the truth in this query. At that moment Barbara was with Andreas. She had promised to come home this evening ...

— Will you play a little? he asked the Judge.

— I shall be glad to play a little for you. It will, unfortunately, only be solo! I am perforce almost always a solo performer. It is never so *agitato* as, for example, trio.

He gave a wry smile at the Priest and played a long, quavering trill. Pastor Paul felt an intoxication, he was miserable, yet ardent, the music filled him with fire.

Was he to storm and chafe the whole day?

Pastor Paul had taken up much of the Judge's time before he could persuade himself to go. Barbara had promised that she would come home this evening, but it was a long while yet till evening. A fearsome loneliness bore in on him, and gnawed his heart, while he

226

wandered through the narrow, winter-sombre lanes. He met a man whose face he thought he had seen before, but where? The man greeted him as someone familiar. He encountered many folk whom he remembered as though from a dream. They all greeted him familiarly. He thought no more of this, but when he came back to Nyggjustova, Magdalena, his mother-in-law, said to him: — Some Kirkjubour men have been here asking for you. They wanted to know if you had come all the way. They were looking for you with lanterns on Reyn last night.

She spoke sullenly and with her usual sour reproachfulness. Pastor Paul's only answer was, Oh! It came into his head at that moment that he should pay his colleague, the Havn priest, a visit. He was not fond of Master Wenzel, yet he was drawn towards his house. One never knew what might happen in that house. He did not think out his intention in going there. But he was in the grip of despair.

Pastor Wenzel received him with some reservations on Heaven's account, and with many kinds of reproachfulness on his family's account. He said nothing directly, but it was clear that he considered Pastor Paul answerable for the scandal that emanated from his wife, and that had now cast its net over the Heyde family. He had a look of unassuageable injury. Moreover the sick and the sorrowful were awaiting his visit — so many were suffering *undeserved* distress, he asked his pastor colleague to excuse him, and out he went. But his wife would be at home and would see that he was given a modest cup of coffee.

— Perhaps it is not a cup of coffee you want so much, after all, said she, when Master Wenzel had departed. Perhaps you would prefer a glass of French brandy, or rum?

For the first time in his life Pastor Paul took in Mme Anna Sophia Heyde properly, and he responded to her at once. She was big, bright and gentle, and there was an intimacy in all her ways that comforted him somewhat. Ach, the little horse in his heart! It immediately felt the touch as it were of a caressing and soothing hand. He straightway made up his mind that he too would be intimate, and open his sorrow to Anna Sophia. He longed, he thirsted for her womanly friendship. He had been so lonely, yes ever since he had arrived in these islands! Barbara had not been his friend, he perceived that at once. She had been his opponent, indeed his enemy, and quite on his own he had had to play against her. Now he longed to talk with a friend — about his enemy, his enemy ...

Anna Sophia looked at him thoughtfully, and in a friendly way.

— This much power you have over her nevertheless, said she. I paid good heed to what happened during the comedy last evening!

Pastor Paul felt a secret pleasure. — There were many others who did too, he remarked.

— Not everyone, not everyone, laughed Anna Sophia.

— So?

— Not Jeppe. She drew a deep sigh and shook her head: — Ah — Andreas! He was much too sure of himself. And when he was quite done with playing Jeppe he had got so drunk that he did not miss her at all. Not until this morning ...

— Is he so negligent of her, then? asked Pastor Paul. He was suddenly downcast.

— Negligent ... I do not know what I should say. Not always, at any rate. He can be *empressé* enough, the good Andreas. And then no-one can hold out against him.

— Ah, yes! said Pastor Paul, and twisted his face as though in pain. I know it well, he understands the art. *Négligeant* sometimes, next *empressé*. Barbara is the same. Believe me, I know how it must be done ... Only I do not do it!

He stared glumly down on to the table top. Nothing hurt him so, as knowing that Andreas could be neglectful towards Barbara and yet be loved by her.

— Take comfort, said Anna Sophia. This game never goes quite by the rules, just the same.

— Ah, yes, he who can be most *négligeant* wins, said Pastor Paul, dispirited.

— Ha ha, you are like all men! You have no idea how we women love to cheat! Barbara especially! She cheats all the time, dear God, dear God! What do you think, now, was that according to the rules, what she did last evening? You did not look so *négligeant* when you walked in on the comedy, ha ha! You looked as though you had been dug up out of the churchyard. Heavens ... and yet she went with you!

Anna Sophia shook her head in admiration.

228

— That was only out of pity, said Pastor Paul, though in a questioning tone.

— Nay, it was in ... ay, in womanliness! She is a lovely nature! Ah, if one might be like her! Mind you ... we other women all love her ... though we ought to envy her. And that is saying much!

Anna Sophia laughed. Pastor Paul said nothing. He sat and burned with longing for Barbara: he emptied his glass and she alone was in his thoughts. He desired her so that it hurt in every bone. He had slept with her last night, and that was more than he could believe. But it was even more improbable that she would come back to him this evening. Yet — she had promised. Alas, he had no faith in that. And yet he did have faith in it, and his feelings were in the most terrible turmoil.

— Where is she? he asked.

— Not here — you may be sure of that. She never shows herself here. Andreas we see little of too. They have haunts of their own ...

Pastor Paul felt as though he was in a landslide of disappointment and dismay. He realized that he had all along assumed that they were here, somewhere in Reynagard. A foolish assumption. Now, in a moment, he felt as though she had slipped right through his fingers. She had her secret ways.

— She is full of lies! he burst out suddenly.

Anna Sophia shrugged her shoulders a little.

— All women are. We have to be. You must not think badly of us for that! When a woman lies it is not the same as when a man lies. Nay, we are another kind.

— I have lost Barbara, said Pastor Paul.

— One never loses Barbara, said Anna Sophia with a smile. But on the other hand one never quite has her. If you could understand that, you could perhaps take it all calmly.

— Yes, that is how she is, said Pastor Paul, angrily. She wants to gobble up everything! She wants to have Andreas, but that does not mean at all that she will give me up. She will never give up any man! Never mind, she will have to choose — in this case!

— She will not be constrained — not by any means.

— I shall not constrain her, but it may be that I shall give her a kick — into hell, as far as a hare can jump in fourteen years!

Pastor Paul stood up. He was beginning to see black.

— She will come back to you again, said Anna Sophia, quietly.

— Do you mean that ... are you serious?

Pastor Paul suddenly became a different man.

— That is as good as certain. I think I understand Barbara, you can surely trust me a little. But now you must take it calmly — you have your life to live! And do not forget either that there are other women in the world.

She stood up and as it were stretched her body a little; she was big and blonde and gentle and ready to smile. Pastor Paul perceived this gesture as a ray of light through the fog and remembered it always — in the way that one has of remembering quite insignificant moments.

He was a little tipsy when he at last broke away from Reynagard. He might well have sat and talked forever about Barbara if the twilight had not reminded him that evening was coming on. Fearful excitement and impatience were beginning to seize his heart, but he was helpless and could do nothing but wait. Here he sat in Nyggju-stova, Barbara's home, as one who belonged to the house. But Barbara, where was she?

His mother-in-law, Magdalena, made supper and vouchsafed him hardly a word. When he hinted that Barbara must be expected soon, she merely put on an ineffably incredulous look.

— But where can she be, then? he asked.

— Do you imagine that *I*, said Magdalena, bitterly, do you imagine that *I* know about her ways or her friends, ever? She is my daughter, that I cannot deny, and I have tried to bring her up as well as I could. But now I wash my hands, Pastor Paul, that is what I have always given you to understand, I wash my hands.

Time passed, and loneliness rode Pastor Paul like a nightmare. Every now and again he thought he could hear someone at the door-latch, and in these moments he was filled with such expectancy that he could see Barbara's shape before him and hear her glittering voice.

— Dearest! Have you waited long? Are you angry with me?

But Barbara did not come, and the weak slap of her mother's game of patience was the only real noise to be heard.

Pastor Paul could not keep still. He went out.

— Say that I have gone down to the Bailie's place, he said to his mother-in-law.

She answered him with a sarcastic nod, and sighed. And began a new game.

Gabriel was cosily smoking a long-stemmed clay pipe. His wife, Suzanne, sat and rocked the little Augustus. Bailie Harme himself had gone to bed, by degrees he had become very frail. But his daughter — it was striking how well she looked, even Pastor Paul could not help noticing this. A fine new radiance had come over her smiling lips and teeth, and there was a roguishness in her eyes that broadened like sunshine whenever she looked at her son. She was an exquisite, dark beauty, and Gabriel was smoking his pipe and displaying such smugness about her that Pastor Paul could fairly hear him say: — Ay, look at *that*, my friend! That is how an intelligent man makes out!

Suzanne, who was sitting by the window and rocking her son, began to sing:

> From my window go, dear man,
> Come another time again:
> Storm and cold, they have driven
> My husband home again.

— What the deuce kind of damned drivel are you sitting and singing to the young one? said Gabriel, annoyed.

Suzanne merely turned her roguish eyes towards her husband and went on singing:

> I am not allowed to sing
> For my child
> As I shall
> And as I can
> And as I will!
> From my window go, dear man,
> Come another time again:
> Storm and cold, they have driven ...

Gabriel walked out — rather suddenly. He made a tour round the Bailie's place. It may, of course, have been on some call of nature that he did so. Suzanne laughed. It was just a well-known cradle song that she had sung. But it was not known to Gabriel. It had never been sung at his cradle.

His good humour had half soured when he came in again. He asked bluntly where Barbara — he begged pardon, Mme Aggersoe! — might be this evening. Pastor Paul answered that she was out but he expected her home soon.

— Pish! exclaimed Gabriel, with a snicker. You will have a long wait!

Pastor Paul had no answer for this, but Gabriel continued in a voice that trembled with scorn: — Never in my life have I known anything so simple-minded as your marriage with her last summer.

Both Suzanne and Pastor Paul were taken aback by Gabriel's manner. He was almost in tears. Malice, anger and old pain twisted themselves together in his voice.

— Let us not speak of Barbara now, said Suzanne, warily.

— Speak about her! Is Pastor Paul not allowed to speak about his own wife, perhaps?

He turned towards Pastor Paul: — I do not know how much you mean to put up with. If I were in your place, then ... God, what impudence! I can easily arrest her for you, if you wish it. And her gallant with her!

— Arrest her? said Pastor Paul. And — and make myself a laughing-stock?

— You are already a laughing-stock, in the devil's name! You could not be more so. Do you want to be Pastor Niels over again? Ay — even worse? She has not ever been so madly lecherous and shameless under all our noses as now! It stares out of her wherever she goes, wherever she is. She is such ... she is such ... a ... a scandal, ptui! And then ... ay, God help us! ... last evening to run off with you, as though nothing had been going on! Ha ha ha, ay, the devil damn me if you are not more gullible ...

— What a busybody you are, Gabriel! said Suzanne, short and sharp. She was red in the face with anger.

— Busy! Busy! It has perhaps not occurred to you that it is my and your father's ... duty and calling to watch over ... over morality, no less! Is it not? But of course! of course! Your sweet housewifely duty is as usual to be on the side of the tart, the whore, the hussy, and invite her in for coffee ... while I am out!

Pastor Paul could think of nothing to say. He was weary, humiliated and despairing, and he had all too clear a picture of how Barbara had lived and shone in this superficial world, while he had been weather-fast on Mykines.

Gabriel went out and came back in again with a flask of brandy in one hand and Christian V's *Norse Law* in the other. With magisterial gravity he laid the heavy tome on the table, asked his wife to bring a glass, filled it and offered it. Pastor Paul drank it straight down, he did so in his need and without dignity. It was the only thing he could do. He could think of nothing to say.

— Let us see, now, said Gabriel, and began to leaf over the pages. Let us see now, what the law says ... m m m m ...

He spat on his fingers and turned with an unaccustomed hand. He was not many months old in the law. — Here it says ... here it says ... let us see now. Homicide. Maiming and wounding, nay. Challenge and duelling. Domestic peace, Church peace, nay. Mischief, risky venture. Nay. He was sweating. Self-defence, nay. On ... on loose behaviour!

He shouted this last, and then snickered: — Indeed, that *is* a good one! A priest's wife! Let us see here: Whoever lies with a woman shall pay her family 24 pieces of silver and the woman 12 pieces of silver and both shall be publicly confessed.

He snickered again. — But if they have no means to make payment — God knows they have none, ha! She has none, in any case! — then they shall be punished in accordance with their means by imprisonment of their persons! But in case they marry each other, then he pays by way of fine four and a half pieces of silver and she half so much and they shall be excused the confession ...

The Priest stiffened and Gabriel too looked the least bit doubtful. But then he said: — Now, this only has to do with unmarried folk. I thought as much, it was far too mild!

He emptied his glass. — There must be an article about married women here — about adultery, I mean! Let me see ... it would not be too much if she were given one whipping at the post, would it?

Pastor Paul stood up. His feelings were in the most violent turmoil. — I do not want her to be punished, I do not want that at all — he stammered, badly: no revenge, none! Though she has ... she has cost me ...

He stood and leaned against the back of a chair and the chair trembled under his hands.

— For there is also this, he went on, at last, and suddenly got control of himself in the notion: I mean, perhaps she will come to a better state of mind.

He uttered these last words despairingly. He began to pace back and forth.

— So she will, just wait and see, said Suzanne, in an unusually agitated tone of conviction.

— Ay, that she will surely do! said Gabriel, sarcastically, between the reading of two paragraphs.

— Well, you will not make her better by whipping her! said Suzanne, fiercely, and stood up with fire in her eyes.

— Be quiet, answered Gabriel, reading eagerly. There is no certainty that there is authority here for whipping her. There is all sorts of other twaddle here. But good God — how she would deserve it!

He leaned back in his chair. — A proper flogging at the post! The day that happens ...

— You are just giving yourself away, you miserable ... said Suzanne through her clenched teeth.

Gabriel looked rather abashed and drank a glass. — I only mean that she deserves a thrashing, that is what I mean, said he.

— What *business* is it of yours, hissed Suzanne. What *business* is it? Here is Pastor Paul standing here, he is the one whose business it is, first of all. He can punish her himself, if he wants to.

Pastor Paul had been sitting crumpled up on the edge of the chair.

— Yes, I do want to! said he. But his voice was strange, and it sounded as though he was swallowing something.

— Have a glass, said Gabriel. Please! Now then, why the devil not give her a beating as all other men do when their wives will not behave themselves? But perhaps you are like Pastor Niels, he would rather be beaten himself!

— If I could get my hands on her! said Pastor Paul, and took a very deep breath. He could feel the anger rise up through his body. He was beginning to see black.

— That would not be difficult, said Gabriel.

— When I do not know where she is?

— Ha! But that is what I can tell you. She and her gallant are holed up together in 'China'.

— Gabriel! cried Suzanne, loudly.

Pastor Paul drank another glass. The anger rose from his bowels and his loins up through his breast and out along his arms. He clenched his fists hard and sighed, softly. His face was chalk-white and stony.

— You will do no good by punishing her, Suzanne cried, suddenly. She spoke in tears, scolding and pleading: You will do no good, Pastor Paul, you will just harden her. I *know* that! I know her! Her mother used to thrash her — oh! The time the sister and brother from Stakkanes committed incest, she herself took her over to the Fort and had her watch the beheading! And afterwards — so that she would never forget — she dragged her home and gave her such a spanking that the whole town could hear it! And you can see, you can see, what kind of fruit that bore! You *can not* punish her, you can indeed *not* punish her, that will be foolishness, i-di-o-tic, that is what it will be! Idiots! Idiots!

But Pastor Paul was seeing black and red. He could already hear Barbara's shriek sound over the whole town, her glittering falsetto break into a wail and shatter like a tower of crystal! He wanted violence and revenge, he seized his stick, Gabriel took the flask and out they both went.

— Idiots! cried and scolded Suzanne after them. Idiots! Little Augustus Gabrielsen Harme woke up and began to cry too.

'China' was a little house where the Royal Stores' seamen would put up when they lay over in Havn. The place had no very good reputation, less on account of the bootlegging that went on there than for certain other causes. At one side of 'China' proper was another smaller house which was a kind of annex, and which fronted on the cabbage and vegetable garden on the west slope of Reyn. Andreas had rented this annex in order to pursue, in its privacy, what were known as his studies. His purposes had, to be sure, been marked at the beginning by some seriousness, but they soon gave evidence that the muses thrived poorly in such near neighbourhood with Bacchus and Venus. Since the New Year, however, Bacchus had not enjoyed such good times, and the course of Andreas' life might have seemed, to those who could not see very well, to have become almost grave.

Pastor Paul and Gabriel stumbled their way out of Gongin into the pitch dark and steep stair-passage that was called Klettaskot. They were both in the grip of an overpowering, terrible anger. Pastor Paul wanted to strike, beat and smash the gallant, Barbara and whomsoever else came in his righteous path. Gabriel had more ambitious plans, he wanted to take by surprise, discover and call down a devil's own scandal and shame on their sinful carryings-on, take them and deliver them over in *flagrante delicto* to the scorn of the people, and settle up with them as a guardian of order. Nevertheless he found that both Pastor Paul and he needed to fortify themselves a little before they got down to work. They stopped, drank to each other from the flask, wished each other every success, and were full of brotherhood. A little narrow stairway led downward to 'China' and the other house. But Gabriel wanted them first to make a flanking movement, and he went around behind by way of the cabbage garden. There he could see that a light was shining in the room.

— Ha! We have them! he snickered, and crept up to the window.

A curtain was pulled across it, but he could peer in through the opening at the bottom. Pastor Paul was beside himself with anger. He recognized the curtain from Jansagerd — Barbara had given it to him to hang on his study window.

— They are not lying down yet, whispered Gabriel, pale with disappointment.

He turned towards Pastor Paul, his face half lighted by the light from inside the room. He peered in again: — But *he* is not wearing shoes. Perhaps they are ready to get into bed now ... wait!

He shifted his position to better contemplate what was going on there. But Pastor Paul would not wait, he went round the house to the door, and when he found it locked he began to hammer on it and kick it and shout.

— Open up, for the devil's skin and bones!

Gabriel was beside him in three bounds.

— Hell and damnation! he hissed: now you have spoiled everything! Now we can prove absolutely nothing on them!

— I will smash them! I will smash them! shrieked Pastor Paul, in a crazed voice.

He broke in a little window with his stick. But the door withstood all his assaults.

— Let me! said Gabriel and began to work at the wooden latch with his knife.

The Priest went on kicking. The noise resounded in the night-empty quarter, windows and doors began to half open, a whole gathering of folk in shifts, wool petticoats and all sorts of intimate clothing, barelegged and in wooden clogs, stood with chattering teeth, ready to run behind every cover, while dogs barked and roosters flew down from their perches and crowed. But the core, the very infection in this uproar was always the Priest's altered voice, cursing and scolding.

Suddenly the door flew open — Gabriel had worked the bolt free. Pastor Paul ran into the dark hearth-room and fell over something, but got right up on his feet again, Gabriel behind him; they went in to the lighted inner room — it was empty. The window was open and out in the cabbage garden fleeing footsteps could be heard. Gabriel looked about with a rapid glance, then in a jump he was out of the window. He was like a ball of energy, everything snapped and crunched under his feet.

Back in the room stood Pastor Paul — with the scent of Barbara in his nostrils, that well-known intimate emanation from her many

237

small things, her clothes, her doings. Yes, Barbara's spirit was at home here! He recognized one of her skirts, that lay thrown down over the bed, a pair of her shoes, her small boxes and caskets, and in the middle of the table — the inkhorn from Jansagerd, his own good inkhorn, which she had given him as a present when he came to Vagar! A great quill stood and curved up from it, and in front of it was a piece of paper, written on. And now he saw other things that he recognized — music-paper, a lute and many of the manly and gallant things that had been unpacked, once, from Andreas Heyde's chest.

He stood a long while fixed to the spot. Right to the farthest out part of his body he was burning in his distress. He supported himself against the table-top, gasped for air, groaned and even whimpered now and again.

— Foxes have holes! he stammered out at last, dully and drunkenly. Foxes have holes.

Before him lay a piece of writing. He read it several times without being able to gather the least meaning from it. The Faroes, it said, are a little group of small islands, lying fully ... miles west of the coast of Norway and ... miles ... of Shetland. The northernmost tip of the islands Captain ... has established as ... degrees Latitude north and ... degrees Longitude west, their southernmost tip ...

Here Andreas Heyde's great work on the Faroes, written by order of the Royal Exchequer, came to a temporary halt. Pastor Paul did not laugh. It merely dawned on him that these lines were written in this room, in the glow of Barbara's tender proximity, and suddenly he took the paper, crumpled it together and threw it on the floor. Then he grasped the lute by the finger-board, swung it round, went out to the hearth-room and broke it in pieces against the edge of the hearth. The strings sang out, rattled and then fell silent. It was a kind of murder. Pastor Paul threw the pieces of the instrument on the fire and heaped the coals up among them. Then he gathered all the music-paper and set it alight, and he brought Barbara's skirt, her hussif, curtains and inkhorn to join them. A nauseating smoke began to fill the house.

Gabriel came in, puffing and cursing softly. He had given up the chase. But Andreas had stuck one of his feet into a dunghill. Gabriel

238

snickered bitterly: he had heard it clearly, and it was a source of triumph for him. He was quite drunk now. It was a few moments before he understood what Pastor Paul was really up to. But then he said, forcefully: — Here, stop this ravaging! I am an official, I can have no part of it. You are drunk, man!

And with that he stumbled out. But first he picked up the crumpled manuscript. He hardly knew himself that he was doing it. His action was almost instinctive. He was a hound for bits of document.

Pastor Paul had ravaged the whole place. His eyes were glazed and witless, his lower jaw hung open. He was beginning to carry the bed-straw in big bunches out on to the hearth. Feverish and sweating he went into the red glare of the fire like a harvester who was harvesting the hay from scandal's couch.

— Foxes have holes ...!

The neighbours watched in consternation as the sparks poured through 'China''s smoke-hole and flew upwards. The crowd grew bigger and bigger, but none dared go in to this crazed man, who was breaking chairs and benches in pieces and throwing them on the fire.

— Foxes have holes!

Then came the *watch*. They were Constable Niels, Niels of the Field, Shrimp, Ole Atten, Rebekka's Poul and the Hinker, all with maces and swords, but otherwise in wooden clogs or tattered half-boots, and not very military in appearance. Yet they were officers of law and order, and their weapons rang as they came down the narrow steps to 'China'. They were rather abashed to be encountering the Vagar priest as an arsonist, but Constable Niels was a punctilious man who always understood his duty. Nor did the soldiers meet any opposition from the poor distraught priest. He followed them willingly.

— Foxes have holes ...! he rasped, as he tumbled into the Corps de Garde's black cellar.

17
Nul ne mérite

L et me, said Barbara, I can reach down much deeper.
And so she did, her arms were bare, they flickered white
through the wavering sea-water. She had a knife in her one hand, and
with it she cut loose a limpet, sucked fast against the steeply-sloping
sea bottom. The shell rolled slowly through the water down into her
other hand.

— For you, said she, and drew her wet arms up out of the water.
Her face was hot, and she was breathless, but her hands were red and
somewhat numb from the cold of the water.

— You are a water nymph, said Andreas. An oceanid!

They were lying out over the black rock at the edge of the sea
below the Fort and collecting limpets. They used them for bait, as in
these summer evenings they would often sit with their rods and lines
and catch red cod and pollock, for boiling and frying.

— Nay, let me rather! said Barbara again, and reached eagerly
down into the water. Your sleeves get in the way!

She searched the rocks deep under water, and leaves of seaweed
wound themselves around her arms. Her hair had fallen over her
forehead. From time to time she peered up through the wisps and
blew at them.

Andreas sat and listened to the cave-like note of the sea as it rose,
gulping and sucking, among the rocks. Barbara's short sleeves got

wet, but she gave no heed to that. She was working in the green depths, her back was stretched with eagerness, and when she looked up from the dark her eyes had the same green glint as the water.

— Ay, she is a water nymph, thought Andreas. He had seen paintings of water nymphs sitting on rocks and skerries, splashing in the waves with white bodies, and sea-green gleams in their eyes. But here and there on their bodies they were red and as though numb with cold from the great wet element, to whose embrace they gave themselves.

He was somewhat confused, as he sat there — as always when Barbara took on a new form in his imagination. Now, here he saw her all at once as one lodged deep in nature, in mighty nature! To tell the truth he needed this. He had come to know her increasingly too well in bed.

The winter had been long. Not that they had had a tedious winter however; on the contrary. It had been a winter full of adventures and escapades and secret rendez-vous, such as not a soul could have dreamed of in a half-underground village like Havn. Especially during the while after 'China' lay gutted, and they had had no fixed dwelling together, they had lived a life after his heart. But now it was summer, and his heart had turned to nature, weary of the dark, and of caresses that had become all too heart-felt.

But look at Barbara, how freshly she had transformed herself into a daughter of nature! She had given him sweet kisses; now with the same grace she would give him salt kisses, and caress him with a wet and numb hand. She would embrace him in the odour of seaweed and the raw stuff of shellfish, and leave him blissful, with fish scales in his hair and clothing. Ay, she was an oceanid! He wanted to lie with her somewhere on this rocky strand.

They went far along the empty shore that day, and in their great desire and forgetfulness of themselves, they let nothing natural be kept secret from the naked stone surface and the changeable, playful ocean breezes.

But afterwards, when Andreas opened his eyes and saw the strand again, and the fjord and Nolsoy's long, sweeping ridge, a strange mood came over him that he could not properly understand. The devil — he was not usually the man to regret a well-achieved purpose!

241

Nor could he see that he had acted otherwise than at nature's bidding! But while he watched the evening sunlight on the small houses over on Nolsoy's familiar isthmus, and on the broad surface of the fjord that lay before his feet like a floor, then he felt that something else altogether was what he had hoped from the nature of this, his homeland. Damnation, it was not Barbara at all that he had wanted! It was *nature* herself that had been his quest! *That* was what he had come to the islands to search out and write about in masterful and useful prose. And here, he had not only wasted a precious working winter in frivolity, but now, while nature was opening herself anew, he was dragging his sentimental gallantry along the strand and fishing for red cod with an Amaryllis, while other men were rowing out to sea or working on the fells.

As they were on their way home they saw a ship sailing in. It was *Fortuna*, on the year's first voyage from Copenhagen, and involuntarily Barbara took Andreas by the arm.

— Are you in a bad humour, Andreas? she asked, softly.

She was hot and flushed, but in her eyes there was a flash of pain, or fear. Andreas was filled with tenderness when he saw it.

— Nay, beloved, he answered.

But later, when they had passed the Fort and could see the town, Tinganes and Vippun, where folk were beginning to gather, she said, very unhappily — I keep thinking that one day you will go away from here.

— Do not think of such a thing now! There is a long while yet. You know how little I have done on my work. And besides, he added, and laughed: besides ... I shall take you with me, my sweet.

Barbara gave a start, a great light kindled in her eyes, but immediately she became deadly serious and asked, in an almost frightened voice: — Is that what you mean to do, Andreas?

— Of course that is what I mean to do.

He tried to laugh, but could not quite bring himself to it.

— It is my mortal most serious intention, said he, in a firm voice. Of course, of course!

Barbara remained thoughtful for a moment, then she quickly brightened up.

— I have no dearer wish in the world! Copenhagen! And Paul, you know ... he will surely ... surely ... he will let the marriage be dissolved and then I shall be free, quite free! That has always been exactly what I have longed for, oh longed for, to get away from here! Do you think ... do you think I can indeed get to Copenhagen?

She was ecstatic, she shone in the light of a prodigious imagining, she fairly danced over the rockiness of Krakustein.

Turf smoke from all Havn's supper fires was rising straight up into the evening's low sunshine, and the town's grass roofs lay shadowed deep green in the golden haze. Voices could be heard from Vippun, and *Fortuna*'s anchor splashed into the still water.

— Ah, if Barbara were to leave the country, thought Andreas. Then I could settle down in peace in this place!

But Barbara, in high spirits, was dancing before him like a great shadow against the red sun.

When Andreas a day or so later visited his uncle, Johan Hendrik suddenly said to him: — Now, Andreas, are you not thinking of going south again soon? How is it — has the Exchequer not set you a time to finish your work?

— Nay, said Andreas, hesitantly. The resolution only says that I shall do it. There is nothing about when.

— Hm. That is bad. It is because they are not ones to hurry themselves in the Exchequer. But ...

— I do not think it is so bad. For to tell the truth it is not going on very quickly, that work ... not as I thought it might.

The Judge limped about, rubbed his thighs, whistled out of the side of his mouth, drummed a little on the table and was very thoughtful.

— You might go on *Fortuna* now, said he, suddenly.

— Now! exclaimed Andreas.

— Ay — do you have something against that? Johan Hendrik smiled a wry smile.

— With an uncompleted work? I may as well tell you the truth, uncle! I know that you will not judge me so harshly as others will.

Well ... it is shameful to have to confess it: I have as yet hardly begun.

He added, turning away: — That is to say: I *had* begun. But all that work spoiled ... Vagar priest!

The Judge's smile twisted into a very satirical grimace. He rubbed his hips violently and then dropped into a chair.

— Tell me straight out, Andreas! Let us assume that you had completed your work but everything else was as it now stands. Would you, in that case, be of a mind to go?

Andreas hesitated a little. His carefree assurance had quite left him, the big blue eyes were faltering in their look. It might have seemed as though he felt himself cornered. But then in one move he drew himself up.

— *Enfin* ! said he. I do not honestly know whether you will like my answer or not, but there is no use my acting a comedy for you just the same. If I could have gone I would have been more than glad to do so. But I can see no way out of this. For I must either go with no report, and I cannot do that, or else I must first finish the report, and I cannot do that either ... not as long as Barbara, anyhow ...

— But then, you might think of breaking off with her?

— That would be hard, but ... ! I did think that she was flightier ...

— Ha ha ha ha! The Judge filled his nostril with snuff, his face was cheerfully distorted. — Flighty! Ho! You are a pair of clowns. You are both flighty. Only you cannot be flighty at the same time. Do you not understand that? When you are flighty, she is not. When she is flighty, you are not. God save us, I thought you would know! How old are you? Twenty-three.

The Judge immediately became serious: — And she is twenty-nine ... Twenty-nine, ay! If she were wise, now ...! But she is not that, she is by no means that.

He stroked his chin and fell to pondering. — After all ... after all, Barbara is in many different ways not ... not especially endowed.

He sneezed and made a face. — God help us moreover, if she had been!

He took a turn up and down on the floor, then quickly stopped and said: — Suppose now, that she had been able to think! ... Then what a witch she would have been — eh, Andreas?

Andreas did not answer. He sat and hung his head.

— Barbara, Johan Hendrik continued, lets herself be run only by her heart.

He stared darkly in front of him. — And it will be a sad story ... a sad, sad story, the day her heart weakens and she must be guided by her reason.

He shook his head: — Tcha! After all, I am sorry for her.

— I am so heartily sorry for her! Andreas suddenly burst out. She gives up everything for me and has not a thought for herself.

He had tears in his eyes: — Gossip, reputation, they mean nothing to her, she is entirely heedless of her own good.

Johan Hendrik was startled for a moment. Then he said, in an unusually caustic and dry tone of voice: You must stop *crying* now, Andreas! For she is even more heedless of others' good. She does what pleases her. And you are intelligent enough to see what shipwreck she brings others into, and herself. Do you never think of the Vagar priest? He may well be unfrocked for neglect of his office and desperate behaviour. They say he has not been sober in the pulpit since the New Year. And you have not done an honest penny's work in the same time. What do you think of that?

Andreas made a helpless, impatient movement of his whole body.

— If I had only written that report I would not hesitate ...

The Judge went over to his desk and began to rummage in a drawer, whistling softly. — Look you, Andreas, said he. It is not because you have deserved it. Nor because I expect it to stimulate your diligence or encourage you in the useful virtues that I have done this work for you. But something had to be done. Moreover, I found much enjoyment in doing it, for all I might have wished that you would be having the enjoyment. If you please, here is the report.

Andreas stared at the neatly-written manuscript that was placed before him on the table.

— Now, you will depart on *Fortuna* will you not? asked the Judge. His eyes were focused in a close scrutiny of his nephew.

— Uncle, you do not think much of me, and you have good reason. But I have some self-respect still.

With these last words Andreas flared up a little, and his big eyes flashed. But Johan Hendrik's features did not change, he merely touched the tip of his nose quickly and said in a dry voice: — Be more exact. Self-respect is such a diffuse notion.

— Am I to deck myself in borrowed feathers? asked Andreas, and struck an attitude.

— Ho, you will stick a few of your own feathers in, to be sure! Flight feathers, in any case! The whole work will need rewriting, you understand. To begin with, because it must be written in your own hand. Then, too, because it needs many improvements, not only in its language and style, in which you will probably find me out of fashion, but also in the argument itself. For in economics, as indeed in all such branches of learning, I deem myself your inferior. It is only in diligence that I, this winter, have been your superior. To put it briefly, this is only the stuff that I have gathered up for you, you must organize it yourself. But that I think you can do much better down in Copenhagen than here — the way things stand now.

Andreas' pale face was more helpless than ever. His eyes again began to glitter.

— Uncle, I thank you that you do not think worse of me than you do, and that you have done all this for my benefit.

— That there does sit a bright head on your shoulders, I steadily refuse to doubt, said Johan Hendrik. It is for that very reason that I ... otherwise, the devil with it!

— But — Barbara? asked Andreas, downcast.

— What good do you hope to accomplish by hanging on with her?

— I have told her that I shall take her with me when I go ...

Johan Hendrik's red, lined and somewhat dusty face pulled itself quickly together into a stony mask. — Barbara in Copenhagen! Ay, there you can in any case be quit of her, eh? Before a month is out I wager that she will be in the whores' prison. Is that what you intend?

— Nay.

— Stupid, cursed flirtation on your part! Does she believe that?

246

— I do not know. Ay, probably. But she thinks it will be a while yet.

The Judge thumped his foot on the floor and then began to pace back and forth. — Weakness, weakness, weakness, he mumbled, damned weakness! You must break off with her, you understand that. Do you not?

— Ay, Andreas whispered. But it will not be easy. It will stab me to the heart, it will.

Johan Hendrik again made one of his great grimaces and stood sunk deep in thought for a while. But then he brightened and said with a cheerful look: — Now then, we shall not be deceived by our feelings, and persuade ourselves that our weakness is generosity.

— Nay, said Andreas. But this will be giving her a terrible hurt.

Johan Hendrik opened his snuff-box slowly. — Now listen to me, Andreas, let us think this through.

He took a pinch of snuff and held it before him between his thumb and index finger.

— *Nul ne mérite d'être loué de sa bonté s'il n'a pas le force d'être méchant.*

He snuffed in the tobacco, made a face and sneezed. — That is to say, Andreas: Nobody deserves praise for his kindness who does not have the strength to be cruel.

Fortuna was lying in East Bay, taking on cargo. Niels of the Field and Shrimp were paddling the big lighter back and forth between Vippun and the ship. It was mostly jackets, stockings and woollen goods that were being carried aboard, harvest of the winter's labour and diligence in all the hearth-rooms of Faroe, heavy hand-knit goods, intended for sale in Copenhagen, Hamburg and Amsterdam for the use of the world's seamen.

— If I am ever to leave these islands, I am afraid I shall not have clothes for it, said Barbara, dreamily. What do you think, Andreas? Will you want to know me?

She laughed softly and archly and grew red in the cheeks. They sat alone together out at the end of Tinganes, near the spot where an azimuth ring had been cut in the stone.

— Clothes! You have such clothing as no-one else has here, said Andreas. And the little you do not have is easy to get in Copenhagen. Look! In a moment the sun will be due west! He pointed to the azimuth ring.

— Ay, it is time to stop work, then; the lightermen will all be going home, said Barbara, absent-mindedly.

He did not want to argue with her. But he knew that the men would not be going home before *Fortuna* had her full cargo. The weather was fine, wind from the north, which meant that the ship would hoist sail and depart during the night. But Barbara as yet suspected nothing.

Andreas' carefree heart was bleeding today from tenderness and shame. She sat so happy beside him and played with her new shining thoughts, the dazzling falsehood of her journey to Copenhagen. He could not bring himself to take it from her, he would let her be happy as long as she could be, he had not the heart to see her alone and abandoned on this shore. Ah, every time he saw her shining face he felt an urge to kiss her and cry in her arms — she whose happiness he was about to murder.

— Do you think I dance well enough? she asked.

— You are naturally a better dancer than any woman I know.

— I danced with an admiral once. That was right here, in the cellar ...

— Ay, you danced with an admiral and after that you married a priest!

— Ach, you always ...! That was long, long afterwards. But do you think now, that I can dance quite ... in the fashion?

— I shall teach you to dance in the fashion. Shall we go up and see Uncle Johan Hendrik? Maybe we can get a little ball going.

— Oh ay, cried Barbara, and was immediately fire and zeal.

They rose and walked up among the Stores buildings. For Andreas, too, a ball was an emancipating project. How he wanted to dance himself out of this! It was the one way to keep his waxen heart from melting on this beautiful and woeful evening. And his uncle, the Judge, should play for it, it was not at all too much to ask that he should play at his own comedy, the old stick. Ay, the queer old stick. Andreas had always been awed by his integrity and had more often

248

than not been cowed into lowering his eyes before his scrutinizing and knowing look. Now he was confused about his uncle. But in his uncertainty he clung all the closer to him. For his moral respect for him was limitless.

Of course Johan Hendrik agreed. A ball could surely be arranged. No doubt Sieur Arentzen would come and play his cello. And many younger ones in Havn would not say nay to a dance.

But when, later in the evening, decked out in their best clothes, they found themselves in the Judge's house, their jollity was rather restrained, and the guests for the most part merely talked softly to one another. It was as though something was weighing on them.

— You are not your usual self, said Barbara to Andreas.

Her eyes were burning in her powdered face. She was nervous. — I do not know, said she, — it is like a ball of shadows.

Outside the small-paned windows the night was still and bright. A rose-coloured streak of daylight still lay across Nolsoy's top, and all the grass roofs of Nolsoy village were lighted on their north sides. East Bay lay far below like a dark mirror. Ducks slept on the sand with their heads under their wings.

— Pshaw! said Johan Hendrik. What kind of a ball is it in daylight? Why did I not think of that?

He went out and came back in with a lighted candelabrum, and then began to light candles around the room, on the bureau and bookshelves. They flickered palely and did not have much effect, but the Judge went outside the house and began to bang the shutters shut on the windows.

— What the devil! called Gabriel from the doorstep. He was one of the very few who had been let in on the secret plan. — Are there some kind of dark doings here this evening?

— I do not know, Johan Hendrik answered. Daylight does not seem to be good for this party. That Andreas is made of soft stuff. Ha! I can not say much for myself ... I cannot bring myself to tell her either. Perhaps it is just as well. But we shall have the devil's own day tomorrow!

— He he he! Gabriel snickered, it is a Satanic comedy you are playing!

— Ay, only let the devil have your little finger! Nothing snarls itself up so, as a lie.

— Never mind, you are frying Barbara in her own grease! Has she ever behaved any better?

— That *is* so! said the Judge, and gave a puff. That *is* so. But just the same ...

He stroked his chin and stared thoughtfully out over the fjord: — Nay, nay ... if we were to say anything now I expect we should never get Andreas away.

They both went in, where jollity was already asserting itself. Sieur Arentzen was screwing up the strings on his cello and trying their pitch with broad sweeps of his bow. Everyone was talking noisily, and the candlelight shone in their eyes.

— Now then, see to it, see to it, said Johan Hendrik, and rubbed his hands together. This is how things should be going!

He picked up his flute and blew a long trill.

— Ay, *now* it is ...! cried Barbara aloud. Enthusiasm broke forth in her voice like warm sunshine. She was happy, childlike, her whole body moved with it.

— Alas, Barbara, we are fooling you, we are fooling you ...! thought Johan Hendrik.

But Barbara clapped her hands and said: — Now I say we should pretend we are a dancing school, for fun. And the dancing master shall be Andreas, he shall tell us when we are not dancing in the fashion. What do we say?

Andreas stood pale in his gallantest dress coat. But when the flute and cello began to mingle their voices his heart kindled and all his carefree high spirits rose in him. He quite forgot that he was to be dancing master.

There was nothing for a dancing master to do — not for Barbara, in any case. She danced with such a queenly bearing and yet with such unrestrained pleasure, so measured a step and indeed such grace, that nothing might be corrected that was more than trifling. She did everything naturally. Nevertheless there was a kind of serious watchfulness in her face; only when she looked at Andreas did her eyes light up warmly, and once, when she reached her hand to him in the dance she asked him tenderly and seriously: — Is this right?

The Judge sat and looked at her; his face was distorted over his flute, and nobody could tell from his lined and ambiguous features whether he was crying or laughing. But Johan Hendrik was not laughing this evening.

Alas, Barbara, we are fooling you, he thought, and his heart shrank up. Never had he seen beauty and naturalness betrayed in this way. Here she was dancing for Andreas, ach, ach, ach, that wind-bag, that lunkhead, she threw burning glances at him, and in a few hours he would secretly sail away from her, like a sneak.

Johan Hendrik blew and blew, the cello sounded its deep notes beside him, the tunes came round and round again, and the dancers who filled his room made the same steps and figures over and over, while the candles dripped and slowly dwindled. It was like a great machine he had set in motion and dared not stop, — a fairy tale with a dreadful ending. Once, during a pause, he brought out wine, every bottle he had, and the gaiety rose. Andreas, too, grew more and more light-hearted and seemed to live only in the present; it was a brilliant, joyous festivity in the dark, shuttered house. But the Judge looked only at his sacrifice with grief in his heart, how intently radiant she was in the midst of her gaiety, how deep she was in her joy, how devout in her dancing. And for a moment he thought he understood her and her doings. She was nature herself, irresponsible, but blind too, easy to fool, and they were fooling her, they were fooling nature vilely in her blind and confident flowering.

Then he looked at Andreas, his nephew, who merely danced and laughed and gave never a thought to anything! That fellow was like Barbara in her bad side, but not in her good. What of *nature* was there in him? Nay, he was not in the least worthy that she should make a gift to him of her divinity, nay, God forgive them all, ptah!

The dance came to an end. The Judge's house opened itself again to the summer night. Its pale light fell blankly on bottles, glasses and smoking candles. It was as though a fairy-tale soap-bubble had suddenly burst. Nolsoy lay day-clear and expressionless, everything was expressionless and still, and involuntarily they all damped down their voices as they crossed the threshold. Nothing stirred in the harbour, gulls were asleep on the roof ridges.

— Then you will come back to me when you have seen Barbara home! said Johan Hendrik to Andreas. I want to have that line taken in before I go to bed.

— Right you are, answered Andreas. He was a little confused at first but then quickly understood what his uncle was driving at.

— Why did you agree? asked Barbara, deeply disappointed, as they followed the lane-way down.

— Ay, but dearest! said Andreas. I could not deny him that. You see, if we do not take that line in now it will be midday before we can get at it again ...

The Judge remained standing in his doorway. He was not sure of Andreas till he had returned. Alas, alas! But ... *nul ne mérite d'être loué de sa bonté* ...

Barbara went to bed, disappointed and somewhat angry with Andreas. An indefinable fear had also come over her. In the last while he had not always seemed his usual self. But she did not want to give in to uneasiness. Moreover, she was dazed and sleepy from the wine and the dancing, and she quickly dozed off.

She half awoke again with the sound of singing. She heard it a long while mingled in her dreams, and felt uncomfortably tormented by it. Then all at once she understood what it was. It was the anchor shanty aboard *Fortuna* — they were weighing anchor! And in the same moment a terrible fright came over her. She was out of bed like a bird, and over to the window.

A whole new brightness lay on Havn now, and on Nolsoy's north-east slope the sunlight was reddening. A great gleam of beauty shone into Barbara's senses, but her thoughts had no time for gladness. Aboard *Fortuna* she caught a glimpse of the men going round the capstan.

— Oh heave, oh ho!

Then the shanty stopped, the sails were already set and *Fortuna* glided silently out of the bay. It was then that she momentarily saw Andreas on the deck. She barely saw him, his form, just as he had looked when he arrived. But it *was* him, for a dead certainty!

She uttered a short cry, a wail of despair, and in the same moment she had pulled on a skirt and was out through the door. She

252

ran down on to the sand ... there was not a person to be seen. *Fortuna* was rocking slowly outwards. She ran like a savage in bare feet over the naked rocks along East Bay. After *Fortuna*.

At one place she had to wade out up to her knees to get past. At another place, in front of the Stores' Manager's house, she scratched her legs to bleeding, climbing up a high stone ledge. She passed the Stores' gateway and ran on out to the farthest point of Tinganes. Then she could go no farther. *Fortuna* glided away. She uttered the same wailing cry, then she ran back along the empty shore.

When she got back to Vippun she met Niels of the Field.

— Ah Jesus, Niels! she called to him: has Andreas gone? And I was to go with him!

Niels stared at her in astonishment. He was not comfortable with this meeting. He had often seen Barbara but never as now, wringing her hands and scalding her cheeks with tears.

— Ay, he mumbled, Andreas was on *Fortuna*.

— And I was to ...! sobbed Barbara. She was beside herself. But suddenly she became another person — a flash of eagerness and cunning persuasiveness began to shine hopefully through her tears, she seized Niels by the arm.

— But you can still get to her, can you not? If you hurry can you row me in a four-man boat, you and Ole and ...?

She looked up at the Stores' gateway, where three Havn men were standing, uncomfortable and glum, in a little group.

— You can surely do that! Will you? Will you?

Barbara's voice was beginning to recover its usual note, it broke into a falsetto of eagerness, and her feet were dancing on the hard stone.

Niels soon understood that it was not a simple matter. — Bless you, said he, hesitantly. It will not do to go to Copenhagen without shoes and something more on top, I know that!

Barbara looked down at herself, how immodestly half-dressed she was, and blushed for a moment. But there was no time for that, she quickly forgot it again. She called to the other men and urged and persuaded with a wet and wildly shining face.

— I shall go home and dress in a hurry! And you get a four-man boat launched and by then I shall be back — will you?

She did not wait for an answer. She ran from them and in through the Stores' gateway. And from there she ran in the sun's first watery rays along the whole harbour in her shift and skirt. Nobody saw this. But one — Johan Hendrik saw her, just as he was coming out of Reynegard. But he did not believe his eyes, only later did he grasp what kind of vision of nature he had had.

After a quarter of an hour a four-man boat skimmed out over East Bay's gleaming mirror. Barbara sat in the stern and put her dress to rights a little. She did not so much as turn to see her mother who, wrapped in whatever pieces of clothing she could pick up, and with fright in her old voice, stood on the sand and called her name. The town had woken up. The early sunshine blinked from windows here and there, opened for curiosity; ay, many folk were already out of doors in slippers. But Barbara gave no heed to all that, she was looking only at *Fortuna*, which, with unfurled sails, like a gilded monument, was standing out into the fjord.

— Fog eastward at sea, Niels of the Field observed, as they were passing the point at the Fort.

— Ay, bless you, there *is* such at this time of year, puffed Ole Atten. They put all their strength into the oar-strokes. The boat scoured ahead over the gleaming water. — It is like a whale-hunt called young Markus, heartily, from the forward thwart: if only the good Lord had sent us the whales!

— Ay, but not now! said Barbara, hurriedly and nervously. She had a hand on either gunwale, she was all but standing on her seat and her eyes never left *Fortuna* for a second. The boat was not going nearly fast enough for her. The sun shone on her left cheek, she was a goddess being drawn in her chariot.

— We are gaining on her! she called.

Niels of the Field kept glancing eastward. It was a summer morning of the finest. But fog lay in great lazy drifts out to sea and northwards among the islands. It moved softly, insinuated itself among the blue mountains, wrapped itself about their feet and left the peaks standing clear and sharp in the bright daylight. It was fair-weather fog, a true sign of summer. But it was not good for visibility, thought Niels. What most made him thoughtful was the great bank that lay behind Nolsoy. Feelers from it were already making their ways over the low isthmus, where the village, Nolsoy, lay. But Barbara did not see, she was looking only straight ahead.

— We are gaining on her! she called again, with hope and jubilation in her many-toned voice. Do you not think we shall overtake her?

The men glanced forward over their shoulders.

— Ay, said Niels, — if all goes on as it is going now, then we shall catch up with her.

— Ah, Niels, said Barbara. You will never promise anything. I know you.

— Promise? God bless you. I will not say too much. Niels was kindlier and more complaisant this morning than he had ever been. But promise ...

Another thing worth noting was that *Fortuna* did not heave to, though they on board must have seen the boat a long while. There was surely something mouldy about this venture, Niels thought. Ay, they had all thought so. This was not why they exerted themselves so, they expected mighty little thanks for their rowing when they got back to shore. But they had taken so many dressings-down already, both from the Commandant and Bailie and now more recently from that Gabriel too. They would gladly take one more for Barbara, *she* had always been friendly towards them.

Fortuna altered course and steered more easterly. She was almost out of the fjord and was nearing Nolsoy's southernmost point, Bordun.

The boat had by now come far out too. Kirkjuboreyn and Nolsoy had stretched themselves out marvellously, and blue-tinting islands, mountains and peaks had come into view, both to south and north. The boat's prow rose and fell as it skimmed over the wide surface of the water.

Row towards Bordun, row straight towards Bordun! called Barbara.

— Current ...! objected Niels of the Field.

— Ah, you and your current! cried Barbara, impatiently: Can you not see that we can make a short cut if we come close to Bordun?

Niels gave in to her — partly. He knew it was a wrong-headed manoeuvre if *Fortuna* was to be overtaken, but his confidence had weakened, he was no longer sure that she either could or should be overtaken. He could see, also, that he was helping a person out of the country who had no pass from the authorities ... now that he thought more closely about it. And never in the world could he believe that Barbara had a pass.

Even so, he rowed with all his might, and so did the others. They could do nothing else under Barbara's eye, she called to them, her eyes shone, she urged them on with her eagerness.

Fortuna was now well out of sight behind Bordun, and they too were nearing that stretched-out steep point. From the harbour it looked very low and flat, now it began to rear up before them like a wall, wild and black. Piercing its outermost end was a hole through which daylight could be seen. Elsewhere the water was dark and green here under the land. They slowly drew so near that they could see sheep quite distinctly as they grazed in sunshine up on the steep, while they lay below in shadow.

The men braced their feet hard against the boat's ribs and fairly rose out of their seats with every stroke.

— Now — now — now! groaned Niels of the Field, in tempo, between clenched teeth. Ole Atten had lost his hat, his white hair and beard bristled, he puffed like a bellows, he laughed and looked like a champion and an old clown at the same time. Young Markus shouted from the forward thwart and Shrimp's face was so blood-red and swollen that it looked as though his eyes would pop out of it on either side. Ah Jesus ... this was how the Havn men rowed for Barbara, they were men, warriors! And the seas washed by them, by both gunwales, and Barbara called and rejoiced and praised them.

But when she looked in towards the land she could see that they were hardly so much as creeping forward. They had come into the current and slowed down as though in a river. Weeping rose up in her throat, she uttered a cry of disappointment and fear.

— Bless you, bless you, do not lose heart, groaned Ole Atten. We are gaining, we are gaining on the headland. It is so short. They win who are patient!

But patience was what Barbara least of all possessed. She rose up, she sat back, she wrung her hands, she shrieked at the men and was beside herself. It was a good quarter of an hour before they had made the few fathoms round Bordun, and were able to look eastward ...

Then it was that it broke. Barbara's face became suddenly quite empty; the men turned and looked over their shoulders and their faces took on the same emptiness. Of *Fortuna* there was nothing to be seen. There was nothing to be seen of anything. Neither ocean nor sky. Nothing but white fog, emptiness, shriek of the gulls. The men rowed on a moment or two yet, as though obsessed, but all at once they left off and rested on their oars. Hopeless. There came an utter stillness in the boat.

In the same moment Barbara burst into a heart-rending passion of tears. The men sat helpless and listened to her dreadful sobbing. The current carried the boat quietly and swiftly back around Bordun into Nolsoy Fjord, where there was no fog. Then the oars were at last dipped again and the stem turned towards Havn.

A crestfallen, sorry sight they presented a brief hour later, rowing into East Bay again. On Tinganes, at the Fort and on every spit of land, stood people and looked at them. Many had watched Barbara's departure, *all* saw her return. She sat in the stern, stiff and chalk-white.

Johan Hendrik, who had stayed by his window, turned away into his room. He had no desire to look at this sight. But otherwise the Havn folk were not averse to making their small remarks over the failed chase they had witnessed. A murmur followed the boat as it made its way in along the shore of the Bay.

— Ay, ay, many a one has burned himself on her. This time she has burned herself. And done it properly ...

When the boat tied up at Vippun, Gabriel stood on the shore and waited, and a troop of mostly young folk stationed themselves around him. Nor were there any windows empty near by. But Barbara's look was such that for a moment Gabriel's tongue failed him. White and numb, like a sleep-walker, she climbed ashore and went right by him up to Nyggjustova. Not until she was out of sight did he recover himself sufficiently that he began to cuss the men. Silent and abashed they laid Barbara's badly-packed and as it were randomly huddled-together baggage up on shore. Gabriel kicked at the things contemptuously.

— So this is the rubbish and tawdry she was going to Copenhagen with, pfuf! Carry this trash up to Nyggjustova, he ordered some youngsters. But you, he went on to the men, you hardly know what it is that you were letting yourselves in for. Had you helped Barbara leave the islands today, you would have followed soon after. *To Bremerholm*, do you understand? Hard labour!

With this he departed. Old Ole Atten's hands — he was the most dutiful of all the soldiers — clenched. But Gabriel went snickering into the Bailie's house.

— He he, now I think, devil eat me, said he to his wife, now I think that the shine has at last gone off Saint Gertrude. Now she is finished, by God, the jade!

Not a word did Suzanne deign to answer him. She merely finished with the bow she was tying and then went straight up to Nyggjustova. On the way she met the youngsters who were lugging up Barbara's poor finery.